# Welcome to Jade's Inn

## By Tammy Godfrey

ISBN-10# 1-63581-032-9
ISBN-13# 978-1-63581-032-5

Published by Vinvatar Publishing
Website: Vinvatar.com

# Table of Contents

# Chapter 1:

# The Break Up

As long as I can remember, I have never had a problem with Thursdays. It's not Friday, but it's close. You're still in the tunnel, but you can see the light. Pretty good shows on TV too. Thursdays were nice, until last Thursday. I hate Thursdays now.

"You're leaving me? Why?" I asked in disbelief.

"I found someone else," Daniel said abruptly, without an ounce of emotion. "I really don't want to get into a big scene right now, Caprice. I know this is coming at you fast and hard, and you're caught completely off-guard, but I want you out of the apartment in a week." Before I even got in a what-the-fuck, he exited out the door like a scared little cheating rabbit.

So there I was standing alone in the apartment we had shared for the last eight months. Okay, we were not married yet, but it felt like a marriage to me. If only he had asked me to marry him, I might have said yes. I thought he was the perfect match for me, but apparently not.

He was strong and tall, and up until now, good-hearted. Daniel is smart too, which is an attractive, and rare, feature in men. Daniel's intelligence was captivating, but it didn't always extend to the bedroom—I suppose you can't always have it all. I loved him, and that's not always easy for me to say.

*Why didn't he feel the same way about me?*

I'm sure he did at some point, but when did he stop loving me? I really was not ready for this. I needed to wake up and start this day over with Daniel kissing me good morning, and nothing but the future to look forward to. This isn't happening.

*Sigh*...shit, This was really happening.

I sat on the couch, the first piece of furniture we picked out together. *What am I going to do now? What did I do? Why is he doing this to me? Hundreds of* questions were swimming in my head as tears fell from my eyes and spilled onto my cheeks.

I needed to deal with the practical for the moment, not the emotional wounds that will be around for the next decade or so.

I really need to keep my jobs, all my jobs, now that they have to pay for my very existence. Rather than sharing it with someone, I have to stand on my own. All four of my jobs are part-time and nothing to be excited about, but they work with my class schedule and that is priceless. I am no longer part of a couple, no longer half of a whole, and neither are my bills. Since Daniel decided to fuck with my status quo in the middle of the semester, finding a vacancy in the dorms may not be the easiest thing. Is it wrong for me to hope that maybe some other couple's world came crashing down around them, leaving an empty bed somewhere. Just like mine...

If I have to find a place off campus, I will also have to find a job that pays more than a part-time salary or I'm screwed. One of my best friends, Dawn, has been bragging about a new job. I'm planning to bribe her with pizza and beer to see if she can throw me a bone with her new boss. However, first it's off to the University Book Store and my boss, Mike. Not all the people working at the bookstore are complete dicks, but Mike is. He is the manager and likes to remind me about that fact every day.

Shortly after I started working there, he asked me out and I said no, because I was dating Daniel. I honestly thought he was used to being shot down by the female species and would just blow it off and move on, but no. Ever since then, my job at the bookstore has been utter hell. I really wish Mike would just get a life instead of making mine miserable, especially today. Mike is a senior this year, getting a bachelors' in Business, with a minor in Philosophy, and the math told me that made him a first-class ass clown.

When I got there, it didn't take long for me to realize that Mike was really being a particularly nasty pain in the ass, and the fact that I was dumped today will not help with me keeping my calm around my boss.

First we got a shipment of school supplies— pens, pencils, paper, all the tools of higher learning, and they came with a display that was to be set up the way the supply company wanted.

I found a spot to put everything together, and when I was two minutes from being done, Mr.

Supervisor tells me in a voice loud enough for the customers and people in the halls outside the store to hear that it was set up wrong. Why did Mike have to pick this day to mess with me? When I finished the display the way he wanted it, which looked completely ridiculous, Mike yelled at me again because it looked completely ludicrous and said I should feel stupid for not being able to follow the directions provided. I needed Mike to stow his crap and let me be.

Maybe if I told him Daniel and I broke up, he would be nicer.

Later when I saw him coming out of the back room, I noticed all the pens in Mike's lame pocket protector were red, the kind of bright red that highlights critical mistakes, like forgetting to hide Mike's favorite candy behind all the others so it wouldn't sell out. Then he took out this lime green calculator, the one with scientific keys that he thought impressed the freshman girls even though he had no idea how to use them and counted the money in the cash register, including the pennies, every fifteen minutes. It was then I figured his mother must have found Mike's dirty magazines last night, and he had to blame someone. Yes, Mike still lived at home. Even though he's told everyone it's because he spends all his time in the basement, it was like he had his own place. I don't know, maybe his cousin Bertha refused to go out with him again.

Damn! He wasn't going to ease up, was he?

Either way, I couldn't do anything right for him. Now he wanted me to take down all the books from the top two book shelves to dust them off, and watch the cash register at the same time.

I was pulling the books down from the shelves while looking at the romance section and trying not to completely lose it, when someone came in. Mike was hiding in the usual place, behind the shelf with the Human Sexuality textbooks, yelling at me to get to the cash register. I managed to run to the customer with a smile pasted on my face that wouldn't fool a child. Once I sold him a pencil and gave him change for a twenty so he could continue "studying" down the hall in the arcade, I headed back to the book shelves. After about an hour of running back and forth, the practical part of me who needed the money lost the battle with the bitch in me and I gave up.

"Mike, I can't do both," I finally told him.

"Well if you want your job you will," he said in an I-am-your-commanding-officer voice. "And if necessary, you will stay late to finish without overtime."

I slammed four heavy Quantum Physics books to the floor and gave Manager Mike a glare with an angry fire in my eyes that could make a brave man cower, and a coward like Mike piss himself. I backed him up into a stack of "Bengal Booster" t-shirts. Now Mike was giving me a scared shitless look. "Mike, since I am certain that you don't have anything to do tonight but take your right hand out on a date, you can do the shelves yourself. I quit!" I turned and stomped out the door.

I decided to deal with not having a fourth job tomorrow. I looked at the time and decided to lose myself in a movie before I went back to deal with Daniel.

♦

When I bought my ticket for the action movie currently playing at the Bengal Theater, I hoped the explosions would help deal with my frustrations and take my mind off of my misery. I walked in and sitting half-way down the aisle was the source of my bad day—Daniel.

Not the lonely Daniel I was hoping for, but the Daniel with a beautiful brunette wrapped in his arms.

*That cocksucker! Is this the bimbo he left me for?*

I had seen her with him before when they did a research project together last semester. My heart started racing and I was shaking when I ran out into the lobby, my tears returning. I couldn't believe the nerve of that prick. We just broke up!

I don't understand how Daniel could have replaced me like that, with no more thought than replacing a light bulb that works with another light bulb that also works—but looks sluttier. I felt discarded and all wrapped up in a sense of betrayal.

Instead of sticking around or confronting him, I headed out into the dark night. I slowly walked across the partly lit quad across Idaho State University wondering how my love life well, my life, managed to fall apart so quickly. I headed back to Daniel's apartment. Not our apartment. Not our home. I don't know if he will be coming back tonight, but I can't let him see me like this. Okay, this is fucking ridiculous! The hell with Daniel, breaking up with me just like that, no explanation just, "You need to leave."

I had to look for a new job and a new place to live. This day had not turned out the way I thought it...huh? That's weird. I suddenly felt like I was forgetting something really important.

The next morning, Daniel had not yet returned to the apartment, chicken shit. I didn't sleep well so I wasn't exactly bright-eyed and bushy-tailed, not that I ever am early in the day. Mornings and I haven't really gotten along since I stopped watching Saturday morning cartoons.

I dragged myself out of the sack with the attitude that there was no possible right side of the bed to get up on. I was off to my first class of the day with all the enthusiasm of a slug on downers.

My first class was Anthropology, which I like except for the walk to the Rendezvous building. From where my apartment is, it's only two blocks, but when you're in a pissy mood you want to kick the ass of anyone who walks in front of you. I made a quick stop to the girl's room to see if I still looked like a puppet from a Tim Burton movie, where I saw a Roommate Wanted notice on the bulletin board for Stevenson Dorms. The rent was in my price range, in other words, low. I grabbed my cell phone and called Sara, the person looking for a roommate, and left a message, hoping she doesn't have a fixation on cute animal posters.

This is because I couldn't bear the thought of anything competing with my Pooh and his friends from the hundred acre wood. After getting off the phone without sounding too desperate, I headed into Anthropology.

Being dumped tends to force one into a state of personal reflection, which takes precedence over the study of Anthropology. I haven't heard a word Professor Henderson has said since I arrived. Instead I started watching the B-movie that is my life, and gave up trying to focus in class.

School in general has not always been my strongest area of expertise. I thought paying attention in high school was a waste of time. I mean not really, but well, yeah...it was. I always *brought notes home saying, Cat doesn't apply herself, and Cat is sleeping in class. It wasn't until* my parents tag-teamed me that I started doing my homework, and I really surprised myself. I even did well on my SAT's.

Believe it or not, I actually thought about the military, for all of about two point five seconds. I really don't like getting up early in the morning. I've changed my major five times, and I still don't know what I want to do. I thought if I got through the basic course work, I'd have it figured out by now. I'm a Psychology major now, but what I really want is a degree in the Arts- Interior Design to be specific.

I love getting a blank room and decorating it. The hard part is getting my parents to help me pay for school. My parents are divorced, but unlike some divorced parents who compete for their children's love by spoiling them my parents fight over who will get stuck with the tab instead. The problem is, I can't stand to be with either one of them. They both drive me crazy. I hate their games. They are still fighting over me like a piece of furniture, or a dog they once owned. I don't know why they won't just help me, or at least give me a little support with my decisions.

My best friend, Geri Lynn Edwards, on the other hand, has known what she was going to be since she was five years old. She always wanted to be Lois Lane, a reporter at the Times. I know Lois Lane didn't work at the Times, but you get my point. She wants to be a reporter, not Superman's bitch. She is currently working on a story about a prostitution ring at the university.

Pocatello, Idaho is a small conservative town so I really can't see a prostitution ring here, but I'm not the one writing the story. Geri is five foot three, a tiny ball of fire who wants to get noticed, either by her three inch heels or her headlines. I've never really understood her motivation to stand out. She has light brown hair and blue eyes. She's not overweight, but she does have meat on her, which gives her sensual curves. I think it makes her look sexy. She thinks she needs to go on a diet to look good. Thin is overrated.

My other best friend, Dawn, is in the same boat I'm in. Dawn wants to be a teacher, but finding money for school is hard. Dawn was taking odd jobs like I did in order to make ends meet, that is, until she came back for the fall with everything paid for. All she's willing to reveal is that she found a job which requires her to work only twice a week and still make good money. I'll talk to her later about it. Maybe there's something to that prostitution ring story Geri is working on after all.

Five minutes before class ended, I was brought out of my self-imposed exile to memory lane when my cell phone went off. Seems I forgot to silence it. Shit shit shit. I made a vain attempt to muffle the Katy Perry ringtone and ran out through the classroom door. I hit the answer button and said. "Hello," in a less than friendly tone.

"Is this Caprice, the one interested sharing an apartment?" asked a bright female voice.

"Yes, and this is Sara I guess. When can I see it?" I said enthusiastically.

"My next class is at two, any time before then will be fine, but I need the rent for the rest of the semester paid up front," Sara said.

I thought about it, and desperation won out. "I can do that," my response was as much of a question as an answer. I can do it if I take all my savings, leaving me nothing in the way of cash until my next paycheck that I don't get for another two weeks.

"Great, so what time would you like to meet?" she asked happily.

"I have to meet friends in an hour, so the sooner the better," I answered.

"I'll meet you in fifteen minutes, Stevenson Hall, room six one four."

"See you then," I said and headed out of the Rendezvous Center then started hiking up the hill to the dorms with my fingers crossed. I really need this to work out.

*Can I afford to do this? Do I have a choice? Why is Daniel doing this, the complete dickhead*? These questions keep swirling around in my head, again and again which does nothing to help me take my mind off of my problems as I make my way up to the dorm. I head into the building and up the stairs, when I realize that Dawn's room is on the same floor, and Geri's is two floors below me. This may work after all...

There was a redhead with more than a few freckles waiting on the sixth floor. "Are you Caprice?" Sara asked.

"Yes I am, and that would make you Sara?" I said shaking her hand.

"Guilty. There is something I need to point out right away," Sara said with nervous concern.

"I moved in with my boyfriend a few weeks ago, and I need a roommate to help keep up appearances. As far as my parents are concerned, I'm a chaste girl still living in the dorms. They would freak if they found out their little girl has shacked-up with a boy. They make up some excuse to visit once a month, but they're really checking to make sure I'm not drunk off my ass, or living in sin. You know the typical nightmares that all parents of college children have."

"I think I get it." I totally did.

"My last roommate was on parent watch until her parents found out what she was doing for me.

They told her I was a bad influence, and since they're paying her bills, I am now looking for a new roommate. I hope that will be you," Sara said eagerly.

We walked into the room, and I took a quick tour. Not a bad place, two beds, two dressers, a restroom, and a roommate who is hardly ever there. "This will work."

"Good, when do you want to move in?" Sara asked with the giddiness of a, well, schoolgirl.

"The sooner the better," I said. "I just have to walk to the bank and get the money."

"You bank at the credit union down the street too?" Sara asked. "Can I walk with you?"

"Sure." Maybe she's afraid that I'll change my mind between here and the bank.

We walked for a while in silence, but I knew she had a question she was dying to ask. Her curiosity finally got the best of her.

"Why do you need a place so fast?" she queried.

"Boyfriend trouble," I admitted.

"Sorry," she said genuinely.

We spent the rest of the walk discussing my new lack of a love life, and how big of an asshole my new ex-boyfriend is. Once we walked to the credit union and through the long line of broke college students, I withdrew enough cash to make my new roomy happy. After a quick review of my new balance, or lack thereof, my financial reality came crashing down around me.

"That son-of-a-bitch!"

"Problem?" Sara asked.

"That cocksucker." I exclaimed.

"The ex?" Sara guessed accurately.

"That sorry-eyed sack of shit!" I went on.

"Okay, Caprice honey," Sara said, putting her hand on my shoulder. "You are making the tellers nervous."

Sara managed to get me out of the bank before I started breaking things around me.

"He didn't just kick me out. He pulled practically all the money out of the account, and all of it was mine! Why did I even put him on my account?"

"Do you want this money back?" Sara offered kindly.

"No...at least not yet," I told her. "Thanks though. I have a friend that I need to see about another job. Let me check with her first, right after I go back in there, apologize to everyone, and change my account number." I wonder what else Daniel had fucked over, and how long he's been doing it to me?

I'm really not looking forward to the lunch time conversation with my friends about all the recent events in my life. They knew Daniel was a shit heel from the beginning. Don't you hate it when your friends are right, and you didn't listen to them? Hopefully, after the first few hundred I-told-you-so's they'll get tired and we can talk about gleeful forms of revenge.

Before the bite to eat, and the biting sarcasm that I knew was coming, I ran back to my ex-place to pick up some of my things and put them in my car, my all-too-small wardrobe before Daniel Dickhead sells it. I also picked up my bath stuff from the crapper. I left the place and stopped by to get Geri, before I was off to the inquisition to have some crow with a side of curly fries.

Dawn was waiting for us at the table. Fortunately, the conversation started out with her classes and her new job. The first thing I noticed about Dawn when I first met her was her blue eyes, bright-sky blue. You wouldn't believe it. It's her eyes that first catch people's attention so I'll admit that she is gorgeous. I'm not gay or anything, but it's hard to be friends with someone that attractive. I sat down at the table, right between my two buds.

"You're not eating anything? Are you dieting?" Geri asked.

"No, I'm not really hungry today," I said. The real reason being I couldn't afford the luxury of school and food at the same time anymore.

"Twilight has always been my time of the day. When the sky is painted like an artist's canvas with reds and golds. This is the time when the night comes alive again," Dawn said.

"Are you okay, Dawn?" I asked.

"Where in the world did you get that from, Dawn?" Geri inquired.

"Julian told it to me," Dawn says in a dreamy sort of a way. Julian, of course. I have never met Julian myself, but if all the hype about him is true, I can understand why Dawn wants to be with him.

"This guy in my class told me about this new exclusive club that's opening tonight," Geri said. "It's called the Bloody Rose, it's a Goth club. It opens tonight and, being the grand opening, they promised to pull out all the stops."

"I'll go if Caprice goes. Will Julian be there?" Dawn asked.

"I'll go on three conditions," I said, "One you introduce me to the amazing Julian. Two, tell me about the new job you acquired that you're keeping under wraps. And three, you buy the tequila. Oh and don't let me do anything or anyone stupid."

"That's four conditions, and Julian is not just a guy," Dawn said.

"Well, what is he then, a god?" I asked sarcastically.

"I'll show you who Julian is and I'll tell you about the job after you go to the club with me," Dawn answered.

"Okay, I'll go. What's the cover?" I asked.

"Nothing, drinks are on the house tonight and they have free food," Geri said.

"So we're back to three conditions," I said standing up. "I'm in."

"Where are you going?" Geri asked.

"I need to move the rest of my things out of my apartment."

"Why are you moving your things out?" Dawn asked with excitement." Oh my God, you did it. You broke up with the bastard. It's about fucking time."

"I didn't break up with him," I said and sat back down reluctantly. Here comes the talk and *the I-told-you-so's.*

"No fucking way, Daniel broke up with you?" Dawn asked in disbelief.

"Yes," I said with a touch of humiliation, and to add to that feeling, the phone rang. It was Daniel. I could tell because my ringtone was our love song—Two is Better than One.

"What! I know what you did to my account you little bastard!" I yelled as soon as I answered it.

"You know how forgetful you are, Caprice honey. I pulled the money to pay for the rest of the bills and rent," Daniel said slyly.

"You're kicking me out, I have to find a new place, and to top it off I've only been in the apartment for five days this month and you're taking all the money for a whole month? And if you call me honey one more time, I will castrate you!" Geri and Dawn watched, not saying a word, knowing better.

"Caprice, I need five hundred dollars more to take your name off the rental agreement."

"I don't have five hundred dollars. I used all the money I had to get a new place," I said with a surprising amount of restraint.

"Well then I'll keep your name on the lease until you can pay to get it off," Daniel said. "I need you out of the apartment in two days. Molly's moving in. Oh, and I know you saw me at the movie last night."

"I am paid up for the rest of the month. If you want me out in two days, you need to pay me back the money you took," I told him firmly.

"I'm not giving you the money and you will be out in two days and you will give me my keys back," Daniel demanded.

"No! I will not! Not until the month is up and my name is off the lease," I yelled and hung up my cell phone with all the anger of a pissed off woman that cannot take any more surprises from her ex. I clammed up, offering no information to my two shocked and nosey companions. They knew I was not in the mood for a Q&A, but that has never stopped them from telling me what they think.

Before they could fire off the first question, I spoke up, "I have to go to my next class, see you tonight." I left Geri and Dawn with open mouths, not knowing what to say. I had three minutes to get to my next class across the quad in the Physical Science building. But instead, I ran straight to my old apartment.

# Chapter 2:

# A Good Place to Start

I used to enjoy being on this bed. It was one of my favorite places before the soul-sucking idiot decided to ruin any chance of a happy future for us. Daniel and I used to spend mornings, afternoons, and evenings here just getting lost in each other. Now here I am, packing all my shit on this bed before the asshole gets back. I wonder if there is something of Daniel's I can take and sell for five hundred dollars so my name won't be on the same piece of paper.

While prowling around the place, there was a knock on the door. I didn't feel nervous, because I knew the prick wouldn't knock on his own door, plus I was expecting Dawn or Geri or both to stop by in case I start on the bastard-boyfriend-ritual-bonfire.

"I brought the marshmallows," Dawn said when I opened the door." Are you okay, honey?"

"No, I don't understand any of this. Daniel was fine the day before we broke up. He planned dinner, we watched my favorite movie, and then we made love in that bed. It was a great night...but then the next morning, he told me we were breaking up in the very bed we just shared. It was like being slapped in the face while your back is turned. I know that doesn't make sense, but that's what love is supposed to be like, right? Looking back on it, it was like a sweet last time for him and a goodbye to me. If I had known, I would have kicked him in the balls before he got his pants back on!" Dawn giggled and I smirked back. "So why are you here, to watch me pack and rant away?"

"I came to tell you about my new job," Dawn responded. "I've been working at Jade's Inn, painting murals on the walls of the specialty rooms, and other odd jobs they have available. I get good money for doing it. I can take you over there and you can see what they have to offer you. I told Sam about your decorating skills. He runs the whole place."

"Right now?" I asked.

"Well after we move all this stuff over to your new apartment and away from your scummy ex. Where is your new apartment?" Dawn asked.

"Across the hall from you."

"No shit! This is so great! Then we can go to the new night club tonight," Dawn said with a new enthusiasm.

"I gotta tell ya, Dawn, I'm not really feeling it. I mean, I'm here packing my year long relationship in these boxes. I'm not exactly feeling social, I'm feeling pissed."

"Come on, Cat, you said you would go, remember? You need a job, you need a beer. I think you just need to get laid."

"All right, you win," I said. "I'll go, I'll go, but no guys! I'm guy free."

"You switching teams, Cat?"

"No, I'm just taking myself out of the game for a while," I told her before she jumped to anymore conclusions." Let's grab these boxes. I want to get the fuck out of here." As I readied myself to leave, I had the strong urge to stick a rotting fish under the mattress, but Dawn came up with a better idea. Dawn asked where Daniel kept his condom stash, then where he kept the scissors. After conducting a cutting ceremony over the bed, we decided to depart. We packed the boxes in the car and headed to the new apartment. We didn't say much on the way over, mainly because Dawn had her iPod cranked all the way up with '80s music she enjoys using to induce deafness in others. When we arrived at the new place, I reached around to the backseat to grab the first box.

"Wait," Dawn said. "We've lifted enough."

"Well, I'm not leaving my stuff out in the car."

"You don't have to; I've lived here since I was a freshman. There are guys hanging around here waiting for hotties like us. Give me ten seconds..." Ten seconds later Dawn showed up with five muscular guys who looked ready to do her bidding.

"Cat step aside, the Bengals front line is here." She opened the back door and the trunk, "Grab a box boys, and follow me."

"Room six one four," I said with a smile.

After the linesmen finally accepted a consolations prize of a six pack and pretzels, they chuckled and left us with five phone numbers for anything else we ever needed, such as a date on the town.

"Ready to head over to Jade's Inn?" Dawn asked with-a-cat-that-ate-the-canary-smile on her face.

"Sure, what type of jobs do they have there?" I asked with fear when the image of a cigarette girl in a tacky outfit, carrying a silly tray popped in my head.

"They're looking for bartenders, room designers, painters, and...other jobs," Dawn said.

"Room designer?" I asked with a mixture of hope and confusion.

"Yes. Someone has to come up with these fantasy room ideas," Dawn said. "If we go now I can give you the tour, check out the rooms, see what they have. Then you can come up with a few ideas and write a proposal. Maybe afterwards you can mix me a drink, you know, the bartender thing. Cover your bases."

"Off to Jade's Inn then," I said "First, a quick wardrobe change. Something less gloomy, and more girly." I have passed this Jade's Inn many times since it's not far from campus. The place is shrouded by trees, so you have to be fairly close to see the whole building. When we turned up the drive, I got a much closer look, but it still wasn't easy to see. Most of the old stone buildings are covered in ivy. During the day, the place certainly has a gothic charm to it, but at night it looks like a place the Scooby gang would investigate.

Dawn was smiling from ear-to-ear, and practically skipping down the cobblestone path. I think she was channeling her inner eight year old that only comes out at Christmas time when she showed me the fountain out in front of Jade's Inn. It had a rainbow of lights underneath, thirty-six jets of water on a timer with a stone bench right next to it. If I can only get used to the *gargoyles lining the roof tops—with their piercing gaze—I could see myself working here. Even* before we ascended the crescent-shaped stairs to the large main entrance, we could hear what sounded like a huge party.

I've been to fantasy themed hotels before, some pretty lame, but this place was immaculate. I'm guessing the blood-red carpets didn't just look old and expensive, I bet they were. The whole place was bathed in a soft light from the most incredible chandeliers and candelabras with real candles lighting the hall.

After I checked for mud on my shoes for the third time, Dawn led me down a hallway lined with original oil paintings. We visited a total of thirteen rooms from the Camelot room, complete with an Excalibur sword in an actual stone, to Cleopatra's Throne room minus the poisonous asp. I particularly like the Parisian room, with the painting of the Eiffel tower, and the Jungle room, which was pretty much self-explanatory. We eventually made our way to the back of the Inn where the new construction was going on. It looked like they're putting in another five, or ten, rooms.

"Here we are," Dawn announced with the air that she was presenting the Queen. "This is your canvas. Come up with amazing, original ideas and the job could be yours," she said with a small curtsey.

Dawn could see I was getting nervous at the prospect of designing a room, so she walked up behind me, put her hands on my shoulders, and rubbed soothingly. It helped. Then Dawn leaned in and whispered in my ear, "Relax...you'll do great. Now if my eyes don't deceive me, there's a party going on somewhere in this place. What do ya say we track it down?" We made it halfway down the hall when Dawn said, "Oh, by the way, when we are here, call me Lisa."

I stopped, but Lisa kept walking, "Why?" I asked. I have to admit, I was afraid of the answer.

"Around here you want an alias, trust me. There are some people who, when they walk through the door, seem normal, but after a while—after a round or three—their true nature begins to seep through their carefully crafted charming exterior," she said knowingly.

"Wow, really?"

"They're fucking weird, and that's the truth," Dawn stated honestly.

"Why Lisa, it seems less exotic than Dawn?"

"She was a childhood friend."

"And..." I prompted, waiting for the punch line.

"And she was a weird five year old," Dawn said without reservation.

"Ok...Lisa, lead the way." We continued back down the hall, walking past the empty rooms that waited to be draped in fantasy themes. Ideas crowded into my brain, some more persistent than others.

"I have an idea, but I don't think they will go for it," I finally said, contemplating the room design.

"Just write it up, you get bonuses if they really like your idea," Dawn said. "The worst they can say is no, then the only bonus you get is a scotch and soda."

"No, the worst they can say is you suck, don't give up your day job," I responded in dread.

We made our way back to the main part of the Inn, where the liquor has clearly been flowing for a while. We strode through the crowd with caution. Most people didn't acknowledge we were there, but there were some that couldn't take their beady little eyes off us.

"Don't look at them directly," Dawn warned.

"Good advice," I said as I averted my eyes from the three hundred pound guy in a leisure suit.

"Sam!" Dawn shouted above the racquet.

"There's my girl," came a deep voice through the crowd. Dawn threw her arms around a large, very well dressed African-American gentleman.

"Have you been behaving?" Sam asked.

"Yes, but only because we just got here," Dawn admitted. "Sam, this is my friend Caprice."

"Ah yes, the young lady who will design her way into our hearts." he then motioned us to the nearest vacant bar stools, and I started getting nervous. Am I really interviewing for a job in a *bar?*

"So what do you think of our little inn?"

My moment of silence was definitely not a way to make a good first impression. I turned around to the bartender, raised my hand for a tall cool one, and quickly slipped on my confident mask.

"I have some ideas," I said.

"All great things begin with an idea," Sam stated as he handed me a paper with proposal labeled on it.

What made me think of Sleeping Beauty at the time? I can't say. There was absolutely nothing in my immediate surroundings that inspired thoughts of fairytales with happy endings. Maybe deep down where my inner little girl lives, I still believed in a Prince Charming and the idea one girl would be enough for him. I may have to tone down the bright and cheery side of the fairytale to fit with the darker gothic themes of this place by channeling Anne Rice's version of Sleeping Beauty. I'm sure Sleeping Beauty could have another side of her persona she didn't show in the light of day. I'm thinking a kinky side she kept to herself, all the while waiting for the charming prince to sweep her off her feet. My new chaste life is running away with my imagination.

*Maybe I should start with something simple, like a see through-bed. It could be like seeing through a coffin, but it's really a bed. I'll drape it with royal looking purple bedding. I see a hot tub, a black marble hot tub, surrounded by a mural of Sleeping Beauty being kissed by the prince. I think a spinning wheel might give it a medieval touch. I can green it up with a few plants here and there, but what I really need is a glass case that displays a beautiful crown. That will be the centerpiece of the room. A Princess bedchamber, very female oriented. That way every guy that comes in will feel like he's receiving a special invitation to a very private place only few men will ever see.*

My blank proposal sheet was quickly being filled by my bizarre imagination. When I finally finished, I handed it to Sam. I hoped he wouldn't laugh and throw it right back in my face.

"Gotta say, over the top, but it's definitely different from our other rooms..." Sam said after a long and uncomfortable silence. "I like it, it could work." Sam stood up, folded the paper in half, and put it in the inside pocket of his jacket. "I'll show this to the owner and see what he thinks," Sam said as he patted the spot where he just placed my proposal.

Sam took my hand and shook it, then turned on his heels and was gone. "Now that the boring business stuff is over and done," Dawn said. "I hear the sweet call of the wild. They're saying...Come to us, Dawn. We miss you...and bring your cute friend. Come to the Bloody Rose as soon as you can."

I returned to my apartment to change before heading to the Bloody Rose for its grand opening. It wasn't hard to find. The crowd was overflowing into the streets. The large neon sign of a bleeding rose, which beckoned to all in the darkened neighborhood, also made it easy to locate. Some preplanning on the wardrobe front is always a good idea, particularly when you are going to a new club. A case like tonight called for apparel that was short, tight, and proudly displayed more skin than it covered up.

Dawn's choice of a tank top—which was clearly meant to fit a ten year old—and the fact that she knew Ronny the doorman and bouncer, got us into the Bloody Rose quickly—pissing off the long line of potential patrons. Her choice of this half an outfit was two-fold. One was to get in the door and the other was to raise the anger of the more pretentious crowd, which included all of the girls staring daggers at us as we entered.

We made our way through a sea of people. I guess it could be described as a black sea of people in black suits, dresses, gothic clothes, and hair to top it all off. I would be willing to bet that most of the black hair was not original, but it went well with the black eye shadow and black lipstick. The black does bring out the body piercings, at least the piercings I could see. I could have imagined the various other body parts that some of these people have pierced, but I really didn't want to.

I wonder sometimes what kind of jobs these people have during the day. Do they look like this normally, or is this a special occasion? Maybe the pierced, dark persona they project now is the real them, and the colorful character that walks in the daylight is the disguise.

A waving hand in the distance brought me out of my heart-felt analysis of the counter- culture in modern society. "Hey guys, over here," Geri shouted above the crowd.  After ensuring that the barmaid, who was wearing less than we were got the order right, my eyes meandered through the mass of humanity. Oh my God! Tall, dark, and handsome didn't even describe him, this...this...holy crap! This was the man of my dreams.

"Julian is very into the gothic scene," Geri said in the middle of a conversation that brought me back to myself.

"Who is this Julian you keep talking about?" I managed to ask, still looking at Mr. Right Now.

"He's the eye candy you're molesting in that dirty little mind of yours." Dawn quipped.

"That's Julian?" I said louder than intended. I couldn't take my eyes off him. He was definitely making my mouth, as well as other things lower in my body, water. Julian had long, sexy, brown hair that made me want to run my hands though it...grab it, pull him toward me, and kiss those luscious lips that look so very seductive. Then there are those deep, milk chocolate brown eyes. I could lose myself in those eyes. I wonder how he smells. That thought was cut *short by my inner voice telling me, Stop that, no guys for you! Don't think about this guy! Remember what happened with the last guy you liked. The voice was right.*

I managed to close my eyes, but he was still there in my mind, in all my senses. Julian's scent was intoxicating, but I was just imagining it, right? I suddenly realized he was holding my hand. My other hand, which had developed a mind of its own, was running up and down Julian's soft, white, silken shirt. My hand managed to stop just short of the black leather pants. I'm glad my runaway hand had some boundaries.

I finally opened my eyes to take him all in. Then it hit me. Julian looked identical to a movie vampire. Not the creepy 1930'skind, but the sexy Christopher Lee kind. The kind you want to share an eternity with.

"Hello Caprice," he said in a deep, yet softly familiar voice with the hint of an Irish accent.

"Hello?" I replied, wondering if—and how-—he might know my name. "I'm sorry, have we met?"

"No, but I know all about you, Caprice," he said. He bowed and kissed my hand and I felt comfortable, relaxed, as if I'd known him forever. The feeling washed over me similar to a warm summer rain, just from one kiss on the hand. Then he gently guided me to the dance floor, and I followed him without even thinking about what I was doing. I thought I was lost in a dream again, surrounded by a mist, and time was standing still just for us. Julian looked into my eyes as I felt him touch my soul. The dance was slow, and Julian bent down to whisper in my ear, "I have loved you for eternity."

Julian's hot breath crept into my mind and soul like a mysterious breeze on a dark night, both inviting and frightening—it was totally amazing. I suddenly stopped breathing. I didn't remember where I was, or even who I was. All I could remember were those words. *I have loved you for eternity.*

What was I doing? Reality and reason fought their way back into my mind. Without realizing it, I found that my hands were running up and down Julian's body of their own accord. Look, but don't touch, was a rule that suddenly sprang into my brain. That's the law of my life and I just broke it big time. Now I'm dancing with him! I needed to walk off the dance floor and run home. Not walk, run...do not pass go, do not collect two-hundred dollars.

I had no mind of my own as my hands rested on Julian's shoulders. Someone shoot me please! Okay, maybe one dance won't hurt. All he wants to do is dance with me. Julian's arms were around me, he was easily over six feet tall, and had the most entrancing chocolate brown eyes. What harm could it do? Wow, he smells like rain. *The smell right before it rains outside. The smell of a new life...*

I buried my face in Julian's hair, and the rest of my body egged me on. I was walking on air. The song ended and I didn't want to stop dancing. Julian placed his hands on my back and pulled me to him. He kissed me so passionately— I wanted to climb into his mouth. At the same time, he ran his fingernails along the outside of my arms causing goose bumps to erupt all over me. He kissed my cheeks and then started nibbling on my ear as he worked kisses along my neck. He couldn't know how much that drives me wild...could he? At this point, it wouldn't surprise me if he did. If he knew everything about me, like how I take my coffee, how much I hate the Dallas Cowboys, whether I prefer tampons or pads. I needed to go outside, to take a deep breath of the night air and bang my head on the nearest brick wall for letting this happen.

I mustered enough restraint to say, "I need a breath of fresh air. I'm going outside..." In my head I told myself to run home.

"Can I join you?" Julian asked.

*"Yes." I said, automatically. Why can't I say no to this guy?*

Outside, the bright moonlight pierced through the darkness and the warm night air brushed my face. I enjoy moonlight.

"Why do you like the moonlight so much?" Julian asked.

"I'm not quite sure. How did you know I love the moonlight?" I replied.

"Let me show you," he said, his eyes letting me know he understood me.

Julian ran his hands through my hair as he put soft, warm kisses onto my lips. Kissing him was similar to the first kiss of a new lover, the feeling of lasting happiness— the happy ever after fairytale you hoped to be true come into reality. I've never experienced anything like that, with any guy, simply by him kissing me anyway.

"I don't think you're ready to know me yet, but you will be, love." Julian said to me like he knew it was a reality. Then he kissed my hand and did this bow that was very graceful and very masculine at the same time. "I will see you soon, Caprice," he said as he backed up and returned to the club.

This could have been the best night of my life...but it wasn't because just at that moment Daniel showed up. "Was that for my benefit, to make me jealous or something?" Daniel asked with an angry expression on his face.

"Trust me, there was a benefit, but not for you." I replied coldly. Was this asshole serious? It's time to put this fucker in his place. "It was a real kiss,

Danny boy, better than anything I've gotten from you!"

"Maybe if you had dressed more like a girl, we would still be together," he replied coldly. I couldn't believe the nerve of this prick. He was giving me fashion advice. I was at a loss. I turned and just walked away.

Daniel called after me as I huffed away. "He's way out of your league, Caprice, and I'm keeping all the deposit on the apartment because of what you did."

As much as I wanted to go back into the club, I didn't really think I could control myself around Daniel any longer. Geri and Dawn were still in the Bloody Rose, probably wondering what the hell happened to me. I called Geri on my cell and told her I didn't feel well. I doubted she bought it, but I needed to be any place other than here. Since the club was only three blocks away from home, I decided to walk.

How long can a three block walk take anyway? I could feel time slowing down. The passing of each second seemed labored as I took each step. I was not sure what time it was, or what day for that matter. The only thing on my mind was my bed, which didn't seem to be getting any closer. And of course two guys—well, one real amazing guy and one asshole. Okay, I need to reach into my brain with a pair of tweezers and pull Daniel's lame ass out of there. Julian on the other hand, he'll be setting up permanent residence right in the forefront of my mind.

*Should I be obsessing about a guy I just met? Maybe he's bad in bed? This, of course, is ridiculous. A man can't kiss that way and not know his way around a woman. I can still feel his lips on mine. I can imagine them exploring other parts of me. I can also see me undressing him...with my teeth.*

Oh God! I needed serious couch time with a fully qualified therapist. I needed to get over Daniel before jumping into bed with the first man...he's not a man...he's a supernatural being not from this world...he was like a dark fay from one of Laurel K. Hamilton's fairy books that makes me go weak in the crotch.

Finally, home. I sprinted up the stairs, convinced that my bed missed me as much as I missed it. When I made it to my room, I flopped face first onto my waiting pillow and newly assembled bedspread. After several minutes, I realized I needed to seek comfort in the warmth of my Winnie the Pooh PJs.

I tumbled towards the light switch in the bathroom and finally found it in my new surroundings. After staring at myself in the mirror for I don't know how long, I came to the conclusion Julian was not standing behind me with his arms wrapped around my body. So why could I still feel him... his touch... his breath? I took one last look and wondered...what could *he possibly see in me?*

Finally, I crawled into bed, pulled the covers over myself, and closed my eyes. I was not going to have a dream about Julian.

*"Caprice, tonight is all for you," Julian whispered in my ear. I was no longer in my bed, or in my pajamas. Winnie the Pooh and Piglet have been replaced by a floor-length, blood red strapless dress. The room, wherever I was, was dark, and out of the darkness came Julian's hand that took mine in his. With the room bathed in a soft light, he led me to the center of the room onto a California king-sized bed that was draped in silky linen the same color as my dress.*

*I know I said I didn't want to have a dream about Julian, but he was slowly taking his shirt off, and I reconsidered immediately. My hands were drawn to his bare chest while his hands made their way to the zipper on the back of my silky, red dress. I closed my eyes when I first felt his warm breath, and then his soft lips, upon my neck.*

*Once the zipper was all the way to the bottom, the fabric hung loosely on my breasts until Julian gently pulled it past my hips, and let it fell freely to the floor, revealing a matching bra and panties. Julian took me by the hand as I lightly stepped out of the dress. He kissed the inside of my palm before lowering me onto the bed. I was lying on my back as I watched him slowly lower himself on top of me, his lips to my lips.*

*Julian slowly moved his hands up my sides with the touch of an artist. His hands continued up my body, until they met my lacy, red bra. He pushed it aside, exposing my bare breasts. My nipples were hard from the pure anticipation of Julian's touch, and I didn't have to wait long. His hands cupped my breasts as his tongue circled one nipple, then the* other. Using his whole mouth, he began sucking then biting the tender nubs of flesh, making me wince in both pain and pleasure.

Julian stood up, taking my bra with him. He dropped it to the floor and then slowly lowered his black pants, revealing his amazing legs and what lay between them concealed behind silky black boxers. I slowly moved my hands up those amazing calves and back to his equally amazing pecks. I just stared at him, taking in the whole package. He came toward the bed and I found that I couldn't move as he approached.

Julian then laid on his back, with a hint of a smile on his face, which I took as an open invitation—free reign to do as I pleased, with whatever catches my fancy. His hint of a grin changed to a lustful chuckle before I leaned alongside him, breathing in his very essence and touching my lips to his.

I ran my tongue along Julian's neck and then slid to his chest. I stopped to kiss his nipples, just as a brief thank you for the attention he had given mine. My lips and tongue continued their journey over the length his body along one leg, and then the other. While I continued my exploration along his body, he promptly removed his boxers, revealing his immense size beneath the black silk.

I stopped and gazed at his hardened shaft. I lightly ran my fingertips along his member, and looked into his eyes waiting for a reaction. When I worked my hand over his hardness, he tilted his head back and moaned—just the reaction I was looking for. My hand continued to work its delicate *magic as I planted kisses all over his abdomen. My lips slowly moved to his hard shaft and I took it into my mouth. A shallow gasp escaped his lips as he placed his hands lightly on my head in encouragement. Slowly, I took him further into my mouth and along the back of my throat. I choked from his massive size.*

*"Oh...yes my love, that's it," he whispered. I am so caught up in pleasing him, His moans of pleasure spurred me on. Julian's hips bucked, matching my movements. When his body began to tense up, and his moment of truth was imminent, he stopped me. With his hand under my chin, he gently tilted my head up and looked me in the eye. "No Caprice, not yet."*

*I have to admit I was somewhat surprised, and disappointed, until Julian pulled me to him and kissed me with conviction. It was not a soft and gentle kiss. It was hard, deep, and passionate. He pulled away, laying me back on the bed, and glided his hand along my front. "You are so beautiful," he told me as his hands continued trailing and removing my red panties. I felt his strong hands travel along the back of my legs, and his tongue trailed down my stomach.*

*My moans of ecstasy became louder and louder and my legs spread wider as his hands and tongue met in my center. He held onto my legs as he finally inserted one finger inside me. I was tight with anticipation and felt every part of his finger as it slowly moved in and out. I ran my fingers through his hair and moved his mouth to where I needed it* to be. His breath was warm and his lips hot as I pulled him tighter against me.

"Julian... Please fuck me," I pleaded in a quiet, yet husky voice. Julian's eyes met mine, and then he stopped.

"I cannot ever just fuck you," he told me before returning his attention between my legs.

With every touch of his fingers, with every touch of his tongue on the skin of my neck, I got lost further and further in the moment. I hoped it would never end. I let out a sigh of disappointment when his fingers left my center and traveled back along my leg, his mouth moving to the same place. I could no longer feel his tongue on my upper thigh. What I felt instead, I'm quite sure, were his teeth. His mouth slowly closed over a length of skin on my leg, and he sank his teeth into my thigh. I lay there in stunned silence. I couldn't move due to my shock at not feeling any pain. All I could feel was a gentle sucking sensation as I watched crimson lines of blood flow to the bottom of my leg and pool on the bed.

Julian looked up at me...with blood on his face...my blood!

I snapped awake out of my dream and shot up, breathing heavily. It felt so real. It still feels real. I can still feel him on me—the room resonating with the scent of rain in his absence. I reached out for the solace of my large Winnie the Pooh bear. I could smell him there too, but for some reason, I didn't mind. I clutched my teddy bear in a big hug and fell into a peaceful, dreamless sleep.

# Chapter 3:

# Everything is Falling Apart

When I woke up, there was a familiar haze I'm sure everybody feels when they are startled awake from a nightmare. Happily, this haze was a pleasant one, unlike the all too common hangover haze which is usually pretty...hazy. This one was nice. I felt the coolness of my soft pillow and smelled the sweet aroma of a rose. A rose?

My eyes snapped open and I was faced with petals from a red rose, but not just any red rose.

A red rose with a note that said *To My Love*.

That was all it said. Three little words leaving one big mystery. How in the hell did it get here? Should I be creeped out? Was I visited by an insane florist who has trouble verbally expressing himself, or maybe a flying flower fairy? The window was open, but this apartment was six stories high. Maybe it was a secret admirer, a flying secret admirer.

Thoughts of Julian...lusty thoughts of Julian and my nasty intentions toward him. The thoughts of my single flower slowly faded away, giving way to thoughts of last night. I could feel his caress, his kiss, and his...teeth. I quickly ran my hand along my leg. There was nothing there but nice, smooth un-punctured skin. I needed to jump in the shower to wash away any impurities left behind by my all too real dream, but that smell of rain was all over me. His scent. I loved the smell, and a shower would take away the scent of him.

Have I crossed a line? I'm skipping personal hygiene for a tall, dark stranger who may very well be a figment of my libido. My journey into the darker recesses of my own neuroses was interrupted by the phone.

"Hello?" I said unsure.

"This is Shane from Fast Lane Loans," said a male voice.

Damn! I need to remember to check the caller ID.

"I'm calling to let you know that your loan is..." he began.

"Past due, I know," I interrupted in a soft voice I hoped generated sympathy from the other end of the line. "I've had a few set-backs recently. I can get you the money on the first of the month."

"I'm sorry miss, but we can only give you twenty-four hours, after that we will have to repossess your car," he said without an ounce of sympathy.

"I'll see what I can do," I said as I hung up the phone, and then I threw it on the bed where it bounced off onto the floor. Damn! I should have used my sexy voice. The phone started ringing again. Clearly I didn't throw it hard enough.

"Hello Geri," I said in relief after checking the caller ID this time.

"Took you long enough to answer," she replied.

"If I get one more call from a creditor, I'm changing my name to Betty Louise and moving to Branson, Missouri."

"Yea, they're dicks. You need to come to the Pita Pit. You can drown your sorrows in Mocha. I'll spike it with a mini bottle of Jack if you want?" she said with all the sympathy I needed.

"You sound kinda eager to see me," I told her with suspicion in my voice.

"We need to talk," she said blatantly.

"About...?" I began.

Silence.

"Geri?" Still nothing. "Is this about last night on the dance floor?" I questioned.

"Maybe," she said in a playful tone.

"Geri?" I was in no mood to play games.

"I'll throw in a free Pita, my treat," she tempted.

There was a brief hesitation on my part, until my stomach rumbled noisily. "I'll be there in ten," I said with a sigh.

When I got to the Pita Pit, there was Geri smiling from ear-to-ear, which can mean only one thing, she got laid by something other than a battery operated appliance. "So what's got your motor running?" I ask.

"Oh my God, Caprice, you won't believe the guy I met," she said with the giddiness of a Catholic schoolgirl who just broke into the sacramental wine.

"Geri, I'm really not sure I want to hear about this," I said hesitantly.

"Come on Cat, after last night I figured you'd be open to anything."

"Open? Interesting choice of words Geri, where did you meet this guy?" I quickly changed the subject.

"Does that really matter?"

"Oh my God, you met him online. Remember Geri, fool me once..." I reprimanded her.

"I know, but that was...an anomaly. Laura, that Goth girl from Trig class, she told me about this online dating site. She said it was great."

"And you believed her?" I questioned.

"I checked it out. You should too," she prompted.

"I have," I admitted. "But it never went beyond the keyboard. According to their high tech program, I'm looking for a truck driver with a PhD in religion."

"This isn't the same site. This one is new and it's cool as hell. It's called Secular Festival dot com," she continued.

I wasn't convinced in the least.

Geri kept trying. "Have you heard about the matchmaking festival in Lisdoonvarna, Ireland? It happens every year around September or October."

"Matchmaking? You mean like in those old movies where a Matchmaker talks a gullible young girl into marrying a daddy approved, rich asshole instead of the love of her life?"

"Okay, you're not getting it," she said with frustration. "The Matchmaking Festival in Ireland is real, and since I can't afford a trip to the Emerald Isle to find me lucky charm, I thought I would surf the net. You just fill out the profile, hit send, and wait for them to kick back a list of names of guys who are willing to stay and cuddle afterword. Oh, and don't post a picture," she warned.

"Why, are you speaking from experience?" I asked with a grin.

"Yes, you can get some real jerks," Geri said honestly.

"Really...let's hear about it."

"Not now, not ever," Geri said quickly. "Seriously Caprice, if you meet someone you like you can send him a photo, just don't post it publicly."

"Lesson learned?" I asked.

"The hard way," she answered, handing me an envelope.

"What's this?"

"It will help you get on the website," she answered as the pitas and drinks came to the table.

"Caprice, I don't want you to get hurt, but Julian is a player," Geri said.

"I know. Every girl including Dawn wants him and would sleep with him if he asked," I said while looking down at my hands.

I took a peek in the envelope. "I can't do this. It's not me, and I don't want a guy anytime soon. What happened last night was a lapse of judgment on my part." Then my phone alarm reminded me I needed to take off to another job pushing ice cream. "If you need me Geri, I'll be at Scoops passing out frozen headaches on a cone." I grabbed my pita as I left for work.

"Better hurry," she said as I turned to go.

"Thanks," I said, handing the envelope back. "I need to go guy free for a while, but if I change my mind I'll call to get that envelope."

I walked through the employee's entrance of Scoops and there was my boss in her dumbass red and white ice cream manager hat.

"Caprice, we need to talk," she said in a voice that indicated I was in trouble. *What the fuck does she want now? I got here with at least five seconds to spare.*

"Can you work a longer shift today?" She asked.

Shane's threats of repossessing my ride echoed in my head, "Yeah, I can do that," I told her begrudgingly. After about two hours of shoving thousands of calories of ice cream into waffle cones, my ass began to drag. I don't know why. It could be not enough sleep, or it could be too much hell-thy-name-is-Daniel in my life. Fortunately, time flew by as business picked up. But, unfortunately, it slowed back down when a boisterous, scary-looking lady started shouting her opinion at the top of her lungs.

The manager's attempt to calm her down was apparently succeeding. The irate lady's anger seemed less random and more focused...right at me. I don't know if her tutti wasn't fruity enough or she counted the one thousand sprinkles and came up with only nine hundred and ninety-nine. I don't know why she was glaring at me like all her troubles were my fault, I didn't even wait on her. She wasn't the only one glaring at me, now my manager was also.

It didn't take a keen sense of cosmic awareness to understand that I was being thrown under the bus here. I approached the irate woman and my boss. "I never said anything to you ma'am," I said in a stern, but civil, voice that I hoped wouldn't scare the customers that didn't hate me.

"No, you didn't have to...you kept rolling your eyes at me," she said in indignation.

Was this bitch serious? "I did not. I didn't even notice you. I was helping the other customers."

"I want this employee fired, now," she bellowed at the top of her lungs.

My boss took one look at me and I could see the cowardice in her eyes surface. She could side with me, a somewhat valued employee, or the bitch monster that clearly eats here too often.

"Caprice, you need to be out of here by the end of the day, you're fired," she said without a moment's hesitation.

"I'll make it easy for you," I said, taking off my apron. "I'll be out of here before she can finish her second Butterscotch Ripple. I quit."

"But I need you today," she said in mild shock.

"Are you kidding? You're more unbelievable than she is!" And with that, I left behind a crazed boss and an ice cream parlor full of screaming kids.

Okay, let's review. In the last twenty-four hours I have been fired from one job and I quit another. I was now Caprice, the arch enemy of Shane and his merry band of repo-men. Ugh, I should have stayed at Scoops. I'm sure after that bitch left I could have convinced my boss to keep me. I was just not in the mood for her shit.

During my drive home, I decided to occupy my mind with math. I'm out two jobs—and if I'm lucky enough to get work at Jade's Inn—I won't get paid for two weeks. This could be the last time I drive this car. Math sucks.

♦

When my Katy Perry ringtone went off, I attempted to put my depression on hold. "Hello," I said with hesitation, hoping it was someone who wanted to give me money and not take it.

"Caprice?" asked a voice.

"Yes."

"This is Sam from Jade's Inn." I suddenly realized how deep the voice was.

"Oh Sam...Hi...thank God," I said with relief.

"Sounds like you're happy to hear from me. You expecting someone else?"

"Oh no, it's nothing. I thought it might be, never mind." I tried real hard to stop the impending babble-fest coming out of me. "What can you do for me? I mean what can I do for *you?" Oh hell, just kill me.*

"Relax Caprice," Sam said in that deep, smooth tone he used. "Jade likes your design. He would very much enjoy hearing your other ideas. Maybe you can come over for coffee and a contract signing?"

"Contract signing...Really?" I asked hopefully.

"Really, you'll contract to do the Sleeping Beauty Room and two more rooms on top of that if you're still interested."

"I can be there in five minutes," I said as I hit the brakes and spun my car around.

"See you in five," Sam said before hanging up.

I'm wondering if it would be too forward of me to ask for an advance. I can't very well *arrive on time to my new job, or my current jobs I haven't fucked up, without wheels.*

Once I was in the parking lot of the Inn, it kind of hit me. My car really didn't fit in here among the classier cars. But hell, it's my car and I need to keep it for now. I jumped out and walked three steps and stopped dead. I looked down at myself. Oh shit, I can't go in there with my Scoops ice cream uniform on. I quickly went back to my car to see if I had any clothes. I found a pair of jeans with holes in the knees and a red tank top. Great, I should have gone home and changed.

I jumped in the back seat and looked around outside to see if the coast was clear. In what took about ten seconds, which was about five seconds too long in panic time, I had my ice cream covered pants off and my holey jeans on. I checked around again and pulled my shirt off, putting the tank top on. I looked more college girly and less pathetic ice cream girly. I slipped my shoes back on and started walking again and felt my ponytail hit my back. I grabbed the rubber band, pulled it out, and whipped my hair down and up in a heavy metal head banger move. I combed my fingers though my hair, hoping it doesn't look too ridiculously scary. I was obsessing. It wasn't like I was trying out for a modeling reality show.

I started up the familiar crescent-shaped stairs and stopped halfway to my destination. I slowly spun around, a complete three hundred and sixty degree turn, taking it all in. I don't know how this place does it. I've only been here once before, but it feels identical to home. I belonged. This place casted a spell and I was under it. It wanted me here somehow.

I walked back down the stairs and chose to take the side door. It's a privileged, private employee entrance. I began walking down the hallway when I heard the music. This wasn't some elevator music being piped through speakers around the Inn. This was live piano music coming from up front. I followed the music and there was Sam, tickling the ivories in a tux and tie. When I look at this guy, I see a linebacker that can crush your skull with his bare hands, and now he's playing piano like it's his only reason for living. I'm not familiar with the tune, but the music is beautiful. It has a darkness to it which both scared and pulled you in at the same time.

I found a shadowy corner and sat down to listen. I could have sat there for hours. I was more relaxed than I had been in days, so naturally, my phone rang. It always seems louder when I'm in public.

I quickly back into the hallway and straightened up, "Hello."

"Hello, this is Kim from Fast Lane Loans."
*Crap.*

"I'm just calling to remind you we close at five, so you still have some time to bring by your payment," she said in an emotionless voice that told me sympathy would not avail me.

"Thanks for the reminder, I guess." There was absolutely no sincerity in my response at all, but I really didn't care at this point.

"Look, I need to let you know that if we repossess your car it will cost you twice as much to get it back," she said kindly. At least she had more sympathy in her voice than Shane did. "You only have one payment left...it would be a shame to lose it now. So we'll see you before five."

So much for sympathy. She made it sound like it's easy to pull five hundred dollars out of my ass and put it on her desk by five.

"I'll try," I said, but she had hung up the phone. Bitch. I hope she and Shane get an STD together.

I stayed out in the hallway and found a sturdy wall to hold me up. I didn't want to cry on the floor. I didn't even hear the music stop.

"Money problems?" a deep, smooth voice asked. I was startled out of my slump and turned quickly to see Sam staring at me with a very concerned look. "Caprice, honey, why don't you come sit down before you pass out."

"Sorry," was all I managed to say.

Sam came up to me with an extended arm. "Tell Sam your money troubles," he said in a soft, reassuring voice as he took my hand and wrapped my arm around his. We sat down on the couch, in the foyer, and I told him my sad little tale of woe.

"Well this isn't a magical parchment," Sam said after I finished. He handed me a few pieces of paper. "It won't make your problems go away over night, but it is a bright spot in an otherwise dark day."

A contract, wordy, but the large number at the bottom was...large. "Is this right?" I asked Sam.

"Yes it is."

"Wow. Any chance there is an advance somewhere in those numbers?"

"Sorry kiddo. But..." he started then stopped.

"But? There's a but?" My sad eyes must have gotten to him.

"But...there is something you may be able to do."

"I'm listening," I said eagerly.

"Dawn is working on a project for us tonight. You can help her with it. It pays well."

"Sure. Any job would be great."

"Well, the first thing I need you to do is fill out an application and you will also need to take a physical." There was a staring contest for a moment. A physical? Was I trying out for the Jade's Inn track team? I didn't have to say a word. Sam knew what I was thinking. "It's Jade's rule, everyone that works here takes a physical. I can make all the arrangements if you like."

"Well," I began timidly, "I don't have a doctor and I really can't afford one," I said honestly.

"Won't be a problem. Everyone who works here is fully covered with medical and dental," he said happily.

"Sounds great!" Wow, a job that has benefits. This is new.

Sam gently squeezed my hand. "Tell you what, you bring me a copy of the completed physical, and

I'll see if I can come up with the money you need to get your car back."

I wonder if Sam and I are far enough in our new employer/employee relationship for me to give him a great big hug. I took a chance. "Thank you," I said, attempting to wrap my arms all the way around his massive form.

"I will see you soon," Sam said as he gently pulled himself away from me.

"Okay Sam. Thanks again." He beamed and walked back to his office and I headed out the front door.

As I walked to my car, I couldn't help but wonder about this mysterious project I volunteered to help with. As nice and caring as Sam is, he wasn't exactly forthcoming with details. If I didn't know better, I'd also say there was some hesitation in his voice when he made the offer. I can't tell if his hesitation was based on a lack of faith in my abilities to do whatever it is I am supposed to do, or if he was just concerned about me. Well, I got to say, my interest was definitely peaked.

I sat in my car and took out my phone. There was one person who could tell me what Dawn was going to do tonight that paid so well, and that was Dawn. I dialed her up and listened to Girls Just Want to Have Fun by Cyndi Lauper until she answered.

"Hi there," Dawn said, as if she was expecting my call.

"Hi Dawn, what are you up to?" I asked surreptitiously.

"Getting ready for tonight," she said without suspicion. Score.

"Actually," I said, "That's why I called, about tonight, about this...project you're doing. Sam told me..."

"I know," she interrupted. "Sam called me about two minutes before you did. I know he wasn't exactly an open book, so we should probably talk first." So much for the element of *surprise*.

Now I'm getting nervous about what Dawn is not saying. "Talk to me girl. What are you not telling me? Are we breaking the law with this project?"

There was silence on the other end of the line, and that's not like Dawn. This job better pay. "Be in my room in two hours." Dawn commanded. She hung up before I could answer.

Any minute now I'll start hearing the narrator guy from the Twilight Zone. I put my phone back in my pocket and took out the business card Sam gave me. This job is irrelevant if I can't get a physical.

I made the call and the doctor's office said there was a cancellation. I can have the time slot if I can get there in ten minutes. I'm really not in the mood to play doctor right now, but a girl's got to do what a girl's got to do.

# Chapter 4:

# Learning

I walked into a very nice, clean doctor's office. After being directed to a chair by a receptionist, who looked like she hasn't laughed in three years, I fill out the pain-in-the-ass paperwork.

"Caprice?" I heard a voice say.

"Yes," I said looking up at the tall nurse.

"Hi, my name is Nancy. Can you come this way please?"

Nurse Nancy? Should I call her Nancy? Nurse Nancy sounds like a porn character. Of course with as short as her skirt is, Nurse Nancy sounds more accurate.

"So you work at Jade's Inn?" Nurse Nancy asked.

"Yes, I'm hoping to start tonight."

"Have you met Sam?" she asked, not looking at me and continuing to fill out some paperwork.

Well that caught me by surprise. I stared at Nurse Nancy in a brief studded silence. "Yeah, I've met him," I finally said.

"Isn't he cute and cuddly?" she asked with a girlish smirk.

"Yeah, in an enormous truck-sized teddy bear sort of way," I replied uncertainly.

"Yes, I guess he is hard to miss in a crowd," she said with a hint of disappointment in her voice. We walked into a back room that was filled with all the typical trappings of a doctor's playroom. It came complete with an examination table with the paper covering that tends to stick to your ass. It also has all the same pictures on the wall of what various parts of the inside of your body looks like, and other pictures of people smiling like they are happy to be under a microscope.

Nurse Nancy directed me to the table. "Okay, you sit here. You're going to have to take a drug and blood test."

"Really, and I didn't even study," I said playfully.

Nurse Nancy put on her serious face, her early playful side gone." If you don't think you will be able to pass the drug test..."

"No I'm clean, the only thing I take is the occasional Tylenol, more frequently than normal," I admitted.

"Oh, before I forget," Nurse Nancy said, "There is one more test you'll need to take."

"Another one...Three mid-terms at once," I quipped as she reached into a drawer and pulled out a plastic cap. "Oh hells. Look, I am not pregnant."

"Sorry, but it's SOP, a Standard Operating Pain-in-the-ass," she said, her playful side showing again.

"Okay...but there is no chance, I'm knocked up." But then I began to think. That last time Daniel and I had sex, was he wearing a condom? I remember when we bought them. I wanted to get the ribbed ones, but he was afraid it would take away from his own pleasure. I'm sure we used one last time...didn't we?

After being weighed in on a scale that couldn't have been right, and banished to a bathroom to piss in a cup, I came out and was escorted back to the exam room.

"Just relax, the doctor will be in shortly," Nurse Nancy said with a smile. "His name is Dr. Andrews. He's not as cool as Sam, but he's all right," she said as she turned and left the room. So I sat waiting and waiting for Dr. Andrews and his instruments of poking and prodding. More waiting arrived, followed shortly by additional waiting. I don't understand why everyone in a doctor's office has such a different definition of "be in shortly." I think it should be like pizza. If he's not in here in thirty minutes, it's free.

With all this time on my hands, I had time to think and come to a conclusion. This is nuts. I'm jumping head first into a job I know nothing about. I need to get my car paid for before I have to take the bus and end up sitting next to Joe Shmoe, wearing a creepy raincoat and talking about his seven cats. It's not like I can get money from the Bank of Mom and Dad. If I can't make this job work...

Filling out the application for the Inn seemed less boring then doing nothing, so I started filling in the standard blanks. Name, address, job experience, and then the education questions *went from standard to none-of-your-damn-business.*

*How many people have you slept with? That's easy, two—sad, but easy. Ben from high* school was my first. I'm still trying to live that one down. Then there was Daniel, and I didn't exactly trade up. It's kind of an odd question for an Inn.

*Are you straight? And the odd just keeps coming. Yes, I'm straight. If yes, have you ever* been with anyone of the same sex? No. I don't think I want to, but I didn't write that down.

*Do you want to have sex with more than one person?* No. Deep down in the horny corner of my brain, I have thought about it, but again I'm not writing that down.

I was able to finish this very bizarre application just as Dr. Andrews showed up. "You must be Caprice," he said with the same smile he probably pasted on earlier this morning.

"Must be," I replied.

"Okay, if you can have a seat up here," he said, indicating the paper covered thing-a-majig. He started taking what appeared to be the less intrusive torture devices out of the drawer. He did a quick check of the heart, but spent too long watching my chest move when he checked the lungs.

"Okay, Caprice if you can lie back," he said.

Oh fuck, I hate this part! I have no doubt this procedure, and the instruments used really did come from the darker recesses of human history—like the Spanish Inquisition. I half expect the doctor to start asking where the top secret plans are. I laid back and started counting the dots on the ceiling.

"Have you been, or are you currently, on birth control?" The doctor asked as he finished his very thorough exploration.

"No, I'm not currently," I admitted. He handed me about three months' worth of samples and told me my tests came out fine. It's good to know Daniel didn't leave me with anything to remember him by. I couldn't get out of that place fast enough. I practically sprinted to the door, waving goodbye to Nurse Nancy on the way. I think she winked at me. I made it to the car with my test results and my new birth control pills. I still don't know why he insisted on those. I started the car and headed straight to the Inn.

I kept my mind occupied on the drive to my future work place by going over the events of the last few hours, the strange questions from the doctor, and the stranger questions on the application. The fact that my new job required me to disclose my personal sexual history leads me to believe my new career path will lead straight to a cell where there sits a new roomy named "Bertha" who thinks I'm cute when I snore. I pulled into one of the last parking spots at the Inn and made my way through the crowd to Sam's office.

"That was fast," Sam said when I walked in.

"There was a cancellation. Here is my clean bill of health and I left my new prescription out in my car." He looked through the forms as I watched him pensively. I was feeling nervous. He opened the drawer in his desk, took out a file with my name on it and put the forms in it. I was officially nervous. "So what happens now?"

"Just one more thing," he said after putting my file away. "I need a video."

"A video? Of what?" I questioned, shocked.

"Of you," he said simply, and offered me a smile.

"What kind of video?"

"Relax. It's just you sitting in a chair and me asking you questions. It's more for a record than anything else," Sam said with a wink.

"Am I fully clothed?" I said half-joking and half-wondering.

"Yes you are."

He led me down the hallway to a room with a sign labeled private. In the short time I had known Sam I had come to trust him, but for some reason I was uneasy. I sat down on a stool in the middle of the room, feeling isolated and alone. Sam sat at a table at the other end and switched on the lights. They were kind of blinding. I could see a camera pointed at me with a blinking red light.

"Okay, Caprice, just relax. Be honest and most of all be yourself," he said sensing my anxiety.

"O-okay," I didn't relax.

"Do you drink?" He asked gently.

"Not very often and no more than two drinks and then I stop, but if you're offering... It's been one of those days."

"No, that was just the first question. Do you smoke?" he continued.

"No," I said.

"Could you be with someone who smoked?" he asked again.

"No. What type of question is that?" I questioned.

"Standard," Sam said holding up the clipboard with a sheet of questions on it. "We have special guests, and we need to be very...particular about who we hire. Can we get back to the questions?" he prompted.

I bowed my head.

"What's your living situation?" he inquired.

"I live by myself in the dorm, but I have a roommate who lives with her boyfriend and she comes over every once in a while to meet her parents there. It's a hush-hush thing."

"Do you like to try new things?" he said changing the direction of the questions.

"Yes," I was hoping he was talking about food on that one.

"Do you have brothers or sisters?" he said changing direction again.

"Yes," I said.

"Which one are you?" he asked.

"First born, big sis," I said with a note of pride in my voice.

"Do you consider yourself a creative person?" he asked, a question much more to my liking.

"I'd like to think so," I answered honestly.

"Do you have traditional values?" Sam asked.

Now that was a loaded question. "I think I should say no, but to be honest, yes I believe I do." Thinking of the applesauce cake I make every year at Christmas time, the thrill of opening one Christmas present on Christmas Eve, and all the other things I think about during the holiday seasons. Come to think of it, I'm a very traditional girl.

"Would you rather have loyal friends or interesting friends?" he prompted quizzically.

"Loyal friends," I said, with as much truth as possible.

"Do you often fall in love?" He asked, looking at the clipboard.

"No..." I said tentatively.

"You have never been in love?" Sam prompted.

"I thought I was once, but not really," I said with a twang of pain in my chest.

"Do you find yourself daydreaming?" He asked.

"No," I didn't even believe myself when I said it. I knew he wanted honesty, but I thought I should leave out details about daydreaming, night-dreaming, and anything concerning the recent fantasizing about Julian.

"Do you believe long established customs should be respected?" Sam switched gears again.

That's a standard question? Who came up with these? "Yes, I always try and respect the customs of other people, even my friends."

"What do you think your friends would say about you?" Sam asked intently.

"I can only hope they'd say I was fun. I don't spend money past my needs. I do have a crazy habit of collecting Winnie the Pooh characters," I finished uncertainly.

Sam turned off the main lights and beamed at me, "Caprice, that's all we need." He stood up, reached inside his jacket, pulled out an envelope and then gave it to me. I opened it up. It was the pink slip on my car. It was paid for!

"Now go talk with Dawn and be back at six," he said before he left the room.

For a moment, a brief moment, I laughed on my way to Dawn's room. It wasn't a loud laugh, more of a suppressed giggle that comes out when you think of something funny right in the middle of class or church.

Dawn was fucking with me.

I'll walk in her room and she'll say "April Fools," or some dumbass thing like that, then she'll laugh her ass off. "Did I scare you?" she'll ask and then I'll seriously consider bitch- slapping her.

These thoughts quickly disappeared, the laughing stopped, and the fear returned. I no longer had to put up with the prick at the bookstore, or push ice cream to patrons who have mastered the art of being truly evil. But I still feel like a prisoner to the economic realities of my life. The burning question is if I'll become an actual, no joke, and prisoner.

I had my pink slip, the car was mine, and the sky wasn't falling. So why did I feel nervous about Dawn's room? Why was I walking slower than normal? When I found myself standing in front of Dawn's door, I realized running back to my car and speeding off was all in my head. This was going to happen. When I knocked lightly on the door, it was probably because I was hoping she wouldn't be there. Unfortunately, she rapidly opened the door.

"Could I ask you a question before we talk about the job?" Dawn asked before I could even say hello.

"Okay," I told her. I didn't know if I felt more relieved or simply more anxious. I think I was jumping between both. Was this a veiled attempt by Dawn to work in the details of the job by hiding them between the lines of a seemingly casual conversation?

"So, you and Julian, dance floor. Spill," she asked in syllables.

"We danced," I answered honestly.

"Needing more narrative here," Dawn prompted.

"We danced, we...kissed," I said flatly.

Dawn pulled me into her room, dragged me to the couch, and stared at me like an eight year old waiting for the end to an exciting bedtime story.

"The kiss was amazing. The dance was amazing. I needed air, so I went outside. I knew if I went back in, there would be more than just dancing and kissing...clothes and inhibition would have been lost. I decided to bail," I finished.

"You wanted him bad?" Dawn said in surprise.

"I wanted him more than bad. That is why I ran away like a scared little girl." When my imagination starts to undress a guy who wasn't even there, I knew it was time to change the subject. "Can we talk about the job now?"

Dawn stood up and started pacing back and forth. She stopped and turned to me. "First, you can't tell Geri," she said as though her pacing had made her come to some kind of decision.

"Why, are you a prostitute?" I joked.

"Paid escort is more PC," she replied without hesitation.

I was silent. I could tell she was waiting for the revelation to sink in, and waiting for me to reply. I didn't.

"The money is really good at the brothel," she finally said.

"You're not bullshitting me are you? What about the hotel? Is that real or just a front?" I was reeling.

"No, Jade's Inn is a themed hotel as well as an...Escort service for certain clientele."

"So Geri doesn't know?" I asked, still trying to recover. I couldn't even think about how ironic it was that I had been joking about this only a day or two ago.

"God no! She'd freak and then try and write the exposé of the century," Dawn said in horror.

"How did you get involved in this?"

"Do you remember when I lost my job at the bookstore for being five dollars short on my till, even though everyone knew it was because I refused to sleep with Mike?" I was bobbing my head remembering. "Well, I went in the direction of a club downtown in order to drown my sorrows and I met a guy who gave me his card, and told me to call if I was looking for work. I was looking for work, so I called."

"Just like that?"

"My rent and tuition won't pay themselves," Dawn concluded.

"I get that...really I do, but..." I fumbled.

"Caprice, the money is great."

"But how did you know that guy wasn't a creep that could have killed you?"

"It was Sam," she said simply.

"It was...Sam? Like Sam, Sam?" I stammered. Dawn just bobbed her head in response. "I work in a brothel and I'm designing a room based on a beloved fairy tale so people can fuck in it?" I asked in utter astonishment.

"You don't think people don't fuck at the hotels in Disneyland?"

"So not the point," I said quickly, and she started looking sad. "Do you like the...work?"

She started smiling again. "I like working at the Inn. Seriously though, you can't tell Geri, she thinks I'm painting rooms there, which I am so it's not like it's a lie...it's more of an omission of certain truths."

"Dawn, you're babbling," I said.

"Sorry," she apologized.

"I came here to find out about this job I'm supposed to help you with, now I'm thinking that maybe I don't want to know."

"It's not that big of a deal," she reassured me.

"I don't think I can have sex for money," I said with my outside voice. My inside voice was *saying you may not have a choice.*

"What if I told you that you won't have to have sex with anyone tonight, and you can still settle the debt on your car?"

"Does it involve me just designing rooms?" I asked with hope. "I can design a dominatrix themed chamber as long as I don't have to...dominate."

Dawn put on her reassuring smirk with a sympathetic expression on her face. "The room designing will happen and hey—the domination room thumbs up—but you won't see any cash for a while. You help me tonight and you get paid tonight, and trust me it isn't minimum wage."

"Are you having...sex?" I asked.

"Yes," she said simply.

"But I'm not?" I cautiously asked.

"No."

"But you need my help?"

"Yes," she stated.

"Hey," I spoke up. "If you're looking for a tutorial, you don't want me. Besides you know how to do...everything. I should know, I've been in the next room before. Remember the freshman mixer?"

With that Dawn gave me an even bigger grin and said "Compared to the freshman mixer, this will be something with long-term benefits, Caprice." I swallowed apprehensively, wondering if the freshman mixer was really something I wanted to relive.

# Chapter 5:

# The First Night

# Working at Jade's Inn

It was six o'clock and I was right on time, punctual. I wonder if I get points for that. I was wearing my game face, but nervous as hell. Sam met me at the door and silently led me to a changing room.

Hanging on the wall was my outfit.

*So much for the girl next door routine.*

It was a black, ivory, contemporary dress with a pull-over V-neck, gather at the bust, cap flutter sleeves, fitted bodice, with a scalloped hem. To top it off—or bottom it off—a black garter belt and fishnet stockings.

No underwear.

This isn't the girl next door. This isn't even girl around the corner and down the block.

"You look...great," Sam said with sincerity as I stepped out of the changing room. He led me down the hall to a room with a gold-plated sign on the door that read "Roman Bath." The sign wasn't lying. This place was amazing with Roman pillars and statues of ancient gods. The half-naked statue pouring water into the beautiful marble sunken bath might have been Aphrodite. She must have been hot in her day.

"Okay, here's the rule," Sam said in his best business voice. "The client is not supposed to touch you. That rule will be followed." If that's a Sam rule, I'm guessing no one ever breaks it. Sam sat me down on an antique looking, long chair with a big pillow. It looked like it was built for a Roman Priestess to recline on while she was being fed grapes from her well-hung minions. It looked cool, and it fit the room, but it was not in the right place. It looked like it had been moved from near the tub, and now it was facing a bed adorned with white, silk sheets. I guess the stage was set.

There was a knock at the door and in walked a six foot two, eyes of blue, short, dark brown haired a guy that looked like a college professor. Sam introduced him as Kurt, which I'm sure wasn't his real name. He was cute, but definitely not my type. However, when his black silk robe opened to reveal his bulging boxers, and there wasn't a hint of embarrassment on his face, I had to be impressed.

Sam turned to me and quietly said, "Remember, he won't touch you. However, if you feel inspired to...help yourself...while you watch, feel free." Subtlety obviously wasn't Sam's strong suit. It's not often that I get an open invitation to give myself a happy. Sam went to leave the room, and when he opened the door, there was Dawn—wearing a floor length, black leather jacket and black lace, wrist length, half finger gloves on her hands. Why was I so focused on those gloves, I have no idea. Sam then took her by the tips of her fingers, held her hand up high, and guided her into the room like an artist putting his models in place.

"Lady, gentleman, I present to you, Lisa." Dawn, or Lisa as far as Kurt knows, waltzed into the room and did a complete turn, her jacket twirling up and showing some leg. Sam beamed and left the Roman Bath, closing the door behind him.

This was awkward. I was a rookie, and it was probably showing. Dawn led us over to this really cool looking stone table and bench that seemed like it was carved right out of the wall. On top of the table was a bottle of champagne and three crystal glasses. The small talk didn't last long. It really didn't seem appropriate, considering. We weren't really concerned about the weather or who was from out of town. We made a toast to the evening, then stood up and moved towards the bed.

Kurt guided me to the fancy chair then moved to the bed himself. Dawn, now standing in the middle of the room, slowly pulled the jacket down from her shoulders, allowing it to drop further and further towards the floor. I don't know how she did it, but she made the jacket appear to move in slow motion as it fell.

When I saw what Dawn was wearing under the jacket, my eyes widened as much as Kurt's. She wore a black leather corset, a skimpy, black, see-through, thong panty and the thigh-high stockings she displayed were also black. I'm not sure what color the high heels were, but I think they were somewhere between black and scarlet.

Dawn sauntered over to Kurt with all the confident attitude of a woman in control. Kurt put his hands gently on her shoulders then moved them slowly down her arms, kissing her in a way that clearly showed he cared for her. She glided her hands across his chest and then lowered herself in front of him, reaching under the black robe. It wasn't long before I saw Kurt's black *silk boxes down around his ankles. Who would have thought he's wasn't circumcised?*

Never saw that before.

Dawn slowly stood up and stared into Kurt's eyes with a wry smile on her face. I couldn't believe how gracefully she moved and how sexy she looked doing it. I couldn't help but wonder how long she'd been doing this. Dawn traced her fingers along Kurt's jaw, from one side to the other, while moving behind him. She lifted his arms straight out and slowly took off his robe completely. There was Kurt in all his naked glory, and clearly he was excited to be there.

Dawn put her hand on his head and ran her fingers through his hair as she came back around and stood in front of him. I found myself anticipating what I knew was about to happen as I watched Dawn putting her arms around his neck and shoulders, pulling Kurt even closer to her. Kurt pulled away and started kissing her cheek, going to her ear lobe and breathing a bit heavy on her as I watched it all. This was better than a sex DVD.

Kurt began to slowly massage Dawn's breasts, pulling them up to expose the nipples over the top of corset. I saw Dawn look at me for a second. Our eyes met, and then she was back to kissing Kurt again.

Kurt started sucking Dawn's breast as he teased her, watching how her nipples were getting hard. Then Dawn started kissing Kurt's neck and working down his chest, moving her hands down to Kurt's happy place. Dawn reached out and took hold of him in her hand. I started thinking of Julian and how much I wanted to do the same thing to him.

Dawn was on her knees now, in front of him, and both of them positioned where I could see everything. Dawn began to kissing Kurt's member, licking it and slowly placing the head in her mouth. Kurt looked into my eyes, but I shyly looked away and peeked back down at Dawn. She pulled away and I could see that Kurt was finally fully erect, and he wasn't small. I watched as she took hold at the base of his shaft. Kurt then ran his fingers sultrily through Dawn's hair, then grabbed and pulled it.

Ouch, that had to hurt, but she didn't act like it hurt. She looks more turned on by it. That's hot.

After spending some time at the tip, she took all of him into her mouth. Hearing the quick intake of his breath gave her the encouragement to go even deeper. She began a slow rhythm that brought out a slow moan from Kurt. He started running his fingers through Dawn's hair. I think it was his way of telling Dawn it felt good to him. She began to pick up the pace and alternated between his tip and shaft. I knew Kurt was close when his hand pulled tighter in her hair. Kurt was trying hard to maintain control. I could see it in his eyes when he would casually look at me, watching me enjoy what they were doing. Dawn's rhythm began to increase until she heard the words, "Baby, I'm coming!"

She slowly withdrew his member from her mouth and stood up. Kurt then laid her on her back across the white silk blankets of the bed, and then slowly traced his hands down her body, pausing to cup her breasts under her corset. He then continued kissing down the rest of her from over her stomach and panties, all the way down to her knees.

He gently pushed them apart and ran his hands back up her legs, over the region of her crotch, eventually resting on her red thong. Then he was quickly under it.

Dawn was excited. I could tell, even from where I was sitting. Kurt moved up to her breasts, moving his fingers over her hard nipples. He kissed her lips, then her neck, then ran his tongue down her front, stopping to play with her navel. When he continued to move his head down, Dawn's legs opened wider. He moved his head between her legs and seemed content to remain there for a while. To my surprise, I seemed envious...and anxious.

Eventually, Kurt turned Dawn over on her stomach. He moved her up to a kneeling position on her hands and knees, pulled the crotch of her panties aside, pressed against her and slowly pushed in. I had to pause and reflect.

*How did I get here? How did I get to this point? I lost a couple of jobs. I lost my car, and now I was sitting there watching my friend getting fucked. I was getting paid for this, and okay I'll admit, I was really turned on too.*

Kurt continued to push into Dawn, thrusting harder and harder with each movement of his body. Her breathing was getting shallower and shallower from his efforts. She closed her eyes and moved her own hand between her legs. When she opened her eyes, she was looking straight at me. Is it wrong that I was even more turned by that?

Kurt's erection appeared as stiff as ever, and he was pounding into Dawn like a jackhammer. He slowed down to undo her bra. Her breasts were now free, moving back and forth, when Kurt put his hands on her hips and continued thrusting into her. I was startled when I felt a hand on my own breast, and was shocked when I realized it was my own.

I started watching the show again, and I left my hand where it was. Kurt slowly pulled out and turned Dawn over on her back. Oh my God. This is like a cross between a porn movie and dinner theater but, no one is eating, so to speak. Dawn lifted her legs high and rested them on Kurt's shoulders as he moved himself on top of her again.

Kurt lowered himself carefully onto Dawn, and pushed inside of her in one movement. I could hear Dawn's intake of breath, and then I heard squeals and moans—not just from her, but from me too.

I could not believe what I was feeling, what I was doing. The room was filled with the musky scent of sex so thick you could feel it, taste it, and choke on it. I pulled my skirt up and moved my hand between my legs. I knew both Kurt and Dawn could see me, all of me, since I wasn't wearing panties. The look on Dawn's face was priceless. I had one foot on the floor and one draped over the arm of the chair. This really got Dawn going. Kurt began pounding into her with greater intensity.

I could tell Dawn was close to finding her release, just like I was. She was able to maneuver Kurt on his back so that she straddled him, and rode him up and down for all he was worth. Her eyes rolled back, her head rolled back, and she exploded in ecstasy. She continued to ride Kurt while she massaged her own breasts, and Kurt thrust up one last time up as he came inside of Dawn. The sound of their moans of ecstasy covered the sound of my own.

*Well, that was different!*

You know when young people, late teens to early twenties, leave home for the first time they think "Wow! I'm on my own. I'm an independent spirit doing things for myself." After about a week or two they get scared, they think "Shit, I have to do everything for myself!" Reality takes a foothold, imbedded deep inside that part of the mind where they used to keep their youthful enthusiasm. They start thinking about home-cooked meals, their little dog Sparky, and good old Mom and Dad, and they give them a call and say, "Guess what I did today?"

I didn't think I'd be making that call.

My eyes were closed, but I could hear talking. I could have opened them, but I didn't want to. If I opened my eyes, the talking people will be naked. If I keep my eyes closed, I can be invisible. If I opened them, the naked people will notice me and they might say, "Thanks, you're amazing." I was not looking for affirmation. I was looking for an escape hatch.

About five minutes after the talking stopped, I opened one eye. This was risky, I know, because if they were still there they might think I was winking at them. They'll think I want to do it again, maybe switch places with someone. Fortunately, my one eye didn't see a room full of pervs...Just one...Just me. Just one perv surrounded by a bunch of Roman God statues. I wonder what they thought of the show. Probably, the one that didn't hide his head in his toga was *Baucus. Was he a Roman god or a Greek god? I couldn't remember.*

I made my way to the Roman sink and cleaned myself off. I put my clothes back on while Venus stood there and watched me. She looked sort of judgmental, in a god-like way. I just can't tell if she was judging my moral character or my performance. She was the goddess of love. Maybe she'd give me two thumbs up.

I stepped up to the statue, "This is between me and you, Neptune," I said quietly. "I enjoyed it."

I did a cowardly thing and put my ear to the door. I couldn't hear anyone—no walking, no talking, and no laughing. Then I did a brave thing and opened the door.

"Hi...Sam," I said meekly.

"Hello Caprice," he replied in that deep soothing voice of his. "Caprice, I'm not going to ask how you're feeling. This was your first time, so I won't ask about your emotional state. Let me just say that the client loved you, which he expressed both verbally and monetarily." Sam reached into his inside pocket.

"This is for you. A four hundred dollar tip, you earned it." Sam chuckled and walked back down the hall to the front desk. I walked the other way.

I got the point of the employee's entrance now. It was convenient. It lets you make a more discreet, stealthy exit, avoiding large crowds and glaring eyes. All I had to do now was make it across the parking lot to my car.

My car. The car I just paid off by watching my friend get laid.

The air was cool, but more importantly it was dark, nature's cover. I didn't need a mask. I didn't have to hide my face like a celebrity coming out of rehab. The night was my friend. But I *was thinking. If I'll continue to work here—in more than a room designer capacity—I need to not feel shame, let alone hide from it. I saw two people enjoy the hell out of each other, and they let me join them. They had a great time and I had, at least, two orgasms.*

So why did I feel so conspicuous? I was alone in a parking lot, and yet, I felt like I was in someone's spotlight.

I didn't hear the footsteps. I did hear a deep voice say, "Do you mind if I walk with you?"

I turned so fast I nearly tripped over my own feet. "Julian! Where did you...were you lurking in the shadows?"

"I apologize if I startled you, honestly, I did not mean to," he said with genuine concern.

"That's okay," I said breathlessly. "Just give me a chance to breathe again, and I'll be fine."

"So...may I walk with you?" he softly asked again.

"Um...we..." My head, my heart, and my crotch were in a three-way battle, and I don't *know who was on whose side. Okay, mister hottest guy ever, what are your intentions? I'm still keyed up from watching the porno which keeps replaying in my head. Dawn does Kurt, and* Julian picks now to walk with me, and then stare at me with those bedroom eyes. How dare *he...wait, walking together with Julian through a dark parking lot? Why did it feel like déjà vu?*

"Look, there's no need to walk with me. I'm fine and there's my car. So why don't you just let me be and..." I began.

"I saw you come out of Jade's Inn," he interrupted.

"Yes, I did. Do you have a problem with that?" I said cautiously.

"No, not at all, I find it interesting. When did you start?"

"I started tonight if you must know." *Why am I telling him this? If he asks about the details, I'm pulling out the mace. Or maybe a rock! Better yet, pull him into the back seat of my car and have my way with him.*

"You appear distracted."

"Probably...maybe...a little," I stammered.

"Perhaps I should leave you so you can return home on your own?" he asked curtly.

"Probably," I said weakly and still tripping while walking as I tried to escape.

"Is it inappropriate if I ask you for a kiss before I leave?" he prompted in the politest voice I have ever heard a person use.

"Probably...not," I said, not sure what my mind was thinking. But, I really wanted him to kiss me. I was lost in those eyes. I would have agreed to anything if he continued to press the issue. He put both hands behind my neck, and gently pressed his lips to mine. The kiss was soft, at first, but there was an urgency that took us both over. I could feel a need, I just didn't know if it was mine or his. I knew I wanted him, in the worst way possible, and clearly he wanted me.

My head won the battle and I pulled away." Okay...well...I need to...go," I said as I jumped in my car, started it up, and left tracks in the Jade's Inn parking lot. Holy crap! I hope I *have batteries at home for what I was planning to do later.*

No sooner had I gotten my car in the parking lot to the dorm, than I sat in it thinking about the evening. I would have ran to my room by now, be in my bed hiding under the covers, waking up from the most bizarre erotic dream I've ever had... But, I was still in my car replaying everything. It's still sinking in. The fact that I watched my best friend fucking, and getting fucked in return, didn't really bother me. What bothered me was the fact that it didn't bother me. I didn't know I was voyeuristic. "Caprice, I would like to introduce you to, Caprice, someone you thought you knew," I said to myself in mock introduction.

I made it up the stairs and to my room, but somebody had gotten there first. There was a note on the door.

*Welcome to the family. Did I put on a show or*

*what? You put on a hell of a display yourself. I
didn't know you had it in you. Can we get together
tomorrow and talk?*

*Love (don't hate), Dawn*

*P.S. Geri will freak if she knew what we are doing.
So shhhhh.*


I crumpled up the note and went inside. I had a
decision to make—bed or booze. I opted for bed
and headed that way. Again, someone had gotten
there before me. On the pillow rested another
note...and a rose.

*I loved watching you tonight. See you soon.*

This one didn't have a signature. A fan letter
from anonymous? Maybe Dawn talked Kurt into
leaving me fan mail, but Dawn doesn't have a key.
The door was locked, but the window was open. My
mysterious flying secret admirer had struck again.

I was in that room for an hour and a half and I
needed to take a shower. A longer one than usual,
much longer, I ran out of hot water. I got dressed in
my cute, non-sexual, PJ's with a Pooh bear falling
asleep over a line that says Sleepy as a Bee, then
went to sit on my bed. I needed to sleep, I really
did. The fact that I now had money to pay my bills
should calm down the practical side of my life. I
should have been relaxed, but looking at my cell
phone it was only...nine- thirty...wow, I thought it
was later than that. I decided to check my email for

classes tomorrow and see if I had anything from Geri because I wouldn't do that match making thing and I knew she wasn't going to let it go that easy.

I turned off the soft, comforting glow from the computer, and had just picked a particularly soft, fluffy Winnie the Pooh bear and the next Anita Blake novel. She's my favorite, when my cell phone rang.

"Hi, Cat, it's me Alex," said the voice on the phone. Alex, who was more Daniel's friend than mine, had often worked out with us at the gym together.

"Hey Alex, what's up?" For a second, I had a flash of alarm, thinking something had happened to Daniel, and Alex was calling to tell me.

"I was just thinking of you and thought I'd give you a call. I hope it's okay. Am I interrupting anything?"

"Just on my date with Laurell K. Hamilton."

"Oh, okay. I hope this isn't too awkward, but I was just wondering if you'd like to go with me some night to Portneuf Valley Brewery. They have great music and food there." Alex was cute. I had never had any idea that he was interested in me, so I was surprised by his request.

"Hello? Listen, if you feel weird about it, I completely understand," he said with a respectful, yet disappointed note in his voice.

"No, no, not at all...I'm just surprised. You know I just broke up with Daniel and I know you guys hang out," I said, trying to be considerate.

"Well, I asked Daniel. I didn't know if he'd object, especially since he and Molly broke up," he said as if this is common knowledge.

*Whoa, did I hear right? Daniel and Molly broke up? Well there was a happy bit of news. It kind of makes me feel tingly all over. I wonder who broke up with whom. If Daniel called it off, did this mean he had come to his senses and realized what a mistake he'd made? What am I saying, I didn't want him back...or did I? And why is Alex asking Daniel if he can date me? He's got some nerve! Daniel can't say who I can date and who I can't. If he knew what I did tonight, it would make his head spin.*

"I didn't know he broke up with her," I said, as the wheels in my brain started moving, cranking out veritable possibilities. Maybe there was a chance we can get together again. Why was I thinking that way?

"Well, she left him," Alex commented. "You probably don't want to talk about it." He sounded hopeful and disappointed at the same time. "I just wanted to call and see if you'd like to check this place out with me." Clearly he didn't know me as well as he thought. I'd have loved to hear more about how Molly dropped Daniel's ass. In my world of imagination, I can see her throwing heavy objects at him before leaving.

"Sure, Alex. I'd love to go. When are you going?"

"How about dinner at the Brewery tomorrow night, if that's not too short notice?" he said excitedly.

"No, that sounds great. I'm pretty open tomorrow," I said in an even tone. But, I was really boiling to know more about Daniel's breakup.

"Okay, I'll pick you up at seven. Where are you staying at, since you moved out?" he asked curiously.

"I'm now living in Stevenson dorms room six one four," I responded.

"I'll see you tomorrow," he said, like Christmas had arrived early.

"I'm looking forward to it, bye." As I hung up the phone I tried to think about what will happen when I see Daniel again. I guess this is commonly known as soul searching. Do I want him back? Hell no. Do I want him to ask me back? That could be fun, and I knew he would ask.

Even though Daniel can't commit to a relationship that is anything close to permanent, I really think he's afraid being alone.

I read until I fell asleep, and once asleep began to dream. Not of Alex. Maybe I'll dream of *Daniel's body on the ground and Molly standing over it with his heart in one hand and his dick in the other.*

It began with a dress. It was a white dress that was snug on the top and about the waist, and flowing below the hips. My hair and the dress were blowing in the wind as I walked outside my dorm, watching as a long black limo approached. It came to a stop and Julian stepped out, wearing a long black jacket and a blood red shirt underneath. He looked incredibly hot, and made my own temperature rise in the dream as he approached. I looked down and noticed my dress was now a blood red that matched Julian's shirt. Julian held out his hand and I grabbed it as he helped me into the limo. Julian was kissing my neck and moving down to my breast until the limo stopped. All Julian said was, "After," which left me thinking of wonderful things. The car stopped in front of the Bloody Rose. We stepped out of the vehicle, went straight inside, and he led me directly to the dance floor. The first dance was slow and all ours. After it concluded, the rules changed.

Julian left me and said, "Let the game begin." Then Julian went and led a hot, young woman to the dance floor, whose mini skirt was as tight as a second skin. Her hair was raven black and it flew everywhere as she spun around. Julian pulled her close, his hips moved in perfect rhythm with hers.

My red dress was now tight and very, very black. It was now my turn to dance with a young stranger. I didn't know his name, but he was tall, he knew his way around the dance floor, and judging by the bulge in his pants, he was more than happy to see me. Our dance was not unlike the young woman and Julian's, and even though Julian knew it, he kept a very close watch on me.

The night went on and so did the game of changing partners. Each dance with the strangers was hotter than the last. I never thought that condoms would be necessary on the dance floor, but I was starting to think it might not be a bad idea for this kind of dancing. I don't know if the object of the game was to make each other jealous or to turn each other on, but it worked either way.

After we danced with nearly everyone in the place, we said goodbye to them and left for the car. Just to put an exclamation on the festivities at the notorious Bloody Rose, I smacked him on the ass.

"That's for every dance that wasn't with me. I believe you're just trying to make me jealous," I said playfully as we moved towards the car.

"It worked didn't it?" He replied.

I answered him with another smack in the rear.

Once inside the car, Julian pulled me into a passionate kiss. I allowed his tongue to pass my lips. His hand was on my knee and slowly started moving up. As his hand reached my upper thigh, his lips found the pulse point on my neck. His fingers slipped into my panties as his teeth pierced my neck. Then Julian looked up into my eyes with blood covering his face...my blood...

I shot up out of bed with my hand on my neck and ran into the bathroom. I was afraid to look in the mirror. When I did...there was nothing there. I dreamed of Julian biting me, and I enjoyed it. The brief pain seems small compared to the intense feeling of pleasure...of being claimed...of being loved.

I returned to bed, hoping to dream of puppies instead of Julian being a vampire. Maybe reading Laurell K. Hamilton books was not such a smart idea at bed time.

# Chapter 6:

# The Day After

I woke the next morning to Dawn knocking on the door.

"Wake up, we need to be at Jade's Inn in twenty minutes," she said in a hurry.

"It's Sunday, can't I sleep today?" I asked pleadingly. "Isn't it sacrilegious in our line of work to be doing our line of work on Sunday?"

"No, we have to get our work assignments for next week, so you can tell Sam you'll not be doing any more assignments because you said it was a one-time thing." Dawn said as I opened the door and let her in.

"Give me five minutes and we can go," I said, and then I thought about it. "Why do I have to go?"

"All escorts, men and women, have a meeting on Sunday. It's the rules," she said like a senior at prom.

"I'm not an escort. It was a one-time thing," I said resolutely.

"All the more reason to go, so you can tell Sam exactly that today. By the way, did you know you got the most hits on the website last night? Set a new rookie record. You have the biggest bid ever for a new girl."

I was going through my closet picking through the limited wardrobe in front of me, when I *thought I heard Dawn say biggest bid. I couldn't have been the bid...and then it hit me like a* Mack truck. "Biggest bid?" I shouted turning around.

"Biggest bid," she said again with enthusiasm.

"Bid? As in bid?" I stammered.

"Did I forget to mention the part about the bidding?" she said with a sly smile.

I was livid, "Uh, let me think. Sex, Roman bath, voyeurism...nope, no bidding," I said irately, then sat down and pulled Dawn with me. "Let's talk about auctions and shit!"

"It's not as bad as it sounds," she said immediately, with her hands in the air in a defensive posture. "It's not like there's a guy in a cowboy hat talking really fast. It's more of a silent bidding process."

"It's not as bad as it sounds," she said immediately, with her hands in the air in a defensive posture. "It's not like there's a guy in a cowboy hat talking really fast. It's more of a silent bidding process."

"Dawn, I really don't want to do this...I don't want to be a prostitute," I said in a whisper as though someone could hear me.

"So you think I'm a prostitute?" Dawn said with an impish twinkle in her eyes.

"No..." I lied. "I don't think that about you." Which, of course, I really did. I mean she's having sex with guys and getting paid for it. If it fucks like a duck...

"Caprice, do you know how many guys I sleep with?" she said with raised eyebrows.

"No, honestly I never thought about it," I said curiously.

"Two guys, the same two guys maybe twice a week. You met Kurt, the other is Sean. Sean is the one I really like. I won't be getting a new guy until Kurt's time is up in about a month," she said bluntly.

"A new guy, huh?" I questioned.

"When I started, both Kurt and Sean wanted me exclusively. They both made a bid, along with several others. I get with the high bidder and work out a deal that essentially makes me his for the next six months. Kurt and Sean bid about the same, but neither had enough. Sam suggested I take both if they agree, which they did," she finished.

"So you're not getting with any random guy that walks into Jade's Inn?" I asked cautiously.

"No. The money talks, but I have the final decision and choice. Sean has asked for another six month extension, which I'm happy to talk about. It's not prostitution if you really like the guy, is it Cat?"

Who was I to shoot holes in her delusion? She sounds like she really likes this Sean guy. He's buying her affection, even if she's giving it of her own free will. Although, I couldn't help but think she'll get hurt in the long run...

"I don't know about this stuff. I don't exactly put the 'pro' in prostitute, but I don't think you're a hooker." And I hope she believed that, even if deep down I didn't.

There was a sudden, dim sadness in Dawn's eyes, but the light quickly came back like a switch in her mind was thrown. She banished the financial aspect of her career choices, and decided to focus on the sex, or more specifically our night of debauchery. "So what did you think about last night?" Dawn asked politely.

"It was good...It was fun... It was...weird in a good...a fun way." I started turning red with embarrassment at the mention of the previous night's activities. "That doesn't go beyond us. Honestly Dawn, I didn't think I was capable of doing...that," I said apprehensively.

"Gotta tell ya Cat, I knew you're capable of doing...that, I just didn't know you're capable of sharing," she said with a wink.

"Our little secret?" I asked tentatively.

"Our little secret," she sincerely answered.

I finished dressing and Dawn averted her eyes. I felt more comfortable, but I'm not sure why she bothered. "I hope they have guys picked out for you," she said.

"Already? They found people for me?" I let that information roll around in my head for a while.

"Sam told me there was a bidding war," Dawn said too happily.

"A war? Are there casualties?"

"All but two, the highest bidders," she then said in an air of seriousness.

"You mean I have to tag team like you have been?" All kinds of imagery just passed through the naughty side of my head, which was smiling widely on the inside. The outer me was staring at Dawn like an uptight librarian. Good cover.

"No," Dawn explained. "You do not have to double dip if you don't want to. You pick the highest bidder. Hell, if you want you can pick the lowest bidder, but I wouldn't recommend it. This is a business."

"And there's no business like showing your business, but I don't know if it's a business I want to know...you know?" I said as I finished getting dressed.

"I know," Dawn said.

"So this choosing between bidders...May I bring up a moot point, I mean really moot," I said, raising my eyebrows again.

Dawn put her hands on my shoulders in an effort to calm me down. "Caprice, I get that you are having issues with the idea of prostitution. But you need to think about it, and we need to go. I'll drive while you think, and while you're thinking, think of a new persona for your profession."

"A new name? I haven't finished using my old one yet, thank you very much," I said in mock offense.

"It's just a stage name, a 'Clark Kent' to get you through the evening, Superman. It's more for your safety, in case a client gets too clingy after business hours," Dawn said as we walked out my apartment door.

"Still a moot point," I reminded her heading towards the car. "But how about...Emily?"

Dawn looked at me as she unlocked the car and seated herself behind the wheel. "I like it. Short, sweet, there's innocence to it...The clients will love it! A name like that could up your bid, Cat."

She started the car, pointed it in the right direction and we took off to whatever awaited us, no matter how scary, weird, bizarre, strange, or freaky it might be. Ever since Daniel broke up with me, it seems like I have been losing control of my life. Oh well, at least I'm only a sort-of prostitute and not a stripper or something.  My car chimed, just to remind me it's riding on fumes. Dawn didn't seem concerned as she was driving. She hauled ass in my newly paid for car while I was supposed to be thinking about a career in the sex industry. I'm still trying to get used to the idea that two guys want me, and are apparently engaged in a financial fist-a-cuffs to see who gets to see me naked on certain days of *the week. Crap, now Dawns got me taking this shit seriously.*

We were getting close to Jade's Inn when it started to rain. The sky grew dark. The world was getting damp, and Dawn, thinking she was being clever, parked at a nearby grocery store.  I guess she wanted people to think we were shopping. Of course it meant we had further to run in the rain, which I didn't mind in the slightest.

We burst through the side door of the Inn laughing and dripping wet. After a quick stop in the ladies room to search for paper towels and hand dryers, we headed down the hall to the conference room. I could smell the food before we even got there.  What a spread! Eggs, bacon, sausage, pancakes, even cereal lay out on the table. If this was a bribe, it was a good start. I looked at Dawn, she looked at me, our eyes narrowed and we raced to the pre-made omelets station. Within a half an hour, I had eaten like it was Thanksgiving. I could have slept for a week, but then Sam arrived.

Sam was carrying some files when he came in, very business-like. He also brought a couple of people—a young man and woman—I've never seen before. They started dishing up whatever breakfast food Dawn and I left behind. Sam introduced the girl as Cathy and the boy as Mike. He introduced me as Caprice so I'm guessing that Cathy and Mike weren't stage names. It doesn't matter one way or the other I guess. The files Sam was carrying had our assignments. Cathy was told she'd be a cowgirl for some guy from Texas. I hid my laugh behind a glass of orange juice. Mike will be entertaining Mrs. Reardon's fantasy of being taken by Zorro. I couldn't even hide that laugh.

"Okay Caprice, you're next," Sam said.

This just stopped being funny. Some people get butterflies in their stomach, like Charlie Brown on Halloween. I got a rock in the pit of my stomach that felt like it was growing by the minute.

"I want you to take a look at these," Sam said.

As he pushed two files across the table to me, I was more than nervous when I took a peek at file number one. Staring back at me was a picture of a blue-eyed, blond guy who looked like every other blue-eyed, blond guy who came in on a surf board.

It's time to see what was behind file number two. I opened it slowly, and closed it quickly as I sprayed orange juice out of my mouth all over the table. Not very lady-like.

"Caprice, are you okay?" Dawn asked quickly as she patted me on the back.

I couldn't answer her. I couldn't say anything.

Dawn opened the file slowly, and closed it quickly, "Holy shit."

My sentiments exactly. I wish I could voice them. I opened the file again, and again Julian was staring back at me.

"It's him isn't it?" Dawn said.

"Yes it is," I replied quietly, staring intently into those eyes. Those eyes were staring back at me. They were intense, and they had depth. He was alive in the picture, and the picture knew I was there. He wanted me. If he could have reached out through the photo with his hands, he would have. But instead, he used his eyes to grab a hold of my soul and held me there.

"Earth to Cat..." asked Dawn from far away.

"Huh?" I asked in the daze.

"I said, did you notice the actual amount of the bid? You are one expensive piece of...and I'll stop talking and fill my mouth with breakfast foods, rather than my foot," Dawn said while shoveling eggs into her mouth.

I managed to pull my eyes from his, and I looked at how much I was worth to a mysterious man I just met. Holy Crap, I am an expensive piece! The feeling of misplaced pride and swelling ego was matched with such a huge dollar sign. This much money would pay for a new car, rent far into the future, and school—Hell, a PhD.

I came today with the idea of telling Sam that I absolutely, positively would not work at Jade's Inn as a commodity. Now I was thinking that I would absolutely, positively, probably think about the potential of considering it.

I turned to Sam. He could see the concern on my face. "Sam, can I get back to you on this?" I asked.

"I understand," he said reassuringly. "But tell me this Caprice, if you decide to participate with one of the gentlemen, which one would you choose?"

I was silent for a moment. Everyone probably thought I was having a difficult time deciding between the two. I wasn't, but let I them think I was. "Do I have to decide now or later?"

"Now would be...beneficial," Sam prompted.

Dawn kept tapping her finger on Julian's picture over and over again. "Cat this is a no- brainer," Dawn whispered.

"Dawn, it's her choice," Sam said firmly.

She decided to keep her obvious opinion to herself, but she kept throwing looks at Julian's file. "Can I continue to mull this over?" I asked as I handed him back the files. When I turned my eyes away from Sam's disappointed stare, I looked down thinking maybe today is the day I finally learn how to turn invisible. I kept looking at my hand and realized it's not disappearing, and then I realized that I didn't give Sam both files. I still had one file. I didn't let it go.

I looked up at Sam. He looked back at me with that I-can-read-you-like-a-book gaze. "Have you made a choice?" he asked.

"Not...necessarily. However, if I'm going to go ahead with this..." I pushed the other file to him.

When Sam opened the file, I could swear there was a sparkle in his eye. "To be fair Caprice, this particular client has specific requests that you need to be aware of before you make your decision."

Cathy and Mike had their attention divided between our confusing conversation and their desire to consume as much food as possible without looking like they're trying to consume as much food as possible. Sam, realizing that this discussion needed to continue in private, asked me to follow him to his office. Dawn looked hurt at the abandonment, until she realized pancakes can be comfort food.

It was a short walk for both of us to Sam's office and an even shorter walk for Sam to the other side of his desk. In my head, however, time passed more slowly. It gave me time to ponder. *Why do we need to talk in private? Could Julian's specific requests be so kinky that they embarrass a Cowgirl and Zorro?*

"The client," Sam began and then paused. "Julian has one main request." Here it comes. "He would like to be...exclusive. He doesn't want you to be with anyone else, inside or outside Jade's Inn. He is willing to pay extra for this exclusivity."

"That's it?" I asked with relief. I was able to expel images of Dorothy with ruby slippers from my mind. "It's not an issue. I'm not looking for a boyfriend."

"Good," Sam said with a smile. "That makes things easier."

"Seriously, is that it? There's got to be more to this private face-to-face."

"He also wants you to wear a ring. He'll pick one out for you in a week or two."

I thought about that for a moment. "So is it a gift or some symbolic marking of his territory? A wedding ring without the wedding...An engagement ring without the courtship...A promise ring without the promise?"

"Since you promise you won't be seeing anyone else, I guess it's closer to the last one. But I'm sure Julian will appreciate it if you would consider it a gift."

"Okay," I said. We're exclusive and I'm getting a ring to prove it. "Anything else?"

"There may be some role playing," he said.

*Well shit! Did he want to be the lion or the tin man?*

"Caprice," Sam said with a serious tone. "In case you haven't made up your mind about working here, you should know that Julian has been using this service for over ten years, and he has never found anyone, chosen anyone...until now."

Sam kept watching me intently hoping to see some facial expression that tells him how incredibly flattered I was, and that nothing made me happier than becoming Julian's one and only. Okay so I was flattered. Being told that someone had waited ten years for me is kind of romantic.

"We told Julian that you're on a six month contract," Sam continued. "So if the first date goes well, he will want you for the whole six months, with an option for two more years."

"An option for two more years? We went from very romantic to very business-like in about half a second. Maybe if all goes well, we can get an extended warranty." The sarcasm was radiating off the walls of Sam's office. He didn't seem amused.

"I understand this is a whole heap to take in," Sam said apologetically. "It is important that you understand the practical side of this business. Julian wants you Wednesdays, Fridays, and several Saturdays. As you know, he is paying a great deal of money for your company. The Inn will get a certain percentage of that money. You will get one thousand dollars a night, and that does not include tip."

Sam turned around and opened a drawer in the filing cabinet behind his desk. I watched him as he was thumbing through the various folders. Do I need to takes notes? Do I need to have a *lawyer review the contract? Do lawyers review those kinds of things? Sam pulled out some piece* of paper and turned back around. "I have a W-4 here that you will need to fill out."

"Wow, a W-4, I guess the government gets its cut of the sex trade too," I said with a grin.

Sam was giving me another serious look. "I want you to really think about this," he said like he was giving me an out. "Once you get into this contract, it's very difficult to get out, Caprice. Do you understand?"

He sounded menacing. "Trust me Sam, I will be thinking very hard about this." Julian was in my thoughts more and more lately. I probably would have gone out with him if he had just asked.

"I need to ask you another question," Sam said.

"You're not going to ask me for references are you?"

"No, nothing like that," Sam beamed. "Can you tell me who referred you to us?"

"Dawn did, that's not a problem is it? She not in trouble for telling about this place is she?" I asked nervously.

"No, of course not, quite the contrary, she will be getting a bonus for it," Sam said writing something on the papers in front of him.

"Cool," I said. "Dinner is on her. Is there anything else you need to know?"

He put his elbows on his desk, clasped his hands together, and rested his chin between his hands. "I just need to know when you think you can give us an answer."

I stood up, looked around the office, and fumbled around in my purse. "How about a week?"

Sam stood up and we headed out of his office, down the hall, and into the conference room. Sam opened the door for me, and there was Dawn. She was in an animated conversation with Zorro and the cowgirl, who were listening to an account related to one of my more embarrassing moments.

"...and then Caprice staggers over to the kiddie pool full of Tequila and...Oh, Hi Cat we weren't just talking about you. How did it go?" she said with false modesty.

"It went," I replied in a serious tone.

"Any epiphanies?"

"Not yet," I said, giving her a look that implied that this topic was not over.

"Want some pancakes?"

I decided not to take the bribe. "I want to leave."

"Okay, hold on," Dawn said, turning to Sam. "Hey Sam any assignments for me, I'm feeling left out." As she said this, Dawn crossed her arms and pouted like a three year old who needed more attention.

Since I'm the rookie here, I don't know how Dawn usually reacts to her new gigs. I'm guessing the small panic attack I experienced wasn't the norm.

Sam beckoned to Dawn, and then pulled her aside to inform her about upcoming assignments. I suddenly felt like a storm of anxiety was filling every part of my being and threatened to break out of me at any moment. I felt nauseous, I felt panicky, I felt like....

"I can't do this!" Dawn suddenly yelled from the other side of the room. For a moment, I thought I had said those words.

"Relax Dawn," Sam told her in a pacifying voice. "I know someone at the club that can help you."

"Help her with what? What club?" I pondered out loud.

Dawn walked over to me, her attitude transformed from upset three year old to angry teen. "I guess Kurt is in the mood for a stripper," Dawn said.

"What's the big deal, Dawn? Last time Kurt saw you naked and willing. You had your legs wrapped around his neck. A striptease seems pretty tame," I commented.

"He wants me to strip at Teddie's," Dawn said in a timid voice.

"Really?"

"Yes, He wants me to strip in front of a crowd while he watches. He wants me to use the pole and everything, Cat. I could break my neck!"

"Do you have to strip completely naked?" I asked aghast.

"No, just down to a skimpy bra and G-string, but can you imagine being on the pole and getting hung up on your G-string? It's like the ultimate wedgie," she said in exasperation.

"Dawn, if it's makes you feel any better, I'll help you," I told her.

"How? You don't know anything about pole dancing," she said bluntly.

"Hey, even if my help goes as far as moral support, and not laughing when you fall on your ass, at least I'll get to keep my clothes on," I said trying to suppress a laugh. As we stood up to leave, I was getting nervous. I then turned back to Sam. "I am right aren't I Sam? I won't have to be involved and naked in this fantasy of Kurt's?"

"No Caprice, you will not," Sam answered and we left. Dawn's stripper dilemma was no longer up for debate, and even though I told Sam I wasn't interested in any guys, I did have a date that night.

"Hey Dawn, do you remember Alex?" I asked her as we got into the car.

"Alex...oh yeah, Daniel's cute friend...What about him?" she said closing the door and starting the engine.

"I have a date with him tonight," I said perking up.

"No way, you do remember the part about Alex being Daniel's friend right?"

"I remember," I said grudgingly.

"Honestly, I don't see him as your type...why go out with him?"

"I'm available, he asked, I didn't want to over think it," I said simply. "Beside, he's not paying me to go out with him."

"So you under thought it?" Dawn said with a smirk.

We talked more about the ramifications of dating the friends of ex's, and Alex's butt on the way back to the dorms. When we got to our floor we saw someone outside my door in the hall. It's was Daniel. Let the groveling begin.

# Chapter 7:

# Daniel wants Me Back

"I can't believe you said you'd go out with Alex." Daniel shouted, after he saw Dawn walk into her room and shut the door. Okay, that's not groveling. I've heard groveling and it doesn't sound anything like that. No, "Hi, how have you been? You look great." No, for Daniel it's straight to scolding me like a child sneaking a cookie from his private stash.

Well, it so happens that Alex is not one of his cookies. "Do the math Daniel, one plus one equals two remember? One, I'm not dating anyone right now, plus he asked me. That equals two of us going out," I said firmly.

Daniel just glared at me. Math was never his strong suit. "I just...I just thought that you would say no to him." He started pacing back and forth, "I don't want you dating him. I want you to call and cancel. Tell him you changed your mind, women do that."

I giggled. Is he serious with this shit? "I'm not cancelling, Daniel."

"What? Yes you will!" Daniel yelled.

"No Daniel, I will not. You have no say in my life...You lost that right when you left me. Let me say that last part again you...left...me," I seethed.

Daniel was silent for a moment. Not opening his dumb mouth was a good look for him, but I knew it wouldn't last. "I want you to move back in." His voice was quieter now, but I still heard what he said. I couldn't believe it, but I heard it. I also couldn't believe he thought I would even consider getting back with him.

"Your new girl dumped your ass didn't she? Alex told me."

Daniel now looked like a kid who had to explain his misdeeds. "I was wrong to leave you for her. I want you back, Caprice," he said. There's the groveling I was looking for. Half the doors on the floor were open now. We had an audience.

"Sorry Daniel, not happening," I said, not ready to budge.

"You'll have to continue paying the rent," he said grasping at straws.

I think all the interested onlookers will be witnesses in my murder trial. "I take it you draining our account, preventing me from paying my share of the rent, was a strategic move on your part so if, or I should say when, your new relationship crashed and burned, you could come crawling back to me but make it look like I came crawling back to you because I feel financially strapped!" I spat at him, and it felt good.

"Caprice, it's not like..." Daniel started, but I cut him off.

"Don't deny it Daniel. Don't even try."

"Cat listen..." he attempted again.

"And don't call me Cat, you're not nearly cool enough. And as far as cash flow goes, I got the money to get my name off the damn lease," I said firmly.

Obviously that's not entirely true, I don't have the cash in hand, but I can't let Daniel Dumb Ass think he has me in his trap.

"I will never move back in with you Daniel. Never!" I'd rather sleep with strangers, or a stranger, than crawl back to that weasel. Before this Neanderthal could give me another verbal clubbing in an attempt to drag me off to his cave, I opened my door, stepped inside and slammed it in his face.

That was so much fun. I opened the door, saw his shocked expression, and slammed it again. He tried the doorknob, hoping I didn't beat him to the lock, but to no avail. Then he started pounding, loud. You could hear the desperation in his relentless pounding, so I had no doubt he would have continued into the wee hours of the morning. Thankfully, one of the curious onlookers convinced Daniel that campus security was on the way.

"This is not over." Daniel shouted. "I'll be back."

I heard him stomping down the hallway amid the laughs of our audience. I opened the door a crack to make sure he was gone. I closed it again, fell back against it, and slid to the floor.

I needed to occupy my mind with something other than bad boyfriends. I decided to do homework. Sometimes it baffled the shit out of me and required my full concentration. I'm sure my dedication to my academic responsibilities will wear off shortly, just in time for me to get ready for my date tonight.

I got two out of the forty geometry problems done before I gave up and started working on my hair. I don't know how long I was in the bathroom, staring at my face, trying to put right what nature made wrong.

♦

I'm in college, a college girl, a college woman, all grown up. I've been on dates, they are nothing new, but when there was knock on the door, I froze like a sixteen year-old on her first date.

I came out of the bathroom and headed for the front door. I looked at myself one more time in the small mirror next to the door and realized I had lipstick on my upper lip but not my bottom lip. I ran back into the bathroom, grabbed the lipstick, and started putting it on as I walked back to the door. When I was done, I threw the lipstick behind the couch and looked up at the clock. Alex was right on time...dammit. I wouldn't have minded if he showed up a half hour late.

I opened the door and was met by a bouquet of daisies and behind them was Alex with the cutest grin on his face. "Hello Alex," I said brightly.

"Hi Caprice, you look great." All I could do is smile back at him, practically beaming. Knowing Daniel was pissed off about me going on this date made it so much more fun to go on.

"You clean up pretty nice yourself," I told him, and I wasn't lying. Alex looked pretty good in his jacket, his fashionably messy hair and flashy grin shining out of his five o'clock shadow. I've known

Alex for a while because he is a friend of Daniel's, and I've always thought he was a good looking guy, not cologne model cute, but he easy on the eyes. I grabbed my jacket and attempted to put it on one-handed with my purse in the other hand.

"Are you ready to go?" he asked, prying the jacket from my hands and holding it out for me.

"Yes I am," I said, slipping my arms in the jacket and smiling. Alex has always been the nice guy. I've never caught him staring at my ass with drool rolling down his chin like some of Daniel's other friends. That's probably why Daniel is so ticked off about my date—he knows that Alex can be a pretty decent guy. As great as Alex is, there really hasn't been any chemistry between us, probably because he is friends with Daniel, so my motivation for this evening may be less than honorable. I have to admit that knowing Daniel is so pissed is a big reason why I decided to go on this date.

The drive over to the restaurant was quiet, too quiet...an uncomfortable quiet. The conversation going on was between the DJs on the radio. I wondered if Alex knew I was sort of using him to make his friend angry. Was I that obvious?

We pulled into an Italian place I had always wanted to try. Daniel never took me there. We sat down without words, continuing our invisible dialogue hoping chemistry would arrive on its own. I thought Alex might ask me how I was doing after the break-up, but he didn't. Maybe he didn't want to pry, but at least he could look at me. His attention seemed elsewhere. If he was staring at some waitress's ass, I'm taking back all those nice things I said about him.

My curiosity got the best of me so I turned around.

"Well shit...Daniel..." I whispered.

Hope.

Hope is a good word. Hope is a word that the glass-half-full guys live by. Hope gives us something to look forward to, like when your team is down by ten but there is still time on the clock, or the soft Christmas present that says "From Santa" isn't just a pair of socks or a sweater, but something cool.  Hope gives us...hope in times of dire distress...like now for instance. I can hope that in my rush to get ready for this date, I slipped in the shower, hit my head, knocked myself out, and I'm just having a bad dream in the back of the ambulance on the way to the emergency room.

But, this wasn't a dream.

I'd settle for a nightmare, but it wasn't that either.

*He's here. Daniel's here at the restaurant, the place he never took me...*

*That motherfucker is really here.*

*What the hell is he...What kind of asshole just...How the hell did Daniel know* where...Obviously I was not finding the answers in my own head, so I looked to Alex. Alex wouldn't have told Daniel where we would be, would he? By the look on his face, no, he didn't.  He looked as surprised as I was. As a matter of fact, his surprised look changed to utter shock. I followed Alex's wide-eyed stare back to Daniel, and then my eyes widened and my jaw dropped.

Standing between the imaginary daggers shooting out of my eyes and their rightful target, was a tight, short, red dress with a blonde inside it. I couldn't see her face because it was currently attached to Daniel's face. When they finally untied their tongues and separated, my eyes widened further. I know her. I've seen her. She's seen me.

*Nurse Nancy?*

Of all the women out there suffering a serious case of bad judgment, why did it have to be my nurse? The fact that the smug son-of-a-bitch was spending half his time glaring at her chest instead of locking lips, and the other half looking at me leads me to believe he was trying to make me jealous. Honestly, I really didn't give a shit who he was playing tonsil hockey with. I just wanted him to do it anywhere but not here. I wanted him to leave me alone.

Alex was clearly not taking this well either. He had that How could he? Look on his face too. I'm beginning to think that there's more back story to this whole Daniel showing up with Nancy thing then I could imagine.

"That bastard," Alex said in a low voice. Yep, more drama, and all the players know each other.

Before I could ask Alex "What the fuck?" the waitress came over. I think she said "Sir" three times before Alex clued in that she was asking if he wanted a drink. "Beer," was all he said without even looking at her.

"Coke for me," I told her. I figured I'd wait until I was safe at home before I hit the hard stuff.

"I can't believe he did that," Alex said to me without looking at me again.

"He's making me uncomfortable too," I said.

"You're not upset about him crashing our date are you?" I asked. "You're upset that he brought one of his own."

"I have had a crush on her for like a year or more." Was he looking for sympathy from me? "Daniel knew I liked her," he said like a whimpering puppy I'm starting to see the big picture here. Daniel didn't want me to go out with Alex. Alex goes out with me anyway, probably because Daniel told him not to, and Daniel knows that Alex likes the naughty nurse. Daniel brings said nurse to the same restaurant that Alex brings me to creating a double mind-fuck.

Men are pricks, and stupid ones at that.

*"Do you want to leave?" I asked with hope. Well look at that, there's that hope thing again!*

"No. No, let's just have a nice dinner and ignore Daniel and...what's her name?"

"Do you know her name?" I asked curiously.

"No, do you?" he asked, hopeful.

Damn it.

My hypothesis that men are stupid pricks just went from theory to fact. I didn't know whether to laugh or...laugh really loud. "Wait a minute," I finally said. "You're pissed at Daniel for bringing the girl here that you didn't have the balls to even introduce yourself to for over the space of a year?"

"Every time I saw her, I just lost my nerve," Alex said finally looking at me long enough to see the expression on my face. It was somewhere between disgust and pity. "Okay, I'm pathetic, I get it," he admitted.

"Her name is Nancy. She's a nurse at my doctor's office." I'm not sure why I offered up that bit of information. I guess my sense of pity outweighed my sense of disgust. I was beginning to wonder if he even heard me when the waitress came back with the drinks.

"Do you know what you want?" she asked. I was about to tell her what I wanted when I stopped and watched Alex drink the entire beer without even taking a breath. If this was a frat party, I would have been fairly impressed. However, this was not a frat party.

"Could you bring me another one of these," Alex asked, again without looking at the waitress. If he had looked at her he probably would have realized that she was pretty cute and I think impressed with his beer drinking abilities. Why didn't I ever see how much of a coward Alex was? He can't even complete a full sentence in front of a waitress. I bet he couldn't ask for her name either.

You got to hand it to Daniel, he played his cards well. Alex was clearly in no mood to even pretend this was a real date anymore. I didn't see any flames or smoke coming out of Alex's eyes, but I could feel the heat. He was pissed. I didn't want to add fuel to the fire by telling Alex this was the worst date I've been on, and that includes when I was twelve and my mom told me that I had to go to a

Disney movie with Timmy, the neighbors' dimwitted son.

My awkward trip down memory lane with Timmy was interrupted by the cute waitress with the nice body that Alex hadn't even noticed. She had a couple of tall cool ones with her, and they weren't on the table for half a second before Alex had one opened and was giving a repeat performance of downing it in one throw. The second one took a few seconds longer. Our waitress had that cute, quizzical look on her face, the one where one eyebrow raises higher than the other and the mind attempts to grasp the odd and unexplainable. She looked at Alex, then at me, then back at Alex. Of course Alex had no clue she was even there. She looked back at me, pointed to Alex and said, "Really?"

"It was on a whim," I told her. I don't think she believed me. "Can we get the check, we won't be staying."

She reached into her pocket. "Already had it prepared," she said, not taking her shocked expression off Alex. She put it down on the table and walked away.

Alex finally looked away from his secret crush and Daniel, and picked up the check. "I guess this really hasn't been much of a date, huh?"

"Not your fault...entirely," I reassured him.

"No, not entirely," Alex said with a less than sincere smile. He looked at me, for about five seconds and then turned his attention back to the Daniel show at the bar. I thought maybe he would suggest we go somewhere else, but he wasn't saying anything. I think he was torn between getting the hell out of there, and beating the hell out of his BFF.

I decided to make up his mind for him. "Let's go. Daniel got his point across."

Alex was able to walk straight out to his car, probably because the alcohol could barely swim upstream against the anger. Getting behind the wheel was another matter. "Are you sure you're okay to drive? You put those beers away like you just walked out of the Sahara."

Alex opened the passenger door for me. "I'm okay to drive." After he shut it, he walked around to the other side and got in. "The question is, how are you?" he asked with concern.

"All things considered, I'm in one piece, mentally speaking," I replied flatly.

"You don't seem too upset."

"Hey, don't get me wrong. I may be all fucking charm and grace on the outside, but on the inside, I'm sticking pins and needles in my little Daniel doll."

"I can't believe he did that to you," Alex said as he sped up.

"Did what, bring a date so he has company when he spied on me, or drive recklessly? Oh wait that's you."

"I mean he dumps you, finds someone else who eventually dumps him, and he returns to try and get you back."

"Hey, he's your friend."

"That's what I thought," Alex said, then questioned, "You're not considering going back to him are you?"

"Not even," I said firmly.

"Good," Alex said while slowing down. "Did you know he cheated on you twice with a girl in his history class? Oh wait, and...and there was a third girl he met at a bar when you had to go home that one weekend to see your parents."

Alex kept talking. I had no idea what he was saying. I had no idea this went on while we were together. I stopped paying attention to him, his driving, the weather outside, and the whole world. I thought of Daniel's cheating ass and why I ever thought I could trust him.

"That rat bastard," I said quietly.

"He can't even afford the apartment anymore," Alex continued. "That's one reason why he wants you back."

"I won't be going back to him or the apartment," I said with certainty.

"Good. There's plenty of fish in the sea," Alex said in the most clichéd way possible.

"There's plenty of fish...Really? You're going to use that line? Those aren't fish they're sharks, big toothy man-sharks. The cute fish are gay."

"Hey, I'm no—"

"Alex, Stop!"

# Chapter 8:

# Close Call

The screeching of the tires echoed throughout the neighborhood, and my head. When the little boy who had run out in front of the car heard them, he froze like a deer in the headlights.

Thankfully, Alex pulled the steering wheel hard to the right and then the left, trying to regain control of the vehicle. The car turned completely around before slamming into the curb. The dying echo of the screeching tires was replaced by a thunderous bang of one of the tires blowing out upon impact. My head stopped spinning about twenty seconds after the car did.

When I finally got my breathing under control, I planned on telling Alex what a dumbass he was, but he was out of the car when I looked.

"Shit!" Alex yelled, scaring the little boy, who left his ball on the other side of the street and ran back home.

I got out and went to the other side of the car, and then saw what was left of the steel-belted radial on the driver's side "Shit!"

Alex looked at me, "Like I said."

"It lost one of its legs. Do we shoot it?" I said, trying to defuse the situation.

"Let me check the trunk," Alex said. "If I can't find a spare and jack, maybe I'll find a gun in there." Alex started patting his pockets. "Keys...keys."

"Alex, the car is still running," I pointed out.

"Yeah..." he said looking completely lost.

"Sweetie, the keys are in the ignition," I said calmly.

"Oh yeah...Sorry... Head trauma." Alex turned off the car, managed to find his way to the trunk, and opened it up. I soon discovered where the term "junk in the trunk" came from. If this was Alex's ass, it would be huge. He pulled out a set of golf clubs, followed by a red cooler. By the sound it made I would say it still had two or three beers floating around in the melted ice that he and his buddies didn't drink the last time they went golfing. Then he pulled out a garbage bag and handed it to me. The smell wasn't the least bit familiar, but I wasn't even gonna ask what was inside. After a few more odds and ends, he was finally able to reach the spare tire and jack.

Alex had three beers. Not even enough for a light buzz where some people are concerned, but the fact that he downed each one in record time leads me to believe he was more than tipsy. That being said, the fact that he got to the right side of the car with the blow out on the first try means points in his favor.

Alex placed the jack under the car and cranked it. Unfortunately, he positioned it in the wrong place. I debated on whether to let him know right away, and possibly bruising his fragile male ego, or just sit back and watch the show. I decided to sit on the curb and watch for a while...I just wish I had popcorn.

"Have you ever changed a tire, Alex?" I finally asked.

"Yes, as a matter of fact my dad taught me how," he said sarcastically.

"How long ago was that?" I questioned under my breath.

"It's been a while. What's your point?" he said with a hint of irritation.

"You have the jack in the wrong place. If you keep going you'll crack the door."

After a long pause and a few choice words under his breath that I'm sure were about me, Alex turned the jack handle in the other direction.

"What about you Wonder Woman, have you ever changed a tire?" Alex asked pointedly.

"It's Dawn who likes Wonder Woman, but yes, many times," I said remembering the previous week's curbside flat and fix. The mechanic offered to mount the tire after he fitted a new one, but being a poor, little, college girl, I learned how to do it for myself.

"Well, so have I. Let me fix this," Alex said angrily. Guys are so toxic at times. I swear he believes if he doesn't do this, his dick will shrink. He moved the jack. Wrong again. I decided to step in before his ego broke a nail.

"Try right here, under the frame. See the metal here?" I pointed.

"Fine, if it makes you happy!" At once, he moved the jack to crank the car up. Clearly his ability to reason was swimming upstream against the beer.

Usually it takes a few dates before you see through the façade people put up when they start going out with each other. But, throw in a variable like a flat tire, and individual's with more annoying personality traits and idiosyncrasies—that they try so hard to mask—come to the surface.

Alex didn't seem like the type to be threatened by a woman's strength and knowledge of the inner workings of a tire jack, but the fact he didn't take off the hubcap or loosen the lug nuts before he jacked up the car tells me that he doesn't know what he's doing. Unfortunately, he doesn't want anyone else to know he doesn't know what he's doing, so he pretends he really does.

He finally managed to get the hubcap off, but when he tried the lug nuts, the wheel kept spinning. This was going to be a long night, but at least there's some entertainment. Alex knew I could take care of this, but after several minutes of a spinning tire going nowhere, the only thing he could ask was if I would hold the tire.

I got down on my knees and started cranking the jack down. Once the tire was level with the ground, I turned to Alex, "Now try." If I didn't know better I'd say Alex wanted to hit me...if I was a guy, he probably would have. Instead of taking a swing at me, he took out his frustrations on the lugs nuts.

After a few strained grunts and colorful expletives, Alex managed to loosen all the nuts. He wanted them all off, but I told him to wait until the car was jacked up again. I don't think he was really getting into the student/teacher dynamic playing out here. He got the car jacked back up, removed the lug nuts and got the tire off, all without a comment from me. But, as he tried to put the spare on backwards, I had to turn around and laugh while pretending to look at the night sky.

"Something funny about the stars tonight?" Alex asked with an acid tone.

"You're putting the tire on backward," I told him without turning around.

With a complete lack of stealth, Alex quickly turned the tire around and put it back on. "It's not backward, see, it fits perfect," he stated in a curt tone.

I turned back around with a smirk. "You're right, my bad," then he put the lug nuts back on and tried to tighten them. When the car tipped on the jack he stopped and lowered the car down, all the while glaring at me like he was daring me to make a comment. I began looking at the stars again. Once he put the bad tire in the trunk with the jack, and repacked all the other stuff, he walked around the driver's side. I'm pretty sure he wasn't going to open my door for me, so I got in myself.

"So about Daniel...you can do better," Alex said picking up where he left off.

*Wow! As if nothing happened. We will pick up this conversation as if there was no blow out* of a tire or an ego? I think he's hoping I'll forget about the last thirty minutes before we reach the next stop light.

"You know Caprice, you're...one of the good ones, one of the good girls that guys take home to meet their mom. You're like potential daughter-in-law material."

"You're scaring me Alex."

"I just mean...I don't get it. I don't understand how Daniel landed with you to begin with?"

"Landed? Are we using fish analogies again?"

"You know what I mean,"

*"Yeah, I'm a keeper," I agreed. I wonder what he'd think if he knew about my misadventures at Jade's Inn. Not exactly Sunday dinner at the in-laws. I wonder what Alex's dear sweet mother thinks of Nurse Nancy.*

We returned to the mutual silent treatment we had shared earlier. It gave me time to reflect on the night's events. My thoughts kept coming back to Daniel and the company he keeps. Not Nancy, but all the other women I learned about after we broke up. I guess I should consider myself lucky I didn't pick up an STD or two.

Alas, the end of my torment was in sight. When we pulled up out in front of my dorm, Alex just sat there. He didn't even ask if he could come in. He's smarter than I thought.

"Good night, Caprice," he said in an utterly defeated tone.

"Good night, Alex," I couldn't say fast enough as I got out of the car.

Then Alex drove off. Good riddance.

I stood there...in the dark...alone. I was alone with my thoughts. I realized, as I was walking back to my room, that I was alone with thoughts of Daniel too. He's naked. He has *sweet honey poured over his chest, his legs, and that thing in the*

*between his legs of his he used to call Hector.
Daniel and Hector are lying in an open field on top
of three of the cutest little ant hills. The army ants,
marching two-by-two, have completely covered him,
and dine on his naked flesh...*

The more I thought about that asshole asking me
to come back and threatening me about the
apartment, the more insects I added to my little
torture fantasy. When the women he cheated on me
with came back to mind, I turned my thoughts
towards scorpions.

I walked down the hall to my room, when I
suddenly noticed an envelope sticking out of the
*door. If it is from Daniel, I'm changing the
scorpions to elephants! After a paranoid
examination* of the envelope, I opened it up.

*My Caprice,*

*You awaken my spirit. My desire for you is
love's pure flame.*

*When the stars are shining bright, I arise from
dreams of thee.*

*You're my muse, translating the language of my
heart.*

*Apart and never parted, as I talk to you, I
converse open-hearted.*

*Many have loved me, but none I have loved till
now.*

*Your voice is like music to my ears, I dream of
touching you as if you're mine.*

*I live in a dream state, where I can see and hear
only you, but I can't feel or touch you.*

*I want to be worthy of your love, please let me have your solitude, so you can see what my heart knows.*

*Yours,*
*Julian*

*Wow! I mean...holy...wow!*
I read the letter again...then again...Is this guy for real? Do people still talk this way, or did he just combine together several Hallmark cards? Okay, he's tall, dark, handsome and mysterious, and I've seen the way he looks at me. His eyes are like a sense of mystery, exciting and scary. I know he wants me, but what part of me does he want? Emily, the Jade's Inn newbie.

That's what guys like isn't it? Fresh meat? A virgin no one else has touched yet? Or does Julian like the real me, the poor little college girl who's just trying to make ends meet by selling herself to the highest bidder? He can't like me for me, he doesn't even know me. Like all the clients of Jade's Inn, he likes the fantasy. I just have to keep reminding myself I'm doing this for a friend.

My downward spiral into self-pity was interrupted by a knock at the door. Who the hell could that be? The way my night was going, it could be a bill collector, or possibly someone from the CDC telling me I'm so pathetic that my life is quarantined. Oh God, what if it's one of *those religious weirdoes here to tell me to repent for my sins of stupidity. If I'm quiet they'll go away.*

"I'm not a Jehovah's Witness, Cat. Open up."
*Dawn.*

I opened the door to find Dawn all dressed up in her lets-go-clubbing outfit. "Hi, Dawn," I said, leaving the door open and walking to the couch.

"I see you came home early," she said, closing the door "Bad date?"

"Bad would have been good," I told her. "What I had happened tonight could be considered horrible on an epic scale."

"Was Alex that bad? He looked cute in a nice guy kind of way," Dawn asked.

"Alex has issues, but he wasn't the bad part, well, not the worst part." I continued.

"Well, this sounds like a story, Let me get comfy," Dawn said, jumping on couch next to me, "Shoot."

"Daniel showed up," I said reluctantly.

"What?" Dawn yelled in disbelief.

"Oh yeah! He didn't say anything, he just stared at us...he and his date...the nurse," I stated weakly.

"A nurse?" Dawn said in disbelief.

"Yeah, Nurse Nancy from the doctor's office yesterday," I continued.

"Nurse, honey, they make soap operas out of shit like this," Dawn said flatly without a hint of sympathy in her voice.

"Tell me about it," I mumbled sarcastically.

"What did you do? What did Alex do?" Dawn asked.

"Alex didn't do anything but stare back and drink like a Viking before a conquest," I said.

"And you?" Dawn asked.

"I thought about throwing my arms around Alex, or grabbing him under the table just to piss off Daniel even more, but I couldn't toy with Alex like that," I said, expressing for the first time what I imagined doing earlier to get back at Daniel.

"He's a guy, sweetie, he wouldn't have minded," Dawn informed me. "You look like you have a serious need for a mental tidy."

"And you have the usual prescription?" I asked.

"Damn straight," she said. "The Bloody Rose can cure what ail's ya."

"I don't know, Dawn," I said. "I was thinking I would stay here and read a book, something depressing like a self-help book."

"Maybe Julian will be there." Dawn pointed out.

Just the mention of the name and I was imagining myself out with him tonight instead of Alex. The date ended with Daniel bloody and unconscious, and when we got home, Julian would be using me as a blanket.

"I don't think so, Dawn."

"But I do know. That's the great thing about having irresponsible friends, they can make all your stupid decisions for you."

"It does take the pressure off," I admitted.

"Think of it this way," Dawn explained. "After that disaster of a date with Alex, your evening can only get better."

"Okay, I bow to your insane Dawn logic, but no Julian," I said firmly.

"Why?" Dawn asked.

"Because if I see him...I won't be able to say no."

The Bloody Rose was packed as usual. Everyone on the dance floor was dancing cheek-to-cheek, mainly out of a necessity for room. The drinks had been flowing for hours, so I'm guessing that no one on the dance floor cared whose ass they're rubbing up against.

I peered through the mass of man and woman and saw two hands in the air—both carrying Long Island iced teas. Eventually the hands made their way through the dance floor and Dawn sat down next to me.

"I hope one of those is mine," I said. I was pretty sure I already knew the answer.

"Actually, hon...they both are," Dawn replied with a scary look of concern as she was not looking at me, but at the recently opened front door of the Bloody Rose. "Oh Crap."

"You better be fucking with me with the way you're looking at me, Dawn," I told her. She pushed both glasses across the table to me, and then she looked everywhere but at me, avoiding my steely glare.

"Dawn, out with it. Whatever it is, I'm sure it isn't your fault."

"Oh, it's not."

"Then out with it," I demanded.

"You have a stalker."

I sat staring at her, waiting for the rest of the story. Instead, Dawn looked back at me and then toward the door. I turned my head and saw, among the humans, that mother-fucking, cock-sucking, asshole, worthless piece of shit, son-of-a-bitch! This is what I am now calling Daniel, even to his friends and mother.

"This isn't just evil," I said with an angry huff, "This is beyond satanic...this is Hitler evil! I seriously think I need an exorcist."

"Do you think that service is advertised in the Yellow Pages?" Dawn asked.

"I'm thinking a hasty, but discreet, exit through the back is needed here, followed by a run through the parking lot where we find his car and flatten the tires," I suggested.

"He'll just replace it with a spare," Dawn said flatly.

"Not as easy for guys as you think," I told her. "Besides, we'll flatten all the tires then the spawn of Satan can't follow."

"As fun as that sounds—and it does—we'll call that plan C."

"And plan A and B?" I asked curiously.

"They're in those glasses in front of you. Look, Cat, you can't play hide-and-seek every time numb-nuts comes sniffing around. He's not worth it and should not have that much control over you."

"You're right," I said, dropping my head on the table. "Okay, you're right. I just need to ignore the prick and hope he goes away—try not to let him get to me...show him that his minuscule presence doesn't bother me."

"Yes, that's the spirit," Dawn said encouragingly. "Drown your memories of Daniel in a tall glass of toxic tea, and then do it again with the other glass. I'll be at the bar getting my own memory eraser," she said walking off.

The memories I planned to drown away with the Long Islands started to flood my mind with a vengeance. As much as I wanted them to go away, they put up a good fight and remained. They kept returning like an instant replay...and replay...and replay.

I took a long drink in hopes of putting off the inevitable recaps of the night's events. It didn't work. Visions of Daniel, with various other women that were not me kept dancing through my head. Dawn was right of course, I can't hide from the bastard. I could just kick him in the balls hard enough to dislodge his Adams apple. I mean, was it the sex? Did we not do it enough?

Was I supposed to indulge the ridiculous fantasy of his by bringing another girl into our bed or something? I take another long drink when a hand appeared on my shoulder.

"Hi, Caprice," Daniel said.

I spit out my tea. I think I got his shoes. I hope I did.

"What the hell are you doing here?" I shrieked.

"I want to talk to you," he said simply as if during our last meeting we had parted friends.

"And I want to decapitate you. We don't always get what we want," I said coldly.

*"I want you back, Caprice." Another pathetic attempt.*

"Like I said, before, you don't always get what you want," I told him. "You don't get me and I don't get to stab you in your cheating neck." Daniel was clearly getting frustrated by my frankness, maybe I was getting through to him. "Why do you want me back, Daniel? Is it so I can stay at home to cover your financial ass, while you run around town putting your dick wherever it will fit?"

"That was one time," Daniel stuttered, obviously hoping I didn't know more.

"Don't insult my intelligence, Daniel...you're not nearly smart enough." I took another drink and stared at him, even though he was trying to avoid my glare. "Don't try and bullshit someone who knows you all too well and friends who know your dark secrets."

I put the empty glass down and picked up the other one. That's when I noticed Dawn on the dance floor. She was dancing...with Julian.

What the Fuck?

Dawn...Julian...Dawn and Julian together? When the hell did this happen?

I thought Julian was scheduled to be my boy-toy. I haven't officially joined the Jade's Inn harem, but I didn't say I wouldn't either. Did Julian have to pick someone else? I know Dawn had the hots for him, but to be fair every woman in the world that wasn't blind would have the hots for him.

I stared at the two of them swaying to the music, and then Daniel moved next to me, reminding me that he still existed. "Cat, whatever you heard about me, it's not true," he lied.

I've had enough of this place and the whole damned night. I took a drink of my tea, and looked Daniel right in the eyes. "Number one, don't call me Cat. Number two, shut the fuck up. Number three, leave!"

"No," Daniel said firmly. "Not until we talk about this."

I was getting more and more pissed when I saw something I needed to see—a friendly face. Sam was walking up behind Daniel carrying a tray full of booze.

"You need some help, Caprice?" Sam asked, looking like he was eager to kick some ass.

"That's okay, Sam, Daniel was just leaving. Weren't you, Daniel?" I said staring daggers at him.

Daniel just stood there trying to look defiant instead of scarred shitless.

"Would you like a drink, Caprice?" Sam offered, eying Daniel like an irksome fly that needed swatted.

I looked at the tall, cold drink in my hand and then at the steely look on Daniels face. Then I threw the cold drink in his cold face. "Yes, I could use another one," I told Sam triumphantly.

Sam chuckled at me and then winked back.

Daniel was livid, but he knew he was out gunned. "This isn't over," he declared, as he turned to leave while wiping his face off.

"Thank you, Sam," I said, giving the big, tipsy, teddy bear a huge hug. Even though Sam was bending down to hug me, I still had to stand on my toes to peek over his shoulder, where I saw Julian and Dawn watching us.

Judging by the smile on Dawn's face, and what comes close to a smile on Julian's, I'm guessing that something was up, and everyone was in on it but me. After I let go of Sam, I took a drink off the tray. I'm not sure what it was, but it was a pretty blue one. I sat down and looked at Sam. "Okay Sam, what's the what?" I finally asked.

Sam took a seat across from me and picked his own glass, some reddish brown thing. "Dawn came over and told Julian and I about what was going on," Sam began, "She was hoping that Julian would sweep you off your feet right in front of this Daniel guy, making him jealous. While Julian was all for coming to your rescue, he wanted your permission before driving your ex insane with jealousy."

"He was waiting for my okay?" I asked smiling.

"Yes, he was," Sam said.

"And he decided to dance with Dawn, while waiting for me to give him the go ahead?" I asked shocked.

"He was dancing with Dawn so he could talk to her, and get more information on this idiot known as Daniel," Sam said taking a swig of his drink.

"So it gives you a chance to come over and play hero?" I inquired.

"I do what I can," Sam said with a smile.

I stood up, walked over to Sam, and threw my arms around him again. "Thanks again, Papa Bear." He hugged me back with a tight embrace that made me feel safe.

When I looked up and saw Daniel staring at me from what he believed a safe distance, I decided to scoot my chair closer to Sam. I then noticed Julian was also staring at me intently.

I'm a bug, a scrawny, microscopic insect under two microscopes. One is looking at me with intense heat, and one with intense cold. I feel like I'm being dissected in my mind, body, and soul.

Julian finally turned his attention back to Dawn and their dancing. I couldn't read Dawn's lips, but they were moving a great deal. I can just imagine the tale they're telling about my night of woe, and my lousy luck with men.

I turned back to Sam. "Julian isn't going to want anything to do with me when he hears how fucked up my life is." Sam learned over and whispered in my ear, "He's not going anywhere, hon. He doesn't scare easily, or at all, especially when he cares so much."

"About what?" I asked curiously.

"Not what...who," Sam replied.

"Who?" I asked, a smooth tone in my voice, but inside it was like a cage of butterflies flying around waiting for his answer.

"You, my dear. He's crazy about you, Caprice. He has been since he first saw you." I was speechless. I looked from Sam to Julian and back to Sam again. Then I looked back at Julian. I had a hard time taking my eyes off him as he was dancing.

"Here," Sam said, pushing a glass at me. "Take another sip. It might relax you."

"What do you think they're talking about now?" I asked Sam after following his order and taking a sip.

"You, of course," Sam said. "There's the idea Julian has of cutting off Daniel's head and giving it to you as a symbol of his affection."

I closed my eyes and imagined Daniel's head stuffed and on my mantle with Winnie the Pooh animals sitting on top—Daniel never liked my Winnie the Pooh collection. I took another drink with a smile on my face. I giggled. I was feeling whimsical.

"You probably shouldn't drink that stuff so quickly, Caprice, it's pretty strong," Sam warned. "It will go straight to your head."

"It probably will," I told him. "I haven't eaten anything all day."

"Why don't you sit here and relax," Sam said." I will go get you something to eat."

As Sam left in search of sustenance, Dawn walked over to the table with her cat-that-ate-the-canary grin. If I wasn't pickled, I would have been nervous. She pulled up a chair and plopped down next to me.

"Wow, Cat, you seem...mellow," Dawn said.

"I do feel less inclined to pursue homicide as a career path," I told her.

"What magic potion helped you reach this moral high ground?" Dawn asked with curiosity.

"Well," I began with a smile. "For starters, my girlfriend tried to get me drunk with two Long Island iced teas. Then I mixed in something blue that I was supposed to sip, but I downed instead," I said with a hiccup.

Dawn put her arm around me. "So I guess my girl just can't hold her liquor. Good to know for future reference and humiliation."

I looked at Dawn and beamed, but it wasn't totally sincere. "So...slow dancing, swaying to the music, that looked like fun. There wasn't a...you know...a kiss..."

"A kiss? No, honey, there wasn't. I wish there would have been, but alas, he has eyes for you," she said with longing.

She seemed pretty sure, even more certain than I was. Did she see my letter from Julian? I *put it in my underwear drawer. Did she go through my underwear drawer? "Okay, Dawn, how* can you be so sure his eyes are just for me?" I thought of Daniel's betrayal and was afraid of knowing the answer to that question.

"It's in his eyes, dear. The way he looks at you."

"And how does he look at me?" I asked quizzically.

"Like he doesn't want to look anywhere else," Dawn said with another sigh.

I took another drink and pondered a man of mystery, and the wisdom of a friend—who snoops around where she doesn't belong.

"I'm beginning to sense that you doubt my powers of perception," Dawn said. "You may not believe this, but I have gained insight into the inner workings of the male psyche."

"Let me hear it," I said giggling.

Dawn leaned over and took a drink from my glass "Well, to begin with it's not always in the eyes. For most guys it's in their pants."

"Because they think with their dicks right? Not a ground-breaking new concept for me Dawn," I concluded.

"You're being too obvious, Cat," Dawn said. "I'm talking about something more subtle, more symbolic. It's the way they wear their pants."

"I didn't think guys put any thought into how they wear pants." As an example, I pointed to most of the guys in the place. For the guys on the dance floor, it's a wonder that their pants were still on, the way they were hoping around in their own loose interpretation of modern dance techniques.

Dawn looked at all the guys and then back at me "There's a method to the madness that is a man's fashion sense, even if he's not aware of it himself."

"Should I be taking notes?" I asked.

"First," Dawn continued, ignoring my smartass remark, "If their shirts are tucked into their pants they're looking for someone serious, they're ready to settle down and have a family."

Dawn looked through the masses and pointed out a guy with baggy pants. "That loser doesn't know what he wants or where his life is going. If you're up for it, he's the guy you date just to have fun—no commitment."

"Okay, professor," I said sarcastically. "What about this guy over here, the one with pants so tight they look painted on?"

"That one's more obvious. He wants to get laid. He's basically showing off, trying to draw your attention to his ass and crotch, which is apparently working since you haven't stopped looking at him. He's a one night stand at best, hon."

I look around for more specimens to examine for purely scientific reasons. Then I found Daniel, still damp. He was an amalgam—tight jeans with the shirt half in and out. I was dating and living with someone who didn't know what he wanted or who he wanted. He was hoping to find a mother-figure who will put up with his shit. I wasn't feeling whimsical anymore.

I saw Julian and Sam talking, and I have no doubt that I was still the topic of conversation. I could tell by the way Sam was smiling at me and Julian even winked, both making me feel very self-conscious. When Sam stepped away, I decided to stare longingly back at Julian, just to see if I can make him feel the least bit little nervous. I put him under the microscope to test Dawn's theory.

*One—Shirt tucked in. Check*
*Two—Pants tight, but not too tight. Check*
*Three—See point number two.*

Some may say that I'm developing an unhealthy fixation on his ass, but it's so cute. My alcohol-induced, very vivid daydream of my hand on his butt was cruelly interrupted by the smell of a burger and fries. Sam kept moving the plate around under my nose until I took my eyes off Julian's backside.

"Eat," Sam ordered. He then looked at Dawn. "Make sure she eats all of it."

"Will do," Dawn said as she reached over to the plate. "She will eat all of it except for this one fry...and this one too." She finally stopped after five.

I devoured my burger like a good little girl, and it tasted pretty good. I followed it up with a few fries before Dawn got them all. By the time I was done, my head felt clearer. I stood up and brushed myself off when I noticed Daniel still watching me. When Daniel moved towards me, I froze. He got closer...and closer...and then stopped about six feet from me.

"Would you like to dance?" said a smooth voice from behind me. I turned to find Julian holding out his hand. I have no idea how he got over here so fast, and I didn't care.

"Yes, I would love to dance with you," I said happily.

# Chapter 9:

# The Big Talk

The dance was slow. We moved back and forth in our own little corner of the world. Julian had one hand firmly on my waist, and I had the other hand resting gently on his shoulder. Our other hands were holding each other lightly. He looked into my eyes, and I looked into his. He looked like a movie star, or at least the star of every woman's wet dream.

As much as I wanted to pull him in closer, close enough to feel his heartbeat, I resisted. I'm not sure what part of me fought the urge. It was probably the rational side of my brain telling my heart...and...crotch, to mind their own business.

I think Julian could sense my hesitation. He was probably wondering if it was his body odor. Trust me, it wasn't. I could soak in that scent of rain all night.  Then a nasty thought popped into my head. Maybe it was because he wanted to buy me.

"What are you thinking, Caprice?" Julian asked softly." You seem...distant."

"I do, don't I?" I replied just as softly. We're a few inches apart, which seemed like a safe distance to me.

"But why?" he asked.

As much as I wanted to be blunt about my feelings of being nothing more than a commodity, I held my tongue. For some reason I thought too much honesty at this point would scare him away. "I don't know," I answered him truthfully. "Maybe I'm being silly."

"Go on," Julian said with a subtle smile on his face that was driving me crazy. I'm sure he was well aware of this. I backed up, still holding his hand.

"Let's say we use A and B to represent you and me." I said. "Well... It seems that A likes B, and A asked B out. However, after A and B's date it, seems that B didn't like A as much as A liked B...With me so far?" Julian bobbed in an uncertain manner.

I started again, hoping that Julian gets the picture. "So where A really likes B, but B isn't so keen on A, this unfortunately means that B tells A Let's just be friends. These things happen in the best of all possible worlds. This is how the story should end, with A and B both going their separate ways, onward to greater and better things."

"This isn't what happens though I guess," interjects Julian, with a hesitative sigh.

"No, A is a really popular guy, don't get me wrong. B is also very popular, though not a guy of course, but you know what I mean. A's friends however, in particularly C, thinks there must be something wrong with B for not liking A as much as she does...I don't think C likes A in the way that A wants B to like him, or for that matter how A likes C, that is in the way A likes B..."

I was looking at Julian to see if he was keeping up with my incoherent babbling.

"Okay..." replied Julian in a non-committed sort of way.

I may be developing a rare superiority complex here. I'm twenty-something, and Julian is at most thirty-something, but even with the decade or so of wisdom he has on me, he can't seem to comprehend my insane, inebriated girl logic, so I continued with the education "So C tells D, E, F, G, H and probably I and J as well that B must like Q if she doesn't like A. Then that being what it is, soon D, E, F, G, H and probably I and J have told K,L,M, N, him, and O, P that B really like Q. "

Julian opened his mouth to say something and but thought better of it.

"Eventually the rest of the alphabet gets to hear that B likes Q even though B denies it. Then C herself likes Q too." I took a deep breath, "I do wonder how many people would find out what B is doing." Taking another deep breath "You know what happens next don't you?"

"B falls madly in love with A, and they live happy ever after," Julian said with a hopeful smile on his face.

I looked at him with disbelief "C knows that B is getting paid to sleep with A and B ends up looking like a slut, and has to go to an all-girls college in a different town, in a different country, follow me?"

Then Julian was silent—The uncomfortable type of silence. I think I rendered him catatonic.

How long had I been babbling? I was beginning to weigh the pros and cons of drinking heavily, when I saw a hint of a smile on Julian's face. I grinned myself, and then I started checking out his shoes.

Julian put his hand under my chin and lifted my head slowly up "Are you uneasy about our...arrangement?"

"Maybe a little," I whined out like a tiny girl in trouble from her mom.

"But you haven't even agreed yet," he reminded me.

"Yeah I know, but I can't help but realize we're here now, together, and I'm not running away. If there's a chance I'll take you up on this offer, then I need to come to grips with the fact that you'll be paying me to...accompany you...places," I finished

"I think at this point Caprice, it has become apparent how I feel about you. At least...I hope it's not just my little secret."

"I kind of have a feeling," I said unsure of myself, "I'm just not real clear on what it is."

"Caprice," Julian began, "I am aware of your...situation, and I want to help. I know your school is important to you, and I don't want you to worry about coming up with tuition and rent every semester, or whatever else may come up financially."

"But doesn't everyone have worries like that?" I asked him, "It's called life. It's a pain in the ass, but the pain is not exclusive to me."

"You are not everyone. We would not be here now, dancing, if you were. I wasn't looking for just anyone." he quietly said.

"Dare I ask what you are looking for?" I said hesitantly.

"Nothing now, I found what I wanted," Julian whispered grasping my hand tighter as he twirled me around once and then again, "I found a dance partner...a girlfriend...a..."

"A lover?" I asked finishing his thought.

"Hopefully, with time...but I want more than that," he stated to my surprise.

"More?" I asked with a nervous curiosity.

"I want a soul mate," he said. "I hope that doesn't frighten you."

"A small amount," I admitted. "What's the going rate for soul mates these days?"

Julian stopped dancing. He pulled me close, held me tight, stared into my eyes and beyond. "I need you! The money doesn't matter...I can give you less, I can give you more...I can give you all the money I own, but I need you."

Like the song goes...and then he kissed me.

My toes curled in my shoes as my right leg bent up. It popped. Even though we weren't dancing anymore, I was still spinning. My lips were dancing with his, and his lips really knew how to dance. This was the moment I wanted to live in for the rest of my life.

I didn't notice when the music stopped, but I did notice when a new song came on. It was soft and all too familiar. It was probably the song that could pull me out of my trance with Julian. It was our song, Daniel's and mine, and it came at the worst time. The kiss stopped and just like that, the moment was over. Everything I'd gone through over the last couple of days came flooding back to me in a rush. I thought if I was standing close enough to Julian, the emotions would go away, but they didn't. I cried, and Julian just let me.

He kissed my forehead, continued to hold me tight, and then even tighter as if his embrace could save me from my pain. I thought for a moment. I could get through this, but then there was a tap on Julian's shoulder. Daniel wanted to cut in.

You've got to be fucking kidding. I thought loud enough that I expected everyone on the dance floor to stop and stare at me.

With a gentle brush of his fingers, Julian wiped a single tear that was trailing down my cheek. He then turned to Daniel. "I'm sure of her answer, but I think it best that you hear it from her." Julian then turned back to me. "Would you like to dance with Daniel?"

I didn't answer. I didn't want to talk to Daniel, or about him. I was hoping between the booze and Julian's amazing eyes, I'd forget that Daniel ever existed. I just shook my head back and forth in a solid no.

"You have your answer," Julian said in a cold, mater-of-fact voice as he stood between Daniel and me. I felt like I was wearing a red hood and Daniel was the big bad wolf.

Daniel noticed my waterworks. "You wouldn't be crying if you still didn't have some feelings for me, Cat." He took two steps back and then turned away walking off the dance floor, but continued to stare at me like a predator does at its prey.

Julian was holding me tighter than before, more like protection, like a great wolf hunter. I kept my face down close to his chest so Julian couldn't see the tears that wouldn't stop flowing out of my eyes and down my cheeks.

We were able to keep Daniel from creeping into our dance again, but I wasn't able to keep him from creeping back into my thoughts. He cheated. I don't know why, but the bastard cheated on me. Then he broke up with me. He didn't make love to me first—he fucked me first, before telling me he found someone else. He told me I had to leave. "Why didn't he love me enough to just stay with me?" I whispered louder than I had intended.

"He's a fool," Julian whispered back comfortingly. "He's a fool who didn't know what he had until it was gone. Honestly, I still don't think he knows. He clearly wants you back, but he doesn't understand why."

"He wants me back so he can cheat on me again. If a guy is going to cheat on you first he has to make you feel like you're the one for him."

"Like I said, he's a fool. He had no idea how lucky he was Caprice," Julian said with a quiet conviction. "I will never make that mistake."

Trust isn't easy after it has been lost the first time, but when I looked into Julian's eyes I couldn't help but believe him. I reached up and touched his face, then gently ran my thumb up over his cheek, my fingers brushing across his lips. Then I placed a kiss on his cheek before I removed my fingers. I grinned.

"What are you smiling about?" Julian asked, and then pulled me in close to kiss me.

"Just about what you said. I am the one...right?"

"Yes, you are." I could tell he meant it, every word.

"So you do not want to have a two girl fantasy, or have someone watch us from across the room? I ask because it seems to be the nature of the business at Jade's Inn."

It was now Julian's turn to smile. "Are we negotiating the terms of our contract right now, here on the dance floor?"

"Wait," I said, "You mean I have the option to negotiate the contract?"

"Yes you do...And to answer your previous question, it's only you—inside or outside of the Inn."

"That's very reassuring." We slowly turned around and around in a circle as the music continued. Daniel and his steely glare came into view for a moment until my back was to him, then it come into view again. His expression never changed, not that I expected it to. "Would you like me to take care of him?" Julian asked without missing a step.

"What?"

"Your ex, would you like me to take care of him?" he eyed Daniel who now looked like the prey.

"Damn." I exclaimed. "When you put it that way, it sounds like you want to take him out back, and put a cap in his ass or fit him for cement shoes. Are you channeling your inner Godfather?"

"I could try talking first," he suggested.

"Good luck, when Daniel gets pissy like this, he's got the intellect of cheese." My thoughts drifted back to the cement shoes idea before I realized that the slow, smooth music we were dancing to had changed to something with a more upbeat tempo. We, however, were still in an embrace and moving slowly to our own rhythm.

"You know the music has changed."

"I know," he said without a care.

"Shouldn't we pick up the beat or move off the floor?"

"I'm fine right here, the other music is still playing in my head."

"If I put my ear up to yours, can I hear it?" I joked.

"You can try."

Before I had a chance to climb him, we were interrupted by Julian's serious sidekick. "Sorry to interrupt," Sam said. "We have...business to deal with in your office—they are waiting for you Julian. If you wish, I can remain here with Caprice."

"Yes Sam, I would appreciate that." Julian started walking away. I couldn't quite figure out the look on his face. I could tell he didn't want to leave, but I could also tell he knew he had to. "Will you be okay staying here with Sam?"

"Why, do you think I need a bodyguard?" I turned and looked at Sam. "...with the temperament of a Pit Bull." Julian's eyes glanced in the direction of Daniel, then back to me.

"Okay," I said. "Pit Bull it is. We'll be fine."

As Julian disappeared through a door behind the bar, I turned to my new watcher. A surprising thought popped into my head. "Why didn't you tell me Julian owned this place?"

"You didn't ask," Sam stated plainly.

We made our way back through the crowd and to the table to find Dawn sitting there holding up a glass in a toast. Two glasses clinked together, Dawn was holding one and Geri was holding the other. Since they stopped talking when I approached, I'm guessing that I was the topic of the toast. Then I saw Sam wink at Geri. That's interesting.

"What's the toast to?" I asked, catching them off guard.

"Hi Caprice," Geri yelled, running towards me, and as my Grandmother always said, "Yea," Dawn said quickly. "Toast, I like toast."

"Uh-huh," I said, sitting down next to Sam.

"Bodyguard?" Geri asked.

Hugging the stuffing out of me. "We are toasting...toast."

"Yea," Dawn said quickly. "Toast, I like toast."

"Uh-huh," I said, sitting down next to Sam.

"Bodyguard?" Geri asked.

"Pit Bull," I answered. "Daniel Dickhead is here to make my life miserable. Papa Bear is here to help keep me from taking Daniel out back, and beating his eyes shut." I sat there trying to figure out at what point I became the damsel that suddenly was in distress. With that thought, just because I find out that my ex has his mail forwarded to the lowest pits of hell, I now need to be protected by a tall, dark, and scarily handsome muscle-bound employee.

"Hey Sam," a voice came from behind. Another one of Julian's employees, an attractive barmaid, suddenly appeared from the crowd of patrons. "I see you're entertaining tonight. What's everyone's poison?"

"On the house ladies," Sam said. "What'll ya have?"

"Vodka Tonic," said Geri.

"Rum and Coke," Dawn declared.

"Shirley Temple," I said. I got a perplexing look from Geri and a smile from Dawn.

"What?" queried Geri.

"Saving the nightcap for someone special?" Dawn asked with a smirk. "Does his name start with J and end with ulian?"

"You're dating Julian?" Geri asked with surprise.

I came up with some bullshit answer, but stopped when I noticed all three sets of eyes looking up above me.

"I'm hoping the answer to that question will be yes," Julian said. He put his hands on my shoulders and stared to massage them. I turned red as everyone stared at me like they were expecting an answer to the million dollar question. I knew if I said anything it would throw them into a gossip frenzy that would go on and on for weeks.

"May I escort you home?" Julian asked, coming to my rescue...again.

"Yes please," I said immediately. It's not like I don't like hanging out with my gal pals, but I was in no mood to answer a good deal of questions about the dating habits of Caprice the *College Co-ed.*

I stood up and we walked to the door, but I could see out of the corner of my eye Daniel was still watching me. Julian guided me through the parking lot and to the most beautiful sixty-nine, candy-apple red mustang I have ever seen. The top was down and the interior was all black, pitch black. He opened my door to let me in this gorgeous machine, and then walked to the other side and slid in himself. He pulled out of the parking lot like the car was a Southern carriage embarking upon a long journey. As we took off down the darkened street, I saw Daniel watching us leave.

I turned to Julian, who was keeping his eyes on the road most of the time, but also on me the rest of the time. "You know Julian, despite all the crap that has happened tonight, it was nice seeing you."

"And I loved seeing you too, Caprice." He reached out and turned down the radio, which had been playing since the car started. "So if it was nice seeing me tonight, then keep in mind that you could be seeing me more often."

"Yeah I know, sign the contract and we're officially a couple. It just sounds strange that a paper has to be signed. Once you got my signature, we date exclusively, we go out, we stay in, and we cuddle exclusively. We even have...sex exclusively."

"If that is a problem—" he began.

"Oh no, I like the idea...of sex...exclusively. Oh God, this sounds pathetic!" I exclaimed.

"Relax," Julian reassured me.

"Well, it's just that, I assume that sex is part of the contract. I mean at that place...at the Inn, I assume sex is part of the job." Julian was just sitting in silence and I was squirming, hoping like hell that aliens fly over and beam my ass out of there.

Julian purred and finally broke the silence, "If you would like to discuss the terms of the contract we can. I hope we can get to a point in our relationship that we can avoid referring to sex as a job."

"I'm sorry, but it does appear that way," I told him. "Don't get me wrong, I have no doubt that it will be a job I really, really love, but still..."

"I understand," Julian said trying to put me at ease. "If you have any questions or concerns about that part of the relationship we can discuss it."

"Okay," I said, with a brave face masking my fear and intense excitement.

"We have established that it's just you and I," Julian began, "What would you say to... making love on top of the roof of the Inn?"

"Wow, outside on the roof? Really? That sounds like fun. But what if someone comes up and catches us?"

"We have to lock all the access doors, you know, so we don't violate the 'Just us' rule," he stated.

"Can we do that?" I asked.

"I can make arrangements," he said with a gleam in his eye.

"Good, you know, if we go through with this," I said warily.

"What about...role playing?"

"Holy crap! From romantic to risqué. Does your car U-turn that fast too?" Two seconds after I said that, I wished I hadn't. A mischievous smile crossed Julian's face and the next thing I heard was screeching tires and my screams. Suddenly we were headed in the opposite direction.

"Can we go back and get my stomach. I need it to throw up." Damn I really need to learn to keep my mouth shut. The smile returned and I closed my eyes, put my hand over my mouth and felt the world shift on its axis. We were now headed back to the dorm...God I hope we get there in one piece. "Let's not do that again. This interior is way too nice for me to redecorate it with the burger and booze I just had for dinner."

After catching my breath, I decided to get back on topic "So...role playing...Let me guess, you be Mario Andretti, and I'd be the chick in the bikini handing you a racing trophy. Or you could be Indiana Jones and I'll be that girl who just screams."

"If that is what you want," he said.

I leaned back and closed my eyes. What I wanted was for him to touch me. And then...Holy *crap... he's touching me!*

Julian's hand was on my thigh. His hand was on my freakin' thigh. I wonder if those nice, strong hands would move up if I imagine them moving up. Higher...higher...higher and inside...

"How about just plain dating for a while?" Julian suggested. "Dinner...movies... dancing, that kind of thing?"

I snapped out of my daydream just before my panties were sliding down. Damn! "Dancing...dancing is good...rocking the night away...and dating...just dating?"

Julian took his hand off my thigh and said. "Having sex with you would be amazing, beyond amazing, but I don't want you to think that's all I want just because you may be working at a place like Jade's Inn. That's why we should just start with courting."

*Courting? Do people still say courting? How old is this guy? "I'm still thinking, but the* dating sounds nice."

"Do you want more money?"

"No! Oh God no...no, the money is fine! It's very generous. I don't understand why I have to get paid just to be with you?" I stammered.

"This may sound old fashioned, but I want to take care of you." Julian said, "And I know you are a modern, independent woman who can take care of yourself, but...I will want to...take care of you," he finished.

That was a tiny little rant, which I didn't think he was capable of. I pointed out the irony of sounding old fashioned when we are talking about the world's oldest profession, at which point we pulled up in front of the dorm. I now became curious about how Julian knew where I lived. I didn't give him directions as he drove. I didn't give him an address. I assumed Dawn told him.

I opened the car door when Julian asked me to wait. He got out quickly, walked around to my side and opened it for me. I've heard about this thing called chivalry, I've seen it in movies, the old black and white ones, but when it really happens, it's kind of cool. It's as if our whole evening had begun together, and we were taking the traditional walk up to my place at the end of the date for a good night kiss.

You never think it will happen to you, but there I was, standing at the entrance to the dorm when out of nowhere there appears, on my right shoulder, a tiny little red woman with horns. She seems trying to convince me to stick my hand down the front of Julian's pants, hold on tight, drag him up to my room, and have my way with him. On my left shoulder, stands woman dressed in white robes, and the cutest little pair of wings, trying desperately to talk me into my room alone and getting intimate with a cold shower.

Julian took both my hands in his, "I know a large amount of things have happened to you today," he said. "Some of it you will want to forget, but I hope that some you will remember forever, how I feel about you and why I want us together."

"I know Julian," I said. "It's not just...physical...despite the arrangements...it's more than that," I whispered in a sigh.

He let go of my hand, and wrapped his left arm around my waist, pulling me in close. His right hand caressed my check and lifted my chin up. Our eyes met, and then our lips. The kiss started soft and gentle, and then became more intense before going back to being soft again.

"Good night Caprice," Julian said against my ear, leaving goose bumps in its wake.

"Uh huh...I mean good night to you too," I stuttered.

With a smile, he turned and walked away.

Yeah, I'll remember this night. My little devil disappeared in a puff of red smoke. "I'm very proud of you," my little angel said before disappearing herself. "Oh shut the fuck up."

# Chapter 10:

# Working at Wolf's Lodge

I had a long night of irregular sleep. When I was lying awake, my thoughts kept going to Julian, and when I was asleep, I was with Julian somewhere on cloud nine. Having a very small amount of sleep, and being frustrated, makes for a long day at school. Calculus makes even less sense when you have an overwhelming need to get laid.

After hours and hours of book-learning, I was off to yet another job. This one at the local Wolf's Lodge, it was bingo night. That's right, bingo. B-I-N-G-Oh, just shoot me. The main room at the lodge was full of about twenty tables with lots of chairs that would be filled with lots of older people who have no life, but can hold their liquor quite well.

I've got the routine down. Put on the ugly apron, take down all those chairs and make sure they face the big board so everyone can see the numbers being picked. For those who can't see the board, even from the front row, they just need to turn up their hearing-aids. I'm a vital cog in the inner workings of competitive bingo. I sell tickets, and when the tickets are sold, I sell them food and drinks...and I watch.

I've been watching these people for a while. It's depressing for the most part. Most of these elderly individuals come in here alone and they leave alone. They come here because they have nowhere else to go and they only go home when they're done. But it's not all bad. Occasionally, I get to see the married couples—a man and wife who have been "man and wife" for like twenty, thirty, even forty years. This might be the only place they have to go, but they don't seem to mind because they're together. They give me hope. I see the empty chairs get filled with mostly hollow souls, and it scares me that I might become one of them someday. I can just hear them now "One of us...One of us..." on and on.

There were fifty people tonight, and since the pleasure of selling tickets and hearing all the dirty jokes from the single men were mine and mine alone—the night was long. Mr. Davidson, a sixty-five year old man who dresses like a forty year old man pretending to be a twenty year old boy and who insists I call him Jack, won the big pot of the night. It took him a couple of hours to finish celebrating, and he finally left with less than half the money he had won.

The chairs were once again empty, and I put them back on the tables. After pushing the broom around for a while, I decided to check out and try to slip out the back before Mr. Davidson returned to ask me out for the fifth time.

The coast seemed clear...at first. There was a figure standing near my car, but it wasn't Mr. Davidson. It was Julian. He was wearing black pants that looked like they were custom made just for him, and I was wearing my heart in my throat.

He was also wearing a great looking white shirt with the top buttons undone. Before I could reign in my imagination of what lay underneath, I saw myself biting the buttons off his shirt like candy, nibbling them off one-by-one.

"What can I do for you?" I asked after returning to reality.

"I have something for you."

"Okay," I said with curious hesitation.

He took a step towards me and reached inside his open jacket. "I know you like Winnie the Pooh, so I thought you might enjoy this." He pulled out a red package with a white bow. Now this guy is great looking, probably great in bed. If he wraps his own gifts, and can cook, I'll start looking for the wedding invitations.

"How did you know I liked Winnie the Pooh?"

"You mentioned it in that video you made for the Inn, if you remember."

"Yes I did, didn't I?" I accepted the gift from him and felt like I was in high school getting a class ring or a letterman's jacket from an admirer...a real hot admirer. I managed to get the wrapping off without looking too eager. I opened the box and inside was a book. A Winnie the *Pooh book. An old Winnie the Pooh book.*

"Where did you find it?"

"I have my sources," he said nonchalantly.

I opened the front cover and nearly fell on my ass. I definitely would have if Julian hadn't *caught me. Nineteen twenty-nine...First edition...Autographed by A. A. Milne and the illustrator* Ernest H. Shepard! Oh my God! There was water in my eyes, and if it started rolling down my cheeks I'd have died of embarrassment.

"I'm glad you like it," Julian said. Yeah too late, he saw that I was crying.

It took a while to catch my breath. I couldn't even look up at him. I just kept staring at the book. "How...did you know I would like this?" I asked softly.

Julian let out a small laugh. "You are the type of person who loves to spend the day in the Hundred Acre Wood, what else would you want?"

I was at a loss for words. I held my book tight with one hand and grasped the back of Julian's head with the other, pulling him down and kissing him with reckless abandonment. I melted into the kiss and poured myself into his arms. I didn't ever want to let go. I fought my body's natural tendency not to inhale as long as I could, but I eventually came up for air.

"Well," Julian said, "If I knew you liked the book that much I would have given it to you last night."

"Thank you so much Julian, you have no idea what this means to me...I...I love it!" I'm not sure if Julian really understood how perfect this gift was. I wanted to take him home and show him, and then show him again.

Julian put his hands on my shoulders, "Caprice, I think I need to tell you that I'm not too crazy about you working here."

"Why is that? Aren't you a fan of geriatric games of chance?" I teased

"It's not the business," he said. "It's the location. This isn't exactly the safest part of town. I worry about you being here, especially at night."

Oh, be still my beating heart. He's worried about me. How sweet. He's not wrong about the neighborhood. This place is located on the wrong side of the proverbial railroad tracks. I can see the tracks from here. This is the old part of town where the buildings have been around for a hundred years and are mostly abandoned. But a nagging question prompted me to ask "How did you know I worked here...I don't recall mentioning it on my video?"

"Your friend told me," Julian said. He pulled me towards him, and we leaned against my car. "I know I've brought up this concern before, but if it's the money, I can help you with that. You know I can."

"I know, and that's sweet," I told him, "But I want to keep at least one job that's my own. Call it a security blanket against my own...insecurities."

"And what could you possibly be insecure about?" Julian asked.

"You...Me...Me and You...Us. I just came out of a very bad relationship that turned out quite sour, and I didn't even realize it until the breakup blindsided me. When I found out about Daniel's harem, it didn't exactly boost my self-confidence."

"And you're worried the same thing will happen to us?" Julian said in a cold and serious tone.

"No...maybe. I just need to know that I have a place to go if things go...horribly wrong. Not that they will. I don't mean to sound so pessimistic. It's just that, I've had this job for over a year. I want to keep it until I know our arrangement can work out."

"So maybe after our first official date you'll quit?" he asked hopefully.

"Self-confidence is clearly not an issue with you. But for me, I'll need more time. I guess I need to know you won't dump me for someone else after a week or even a month." I was holding my ground on this.

"How does three weeks sound?"

"How about three months?"

"Until you leave this place for good, I will be here every night that you are," Julian assured me.

"My bodyguard in the shadows," I said with a sly smile.

Julian led me to the driver's side of my car and opened the door for me. I had already stepped in when he took me by the arm. I turned and was met with a kiss. I felt longing in those lips. My legs shook and I slowly lowered myself to the seat and he closed the door. He bent down and I lowered the window.

"Daniel was a fool," was all he said before kissing me again and walking away.

I know I should be creeped out, but I couldn't help but be both flattered and horny at the same time. I decided to put my dirty mind in the glove compartment and think about my new Winnie the Pooh book. I started driving faster and I couldn't wait to get home and read it.

I managed to make it up the stairs, skipping every other step, without falling. I was in a hurry to get to my room, but I came to an abrupt halt when I once again saw a figure, this time standing by my door. It wasn't Julian—which was unfortunate—and it wasn't Jack the wannabe twenty year old, lucky bingo player, come to ply me with more liquor. Even that would have been ten times better than seeing Daniel.

Since the weasely little bastard hadn't noticed me yet, my first impulse was to turn around and flee, but since that is my room—and inside my apartment there are a robe, fuzzy slippers and tea pot that were waiting for me, not to mention my new Winnie the Pooh book—I decided to keep going.

"Hi Cat, having a good night?" he said with a chipper note in this voice.

"I was," I said in disapproval.

"Are you still pissed about the Bloody Rose last night?" Daniel asked with a mischievous smile. "I've forgotten all about it," he lied.

"I sincerely doubt that," I told him. I'd been living with Daniel for eight months and I know when he is lying to me and when his not. Right now he doesn't want to be alone and I'm the one he thinks he can get back. Well, not this time. "I can still smell the booze in your hair. Still using that cheap shampoo?"

I was wondering if I could quickly open the door to my dorm room, get inside, and then slam it closed before he had a chance to get in. Maybe if I close the door hard enough I can take a few of his favorite fingers with it. I put my hand on the door knob, but before I could even turn it, Daniel's hand was on mine.

"I really want to come in," he said, "I want to talk about us, about getting back together."

"You want a booty call Daniel, and if you don't remove your right hand from mine, you'll be stuck with using your left hand to satisfy that booty call," I growled.

"It's not like that Cat, I just want to talk," Daniel said in that smooth, quiet voice he hoped I would find charming, and not the least bit annoying as hell.

"Okay," I said vigorously, "For the learning impaired, don't call me Cat. And do you even realize that what you're doing is stalking? The only way I will ever go out with you is a quick trip to the nearest police station."

Daniel pulled my hand off the door knob and held it tightly, painfully. "Cat...Caprice, don't be like this."

My breath caught in my throat. I couldn't believe I was nervous and scared. I didn't know why. I've been repulsed by this asshole, but never afraid of him. While he was holding my one hand, I was running the other through my purse trying to find my cell phone.

My state of panic became more noticeable when I saw the door to Dawn's room open. Dawn will be my savior, or at least my witness. When Sam came out of the room I was shocked and relieved...and shocked.

"Let go of her," Sam ordered in a low growl that resonated with authority. Daniel released my hand, very quickly. Sam had an intense look in his eyes as he glared at Daniel, then he turned to me and said, "Do you need any help?"

"I'm not the one that needs help...Daniel here is the one with the learning disability. I have told him more than once to leave me alone, to stop following me, to stop being the creepy ex lurking in the shadows."

Sam moved between Daniel and me, and then kept his eyes on Daniel without saying a word. He didn't have to. Daniel stepped back, but tried to look at me "This is dumb Cat. You're upset about the break-up. In time, all this that we're going through will make our relationship stronger."

"Are you for real?" I cried, stepping forward. Sam turned to me and held me back. "I'm not upset about the break-up you dumbass, I'm upset about the cause of the break-up, that would be you! The break-up works for me, now get the hell out of here," I spat.

"I'm going," Daniel said reluctantly. He waited until he got to the stairs before turning back to us. "This isn't over Cat." Then he sprinted down the stairs and out of the building, before I could yell after him.

Sam kept his eyes on the stairs even after Daniel left, while I was fumbling with my keys trying to get them in the door. I lost count of how many times it took for me to get the door open, but I managed to do it, somehow, through my shaking. That's when Sam turned to me and asked to come in.

"Of course Sam, please," I invited emphatically. "You don't even have to ask. You're my hero. You're my Super Sam."

Sam came into my apartment and closed the door. "I think we need to talk about this Daniel guy because he's becoming dangerous, Caprice."

"You picked up on that too?" I said. "I'm just glad you were here." Then I stopped and thought for a moment. I put my new book down on the table and turned to him. "By the way, why are you here?" I asked.

"I had to bring Dawn home...she had a bad night, or too good of a night depending on your point of view. When I got here, I saw Daniel lurking in the shadows like a panther waiting to pounce on its prey," he explained.

"How long do you think he was out there?"

"I have no idea."

"What can we do?" I said desperately, in a panic. I was still shaking.

Sam took me by the hand. He guided me to my couch and we sat down. "This sounds scary and I don't mean to frighten you Caprice, but if you just say the word, you'll never have to see him again."

After saying this he just stared straight at me, unwavering, not even blinking. I shivered, but I couldn't tell if it was from the fright I got from my encounter with Daniel, or from Sam's presence. I could tell by his look and his tone how serious he was. He could take care of Daniel without giving it a second thought, with no more remorse than he has for the dead bug he scrapes of his shoe.

"Before you do something that will make me feel guilty..." I shut up and started thinking of Daniel getting a really bad circumcision that cuts off all of his nether regions. I got a smile on my face off of that. "Why don't we hold off? Chances are all Daniel needs to find is some hot young thing in a bar—or under a rock—and forget all about me."

"Well, I don't like it, but I'll trust your judgment on Daniel. But, if he does come back tonight, or anytime, just call me okay?" Sam said, sounding like a big brother. He handed me a business card with his number on it, and then put his hand on my shoulder. The warmth of his touch was reassuring, and I could see the concern in his eyes "Look in on Dawn once in a while, she's not feeling well."

"Yeah, a touch of brown bottle flu?" I asked.

"I think it's just the normal type of flu or possibly food poisoning."

"After I wash the day off of me, I'll check on her," I promised.

"Thank you," Sam handed me the key to Dawn's dorm room and left me alone in my own abode.

Once Sam was gone, I planned and organized the rest of my evening with my long, luxurious shower. Which was longer and more luxurious than usual, as I broke out the fruity smelling body gel and my loofah sponge that reaches everywhere— and I do mean everywhere. If this thing had fingers, I'd make it my boyfriend.

After pulling myself away from the loofah, I moved on to the next phase of my plan which involved a green Winnie the Pooh pajama top, blue spaghetti boxer shorts with blue trim and cute little piglets on them. Some may say the Eeyore slippers are over the top, or I have an unhealthy obsession with these cartoon characters, but, since no one is here but me, I don't give a shit what someone might say.

After making myself a nice steaming cup of hot chocolate, which may or may not be in a novelty mug from the hundred acre woods, I curled up with my first edition and was ready to read.

*Oh Crap! I promised to check on Dawn. Crap...Crap...Crap!*

To make myself feel less guilty for not checking on Dawn right away, I poured another cup of hot chocolate, grabbed Dawn's spare key, and quietly made my way to her room. Since my hands were full of chocolaty goodness, I turned around and knocked on the door with the heel of my slipper. There was no answer, and I didn't want to try kicking harder, because if Dawn thought I was the landlord, she'd try to sneak out the window. I carefully put the two cups of hot chocolate on the floor without spilling a drop, because that would be sad, and I opened the door with the spare key.

I peeked through the slightly opened door to her bedroom and saw Dawn sound asleep. She looked sweaty like she just had a rough night of sex, or for her a typical night of sex, but she also looked pale.

"I know you can't hear this," I whispered. "But I want to apologize for saying you were suffering from a bout of 'brown bottle flu'. I know you weren't there when I said it, but I'm sorry anyway." I set the cup down on the nightstand. "Here is a nice cup of chocolate apology when you wake up." I put my hand on her forehead. She felt cold and clammy so I decided not to give her a kiss goodnight. I went to the kitchen and got a glass of water and put it on her nightstand next to the hot chocolate. I pulled the blanket up around Dawn's shoulders and left her to whatever bizarre, flu-driven dream she may have.

I tiptoed out of Dawn's room and started back to mine. When I reached my door I noticed Karen, or is it Sharon, at the end of the hall. I've had a few classes with her and she seems to pay more attention to the other guys, particularly the male professors, than she did to the subject we were studying. At this point she was waving emphatically to someone, trying to get them to hurry. My guess is it's a guy...or two.

When the mysterious suitor showed up at the top of the stairs it turned out to be just one guy, one lone mother-fucker. I thought Sam had scared this asshole away, but Daniel was back and heading into what's-her-name's room. I'm not the least bit surprised. As a matter of fact, I'm relieved that they found each other. Maybe she'll turn out to be that one fantastic fuck that Daniel has been looking for. Perhaps now maybe he'll leave me alone.

Even though Daniel found his slut for the evening, I still locked my door and put a chair under the doorknob. No sense taking any chances. Once I reached the point where I felt as secure as I could be, I rushed back to my bed and my book. I'm sure it must have missed me more than Daniel.

# Chapter 11:

# A new Day

*I was suddenly sitting by a pond, running my fingers through the soft green grass beneath me. I was right on the bank, so when I leaned over and peered into its crystal clear water in front of me, I could see all the way to the bottom. I lay back until I felt the moisture of the grass on the back of my neck. The daylight that shined so bright in the world around me was disappearing as night came, just as soft as the day had been. I don't know when it changed from day to night. I didn't notice. I also didn't recall how I got there, or when, but the surroundings were familiar. I'd seen this place before somewhere...in a story...in a book...about a silly old bear.*

Okay, clearly I was dreaming, but it felt so real, right down to the breeze that was neither *warm nor cold. I was momentarily mesmerized by the light coming off the pond, but I could suddenly feel the presence of someone behind me. I felt safe and didn't turn around, just lay there facing the pond and waited for him to speak.*

*"Caprice, can you hear me?" Julian asked with uncertainty.*

*"I can hear you," I replied simply. I continued to look out over the pond for a moment or two, and*

*then rolled over to catch his gaze as he peered into my eyes. It's just as easy to follow the moonlight in his green eyes as it is on the pond.*

*"I've been trying to reach you," Julian said softly as he moved closer to where I sat.*

*"Just a few more inches and you'll reach me," I told him, then tensed up and grimaced. I tried to relax, but I don't think I was pulling it off. Julian putting his hand on my thigh didn't help.*

*There was a fleeting look on Julian's face that told me he was aware this was a dream, and that this was my dream. A smile played across his lips. I like it when he smiles. Even when it's smug, he still looks good.*

*Julian moved his hand up, pushing my silky red dress higher, and I noticed my innocent Winnie the Pooh pajamas had been replaced. I didn't know where this red dress came from either, but it was absolutely adorable. His hand went from the outside of my thigh, to the inside, and continued up. His magic fingers made their way between my legs, back to the outside of my dress, across my stomach and left goose bumps all over the surface my skin. When his fingers made it to my right breast he made my body shiver more as his hand slowly caressed around my neck to the back of my head.*

*He gently pulled me toward his lips. The kiss was soft until my hand made it behind his head. I pulled him in tightly and the kiss became more aggressive, passionate, and I felt a hunger I had never had before when his mouth opened to mine.*

*My assertive approach took Julian by surprise, putting a dent in that self-assured persona he tries so hard to maintain. He kissed me back with the same intensity, but I don't think he knew where this was going. Honest, I didn't either, but I couldn't wait to find out. My tongue found his tongue, and my hands found his chest after they liberated him from his shirt. I felt him shiver when my nails scraped over surface of his skin. It was so cool. I did it again. His hands grabbed my fancy new dress and pulled it over my head. His lips found the pulse point on my neck, which he kissed, sucked, and drove me nuts. His hands moved down my back, lightly tracing down my spine to my ass. His lips soon followed, kissing their way down my torso...down...down...*

*"Your boss is calling answer the phone, before you get fired...Your boss is calling answer the phone, before you don't have a job...Your boss is calling answer the phone, before you..."*

"This better be important," I yelled in absolute frustration as my cell woke me from my dream. I bolted upright in bed and looked around for that dammed phone. When the ring tone went off again I froze. "Holy shit, I'm late for work."

I grabbed my phone with one hand, started taking my pajamas off and then put my cell to my ear. "I'm sorry Cindy...I'm sorry...Mr. Sandman was playing a cruel joke and made me over sleep. I'll be there in ten minutes," I said hurriedly.

There was a pause on the other end of the phone. I could hear the inner working of her mind trying to come up with the funniest way to fire me. "See you in ten minutes," Cindy finally said and hung up.

Okay, cool, another bullet dodged. I dropped the phone on the bed, and quickly got dressed in whatever jeans and T-shirt I could find closest to me. I hoped they were reasonably clean. I started hopping on one foot across the room while trying to put a shoe on the other. I left my room and was attempting to put my hair in a ponytail as I ran haphazardly down the stairs.

So here I was, in my car breaking various laws like speeding and reckless endangerment at four thirty in the fucking morning. But in the cut-throat world of baking, you got to start early. I was able to run the last two red lights without garnering too much attention, but there were too many cars at the next light. I thought I better call Cindy to let her know I really was on my way, and I didn't just turn over to go back to sleep. You do that once and everyone thinks you make a career out of it. It's so not fair.

I checked my pants pockets. No cell phone. I checked my shirt pockets and realized it didn't have pockets. I thought I may have put the phone in my purse, which would be okay if I had remembered my purse. You see, nothing good can come from a day that starts at four fucking thirty in the morning.

The good news upon arriving at the bread store was that I arrived without a ticket. The bad news is that I arrived without my phone, my purse, and as it turns out, without my text book for my first class. After getting out of the car, I put my hands on my head to make sure I didn't leave it at home as well.

The good thing about working this early at a bread store, besides a steady paycheck, is being slammed in the face by the overwhelming smell of freshly baked bread. I started saying sorry before I even walked through the door. I grabbed an apron and begun grinding the grain for more flour when Cindy came up, "Well aren't you the brave-little-late-employee," Cindy said.

"Brave." I exclaimed.

"Your choice of attire, while fashionable in the outside world isn't real practical in the bread-making business." Cindy said with a smile.

I took a quick peek under the apron at the black T-shirt. Black clothes and flour don't play well together. That's what I get for dressing while I still have one foot in la-la-land.

Cindy did an admirable job of keeping her laughs on the inside, "Okay, you have two choices," She said. "One, go to class looking like you're in serious need of industrial strength dandruff shampoo, or two change your shirt."

"I was late enough as it is," I told her, "I don't want to have to run home for a wardrobe change."

"Not to worry," Cindy reassured me, "I have a couple of spare shirts in my office."

I knew there was a reason I liked her. After slipping on my new shirt, I went back to the grind of grinding flour. Around eight o'clock, I finally felt caught up so I borrowed the boss's phone and called Geri. The loud sound of the grinder was still echoing through my head, so it was hard to hear her when Geri answered her phone.

"Hello!" Geri yelled.

"Hi Geri."

"Oh, Cat, it's you. Been at the grinder again haven't you?"

"Nose and all, can you do me a favor Geri?"

"I suppose," she replied, "If properly persuaded,"

"You'll have my everlasting gratitude," I said, "I'll even throw in a tall, dark stranger if I can find one."

"Don't give me that shit. You found one, you're just keeping him to yourself," Geri said with sarcasm. "Maybe he has a tall, dark brother I could borrow."

"I'll ask. Can you help me?" I asked again.

"What do you need?"

"My books for class and my cell phone," I replied bluntly.

"Books and cell, what happened?"

"I overslept, I was in a rush," I didn't want to go into detail as to why I overslept. If I told her about the dream, we would be on the phone for an hour. As much as I would like to relive the dream, there just wasn't time.

"Where's the key?" Geri asked without hesitation.

"On top of the door frame."

"Okay I'll see you in class," Geri said. "I'll be the one holding your book and you'll be the one with the white chocolate, red raspberry scone."

"Okay," I agreed "One scone made to order." I said and hung up, going immediately back to work.

I do believe time does, in fact, move slower when you're busting your ass before sunrise. There is a cute theoretical physicist at the university, and I plan on asking him to investigate this phenomenon work-related time distortion. Non-morning people like me want answers, particularly on days that started like this. It helps to improve my mood when a boss like Cindy gives me a shirt instead of firing me, and friends like Geri who cover my ass when I leave my brain at home.

After stalling, and even moving backwards, the clock finally clicked forward to eight thirty. Time to stop working the muscles and start exercising my patience with a day filled with boring classes. I gave Cindy back her shirt and she gave me a couple of loafs of bread and a few scones. The sad thing for today is that after I attend two of my classes at the institute of higher learning, I'll watch my friend dance and get intimate with a pole...Yay for me.

I assume more traffic laws were broken on the way to class because I got there fifteen minutes early. I parked, ran to the rendezvous, but did not have time to stop for coffee. I saw Geri in the back row, and there I was, a friend bearing scones, but no café latte.

As I approached Geri, I was overcome by a familiar scent. The closer I got, the richer the smell became. Geri reached behind her and brought out two cups, both with steam rising to the heavens. Coffee. Thank the caffeine gods and their angel, Geri.

"Okay," Geri began like she was delivering the lector for today's class. "I could start by asking probing questions that will eventually reveal all the details of the past that lead you to this lowly state of showing up without books, phones, or coffee. The thing that will hold off the inevitable embarrassment is a white chocolate, red raspberry scone. Do you have the goods?"

I handed the scone that Geri desperately wanted and she swapped me for the coffee I desperately needed. Geri giggled, licking the raspberry from her thumb. "Now the cool reason for your absent-minded behavior would be a night of uncontrolled passion, but I'll guess that it's something duller like nerves about designing your rooms tomorrow for Jade's Inn."

"Yes," I said between gulps of coffee. "Yes that is it exactly, guilty as accused, detective."

"Okay, Cat, you caved way too easy. What's the what?" she said intuitively.

"No that's it. I have a meeting tomorrow to find out if I get the contract to design the rooms."

"And..." Geri asked with a smirk.

"And that's it. I have a business meeting... about...business," I said flatly.

"A meeting with a businessman," Geri added.

"About business," I emphasized again. "Of course," I said quickly." What else would we talk about?"

"Ohhh... I don't know," Geri said. She started picking raspberries out of her scone." Maybe you could talk to big Sam about coffee, dinner, night caps, breakfast..."

"Hardly an appropriate topic for a business meeting," I pointed out sternly.

"Look sweetie," Geri said, putting her hand on my knee. I'm not sure if she's being condescending or if she's just flirting with me. "When the businessmen on the other side of the meeting table looks like a dark, Greek god, any and every topic is suitable for discussion."

My mind quickly went back to the amazing dream I never got to finish. The whole of my vivid imagination was filling in the blanks and coming up with a steamy, yet happy, ending. Geri was staring at me trying to determine the nature of the smile spreading across my face. Before she could ask more personal questions, the professor entered the classroom.

Our convention about sex and business, and the business of sex, was replaced by some incredibly boring psychology. I kept hitting the rewind button on the dream until the class finally ended.

As we stood up, Geri handed me her note book. "I can sympathize with you about the whole new job thing Cat, and since you thought about it all through class, and nothing else what so ever, you can copy my notes."

"You are a lifesaver Geri," I said thankfully.

"Yeah that's me, a tasty little round piece of minty goodness," Geri said.

As far as I could tell, the next class was just as boring as the last one. I did manage to make it home without getting lost or running over a nun's puppy at least. When I finally opened the door to my apartment, there was Dawn with my slippers in one hand and a beer in the other.

"Geri tells me your day sucked," Dawn said bluntly.

"Geri told you?" I said with a groan.

"When you learn to travel faster than a speeding text, you can break the news of the day," she quipped.

I grabbed the slippers, but she held onto the beverage, "The beer is mine," she said pulling out of my reach like I was trying to steal her first born.

"It's too early for you," I told her after finally grabbing the beer and putting it back in the fridge.

"Oh, sad now," Dawn whimpered. "Tell me, what is it that has turned you into the Grinch-That-Stole-Malt-Liquor?"

"I had a dream," I said simply.

"I take it that it wasn't anything noble like Dr. King's speech," Dawn said with a grin.

"It was intense," I admitted, "It was amazing, it was...short."

"Short?"

"No, that wasn't short," I told her knowingly. "The dream was short, it ended before..."

"Oh, I get it," Dawn said. "Premature awaking, I hate when that happens, let me guess, Julian was the leading man in this short story?" I turned red but said nothing. "Well that's a big yes."

"New topic," I said quickly. "How are you?"

"Whiplashed from changing topics so fast," Dawn whined, rubbing her neck. "I'm feeling better than I was when I woke up after me and Sean were going at it like horny, little, chocolate Easter bunnies."

"You weren't feeling good about it?" I said.

Dawn then continued, "I was feeling great, orgasmic. Euphoria...then drained. Our nights together always seem to end too early, and yet I feel like I slept with the entire Boston Marathon."

"Have you been eating your spinach?"

"Yes mommy bitch," she replied." How is the rest of your day looking, Cat?"

"Why?" I asked, already knowing what Dawn was getting at.

"You know the answer," she said before sticking her bottom lip out and batting her eyes. I folded my arms and said nothing. I had nothing left to do, but doing nothing sounded better than watching Dawn short stroke a pole, so I decided to be a pillar of strength, and keep my mouth shut. Dawn's lip came out further and now quivered.

"Please tell me I'll be there for moral support only," I said, feeling the cracks in the pillar appear.

"No promises," Dawn said with a wink.

I just stared at her, she just stared back, and then I narrowed my eyes.

"Pleeeeeeaaassssseeeee!" She begged after a long pause.

"Fine," I said after some hesitation. "However, I'm not riding the pole with you."

"Thank you. Thank you. Thank you." she shouted jumping up and down. "I'll pick you up at two this afternoon."

I was running late.

If you want a computer in the lab, you have to get there early. I mean really early, like those geeky kids that show up to the latest sci-fi flick six hours before it starts. The best chance I had of getting to a keyboard was a pimply-faced freshman that hasn't been laid since he lost his virginity during a freak high school hazing incident. One smile and I get his computer. A smile *and ass-shaking and I can get his password and pin number, I think inwardly with an evil smile.*

I could go to the smaller lab at the Student Union Building which is closer, but it is much smaller. It gets noisy and smelly when the jocks show up after practice, but before a shower. They want everybody to think they are finishing homework, but they are really checking their email to see if the drunken girl from the frat party, whose name they can't remember, sent them an encouraging come hither message. The last time I was there I got pinched, prodded, and proposed to, so I decided to try the Rendezvous Center instead. If it's too crowded, I can always get something to eat.

I was on my way over there, computers and proper freshman flirting techniques on my mind, which lead me to think about guys flirting with strippers and Dawn's illicit proposal. I began thinking about ways of getting out of the trip to the club, like contagious diseases that pop-up out of nowhere, when my attention was diverted by a cheerleader that wasn't so cheerful. She was a young girl that looked like she was still in high school, crying and making her way to a bench outside the entrance. Once she got there, she was looking around and trying to pretend that she wasn't crying. I watched her for several minutes while she was rummaging through her backpack like she lost something, but I suspect she was just trying to hide her tears.  I had a choice—homework that was already late anyway, or some strange girl crying over a breakup or a misstep on the cheerleader pyramid. Hmm...I suppose I could always try summer school. I made my way over, trying for inconspicuous. Cheerleaders can be high strung like wild animals, and I didn't want to spook the girl.

"Excuse me. Uh. Hi. Are you okay? Can I help you?" I asked the young woman. She wasn't exactly out of place. I remember seeing something posted to various billboards around the campus about a high school cheerleading competition. This girl looks like the typical cheerleader...average height, maybe five feet and six inches, tall and skinny. I guess they have to be skinny if they will be tossed around like a rag doll on the human pyramid. Her dish water blonde hair was pulled back in a ponytail, which made it easier to see that she was, in fact, crying. With her hazel eyes and freckles, I bet she looks much better smiling.

"I'm sorry," she sobbed. "I don't mean to be blubbering like a baby. I must look pathetic," she said as she wiped her face.

"You're fine, don't worry," I told her. "Most of the people on this campus are too self-involved to notice. Is there something I can do?"

"I don't know," the girl spat out suddenly. "It's just that...I'm lost and...guys suck!" She kicked a rock by her foot and sent it rolling over to the other edge of the side walk. Wow, this *will not be easy, I surmised.*

"I can help you get to where you need to stay," I said helpfully. "But as far as the guy thing goes, the fact that you know they suck means you are a wise and intelligent young lady that has discovered a deep, meaningful truth while still in high school. I didn't learn that nugget wisdom until a few weeks ago." I managed to get a smile out of her. "So what do people call you besides 'Hey cheerleader' when they see you?" I asked.

"I'm Elizabeth," the girl stated.

"Nice to meet you Elizabeth," I said with my hand extended. "I'm Caprice, but my friends and new acquaintances call me Cat. So where is it that you need to go?"

"I have to find the Physical Science building, room one zero six," Elizabeth said, again wiping the tears from her cheeks.

"I have to admit, and I mean no offense, but I never would have guessed by the way you're dressed that you were looking for a science building. You're in luck. We're not far from the Physical Science Building. I can walk with you there if you want." I don't know if I just felt sorry for this girl, or if I was hoping for a boost to my daily karma. I reached into my backpack and grabbed travel pack of tissues and gave it to Elizabeth.

"Thanks," Elizabeth said. "I would really appreciate it if you could come with me. I know we just met, but would it be weird if I asked you for some advice about guys?"

"I don't know if that's a good idea, considering my recent history with the opposite sex. Any advice

I would give would have to come with a disclaimer. I guess I can listen and give you some advice, that may or may not help, as long as whatever I say won't be held against me in the court of public opinion," I said hesitantly.

"I understand," Elizabeth said. "All I need is to have someone to tell me if I did the right or wrong thing today. See my friend Becca is really into this boy named Josh, and has gone out with him a few times, but the thing is, he's my boyfriend. Becca is dating his twin brother Jaden, but she thinks she's dating Josh and I'm dating Jaden."

"So let me make sure I have this straight. You're dating Josh and your friend Becca thinks she is also dating Josh, but really she is with Josh's twin brother Jaden. Do I have that right?"

"Yes."

"You're making this up aren't you?"

"I wish, but no. I know this sounds like a bad MTV reality show, but it's my pathetic high school existence. To make it worse, my prom is coming up. The big night. The main event. The one night every teenager looks forward to, and I want to go with Josh. I told Becca today what's going on and she told me I was lying to her. Can you believe that? I've been friends with her for over five years and she believes a boy over me. I want to scream," Elizabeth said looking very close to screaming for real.

She didn't take one breath during that fit, so I chimed in "First, relax. A cheerleader throwing a tantrum isn't cheerful, it's simply disturbing," I informed her. "Telling Becca what was happening was the right thing to do, but she probably feels like a fool not knowing these guys did this to her, and so she lashed out at you. It may be time to play the ultimatum card and have this Josh guy and his brother tell your friend the truth. If they don't, tell them you will go to the prom with the richest football player at your school."

"I don't know, I really want to go to the prom with Josh." Elizabeth said hesitantly.

"If you don't stand up for yourself now Josh will keep running over you and you don't want that do you?" I asked.

"No I don't," Elizabeth finally said.

"Also, if your friend doesn't believe you then maybe she's not as good of a friend as you think she is," I finished.

"Thanks, you're very helpful." Elizabeth said. I hope she still thinks so when she goes home. I basically advised her that it's okay to drop her boyfriend and best friend all in one day.

"Feel better?" I asked.

"Yes," She said.

"Come on I'll show you where the Physical Science building is," I said "Why are you going there?"

"Science competition," Elizabeth stated.

"Really," I said. "Studying the aerodynamics of pom-poms and cartwheel routines?"

"Don't let the cheerleading outfit fool you, I'm a real science geek," Elizabeth said. "The cheerleading competition and science competition just happened on the same day."

"That's a happy accident, huh?" I said. "Well if the judges for the science competition are science geeks themselves, I'd keep the cheerleader outfit on. Trust me, it will work in your *favor.*" *A cute, geeky, cheerleading science student...Wow, the lines between high school cliques are really starting to blur. Have I been out of high school that long?*

We made it to the physical science building and tried to open the door. Instead, it opened by itself and nearly took my hand off. A rather high strung girl, whose brown hair was frantically flying everywhere, came out and grabbed Elizabeth by the shoulders. "Where have you been? I've looked everywhere for you!" she said in a high shrill pitch that frightened several birds out of a nearby tree. She was wearing a lab coat that failed to completely hide the cheerleading outfit *she had on underneath. What type of school do they go to?*

Elizabeth turned to me and asked, "Do you want to come inside and watch cheerleaders doing experiments? It's not as scary as it sounds."

"Sure," I agreed, realizing that my attempt to do my homework had been foiled again.

"Cat this is my BFF, Tia. Tia this is Cat." Elizabeth then turned to her friend, "Tia, did you tell Becca what was going on with the guys?"

"Yes, I did," Tia said in frustration, "She doesn't believe me either."

"If they don't have this fixed in twenty-four hours, I'm finding someone else to go to prom with," Elizabeth said with new found determination.

I could see this boy-bashing conversation lasting all afternoon and into the night. "Come on let's get inside," I put my arm around them both. I have to admit I did enjoy hanging around people that make me look like the responsible one.

We walked into the building and into a large room full of wide-eyed overachievers who probably consider slitting their wrists whenever they see a minus sign after any A on a report card. We were greeted by an older woman who brought Elizabeth a lab coat to match everyone else's attire. She led Elizabeth and Tia to the stage area and had them sit behind a long table. I went and sat down looking at my cell to see what time it was.

I saw Elizabeth jump out of her chair and run up some nearby stairs, then hug an old man who I assumed is her dad or grandpa. She saw me in the distance, which was cool as long as she didn't draw too much attention to me.

Just don't point at me kid.

She pointed at me.

And now she's pointing and waving. I reluctantly wave back.

Elizabeth came running down the stairs to where I stood, "Thank you for helping me today," she said after releasing me from quite the formidable bear hug. Before stepping away, she took hold of my arm. She was beginning to look pale when she gave me a strange gaze. "You know my uncle Julian? The one you're falling in love with?"

"What?" I said.

Then Tia came up saying "Pay her no mind. Elizabeth hasn't had lunch and gets dizzy from not eating," she explained. Elizabeth just held on to my arm until her dizziness was over.

"Here is some tomato juice, honey," an unfamiliar voice from behind me.

"Thank you mom," Elizabeth said taking the purple water bottle and drinking from it, "I'm fine now."

I gave Elizabeth a weird look. "Uncle Julian?"

"He's falling in love with you too...you're one of us and you don't know it."

Elizabeth's mother took the bottle back from her daughter and gave her a weird look.

Elizabeth and Tia returned to the stage for the competition. "Good luck," I told them.

I turned to see Elizabeth's mother looking at me, then at her daughter and then back at me.

"Thank you for helping with my daughter," she said and held out her hand. I shook her hand and she smiled "We will meet each other again."

She headed back up the stairs, which suited me fine. Could that have been Julian's sister or *sister - in-law? Small world. I'll ask Julian about it next time I see him, if I remember.*

I found a seat in an obscure corner of the vast room, which had assorted tables and chairs that wound up the stairs of the auditorium. While my plan was to look interested in the proceedings, to tell the truth I really didn't care. I can remember the straight "A" kids in school when I was there, and their knowledge of science was impressive, but as much as I like a diversion, the thoughts of a cheating boyfriend and a strip-teasing girlfriend were overwhelming the thoughts of brainiacs in cheerleading skirts.

*A diversion can be nice though.*

A diversion...great.

A diversion is just what I need.

A diversion is just what I got.

Damn!

What she said about Julian stuck in my head. What the fuck? I need more answers to what just happened, but the competition started and continued for a long time. Or maybe it just seemed that way because I wanted it over. I had no idea how it was going. I was watching the people in the upstairs section of the auditorium more than the kids on stage. I'm not sure how much time passed when I heard loud cheers from the stage, and since Elizabeth and Tia were jumping up and down, I can assumed they kicked ass in the competition. I knew those outfits would go a long way with the judges.

I was happy for the girls, I really was, but my mind keeps jumping back Julian. I closed my eyes, took a deep breath and mustered all the courage to walk up and ask all the questions who? What? Where? Why? I stood up- I took a step forward, stopped and then started walking again. I was going to do this. I was ready, willing and then...my phone goes off. It was the reminder that Dawn put on my phone, and it wasn't just an annoying beep or funny ring tone. It was Dawn's voice saying, "Hustle your ass girl...it's time to be schooled by the professionals." Shit.

# Chapter 12:

# Pole Dancing Rehearsal

The things we do for friendship. We watch them have sex with guys and we watch them have sex with poles, all out of some misguided sense of moral support. When I say "we" do this for friends, I should say "I" because I don't know anyone else crazy enough to go to these types of extremes. I miss the days when your loyalty to your friends was evidenced by backing them up when they trash-talked a boyfriend, or praised a one-night stand, or even traded your favorite doll clothes with each other.

I continued to reminisce about the good old days, which were about a month ago, when we pulled into the parking lot of Teddie's. The building itself is unassuming, in the fact that it looks like any other building. The fancy neon sign that flashed Bikini Dancers was a beacon in the night for those guys who couldn't get a date without paying for it.

Dawn and I stepped out of the car and just stood there, overwhelmed by the sound of outdated dance music and the smell of stale chicken wings. There was another odor that was unfamiliar and I wanted to keep it that way.

Maybe it was the shift in the wind that brought down the wall of various aromas, or maybe it was just Dawn taking my hand which helped me muster the courage to walk straight into the club. It was dark at first, but thankfully empty of male customers, which was a relief for both me and Dawn. Our eyes adjusted to see tiny lights—lots of them—as well as some red and white lights and...a woman.

"Are you Dawn and Caprice?" she asked in a kind, jolly, old voice that belonged in another decade. I was curious how she knew my name, but I said nothing. Dawn was also speechless at first, but she realized this was her party.

"Yes." was all Dawn managed to squeak out.

"Speak up girlie!" the woman said with a welcoming smile, "This is no place for a girl who's shy."

Dawn took a tentative step forward and held out her hand "Yes, I'm Dawn and this is my friend, and moral support, Caprice."

"Pleased to make your acquaintance," she said, shaking Dawn's hand forcefully. I kept my hand at my side, but she managed to find it and squeeze the shit out of it. "Nice to meet you too, moral support. Call me Sweet Sue. I take care of the girls here. They call me Sweet Sue, so can you girls."

I started rubbing my right hand with my left until the feeling came back while Sweet Sue was leading us on a tour of the place. She walked with confidence like the place belonged to her and so did we. She had that, "Don't fuck with me," air about her that made me feel protected and owned simultaneously.

I was hoping that the large open bar will be a stop on the tour, but we passed right by it and headed towards two ominous looking black doors.

"So you want to be a pole dancer? Well it's a fine art to learn," Sweet Sue said after we entered a dark room beyond the doors. I never thought of pole dancing as an art, but I'll defer to her experience. She looks like she's been around the block a few...hundred times.

I heard the click of the light switch and the room lit up, not brightly but dimly. There were small lights lining the wall that looked similar to the lights around the open bar. In the center of the room was a stage and in the center of the stage were, what I can hope were, two reasonably clean poles. Surrounding the stage were a number of chairs, and the set up reminded me of a class in school where the teacher tells the students to put their chairs in a circle once class is finished. I wonder if the girls here feel the same.

Sweet Sue took a step forward, raised her hand and snapped her fingers. Suddenly two spot lights flooded on stage and they lit the stage so brightly, it made the rest of the room look like the kind of ominous dark that invites the sleaziest of activities. I can see this as an advantage to the patrons sitting comfortably in the chairs not wanting to be noticed by the other guys, or pole dancer who may have been his high school teacher.

All was quiet for a moment and then the silence was pierced by the distinctive sound of high heels walking onto the stage. "This is Misty," Sweet Sue said, "She is one of our best pole dancing artists.

She will be your instructor." Well what do you know, she was a teacher! Miss Misty began a slow provocative walk to the front of the stage, every move deliberate, including the way she took off her silky black robe revealing a very skimpy red string bikini. She had her eyes locked on Dawn and me, and never took them off. Honestly, I didn't notice when she threw the robe to me until it was covering my head.

The sound of her stiletto heels echoed throughout the dark room as Misty strolled back to one of the poles and started to swing around by one hand. That's when the music started. It was a song I haven't heard in a while, "Do You Want to Touch Me?"

Not wanting to be heard, I took advantage of the loud music and whispered to Dawn, "She's an artist?"

"A fucking artist my ass," Dawn replied with quiet cynicism.

The shared sarcasm that was evident on our faces soon faded away as we watched this woman dance and defy gravity itself. By the time she was done, I had a new appreciation for the art of pole dancing, not to mention the meaning of the song. However, I was also convinced that

Misty was a contortionist in her past life.

"She's an artist," Dawn and I said together, "In heels!"

"Okay students," Misty said, "Are you ready for today's lesson in how to drive men so crazy they can't help but throw money at you?"

"Yes please," Dawn said and jumped on stage in a single bound. Misty took her by the hand and led her to the pole on the right, while Misty took the pole on the left.

"You're Dawn right?" Misty asked.

"Yes, ma'am," Dawn replied.

"Ma'am?" Misty said in surprise. "That's cute. Well Dawn, swinging on the pole is easy because the pole turns on its own, all you have to do is learn to look sexy while holding on to it."

Misty made it look easy and even said it was easy, but for the next ten minutes I was enjoying the slap-stick routine Dawn was putting on. If I didn't know better, I say Dawn's pole had one hell of a sense of humor. Dawn's ass probably wouldn't agree. Just as Dawn was getting the hang of not falling down, Sweet Sue came out with something to make Dawn's death defying act even more death-defying "Here you go honey," Sue said. "Eight inch heels, compliments of Sam."

"Well isn't he just a darling little perv," Dawn said holding the heels out at arm's length.

Then Sweet Sue turned to me with a smile that I absolutely did not trust, "What's your shoe size dear?"

"Oh I don't need shoes. I'm just here for moral support, remember moral support," I said speaking very fast.

Sue looked at my feet, "Size seven."

Dawn was giving me the puppy dogs eyes while I was shooting daggers back at hers, then Sweet Sue came out with my eight inchers. Dawn and I sat on the edge of the stage comparing our new torture devices. Dawn's fit just right, making her look like a slutty Cinderella and if I clicked my ruby red ones, I could be magically transported to The Little Whore House in Kansas.

"Okay Cat, let's get going," Dawn said with renewed enthusiasm. I continued to sit on my ass with renewed hesitation. I did become concerned when I saw Dawn whisper something in Misty's ear, but my resolve was iron clad. I was not moving.

My iron clad resolves, disappeared when I heard "nineteen-ninety-nine" by Prince. I can say no to Dawn, to Misty, even to Sweet Sue as long as I have a running head start, but I can never say no to Prince.

Dawn knows that. Dawn's a bitch.

I know how to dance. I also know how to get my groove on, particularly when Prince is playing. Misty took it upon herself to show us how to blur the lines between dance and simulated sex. Every time Misty made a seductive move, Dawn and I tried the exact same thing. While it was clear who the professional was, and who the bumbling amateurs were, I found myself enjoying the experience, maybe a little too much.

Trying to stay with the beat and maintaining my balance in my new shoes was becoming more of a challenge because my attention was diverted to this incredibly hot woman on the stage.

Her moves were becoming harder to follow as she was in a seductive world of her own. "Misty, go change for the next part of the training." Sweet Sue said. Misty grabbed the robe and headed to the black drapes.

"Nineteen-ninety-nine" was over and I was sorry to see it go. A new song started I was not familiar with, but it fit the style and mood of the club. The lights dimmed and a red spot light overhead lit the center stage again.

The Naughty Nurse and the Catholic School Girl are stereotypical clichés of every horny guy's fantasy, but the queen of the costume fantasy ball is the cheerleader. When Misty walked out in a blue and orange outfit, complete with pom poms, it was obvious she had mastered the persona.

Misty moved with an intense sensuality that was in perfect timing with the music. It was as if she were under a spell, like a snake enchanted by the music of the snake charmer. The first article of clothing to come off was Misty's top. How she did this while holding the pom poms is beyond me. Her hips and her mini-skirt swayed back and forth in a hypnotic fashion that could freeze a man in his seat looking stupid, while drooling down the front of his beer-stained shirt.

Misty moved to the edge of the stage, turned and faced the poles and bent over. Wow, *leopard print panties—I'm not even surprised. She straightened up, turned back around and* lowered the pom-poms to reveal a matching bra. She brought the pom-poms back up, and somehow the bra dropped to the floor.

"Can you come here to the front of the stage, Caprice?" Misty asked, abruptly ending her erotic dance trance.

"Um...Yea...no...why?" I stammered.

"Let's call it...hands on training," Misty replied with a smile.

"Uh, wow...um...I don't..." I stopped for a moment in a desperate attempt to familiarize myself with the English language. After I collected my thoughts, I gave it another shot. "Okay look, no offense and I'm really flattered, but I don't..." Okay, I lost my train of thought again.

*How do I say this without insulting her? I don't want to hurt her feelings, so I decided to do the* fair thing, throw my friend under the bus. "It's Dawn here who is the real student...maybe she could...you know...do the hands on thing," I said.

Misty's mouth spread in a smile while Dawn's just dropped open. Misty turned her piercing gaze from me to Dawn "Alright, Dawn, you just got moved to the head of the class. Please, take your place."

While Dawn made her way to the front of the stage, she looked over at me, squinting her eyes in a failed attempt to shoot burning lasers at my brain. "Okay...teach...here are my hands,"

Dawn said, holding them up, "Where do you want them?"

Misty did another seductive walk to the front of the stage. I'm beginning to think it's the only way she knows how to stroll around. She probably makes her parents nervous every time she walks through the door at Thanksgiving. "Now Dawn," Misty began, "I want you to hold my skirt here," It was at that point that we noticed Misty's skirt opened on the side with Velcro. You have to admire the convenience. With some hesitation, Dawn took a hold of a small corner of the Velcro opening. Staying in time with the music, Misty twirled to the center of the stage, leaving Dawn holding the skirt.

Now every guy in the imaginary audience could see Misty's tiny bikini top and thong, and she displayed them with pride like she was waving a flag. She finished her patriotic floor show hanging upside down hands free from a pole. She came off the pole and landed on her feet with the grace of a ballerina.

"Let's see what you got honey," Misty said with a smile. That's when Dawn turned the puppy dog eyes on big time.

I quickly held up my hand "The part of the horny patron will be played by Caprice, that's me. The part of the slutty stage siren will be played by Dawnie, which would be you." I firmly sat back in a chair near the front, put my elbows on the stage and started to clap. "Let's go, I've got dollar bills ready to be stuffed in your underthings."

"Okay Sir," Dawn said, "Just relax and enjoy, keeping in mind that I'm new and dressed in street clothes, not a cheerleader outfit." Dawn looked cute trying to look sexy while unbuttoning her blouse. I practically had to swallow my lips to keep from laughing, which is probably why Dawn threw her shirt at me when she finally got it off. She took a few turns on the poles, even trying to hang upside down.

Dawn walked back towards me, obviously feeling more relaxed. She put her thumbs inside the waistband of her pants and moved them around her waist. Next she unbuttoned her jeans and slowly pulled down the zipper, while looking at me like I was a giant sized banana split. Then she opened her jeans more and I could see she was wearing her favorite pink panties with the smiley face that has a tongue sticking out towards the crotch. Dawn turned around, bent over and dropped her jeans. She stepped out of them, spaced her feet apart and stared at me through her legs.

Dawn turned back around to face me and squatted down with her legs open. She ran her hands along the inside of her thighs, back and forth, slowly and provocatively stroking her leg.

She was lost in the moment. I think this amateur stripper just turned pro. My surprised look turned to utter shock when Dawn lowered herself from the stage to my lap, straddling my legs.

She brought her lips to my ear. "I did it," she whispered. Then she squealed "I did it!"

"Yes, yes you did," I told her, "And you still are."

"Huh," Dawn looked at me with wonder and I looked at her with a smile. We both looked down. Dawn blushed when she realized her hips were still gyrating. "Oh shit," she cried and jumped up. "Sorry."

When Dawn found the courage to look at me again, she grinned. At first I thought it was a veiled attempt to hide her embarrassment, but the more she looked at me the more I realized she was a devious little bitch with a master plan.

"Your turn," Misty said with a cheesy smirk.

"My turn?" I said shocked.

"Your turn," she said firmly.

"It's not my turn," I said emphatically.

"Yes..." she stated.

"No...." I replied.

"Well I've had my turn," Dawn said, attempting to use logic to make her point. "Misty has had her turn. Do you want Sweet Sue next?"

"Ok it's my turn," I said quickly.

"I heard that," came from Sweet Sue's voice from a back room.

With a sigh I unbuttoned my top.

"Wait for the music, Hon," Misty said. She raised her hand, and like magic the music began.

To my pleasant surprise, Dawn stayed on stage. She moved to the music and I followed her like an uncoordinated shadow, following her every hip thrust and leg lift. Before I knew it, I was down to my bra and panties, swinging on one pole while Dawn was on the other.

The music stopped, but I didn't want to. The feeling of being nearly naked on a stage and swinging on a pole was beginning to turn me on. By the time I was dressed, I found myself missing the experience.

Just as we jumped off the stage, Sweet Sue came in, "Good show ladies. If I was a man I would want a three-way party. You two ever find yourselves looking for a job, come see me," Sue said as she vigorously shook our hands. I wish the visual of the three-way party with the male version of Sweet Sue would have left as well.

Misty took our hands much more gently, and even gave both Dawn and I a kiss on the cheek. "Call and let me know when your big show will be so I can be in the audience. A friendly face sometimes helps." With that Misty left, and Dawn and I were finally alone.

Where does one go after a day of debaucherous practice? Why shopping, of course! I'm not talking about eggs, milk or feminine hygiene products. I'm talking about Daisy May's. The name implies a nice place to buy flowers for your grandma's new hat, but inside you can find the latest in the newline of vibrators, whips, and other assorted sex toys you may find under the floor board in your grandmother's closet.

Dawn and I weren't there to buy a girl's best battery operated friend, at least not this time.

We were looking for work clothes for Dawn's "new job." Not only do you have to stay on the poles, but you have to look hot doing so, and hot usually translated into skimpy and see-through.

Depending on your mood, or more accurately how long it's been since you've gotten any, will determine whether you are amused when you walk in Daisy May's, or whether the experience is purely cathartic. When we walked in I closed my eyes and took a deep breath, taking in the familiar scent of my panty drawer, and just a hint of latex. Dawn on the other hand headed straight for the French Ticklers.

"How can I help you ladies?" called a voice from behind the mannequin dressed as a dominatrix. When I turned to look, I saw who I thought was a teenage girl that should be at the mall food court flirting with the kid that sells pizza by the slice. I'm sure she meets the minimum age requirement for selling sex in a bottle, but I wouldn't bet my last chocolate bar on it. Her long brown hair was in braids and she wore jeans and a Twilight T-shirt that showed her devotion was split between Jacob and Edward.

"I'm looking for a certain...type of clothing," Dawn said with reservations. Clearly she thought this girl was sixteen as well.

"And what type would that be?"

"Well..." Dawn hesitated again. "It's for work."

"Stripper clothes," the kid declared with a confident knowledge of all thing's slutty. "Right this way."

We walked to the front counter and the girl took out a large book that said Costumes. This was a very organized binder that had each section labeled. What a selection, Comic Book Characters, Fairy Tales, School Girls, S&M, and Professional Women. Dawn and I were both intrigued by this last category. We opened the section expecting to see women dressed as hookers, but found a librarian, airline stewardess, nurse, and teacher. Men's fantasies can be strange and varied.

"All outfits you see here are rip away," the young clerk said.

"That saves time," Dawn commented as she turned back to the "Comic Book Heroes" section. "I want to see this one," she decided.

"Wonder Woman?"

"Yeah," Dawn said paying more attention to the book than me.

"Why?"

"You know what a fan I am and...Kurt likes her."

"How do you know what Kurt likes?"

"He told me. We do talk you know," she said rolling her eyes.

"You talk... about Wonder Woman?" I asked in disbelief.

"We talk about things," Dawn said. "We watch TV, we cuddle. Guys don't want sex all the time, it just seems like they do."

Well my ex, Daniel, was obviously not a typical representative of the male population. He thought of nothing but sex. He'd fuck anything and it didn't necessarily have to move. I still feel stupid for not seeing that.

While I was busy feeling sorry for myself, Dawn was busy trying on one of the Wonder Woman outfits. When she stepped out of the dressing room all I could say was "Linda Carter would be proud."

The outfit was very authentic, right down to the lasso. I could see how that could come in handy in a guy's sex fantasy.

"You'll want this," the sales girl said handing Dawn a roll of tape.

"What's this for," Dawn asked

"It's two-sided tape," the girl said. "You'll need it to keep from giving the crowd a premature show, especially when you're hanging upside down."

"And as we all know," I said in a sarcastic tone. "Wonder Woman was always well known for hanging upside down from poles."

Dawn ignored my jabs and moved toward a table with a wide assortment of panties. She look at each one, sometimes picking one up and holding it up to her hips "I'll need something for underneath, something fitting for a grand finale when Wonder Woman drops the bathing suit."

"How about this," I said holding up a red, white, and blue G-string. "They complete the whole patriotic look."

By the time we got to the counter to pay for the new ensemble, Dawn was looking pale. No, downright sick. "Dawn are you alright?"

"I can't do this," she said hesitantly.

"You don't have to buy Wonder Woman," I told her. "What about Super Girl? Her outfits are over there?" I said encouragingly.

"No, I can't do...the routine, the stripping," Dawn said as though she were trying to keep from vomiting.

"What do you mean? I watched you earlier on stage, you were great."

Dawn paced nervously, "It's all those men. I can't do this in front of all those horny guys staring at me. I need to call Sam!" Dawn reached in her purse and took out her phone, and then she walked outside.

I could see Dawn walking back and forth outside the window pleading her case with Sam. I wandered over to the back wall to look at all the new shiny vibrators, big and small. I was beginning to wonder if they let you try these on like they do with the outfits, but then Dawn came back with that "I need-a-favor" look.

"NO," I said immediately.

"I didn't say anything," Dawn stated.

"NO!" I said again firmly.

"But you don't know..." she began again.

"It's instinctual," I told her. "I trust my instincts, and my instincts tell me you walked out saying you can't do the stripping, then you come back in with this 'Help me' look in those beady-little eyes."

"My eyes aren't beady, they're round and pretty," Dawn said defensively.

"Not when you want something," I countered.

After a long pause, Dawn finally spoke again." Sam thinks that if I have a partner on stage... you know a pal, a true blue friend to strip with me... I might feel more at ease. And with a smoking hot body like yours...."

"Stop...stop," I pleaded, "You're embarrassing yourself."

"Sam said he would pay up the money for the outfit of your choice and three hundred dollars on top of that," Dawn said temptingly.

"Okay, first flattery and now bribery," I said with disgust, "Have you no shame girl?"

"You've known me for all this time and you can ask that? So what do you say? Pretty, pretty, please with chocolate and cherries on top!" Dawn practically yelled.

How do I get myself into this shit? Am I paying some karmic penance for a past life full of evil deeds? Maybe I was a televangelist taking people's hard earned money by day, and putting it in a strippers G-string by night. Man, payback can be a full-circle bitch. I'm getting sad eyes from Dawn and the store clerk now.

"Just...stop...wait," I demanded. I turned and walked into the fitting room. These rooms were not made for pacing, at least not back and forth. They're more equipped for tiny little circles with brief stops to look in the mirror to continue asking yourself why. I could hear Dawn rustling outside the fitting room door.

"Dawn?" I said after a moment.

"Yes," she replied with both hope and fear in her voice.

"If I say no to this, does that mean you won't go through with it? You'll call it off?"

"Yes," she replied again, sounding even more timid.

"Dawn?" I asked.

"Yes," she said with apprehension.

"You kinda suck," I opened the door gave her a not happy look.

"Is that a yes? I heard yes," Dawn said as if I had just announced that Christmas was here.

I didn't answer. She can sweat longer while I went through the pros and cons. First the pros.

*One, Good money.*

*Two, Helping a friend in need.*

*Three, Good money.*

*Now for the cons.*

*One, stripping down to my unmentionables in front of a bunch of salivating horn dogs.*

*Two, same as one. It's worth counting twice.*

*Three, what would Julian think? Should I care? Maybe he's a patron of the art of stripping, but what would he think if he saw me up there driving the guys into a sexual frenzy?*

I've been avoiding it, but I finally turned and looked in the mirror again. Why do mirrors have to be so fucking honest? Why can't they show you what you want to see? I imagined strong, confident woman instead of the person reflecting back at me. Then I imagined myself in a cheap stripper outfit. I like Julian, I really do, but I'm not sure about this setup where I'm a date on a payroll.

*Wait a minute. That's it! What if Julian wouldn't like seeing me strut my stuff across the stage letting stranger ogle my goodies? What if he would hate it? What if he wouldn't want anything to do with me after a night of near nude dancing? He may tear up the contract before I* had a chance to sign it. I didn't just walk out of the fitting room, I was strutting.

"I'm all yours, Dawn," I said with a smile on my face.

"Really? You will?" Dawn jumped up and down like an eight year old who was just told she's going to Disneyland. She threw her arms around me, squeezing what little air I had in my lungs out, and started unbuttoning my blouse from the back "You need an outfit."

It was back to the book for more short-skirted school girls, nurses, cheerleaders, and super heroines, but there was one outfit in my mind that I was considering when we were practicing with Misty. At the time I honestly didn't think I would actually be doing something like this, but when I was on stage, a fantasy was playing out on the screen of my dirty little imagination. I'm sure just about every women has wondered what it would be like to strip on stage in front of strangers, at least I hope most women have. I'd hate to think this perverted little fantasy was an exclusive to my depraved mind.

The ruby slippers from the club looked fantastic on me, and while some may be shocked by the idea of sexualizing the beloved character of Dorothy, I'm sure most guys, the straight ones at least, have been turned on by the innocent, pony-tailed girl in the cute, blue-checkered farm dress. Yeah, she was winey and probably tripping on beds of mushrooms, but she could work it on that yellow brick road.

"Do you have anything in a Dorothy?" I asked our new store clerk friend.

"Of course," she replied without hesitation. She went to a rack in the corner and brought out three blue and white-checkered dresses. The first one was too slutty, the second dress was too big, and the third one was just right. I came out with the dress on and basket in hand.

"Wow," Dawn exclaimed. "What do you have in the basket little girl?"

"Lotions, latex and lots of vibrators," I told her. I took the dress off and brought it to the counter, along with a red G-string and bikini top. I took out my wallet, but the girl waved her hand.

I looked up at her. "Compliments of Sam," she said in acknowledgement.

We both got in the car, our minds reeling with thoughts of what's to come. You can hear the inner workings of Dawn's mind going through the routine. One, two, three, kick, one, two, three, *flash.*

I would like to say that my thoughts were on more important things like world hunger, my grades, the red light Dawn just ran...but my thoughts just kept coming back to the same dilemma… Julian's opinion about me and my decision to express myself through the art of erotic dance. I don't even know if he will be there. Julian seems to like doing business at night for some reason, and while I'm sure I'll be pissed at Dawn for talking me into this, at least she set it up for us to go on after midnight. I think she was hoping that by the time we make our debut, those remaining in the crowd will be too hammered to remember what we look like.

"I have a surprise for you," Dawn said.

A surprise. Seriously? What could possibly come after 'I work at a brothel. I'll strip for fun and money, and so are you.' I waited a moment but she didn't say anything.

"What is it," I finally asked even though I felt like putting my fingers in my ears and saying "La, la, la, la," really loud.

"First we have to get our mascara and eyeliner from our rooms, and then I will show you."

My sense of self-preservation finally kicked in.

"Dawn, I love you, but I really don't need any more surprises today." I was hoping that

Dawn would be overwhelmed by our friendship and a sense of fair play, but she didn't say anything. When she is quiet and contemplating, that's the time to be afraid. The terrifying silence lasted until we reached our dorm. We went inside to get our makeup, and I have to admit, I was hesitant to come back out. After deciding I will convince myself later that this night will be just a bad dream, I went back outside to meet Dawn.

# Chapter 13:

# Finding Out the Truth

"Can I ask where we are going?" I queried.

"Relax, we will be there in five," Dawn said. Okay, now she is just playing with me like a puppet on a string. She is expecting me to play guessing games until we finally get to the end of this magical mystery tour. Not me...not this time...I'm shutting up.

"Did you call Sam to see if Julian can come tonight?" she finally asked with impatience.

*"I forgot." I admitted. Shit, who am I kidding? There is probably no way he can get out of any meeting tonight.*

"Well there's no need to fear," Dawn said. And then quieter she added, "I called Sam and asked him to call Julian."

"Thank you. Now where are we going? Please Dawn, tell me. I'm starting to get nervous."

"Breakfast at Tiffany's," Dawn finally said reluctantly.

"Excuse me?"

"Breakfast at Tiffany's," she said again, but more bluntly this time.

"We're going to an old movie?" I asked, "Or do you know a girl named Tiffany who is serving up eggs and bacon at this hour?"

"I know this girl named Tiffany from my statistics class," Dawn explained. "She has a hair salon on Fifteenth Street. We need to get dolled up for tonight and I know that Tiffany will take care of us. She's very imaginative when it comes to hair. She also has a stylist named Tiffany that works with her and can do wonders with makeup. There is also another girl, Tracy, who does nails," Dawn concluded.

"Sounds like a full service salon. I have to admit, I've never had my nails or makeup done by someone else," I looked at my nails. "Frankly, they are not long enough to do anything with."

"Tracy will take care of that. Your nails will be so long they scare the shit out of the bravest man in the club, whatever length. Trust me, these are the people that work for Jade's Inn, they help us look even hotter than we are," Dawn said happily. I snickered and felt relieved her surprise was something simple and didn't involve criminal activity—or any further sacrifice to my virtues.

We pulled up to a house that looked more like, well, a house than a salon to make hot women look hotter. It was an older place with a white picket fence lined with flowers and green vines. With some salons, you can smell them before you open the door, but if I didn't know this was a salon, I would think it was a New Age store. We walked through the gate, which had lavender growing around it, as we followed the stone path to the door, when Dawn stopped. "Just a heads up, let Tiffany do what she wants, it's easier that way," she said in warning.

"Why?" I asked nervously.

"Because she's an artist," Dawn said with a wink.

"Really? Like Misty is an artist?" I teased.

"Yes...well no, not exactly like Misty. Tiffany knows her way around a head of hair. She's awesome at what she does and she will ask you questions, but she knows the answers, which is why it's best to let her do what she wants. I guarantee you will look amazing."

Dawn was the first to walk through the door, leading the way into this land of bossy hair dressers. The interior of this place, like the exterior, did not look like the typical hair salon. For one thing, there were more plants inside. There were separate stations where you could find sinks and hair dryers, but each one had its own mood lighting and mood music. I also noticed different doors with fancy lettering on them saying things like "Tanning," "Massages," and "Facials." My imagination, which lately could be found in the gutter, went wild in this strange place.

Dawn took off her shoes, rolled up her pants to her knees and sat in this cozy-looking chair that had tub of water in front of it. Then this beautiful blue-eyed blonde, who had a flower painted on her cheek, sat on the floor in front of Dawn and poured various bottles of what I can only guess were "potions" into the tub. The young lady then paid particular attention to Dawn's toenails, so I'm guessing this must be Tracy.

"So, what's your character going to be?" Tracy asked while massaging Dawn's feet.

"Wonder Woman," Dawn moaned in satisfaction.

"So, red, white and blue on the toes and fingers?" she questioned without looking up.

"That works," Dawn replied. "But take your time..."

I sat in another chair, then a woman came through a back door, and over to me. "Have you ever had highlights in your hair?" she asked, reaching out and feeling the texture of my hair. I knew this woman was Tiffany because Tiffany was the hair expert, and she was running her fingers through my brown locks. She massaged my scalp like it was clay, like she was preparing to create a sculpture. She had gorgeous, long, red hair that went down to her waist. I'm guessing her name at home was "Mom" since she had a picture of three kids taped to the mirror.

"I don't think I need highlights," I told her. "I'm doing the Dorothy thing on stage. I think Glenda...Good Witch of the North was the only one with highlights,"

"Think of it this way, Miss...?" Tiffany prompted.

"Caprice," I told her. "My name is Caprice, but my friends call me Cat."

"Think of it this way Cat. When you're on stage, you own that character. You can make her look any way you want. Maybe if she had a wild streak of hot pink in her hair, she would have had the courage to stand up to that bitch Miss Gulch and kick her ass."

"You can highlight it, but only trim it okay," I said. "Wait, what color?"

"Don't you trust me?" Tiffany asked. "I'll make you look beautiful."

I don't know this woman who was still running her fingers though my hair, but Dawn trusts her and I trust Dawn...for the most part. However, this is my hair we're talking about. "Can you show me the colors you're putting in?" I asked hoping not to offend the artist.

I saw Tiffany smile in the mirror, fully aware of my fears. "Sure," She strolled to the back room whistling "Over the Rainbow," and returned with a book that had a myriad of different hair styles and colors. She turned to a page in the middle of the book that showed a two-tone hair color of milk chocolate and a dark chocolate. "What do you think?" she asked.

"I like it, and now I'm craving some chocolate," I said. Tiffany returned to the back room, this time whistling "We're Off to See the Wizard." She came out with the hair colors and a crystal tray full of chocolate.

"What the fuck?" came Dawn's voice, and with that she bolted up out of her chair and walked on her heels with cotton between her toes over to my chair, grabbing a hand full of truffles.

Two hours and an untold number of calories later, my hair was done. I have to admit, Tiffany was an artist—it looked amazing. Dawn came over to show me her patriotic finger and toe nails. All I could do was salute. We switched places and it was my turn to roll up the pant legs.

My new hair style gave me a renewed sense of self-worth. I was ready for anything. "I'm thinking ruby red on the fingers and toes," I told Tracy.

"How about French nails with red tips," she suggested.

"As long as there's red in there somewhere," I replied.

My nails were shiny and my hair was awesome. I sat down at the final station, makeup. Her name was Tiffany and her hair was straight and jet black. For the last several hours, she had been listening to God knows what on her IPod, and waiting patiently for me to walk into her lair so she could express her creativity...on my face. Before I sat down Dawn joined me.

Dawn put her hand on my shoulder and pointed to the chair "You go first, Dorothy."

"Why?"

"Call it a practice round," Dawn chuckled.

"You funny girl, Wonder Bitch," I told her.

I bravely took my seat and turned to Tiffany. "There's an extra tip in it if you don't make me look like the wife of a Texas Televangelist." Tiffany's smile came and went quickly as my sense of self-worth waned. I kept my eyes closed through the entire ordeal, so I don't know how long it took. But, after what seemed like days I heard, "Okay, hon, you're done."

I opened my eyes to a pleasant surprise. While this girl looked like she could get lost in the crowd at a gothic rave, she knew how to wield makeup as if it were a sword, and gave my face a subtle, but classy look. After she made Dawn look equally impressive, we received a business card from Tiffany, and an assurance that anytime we came back for their services, we would get a great deal.

We looked the part. We were ready. The only thing left to do was to show up, get dressed, and then get undressed. Lucky me.

From what I have heard, the dinosaurs that once existed here on Earth were destroyed by a meteorite that struck the planet. As Dawn and I pulled up to the club, I was wondering—and really praying—that history would repeat itself, and another fiery ball of death would fall from the heavens in the next five minutes.

We managed to make it to the back dressing room without being groped by eager customers.

Once back there, all I could think was how much this place was a perv's paradise. When we arrived in the Teddie's backstage dressing room, I was amazed at how uninhibited the women were. In a short time I saw a school girl with her skirt up, a cheerleader with one leg up, two nurses listening to each other's heartbeats, and a couple of girls completely naked just relaxing on a sofa. Some of the ladies gave us a friendly smile, some sultry smiles, and some gave us suspicious sneers. "Relax ladies," soothed a familiar voice, "They're just here for the night."

Misty stepped from behind a curtain wearing a black top and mini-skirt with thigh-high white stockings and a garter. "It's a fantasy play for a boyfriend," she explained.

Dawn and I were clearly nervous about our debut as stage sluts, for lack of a better term. We were trying to burn off some of this nervous energy by pacing back and forth in a back room, which served a secondary place of practice for walking in eight inch heels. I wonder if there is a good health insurance program for this kind of work. Every time we passed each other while pacing, we would give each other a reassuring look and smile, letting the other one know that each of us was there for moral support of the other. Originally, I was supposed to be her moral support, not her partner, but now I'm her rock to cling to and she is mine. Dawn is morally supporting my efforts to morally support her. I still don't know how the fuck that happened.

Misty suddenly put her hands on our shoulders and said, "Ladies, you need to relax, they can smell your fear out there."

"Who can?" Dawn asked, more nervous now than she was before "The girls back here or the guys out there?"

"Yes. Now sit down, relax, and think about—" Misty began.

"Don't tell us to think about the crowd in their underwear," I interrupted. "Some of those guys weigh better than three hundred pounds. I would rather imagine them in snow suits!"

"I will say that you can imagine that the only people out there are the loves of your lives," Misty said. "And if that doesn't work, imagine the money. The better you are, the better the tips."

*"The love of my life..." I did not need to hear that. Do I have a love of my life? I mean, other than Johnny Depp, I have never had a love of my life. How do you know? How do you define it? Is loyalty*

*the most important factor? Maybe I should get a dog. The love of my life could be a Doberman. A Doberman that eats ex-boyfriends. Feeling less nervous now, and* sorrier for myself than I was before, I wandered over to the drapes on the side of the room. What the patrons of this place don't know is that in the back room, behind these drapes, is a very large window that looks out over the stage. From the other side it just looks like a very dark mirror. I peeked behind the drapes to check out the crowd.

My jaw dropped.

He is not the love of my life.

*Daniel.*

*God, why is he here? Why is …. he…here.? Now? Tonight? How did he know about this place? Maybe he is so distraught about losing me he came here to drown his sorrows, and his dick. Maybe he just wandered in, not knowing what he would find. The stupid part of me hoped* that was true, but the smart part of me was sure it wasn't. The smart part of me understood that this was probably not his first time at this particular rodeo. Where's my Doberman when I nccd him?

I turned to Misty and she could tell immediately that something was wrong. "What's the matter Cat? You look like you've seen a ghost...or an ex," Misty giggled.

Pointing at Daniel I asked, "Do you know him?"

"Oh yes, that's Antonio, he's one of our regulars," Misty said.

"No," I said pointing at Daniel again, "That one sitting up front and drooling."

"Yeah, that's Antonio. He claims to have some girlfriend that doesn't understand him."

"Antonio!" I said in shock, desperately trying to process this new information.

"Yes, although I have a feeling that his real name isn't Antonio. Guys that come in here give a fake name, thinking they're being clever, and they tell a sob story about how they are so misunderstood at home, looking for reassurance that they hope to find at the bottom of a bottle or in a strippers' panties. I think if women could understand men more there wouldn't be any strip clubs," Misty concluded.

"That's bullshit," said a thunderous voice from the corner. This woman I have never seen before, suddenly stood up and walked towards us. She was chubbier than most of the girls you would see on stage. She was about five foot two inches, five foot ten inches in heels. She had brown hair that may or may not be a wig, but I could tell that the green in her eyes came from contacts. There was skill and confidence in the way she walked, like she was comfortable with her plus size and didn't care what anyone thought. If anyone were to comment on her appearance, she looked as if she would give them the opportunity to learn what it feels like to wear eight inch heels as a butt plug. I wish I had her confident attitude.

"Candy, please don't start," Misty said, then leaning into my ear as she whispered, "She's an Anthropology major who thinks she knows..."

"Men love to see women's bodies," Candy interrupted. "It's been that was ever since they dropped from the trees and started walking upright. The more they see the better, and in a place like this they don't have to ask or beg. They just need to keep their wallets open. It's a win-win."

Candy then sat down and looked up with a distant stare I recognize from many professors.

"See this place has a calming effect on them. Not like they're bored, more like they can be themselves. They can sport wood or spout bullshit or both, and not be judged for it. Most of these men are professionals who have successful, yet highly stressful careers. They work hard, but fantasize about killing their bosses or running away with their secretaries. But, instead they come here to loosen the tie. You can guess what their fantasies then become. It's also a great place to do business since everyone is usually in a jovial and pleasant mood. What client will say no with tits in his face and booze in his belly?"

"I'm sorry, but I still don't get this shit." I asked, "Why does some asshole like 'Antonio' out there come here? What does he mean his girlfriend doesn't understand him?"

"Antonio is typical of most guys here," Candy said. "Guys that couldn't get a date on a dare, but they come in here and they're treated like Brad Pitt as long as they can afford it. They have hot women—like myself—mostly naked, hanging all over them, and they think they have a shot. On the rare occasion that they think with their larger than life ego, they know there is no way in hell that they are leaving with any of these girls, as much as their little brain is thinking score. Their logic is straight forward. They can go to a dance club, spend one hundred dollars, and come away empty handed, or they can go to a strip joint, spend one hundred dollars to see nude women, and come away with a sense of satisfaction. So why not hedge your bets and ensure the desired outcome?"

"And here I thought the little dears just wanted to get laid," I said dripping with fresh sarcasm, "If they are dancing with some girl they just met, they're thinking of fucking, not talking—an activity they could be doing at home with a girlfriend or wife or...girlfriend."

"I think we can all agree that men are pigs, slime, slugs, and when those pigs, slime, or slugs come in with tens, twenties, and fifties, I can deal with the pigs, slime and slugs successfully," Misty stated.

"I'm beginning to think you're right," I said sadly, "I always thought there were a few decent guys out there, but I'm beginning to wonder."

"There is honey," Candy said in an understanding tone that was a break from her original
lecture, "We call them anomalies. They tend to diverge from the norm..."

"You know, we go out with these guys and we catch them staring at the other women in bikinis and mini-skirts, and we have to slap them on the back of the head to redirect their attention back on us. Imagine what they are doing when they are not with us," said Misty who sounded like she was speaking from experience. I sat down on a nearby chair, thinking about how many times Daniel's been here while we were together.

While she was taking a journey down bad memory lane, I started thinking about the way Daniel looked at all the girls when we were together. Then I started thinking about Julian. I've only known him for a short time, but I can't remember him staring at any other woman when I was with him. He just looked at me and only me. He couldn't take his eyes off. I'm just not sure if it was because of my radiant beauty or because he pays me in order to watch me like a radiant trophy.

"It's just a sex act, no emotion," Misty continued. "Women need to be prepared to accept this fact of life so it doesn't drop us on our asses."

Since my mind had wandered I really wasn't sure where the conversation had gone to.

"What do we need to accept? What is just an act of sex? We just dance seductively, take most of our clothes off and continue to dance seductively...on stage...out of reach," I said pensively.

"Men pay for simulated sex on stage in order to totally control the encounter and get something that their wife and/or girlfriend won't give them. Sometimes this involves more than a lap dance," Candy said, "Men pay for women because they can have whatever and whoever they want for the right price."

"Excuse me. Hello. Remember, no contact no touching from hands, arms, lips or...anything else." My voice went an octave or two higher, and I started to panic when I heard the words "Sex on stage." I can tell by the smiles on both of their faces they picked up on this.

"Some men, usually the richer or more desperate ones, will expect and pay for more than just close up view of an erotic dance," Misty said me. Now she informs me of this, not earlier during our practice when I had enough sense to run and hide in a convent. "Lots of men come to places like this so they can do things with us, like lap dances, which women would not put up with," Candy stated as if this were a normal facts of life.

"That's horse shit. These guys are too little, coward, chicken shits to ask their girlfriend to do something different in bed, for free. But, you're telling me suddenly they seem to find the courage to go find some stranger and pay her to do it," I said more angrily than I had intended.

"Listen honey," Candy said, taken aback by my outburst, "Men want three things from a woman. They want them to act like the girl next door, be the perfect housewife and mother, and parade through the bedroom like the streetwalker from the other side of the tracks. Have you ever looked at Betty Crocker, or your grandmother for that matter, and thought 'That woman must be a werecat in bed?'" I shook my head then Candy asked "Have you ever asked your boyfriend or lover what he really wants in the bedroom?"

"Yes, I have. I asked him, but he didn't always tell me," I said thinking of the last time Daniel and I had sex. "It's like I'm supposed to guess and if I don't get it right, then I find out that he comes to clubs like this and his every dream comes true." I'm starting to really get pissed off thinking about how Daniel would just grab me wherever we were, and have his way with me.

It never really bugged me until now, but I'm glad it finally does. This night has been very educational...and it just started. Someone yelled "Candy you're next," and she walked out on stage, and seemed happy that she didn't have to continue with our little talk that was clearly irritating the hell out of me. Maybe she's having second thoughts about the Anthropology lesson

"How do you know him?" Misty asked after Candy left.

"Who?" I said.

"Antonio," Misty prompted.

I hesitated at first. "He was my boyfriend and roommate until a week and half ago. And his name is not Antonio, it's Daniel," I said looking down at the ground. I had questions and I don't know if I really wanted the answers.

"I'm sorry, Caprice. I'm not sure if it's my place to say anything but I feel that you should know that Antonio...Daniel has been with over half of the girls in the club."

I hesitated again, this time long enough that Misty knew exactly what I would ask next "What about you? Have you slept with him?"

"No, Cat," she said. "God no, believe me. For him it was just a lap dance, that's all, but he always wanted more." I was still looking at the floor when Misty took me by the chin and raised my head, and my eyes met hers. "You're better without him, Caprice."

"Yeah well that's a given," I said then changed the subject, "So, what's a lap dance?" Misty didn't miss a beat. "A lap dance is an erotic dance that begins on the stage and ends up in the guy's lap." Motivated by the quizzical look on my face, Misty beamed, walked over to me in a very seductive way and straddled my legs. "Would you like a demonstration?" Dawn walked over and sat about five feet away waiting to see what I would say. I could see the double-dog-dare-you look in her eyes.

"All right," I said to Misty. "Purely for educational purposes," I stated towards Dawn with an I-accept-your-challenge stare.

"To begin with," Misty said, "You start the dance by moving slowly in view of your client, but just out of his arms' reach. The big difference between this dance and the one you do in front of the whole audience is that you're not doing this in front of the whole audience. It's all about you and your client. It's important for the client to feel he or she is the only one that matters to you at that moment in time. Once you have them believing that, they will be emptying their wallet and bank account for you honey."

Misty moved in closer...inch-by-inch. "Once you get their attention, which usually doesn't take long. You can move in closer to your target. Now, there are rules to this dance. Rule number one is that you can touch them, as a matter of fact, it's kind of expected. Rule number two is they cannot touch you unless you allow it."

Misty ran her hands up along her face and slipped her middle finger into her mouth, moving it in and out in a suggestively slow manner "This drives the guys crazy, if they are looking at your face. They usually have their eyes glued to your chest or your G-string." With that, Misty put her hands on my knees, squatted down, and opened my legs. As if I wasn't in enough shock, she took my hands and ran them down the front of her shirt. Tilting her head back, Misty then ran her hands along my inner thighs and leaned forward. "Don't say a word, you don't have to, this is about having control over them, Caprice. At this point you control everything."

Misty then stood up between my legs and looked me straight in my eyes before winking. She pushed my legs together and then slowly sat down on my lap with her legs wide open in *front of me. Wow, there's that G-string she was talking about. She finally took both of my hands* in hers and then moved her fingers up my arms, over my shoulders, and ran her hands seductively through my hair. I can only gather by her smile that she finds my scared-shitless look  adorable.

She stood back up and I let out a sigh of relief thinking that we were done with today's lesson in how to torture the new chick every time she turns around. But then, Misty suddenly sat back down on my legs and leaned back into my chest. She took my two hands, and back to her breasts they went. I'm numb with shock.

"Remember, this part is purely voluntary, but you can cup them," she said as she rubbed her ass into my lap. "This is the main part of the lap dance. Just keep grinding until you feel a huge bulge in the client's pants." Misty slid her hands behind her waist and ran them along my sides as I leaned my head onto her shoulder. "Now of course when you are giving a lap dance to a woman, you won't feel the bulge, so just keep grinding until she asks you to stop or she asks for more."

Misty rose up off of my lap and turned around and slowly ran her hands back up my thighs. Wow. Her hands began pushing my skirt up higher and higher to the top of my waist. Once she caught a glimpse of my ruby red G-string, she stopped. "Well Caprice, you get the point right?"

"Huh?" I stammered, "Oh right...right." Every attempt I made to control my breathing was in vain.

"Sometimes couples will have us perform lap dances on one partner or the other as a teasing kind of foreplay, fuel for the fire that's to come later," Misty said. "I think this is the end of the lesson on lap dances for today. Now class, any questions? Comments?"

"Holy shit," Dawn said, nearly tripping over her tongue. "What a show! Is there a line to be next? I want a turn."

Misty stood in front of Dawn and I, with her arms held out wide "Lap Dances. They can be the difference between a glass of champagne with strawberries and not making your rent for the month. If you want the tips, and who doesn't, then grab the guy or girl that came to see you, or the stranger that can't take their eyes off you, and start the lap dance on stage. It will drive the crowd crazy."

Walking over to the viewing window, she beaconed for us to follow, saying "You've had a chance to experience a hands-on demonstration. Now, how would you like to see an actual lap dance?" Misty moved over to a curtain on the side of the room and stood there like one of those women on a game show that reveal a fabulous prize, or simply just a bunch of crap. She grabbed the curtain and strutted off to the side, revealing a window into another, more secluded room. In the intimate space, there were long red couches with poles next to them and round red couches with poles coming out of the center. Poles seem to play a central role in this room. It was darker than the main room with a stage. Maybe it's to set the mood or to hide the embarrassment. The guy sitting on the round couch, however, did not look like he would embarrass easily...or at all. He was a big biker guy who probably had a hog in the parking lot and a Harley tattooed on his ass. The girl from the club that was grinding up and down on his lap, with zeal and enthusiasm, may have been a biker babe, but I really couldn't tell because most of her clothes along with her inhibitions were strung along the floor.

I was entranced by the 3-D porn show I was watching through the window, when I heard Sweet Sue call out for Misty to get ready. She strolled over to the door, but before she left she turned and smirked. "Watch and learn, ladies," she said with a wink. The expression on her face changed, her whole demeanor changed, from teacher to professional.

I found respite in a nearby chair and started trying to calm my nerves and slow down my erratic breathing. I allowed my mind to wander and my imagination to soar, trying to come up with a way to put all the new stuff I just learned to practical use. I can see myself giving some guy a lap dance while an angry Daniel sits nearby watching. I could ask some of the burlier bouncers to hold him down if he tries to run away like the little weasel I know he is.

"Do you really want to do a lap dance on stage?" Dawn asked.

"Yes," I said with conviction.

"Okay girl, talk. What is wrong with you tonight? When you showed up here you were fine, nervous but fine. Now it's like your sanity has left the building. What would ever possess you to do a lap dance on stage in front of tons of drooling guys?"

I stood up and jerked the drapes aside. "That fucker right there!"

"Holy shit!" Dawn yelled, "What is that doing here?"

"Apparently the same thing he always does here, sits, drinks and enjoys the show," I spat. "I have been informed by my lap dance instructor that Daniel is a regular who also goes by the name Antonio and tends to leave with some of the local talent," I said bitterly.

"That fucker!" said Dawn. "And you want to give some lucky son-of-a-bitch the lap dance of his life just to piss off Daniel. I can appreciate that sadistic revenge, but it would be so much better if the lucky guy on the receiving end was Julian," she finished with relish.

"Yes, it would," I said with a gleeful smile on my face.

"What if Julian doesn't show up?" Dawn asked apprehensively.

"Then I'll pick someone else out of the crowd, someone big, handsome, and that doubles as an underwear model," I said with an evil grin, "I need to do this now Dawn, the timing is right."

"I totally agree, but you may have to compromise dashingly handsome for cuteness. This place isn't exactly 'high class' darling." Dawn took a look out at the stage and then turned back to me, "Okay, not sure Kurt was expecting an extended show. What do you want to do?"

"What do I want to do?" That's a good question. I didn't say anything. I just kept thinking about what I wanted to do, and the only thing I could come up with, besides the lap dance, would get me twenty years with good behavior.

I heard a sigh from Dawn, followed by a chuckle. "Anytime I can fuck with a guy's mind I'm in," she said with a winning grin.

"You're a good friend, Dawn" I said. "What did I do to deserve a friend like you who would dry hump a stranger just to help out a friend?"

"Yeah, you lucked out there." Dawn said "Besides, you're the good friend. You are my inspiration when it comes to dirty deeds done dirt cheap." She slapped her hands together and rubbed them back and forth in a malevolent way. "Now tell me what we are going to do."

# Chapter 14:

# The Show Must Go On

The sound of cat-calls, clapping, and fat guys valiantly trying—and failing—to give Misty a standing ovation filled Teddie's as she left the stage. Misty and this other girl who started off the show as a fully dressed, sultry secret agent, walked to the back room completely bare. "Okay ladies," Misty said with a smile, "I got them revved up and ready to rush the stage. Have fun," she said with a knowing wink.

*We're up. It's our turn. Okay God, I thought, if it's in your nature to strike down places like Sodom, Gomorrah, and Teddie's with fierce bolts of lightning, now would be the time. Alright, I can't think that way. I have a purpose here. A mission. Payback is a bitch and so am I.*

"Let's go," I said to Dawn. I kept running that quote through my mind I once heard,

"Revenge is a dish best served cold..." I have no idea what it means. A smile crossed my face, a smile born from nervousness and determination. I took Dawn by the hand and walked out.

Upon our entrance into the world of erotic dance, we were first greeted by the bright lights of the stage, and the suspicious smells of...well...a strip club. When my eyes got used to the lights, I beheld a room full of men and women, but mostly men, staring back at me and Dawn. They dared us to entertain them with their gaze, to turn them on. Then the music started. I wasn't familiar with the music, but then again I'm sure it is impossible to find a piece of music that is complementary with Wonder Woman and Dorothy both taking their clothes off. I could tell the audience couldn't care less about the music. They were more interested in the skimpy outfits and whether we could move effortlessly in these eight inch heels that were designed by the antichrist.

I closed my eyes. I swayed to the music. I was trying to get into the right mindset. I need to *think like a dancer, a stripper. It's like I'm an actress playing a character. This isn't me. But that's what every actress wants isn't it? To play someone different from themselves. To make-believe...It's all pretend. I could feel myself moving around the stage with an easier flow. I was getting into it. I saw, there was, the pole. I've practiced this. We spent time practicing the spinning, and practicing not throwing up or not falling on our ass. I can do this, I just need to focus. I need to get a grip, a good tight grip, and smile through the fear. I danced my way to the pole like I knew exactly what I was doing.*

*Then I grasped the pole like my life depended on it and managed a few simple turns. Was I being seductive? Was I alluring, making the audience want to ravish me? Who gives a shit? At this point I only cared about not giving in to gravity.*

I was picking up momentum. My feet left the floor. I was airborne watching the rest of the world, which at the moment was a club of half-drunk people with big eyes glued to me, spin around and around. In my circular travels, I saw Dawn also hanging on for dear life from a second pole on stage, and I saw strangers waiting for her to fall...and I saw Daniel. On the first spin around, his eyes were wide, on the second spin his mouth was open wide. I believe I got his attention. Good, now he will know what he had and will never have again, and it will eat him alive if there is any justice in the world. I came off the pole with a smug smile and an equally smug sense of satisfaction.

It was now time to use my feminine wiles to get the attention of the rest of the patrons, at least, the ones with the cash. It was time for a sexy walk around the stage. The pockets in my Dorothy dress, which was several inches shorter than the original, started to fill up with money.

One dollar bills mostly from the cheap bastards in the front, but my garter belt, the accessory I'm sure Miss Garland left out, was pinning down fives, tens and even twenty's I suspect came from the oriental gentlemen in the nice suits. I strolled over to Dawn as she was still spinning, and I thought I could give the audience thrill. I put a twenty in my mouth and kneeled down. Dawn came slowly around and opened her mouth and took the twenty from me like a pro, like we'd rehearsed this a hundred times.

I took another sultry stroll on the not-so-yellow brick road, collecting more money and scanning the crowd for the one guy I was hoping to see, Julian. But he wasn't there, at least not where I could see him.

I needed to find some guy to dance with on stage—that's where the real money is—and hopefully drive the final nail in Daniel's coffin of regret. It goes without saying that Kurt is off the menu. I don't even have to ask Dawn, I knew she would say not only "No," but "Hell no!"

Besides, the way Kurt is drooling over Dawn and hasn't taken his eyes off her since we started, I'm sure he wouldn't agree to it either. So I continued to scan the crowd, not necessarily like a kid in a candy store searching for the best looking lollipop, but more like a registered voter picking the lesser of two evils.

The trouble with this place is that most of the guys remind me of the one person I want to forget—the one person I would never be caught dead with again. I mean, what are the chances each of these men having a wife or girlfriend at home completely unaware their guy is ogling my every move, and growing more impatient for me to drop the dress completely? I could try and bring one of the girls up here, there are a few that look as eager for the unveiling as the men are, but that wouldn't drive Daniel crazy with jealousy. It would just drive him crazy. I decided to take another twirl on the pole while Dawn walked the stage to take the hard earned cash of the drunker patrons. On the first turn around I noticed Daniel, who looked less shocked and more angry. The plan was working.

On the second turn around the pole, I didn't notice Daniel. I didn't notice anyone...except Julian.

"Thank the gods he's here," I said walking over to Dawn and whispering.

"Yes, the gods of erotic dance are smiling on you honey," Dawn said as she danced around me, running her hands through my hair. The approving sounds of the crowd filled the room, but I couldn't tell if Julian joined in the show of appreciation. I decided not to look at Julian. I didn't want to because I was afraid he would leave. He would see the fear and concern in my eyes, and I the disgust in his. I don't think I could handle that. I decided to focus on the opposite side of the room, but there he was again, watching me, seeing me like he never saw me before. I couldn't tell how he felt about my being on stage. His poker face wouldn't reveal his inner most feelings, not in public anyway. Dawn maneuvered herself in front of me so we were standing face-to-face.

"For a while there, I was afraid he wouldn't show up," Dawn said in a low voice as she danced, "Let the show begin." Dawn backed me up against one of the poles, put her left hand on my shoulder, and wrapped her right leg around my waist. Dawn was really getting into this. Who knew she was such a method actress...at least I hope she was acting. She ran her right hand up my arm and put it on my other shoulder. She then moved up with her left leg and wrapped it around me, pinning me against the pole. With a smile on her face and a shocked look on mine, she put her hand behind my head and pulled me to her chest.

I thought, while my face was buried in Wonder Woman's ample cleavage, if I could pull this *off, maybe Julian wouldn't want anything to do with me. He'll see me as just another girl stripping on stage for money, and I can stop worrying about the whole paid-escort-dating-with-a-contract-thing. Did I want to be an escort? Did I want Julian thinking of me as his escort, or thinking of me as a stripper for all to see? I know this strip and dancing gig is a one-time thing, a* favor for a friend, but it concerned me what Julian thought, and it showed on my face.

"Are you okay?" Dawn whispered. "Can you do this?" she said with a concerned look.

"Yes," I said, pasting the most convincing fake smile on my face that I could muster. Maybe *he'll like it, maybe he would love to see me up close and personal if I'm dancing just for him in a* private show. I needed a guy to flaunt my goodies for in order to drive Daniel insane with jealousy. I'm hoping he will rip his eyes out, knowing that what he sees tonight, he will never see again. When he sees me all over an absolutely perfect specimen like Julian, he will then rip his heart out along with his eyes. Oedipus complex not included.

I looked back over to where Julian was, but of course he wasn't there anymore. The sneaky little shit was now sitting with Kurt.

After a quick swing around the stage with her magic lasso, Dawn sauntered back to me, coming up from behind. She put her lips close to my ear, giving the impression she was giving me a hickey, but instead sweetly whispered something in my ear about how she wanted to bring her boy-toy Kurt on stage. Dawn strutted off stage left, and I danced my way off stage right. We picked up two relatively clean chairs and brought them back to the center stage. Dawn then made her way to the front of the platform with her patented cat-that's-about-to-eat-the canary grin, squatted down with her legs apart, and pointed her finger straight at Kurt, encouraging him to come up on stage. He did so with enthusiasm.

I decided to let her and Kurt share the spotlight alone, so I walked off the stage down to the darker, more dangerous floor, where the eyes and hands of the wild animals roam. I had hoped all eyes would be on Dawn, and some were, but when the object of a guy's lust is walking within arm's reach, they will reach. Each one of them I walked past was hoping I'd stop for a private show.

I was carefully making my way to Julian, but in order to get there I had to walk past Daniel, and he was watching me the entire time. My intent was to just stroll right past him like he wasn't there, he didn't exist, and he didn't matter. But his intentions were different. Daniel reached out and took me by the arm and held me strongly, saying nothing. When I turned and glared at him, also saying nothing, it was as if I didn't need to, and he quickly let go.

When I turned to Julian, his eyes were filled with penetrating anger fixed directly on Daniel.

However, when I got closer, close enough to touch, close enough to smell, his attention was brought back to where it was supposed be—on me and my cute outfit. His dark eyes widened when I took my farm girl dress in each hand, curtsied, and pulled the dress up slowly, past my knees, along my upper thighs, and then let go, dropping it back to where it originally was. Julian leaned forward just hoping I'd meet him halfway, which I did before pushing him back into his chair. I didn't have a mirror so I couldn't tell for sure, but the smile I had on my face was a smile I'm sure I've never had before. It was the smile of a seductive predator consuming more than willing prey. I lifted my dress again as I stepped forward, lowering myself onto Julian's lap.

I leaned myself forward, and whispered, "I can't tell you how glad I am that you're here," in his ear. I slid my hand back along his muscular legs, rotating my hips in small circles. His familiar scent of a breeze after a light summer rain filled my senses and my soul. It was that very scent that gave my hips a will of their own as they started moving back and forth with more intensity. I moved my hands up my legs, bringing the dress up with them, and started massaging my breasts in gentle circles.

"This is a different..." Julian mumbled breathlessly. "I haven't seen this.... this is new." I couldn't help but smile, but I also wondered if this new perspective was good or bad. "Do...do I get an encore after the show?" Julian stammered in amazement. I let out a small laugh at the look on his face. He is so cute when he is at a loss for words. While his mouth was having difficulty expressing itself, another part of his anatomy had no trouble expressing its elation at my persistent grinding.

"If you'll like a private repeat performance, I'm sure something could be arranged sir," I said in a low sultry voice before kissing him on the cheek. I then stood up and extended my hand.

Julian stood up, his long un-tucked black shirt hiding any potential embarrassment, and took my hand then kissed it. You could hear the two female bartenders say, "Ah," as I led him on stage. I could feel Julian's attempt to let go of my hand, but much to his surprise, I didn't let go of his.

Much to his shock, I pulled him up the stage stairs.

Julian knew where I was leading him, and he was hesitant at first. "I do have one request," he said softly as he sat down on the chair and the crowd cheered us on.

"Anything," I told him with my backside to the audience, and more importantly to Daniel.

"I only want you to dance for me," he said looking at me intensely. "Not Dawn and you don't touch Kurt, only me, Caprice," Julian said.

Well, that was probably the nicest thing anyone has said to me all day. "Give me a moment," I said.

I started to walk seductively to center stage, and Dawn met me in the middle with the intent of switching partners, but as she move past me I took her by the hand and twirled her around like Fred Astaire did to Ginger Rogers, and held her in my arms as I kissed her lips. Judging by the reaction from the crowd, this was the high point of the evening. I kissed my way down her neck and back up to her ear and quickly relayed Julian's wish for a one-on-one session with me only.

Dawn held me close, running her hands down my back and promptly grabbed my ass. "No problem honey. Have fun. Make me proud."

I blushed...I couldn't believe it, I was as ruby red as my shoes. I walked behind Julian and crouched down, more to hide than anything else. When I was sure that my normal color returned to my face, I stood back up and moved in front of Julian. I gave him a quick wink to let him know all was well in the world of erotic dance, and his wish was my command. I turned around, lifted my skirt, and sat comfortably in his lap, grinding back and forth, up and down to the music.

After grinding my ass against him, I brought one leg up and rotated my ass on his lap and brought my leg back down so now we were face-to-face. I took Julian's hands into my own and put them on my hips.

"Hold tight" I whispered. I leaned back, far enough to allow my hair to touch the floor. I then wrapped my arms around Julian's legs, and then continued to slide my hips back and forth in my new position.

When the blood began rushing to my head from being upside down, I thought it was time to come back up. This crowd isn't dumb enough to believe that my passing out is some sort of artistic dance move. I admit that my attempts to climb back up Julian were less than graceful, and Julian noticed too. So, with the air of a true gentleman, he reached out and pulled me up, and close...very close. I leaned into him "Hi," I whispered, "Are you ready?"

Julian stiffened, it was subtle but I felt it. I think I made him nervous. Score! "Ready for..." he said faintly.

I slid my hands down the front of his shirt, over his chest, and down into his lap. Then I brought them up the front of my dress, over my chest and inside the collar of my cute little outfit.

"We're not in Kansas anymore," I said and pulled. The top of the dress easily came off in my hand and I held it for a moment or two then let it drop to the floor. Julian's attention was drawn to the ruby red bra that fit like it was two sizes too small. By the sounds of the audience, their eyes were locked in the same place. I once again felt Julian's appreciation for my talents, so I placed my hands on his shoulders and returned to the grind.

I stood back up and started to play with my hair. Guys like that, I know they do. I turned around again, sat down, and leaned back into him and didn't move. He was like a hard yet incredibly comfy chair. I then reached down and took his hands to bring them up and put them *subtly on my chest. Holy shit! He had a firm but gentle hold of my breasts. Okay, it was my idea,* but wow, he's squeezing. There was definitely squeezing involved. I responded by rotating my ass harder and harder into the huge bulge in his pants. Taking a page from the "Misty book of Erotic Dance," I slid my hands behind his neck as I leaned my head onto his shoulder. I did not want to move. I was relaxed, safe, at home in his embrace, but the show must go on. I rose up off of Julian's lap, slowly ran my hands up my thighs, and lifted my skirt up. The crowd went wild. I stood next to Julian and held my skirt out for him. He took it, and I pulled away. Julian was holding my skirt while I was dancing in my red G-string to the cheers and whistles of an appreciative crowd. Dawn, not wanting to be left out of the fun, had Kurt do the same thing with her Wonder Woman costume. We were both dancing around each other and around our wide-eyed gentlemen, and the crowd yelled louder than before.

All good, crazy, outlandish things must end. The show was about over and we needed to get off stage. I held my hand out to Julian and he stood up and came over to me. I walked him off the stage, kissed him, whispered "Wait for me" and slapped his nice, firm butt as he walked away.

As much as I wanted to leave with him, to run off into the darkness of the club and out into the darkness of the night, I knew Dawn still needed my help.

Keeping in mind Julian's no Kurt rule, I focused on Dawn's dancing routine, as strange as that sounds. I danced circles around Dawn while she was riding Kurt's lap like a cowgirl on a mechanical bull, and she couldn't take her gaze off me. They followed me around with wonderment and concern and a real need to know just what the hell I was thinking. I answered her unasked question with a kiss on the lips. "Wow, what was that for?" she asked in a loud whisper.

"It's an attention getter," I answered.

"You had my attention at 'Hello,'" Dawn admitted.

"Not your attention, but thank you. I mean the attention of the crowd. We need to keep them entertained while we figure out a way to get off the stage, starting with Kurt," I stated.

"Leave that to me," Dawn said with a smile. With that she sauntered over to her awaiting boyfriend and sat on his lap again, facing outward. She continued her aggressive grinding while she wrapped her arms around his. Then she slowly stood up, her hips pressed tightly into his, bringing him with her. Kurt was trying to keep up with Dawn's rhythmic motions, but it was starting to look less sexy and more awkward. If these two ever entered a dance contest, they would be the first tapped out. Becoming aware of this, Dawn stepped away from Kurt, turned to face him, and bowed. She then spun to the audience and bowed again. How her breasts stayed in in her skimpy little Wonder Woman top I will never know, but I can say two way tape hurts coming off and doesn't hold you in as much as you want it to. She took Kurt by the hand and walked him off the stage, then returned to me.

At what point does my obligation end? This is a question that I had been asking myself for the last couple of minutes. This all started because Dawn's boyfriend gets a woody watching his girl strip for the masses. I joined the party because Dawn's puppy dog eyes insisted. But is the show over? Is some naked fat lady going to come out and sing? The audience certainly doesn't think so. They're practically leaning forward with anticipation, waiting and wanting more. The music was still playing. Dawn and I looked at each other and we both knew we had to come up with a finish.

When we both realized that a finale was inevitable, we moved to the poles and swung again. If synchronized pole dancing was an Olympic cvent, we would definitely be in medal contention.

Dawn was near the top of her pole, bent over until her head was below her feet, and lowered herself down until her hands were placed on the stage and her feet were together above her. I stepped off my pole and walked over to Dawn. Because of our positions, I was staring at her feet and she was staring at mine. I put my hands inside her ankles, bent my knees and slowly lowered myself down, bringing my hands down the inside of her legs, moving them apart as I went. My hands and face moved closer and closer to her center. Her legs moved wider and wider apart.

The audience became more and more silent. You could hear the entire collective breathing of the audience. The Oh my God look on Dawn's face was priceless. I was merely an inch away from what would be a major shift in our relationship.

"Are you ready?" I asked Dawn.

"Ah.... . for, um.... what?" she asked with trepidation.

"To run," I said before she could answer. I reached down, took her hands, pulling her up to her feet, and quickly dragged her off stage. There's an old adage in show business to "Always leave them wanting more".

The show was over. We were done. We made it out and lived to never tell our grandchildren.

When we got backstage, we walked in to a standing ovation from the girls who worked at Teddie's. It feels surprisingly reassuring to receive a round of applause from a room full of naked women. Dawn came out of her stunned silence. "Thank you for saving my ass tonight. That was a...unique finale. I wasn't sure how I would get off that stage," she said looking at me in relief.

"No problem, thank Daniel for the inspiration," I said "So what's next?"

"Kurt and I are going find a hotel where he can show me his appreciation for an amazing show," Dawn said, then continued, "Especially for the fantastic finish."

I was trying to hide my envy as I said "I'm not sure where the night will lead me." I didn't want to mention out loud that my night will probably lead to my battery operated boyfriend and dreams of Julian in various stages of undress.

"Courage Cat," Dawn said. "After tonight you can do anything or anyone. You were the star."

Dawn and I were getting dressed when we heard whistles coming from behind us. "That was amazing ladies," Sweet Sue said as she approached. "You two can come work for me anytime. I mean that sincerely. Please come and work for me."

"I don't know," I said hesitantly. "Maybe we should retire while we are still on top."

"Well just remember, the door is always open," Sweet Sue said. "Oh, by the way Cat, you have a gentlemen caller wanting to come back and say howdy. Now of course that is not permitted, but since you're new and since you're a one show wonder, I will let you meet him at the stage door."

*Julian. Could the gentlemen be Julian, coming to say how much he loved the show? Julian coming to say how much he hated being in the show? Should I sneak out the bathroom window before it's too late? I decided to muster up my courage and face my gentleman caller. I made my* way to the stage door and opened it.

That's no gentleman. That's Daniel.

"Cat," Daniel said grabbing my arm. "Can we talk?"

"Don't touch me!" I said pulling out of Daniel's grip. "I don't belong to you."

"Look Cat, if the only reason you do not want to come back to me is because you want to work here, I can live with that. It's okay, really. It's kind of cool," he said practically drooling.

I wanted to place my ruby red shoes squarely between Daniel's legs, but instead I just beamed after noticing Julian step out of nowhere, once again. He was behind Daniel, towering over him with a look of pure unbridled anger. He grabbed the wrist Daniel was holding mc by.

Daniel quickly let go as if he was burned by Julian's touch.

"I'm only saying this once. Stay... away... from... Caprice," Julian said. He didn't raise his voice. He didn't have to. He spoke in a whisper you could not only hear, but feel. The sound of his voice went all the way to the bone, as if you were being commanded by a cold winter wind.

"If you put your hand on her again, you will not live long enough to regret it," he said, separating each syllable as he spoke.

Daniel's face was drained of all color, and for the moment his voice escaped him. I must admit, I was afraid myself, but that feeling of fear was nothing compared to the feeling of wanting to jump this guy and do unspeakable things to him that are probably illegal in a rural, conservative state like Idaho. Julian released Daniel's wrist and turned his cold stare to me, but with his cold manner gone. "I hope I didn't frighten you my dear."

"...Nooo," I lied. "No. I'm okay, and you're.... okay. I'm just...I'm.... going in the back of the stage, to find...the backstage," I stammered.

While Julian's attention was on my less than stealthy exit, Daniel managed to slip away from Julian and find his voice. "This is not over Cat," Daniel said. "Me and my ten friends can wait all night for you to come out." The ten friends thing was a bluff Daniel has tried before when his mouth gets him in trouble. The brief smile on Julian's face told me that he was well aware

Daniel was full of shit.

I made my way to the back to find Dawn waiting for me, apparently having witnessed the showdown.

"That was so fucking cool," she said with breathless excitement. "That was like Terminator 'I'll be back' cool. Julian really likes you!" All I could do was smile at her and admire her giddiness in the face of a potential bloodbath. "Well," she said "It's time for me to go burn some of this energy I have. Between your show on stage and Julian's show backstage, I can't promise I won't be thinking of you two instead of Kurt." With that, Dawn turned and skipped away. Yes, she skipped. She was skipping away.

I returned to the back and found the couch. I had to sit. It's been a long, strange, scary night and I needed to take a moment or two...or twenty. I knew Daniel was still out there. Julian scared him enough to leave marks in his underoos, but he was still out there. Daniel doesn't understand the trouble he's gotten himself into. He doesn't understand Julian was not kidding. That's because Daniel's a moron.

I was leaving when I heard running. I turned and saw Dawn coming back into the room. "I thought you would be halfway to the Cloud nine hotels by now," I said.

"I have a message from Misty," Dawn said with an uncontrollable, girlish giggle. "The show isn't over." Dawn reached for the curtain and pulled it back to reveal a horrific scene. Misty was giving Daniel an enthusiastic lap dance. Misty was really grinding into him, and Daniel was really enjoying it. He was looking at the mirror on his side, and he had a smile on his face that said "I know you're there and I know you're watching."

I really do not know what Misty was doing or why she thought I would want to watch this. Business is Business I guess, and he was a client—A creep, but a client. But honestly, I was surprised she would do this to me. Misty stood up and I turned away when at that moment, order was restored to the universe. The bulge in Daniel's pants became a target, and Misty's knee found that target. It was a shot heard round the club, followed by a squeal that was probably heard round the entire city.

"Damn that had to hurt," I snickered with a smile.

"Damn that's going to leave a mark," Dawn said. "Probably marks...I mean...after all..."

Misty came through the door and winked at me. Sweet Sue soon followed "What the hell happened?" she bellowed in anger.

"I slipped," Misty said.

Sweet Sue turned to me and Dawn just as we wiped the smiles from our faces. She turned back to Misty, who was still smirking. "Well try and watch your footing next time," she said and walked out, but not before winking at me too.

I must admit that I did not have the highest opinion of the women who "dance" at places like this before, but now I know they look out for each other, I'm becoming rather fond of the world of erotic dance. Dawn and I were there for only one night, but I felt like we belonged to this sisterhood of sluts. I mean that in the most endearing way possible. And hey, we made four hundred dollars that night. Not bad for a couple of amateurs.

I walked out of the back, no longer worried about coming face-to-face with Daniel. I had a suspicion he won't be looking anyone in the face for a while. After coming out the door, I thought I might have encountered an admiring crowd looking for autographs or souvenir panties.

But, the only one waiting by the door was Julian, with his arm extended in a gentlemanly fashion. I hooked my arm around his and we walked out of Teddie's.

# Chapter 15:

# After the Show

We walked across the parking lot to Julian's classic, what I would guess to be nineteen sixty-six, dark blue and beautiful Ford Mustang. I have never been the type of girl to put out just because the guy's car is cherry, but damn this was a nice ride. This fine piece of machinery made me forget asshole what's-his-name inside.

This was not the car he had before. Is it polite to ask a guy how many cars he has? Is that like asking about the size of his....bank account? Oh what the hell. "How many cars do you have?" I blurted out. Hey, I just danced on this guy's crotch, so I guess being politically correct is not an issue.

"Ten."

"Why ten?" I asked.

"Cars are like accessories, you need more than one depending on the situation, the weather conditions...mood," Julian chuckled.

*Mood...guys have accessories for moods? Who knew? Rich guys have rich accessories* for rich moods. "So Mr. Moody, where are we going?" I asked as I sat carefully in the seat, not wanting to scratch the fine leather.

"First, a question?" Julian said after he got in the other side. "Why was Daniel there? Did you call him?"

"That's two questions," I pointed out. "First, I do not know why Daniel was there. Second, no, I did not call him. I had no idea he went to places like this until tonight," I said with an air that implied murder.

Julian started up the car and it purred like a cougar. It wasn't loud, but it distracted me enough to say "Huh, what did you say?"

"I said that I know our arrangement is not set...yet, but as a favor would you please not do another performance like that again in public?" Julian asked. "I realize you did it to help Dawn out and I understand that, I really do...But Cat, you looked like you were really enjoying yourself."

"I was," I admitted, "I didn't think I would, but I did have fun. I got caught up in the moment. I have never been a girl that guys looked at that way. It was weird, scary, and yes, exciting." I decided not to tell him Daniel was the inspiration for most of what I did tonight. It would be so easy to take my words the wrong way.

"If you have other ideas like that, we can work something out," Julian said. "You know...a private show. Just tell me what you want."

"What do you want?" I asked in my best seductive voice.

"I want a relationship," Julian said, "You know, with normal role play and fun. No threesomes or people watching, I'm selfish that way. You can still feel free to shake what your mother gave you."

Oh my God! Did he really just say that? I had to respond "Honestly Julian, what you saw tonight, as much fun as it was...it was not the real Caprice, I did it to help a friend. And to be honest again, it was easier when I saw you there. I don't know if I could have gone through with the whole thing without you in the audience. I was so ready to turn tail and run until I saw you."

There was a moment of silence. It wasn't uncomfortable, just...quiet. Then I thought for a moment. "Out of curiosity, what type of role playing are we talking about?"

"Well, there are several...types. If you want I could give you...a list?" Julian said with an uncharacteristic stutter. I remained silent for a moment, partly because I was shocked, but mainly because my silence was making him nervous. I can be such a bitch sometimes.

"I see," I said finally, "Well...."

"I apologize Cat, if I embarrassed you. I did not mean..."

"Relax Julian," I said. "I am just teasing you." I reached over and put my hand on his upper thigh, giving it a squeeze, just to see what kind of reaction I could get. Julian's reaction was unexpected and sudden, and so was the car's.

Julian jumped.

I jumped.

The car jumped, and its tires screamed louder than I did.

The car was fishtailing all across the road while I was frantically gripping my car seat with one hand and gripping Julian's leg with the other. No matter how hard I held on, I couldn't stop the world outside from spinning. Julian was frantically pumping the brakes and turning right, then left, then right in a desperate attempt to regain control of his classic nineteen sixty-six, dark blue beauty. Control was finally regained when the car came to a sudden and abrupt stop in an off-road ditch.

It suddenly got quieter, probably because I wasn't screaming at the top of my lungs. Instead the air was filled with the sound of the running car and my hyperventilating. When my heart rate finally got down to a respectable level, it jumped right back up again when Julian put his hands on my shoulder, and then my leg. "Are you okay Cat?" he asked in a quiet, panic-filled voice

"Did I hurt you?"

"Yes," I gulped. "I mean no. I mean yes, I'm okay and no you didn't hurt me."

"Are you sure?" he asked a second time with concern in his voice.

"Yes, of course," I reassured him. "I may sound like I have a traumatic brain injury, but I'm really okay," I managed to unhook the seatbelt, looked around, and asked "Where are we?"

"I'm not sure," Julian replied.

"Well, can we get out?" I said looking doubtfully at the car's position in the ditch.

"Only one way to find out," and with that, Julian pressed the accelerator and the silent hum of the engine was replaced by the squeal of a tire that had no intention of moving. Julian let out a frustrated sigh and looked at me. I don't know if he was looking for an answer on how to get the hell out of the ditch, but all I could do was give him a reassuring smile. He gave me a half-hearted one in return before opening the door and stepping outside. I watched him as he walked around the car a couple of times and then walked up to the road. He looked angry, angry with himself, and he didn't want to look back at me. Oh God, he must be mad at me for all of this.

I opened my door and carefully made my way to the road where he stood "So I'm thinking that we should make a public service message about the dangers of unexpectedly grabbing someone's leg while they are driving a high performance muscle car at night." Julian just kept looking down the road and not at me. Is he really mad at me? But then I said in an apologetic voice "Look Julian, I'm sorry, this was my fault. I shouldn't have grabbed you like that, or at least I should have given you a warning. You know, I could have said 'Hey, do you mind if I grab your leg?' or something similar."

"You did catch me by surprise," Julian said softly, but he didn't look mad, far from it, he looked really pleased. "But I'm afraid the fault is mine, I should have been able to control the car and avoid this ditch."

"What do you mean?" I asked. "You kept the wheels on the road, for the most part. You didn't turn cute, furry, little-rodents into road kill. I think you did a great job of not killing us," I said, genuinely meaning it.

"I appreciate the vote of confidence, but I'm afraid we're stuck here Caprice."

"Well don't think of it as stuck," I told him. "We stopped to smell the metaphorical roses, to breathe in the cool night air, to marvel at the captivating moon. It's kind of romantic if you think about it, being out here...alone...freezing."

Julian opened his large jacket and wrapped it around me, holding me close to his side. I could get used to this. I could live here in his arms for eternity. "You are shivering." Julian noticed. Let's get back into the car and try and call someone." I reluctantly moved with him, wishing I could just stay right where we were. He opened the door like a gentlemen and I got inside.

"Well this is romantic too, I guess," I said to Julian after he sat down. "You can still see the moon through the rearview mirror." Julian beamed at me before looking into the mirror. I could see the light of the moon reflect off the mirror and onto his face. God, he looks good in any light.

He looked back at me and I giggled again. "Just a heads up, I'm going to put my hand back on your leg," I told him.

"Oh...kay," Julian mumbled.

My hand was on his leg. My eyes were locked on his eyes and before I knew it my lips were locked on his lips. I don't know if I pulled him to me or if he pulled me to him and I didn't really care. I could feel us both trying to pull each other closer. Even though it was getting hot in the car, I wanted to be wrapped back up in his jacket, in his arms.

My hand moved up his leg...his hand moved down my neck...our hands kept moving...and then stopped. Our eyes opened...wide. Julian jumped back into his seat and I jumped back into mine. "Excuse me...," Julian muttered, "I'm sorry..."

"Don't be," I said. "It's just the heat of the moment."

Julian took out his phone, "I need to call for a tow. Maybe I can reach Sam."

I could hear the click of each number as he dialed. I watched as he brought the phone to his ear and I could hear the phone ring. That's when a hand came up and took the phone from Julian.

I'm pretty sure it was my hand. It was my hand that took the phone and my hand that threw the phone out the window. It was my hand that returned to his leg. What was my hand thinking? What were his hands thinking? They picked me up out of my seat and put me in his lap. Our lips smashed together, devouring with hunger that surprised us both. The kiss grew more and more intense. With every deep breath, I inhaled that sweet scent of rain that came off Julian's incredible body.

I put my hands on both sides of Julian's face, trying to pull him closer. I wanted all of him closer. I could feel each of his strong fingers move up my back and through my hair. His fingers really seem to like my hair. Two can play at that game. Julian has long hair, long beautiful dark brown hair which he seems to always keep in a ponytail. Running my fingers through a ponytail *is not as much fun. This thing has got to go...*

I had to move quickly, before he could protest, not that he could with my mouth covering his.

With one swift move Julian's hair was set free, Free to flow over his shoulders, free to flow over me if he wanted.

After who knows how long our lips finally parted. "So is this on the list of role play games?" I asked breathlessly.

"No...No role playing," Julian said, "Just me and you... Are you playing a role?"

"No," I admitted. "Although, I do feel like a high school girl on my first car date."

"I wouldn't know how to play that game," Julian said.

"To be honest, me either, this is a first for me, you know, in a car. But I think we would be more comfortable in the back seat," I said glancing towards the seat behind us.

"I would have to agree," Julian admitted, "But are you sure about this?"

"Of course. The front seat is small. It's simple logic and logistics," I said as wicked thoughts ran through my mind.

"No," Julian said with honest seriousness of his voice, "I'm not talking about the backseat. I mean this whole thing. Us here, now? Are you certain?"

"Shut up and get back there," I ordered, "And take your jacket off."

"Are you joining me?" he questioned uncertainly.

"Yes, I will be back there in a minute," I said, "I just have a treat for you, and you don't have to close your eyes. You don't want to close your eyes because that would just defeat the purpose."

That look of desire that he wears so well was briefly replaced by puzzlement. I reached behind me and turned on the radio, hoping for thoughts of a nice romantic tune, or something hot like Pour Some Sugar on Me I can strip my clothes to. Instead, I began taking off my jacket to the beat of Hey, Hey we're the Monkees. One way or the other, this was going to be memorable.

Stripping on the stage is much easier than in the front seat of a classic car, but I did manage to get my jacket off without injury. Before continuing, I looked around to see if there was anyone around. Once I felt it was safe, I looked at Julian with a smile and slowly unbuttoned my shirt.

The farther down I went, the more of my lacy pink bra showed. I tilted my head to the side, letting my hair flow down in front of me, and I bit my lower lip. I have been told this drives the guys crazy.

My shirt was off, and once I found my courage, my lacy pink bra followed. My hands roamed over my breasts, slowly caressing. My fingers pinched both of my ever-hardening nipples. The combination of the cool night air that made its way into the car, and Julian's lustful gaze made them harder. Sometimes my eyes were closed, lost in the moment. Sometimes my eyes were open, lost in his stare—a deep penetrating stare that travelled between my eyes and my breasts, and followed my hands as they moved down to the button of my pants.

The button came undone easily with one hand while I turned off the radio with the other. I brought my hand back around to the zipper. I wanted Julian to hear the zipper as I pulled it down slowly. Once it was all the way down, I pulled the top of my pants to the side, allowing him to see that my panties were just as pink and lacy as my bra. With Julian's eyes squarely fixed on my hands, I thought it was time to blow his mind, so I pulled the top of my pants aside more and slipped my hand down the front.

I was on my knees, swaying my hips back and forth trying to look seductive, trying to look like I knew exactly how to seduce with sultry confidence. In my head however, I was wondering if there was a way to look classy while trying to remove your pants in a small car. There wasn't. I dropped my ass down in the passenger seat, lifted my legs in the air and pulled my pants over my hips and pushed them off my legs. "Help, please."

Julian came from the backseat and took hold of my pants and pulled them off. And so there I was, lying on my back wearing nothing but pink panties and a smile, with my legs resting on Julian's chest. While I was thinking about the cause and effect that brought me to this unflattering position, Julian was grinning from ear to ear, probably thinking about how he can bring this moment up in future conversations for the purpose of blackmail. He put his hands on my ankles, which sent a shockwave through my entire body. My ankles have always been sensitive to the touch. He moved his hands down my legs and then held his hands out to me. I took a hold of them, and he pulled me up as he sat back down. I landed squarely on his lap.

I could tell right away that Julian was enjoying my little show, but I noticed a problem. Julian, as always, was impeccably dressed and I was impeccably naked, but for a skimpy pair of see-through panties. Clearly the advantage was with the man, so I needed to call upon my special womanly powers to remedy the situation. I put my hands on his chest and leaned in, allowing him to get lost in my hypnotic hazel eyes. With our sensual staring contest underway, I slowly unbuttoned the middle button on his silk, probably imported, shirt. I hope he didn't pay too much for it. I put my hands on the inside and pulled, sending little buttons all over the car. Maybe I can find him a new one on EBay.

I pulled off his shirt and jacket with one smooth move that surprised me. I used to do it just for fun with neighborhood kids when I was a kid, but they were skinny little shits so it was easy.

Getting Julian's shirt and jacket over his ample chest, shoulders and arms was tasking achievement that I knew Dawn and Geri would appreciate, since I had planned on telling them every detail of whatever happens tonight.

I thought once I got Julian's shirt off, he would help by taking the rest of his clothes off, but no, all he did was reach around me and pull off his shoes and socks and lean back down in the seat grinning and waiting. I guess that was my cue to proceed with total abandon. Julian is a tall man, compared to most of the guys I have known through the years, and the back seat of a nineteen sixty-six Mustang, while nice, isn't exactly a changing room at JC Penny's. I was pulling his pants and underwear down slowly, giving Julian the impression that I was being seductive rather than giving myself time to consider the geometry. Once his pants and underwear were down below his waist, revealing the excellent prize inside, I stopped.

I forgot the geometry.

I forgot my own name.

Julian, noticing my stunned silence, put his hand behind my head and pulled me into his waiting, slightly parted lips, pressing my bare chest into his. I felt his tongue exploring my mouth while his hands explored everywhere else. They ran up and down my back, sending shivers of pure electricity from my ears to my toes. When those wonderful hands made their way to my breasts, the electricity went straight to my center, causing my hips to rotate, slowly at first, but when his mouth moved from my lips down to my neck, and the tip of his tongue pressed into my pulse point, all my inhibitions went straight out the window and into the night. I moaned softly and ground my hips into his—seeking for what only he could give.

Julian appeared to want me, need me as much as I needed him. I didn't want to wait anothersecond and neither did he. He reached down between my legs and his nimble fingers pulled the crotch of my panties aside. He entered slowly at first, raising his hips with each stroke. I threw my head back, welcoming every inch of him until he was buried deep inside me. I began moving my hips faster and faster, riding his entire length. His hands moved to the small of my back and I leaned back into them, bringing my breasts up into full view—a feast waiting to be taken. Julian leaned forward and put his mouth over one nipple then the other, licking, sucking and biting, sending me over the edge as my orgasm shook every cell in my body.

We were both breathing deeply. The windows were fogged up to the point where we could no longer see the moon. The only thing we saw was the longing in each other's eyes. I leaned forward, wrapped my arms around Julian's neck and pressed my forehead against his. I raised and lowered my hips with a new driving passion. A moan escaped my lips every time I pushed down on him, followed by a sigh every time I raised myself up. I moved myself faster and faster until Julian grasped my hips and pulled me in tightly to his body. "I'm coming," he whispered.

The feeling of his release inside me brought me to another shattering climax. We held each other tight until the incredible sensations subsided.

I dropped onto my back. "Oh...my...God!" I finally managed to say after a while. "Have I ever told you how much I like Mustangs? They really turn me on." Julian just beamed and seemed out of breath as well. As we lay together in the back, I knew this was the best sex I had ever had. But I realized that was only the beginning, and there was so much more to come.

*To sleep perchance to dream, say there's the rub. Was it a dream? Am I still dreaming? Is Julian's hand rubbing in just the right spot merely a*

*wishful figment of my dirty little imagination? If this is a dream, I hope I took an extra-strength sleeping pill. That's right Julian,* right there, that's the rub. Shakespeare knew his shit.

My heart pounded louder and louder. "Are you there my girl?" I heard Julian ask.

"Huh?" I questioned.

"Time to wake up and spill," he said.

"Huh?" I was completely confused.

Julian didn't sound like Julian. Julian sounded like an annoying so-called friend who doesn't know when to let sleeping dogs lie. Another pounding at the door brought me out of last night's memories and into a cold harsh reality that screamed for silence and coffee. Dawn knew I was there. She could probably sense me, or worse, smell me, but I didn't jump out of bed. She can wait. Then I heard the click of the lock and the door opened. I gave her a key. What was I thinking? Nothing good can come from a girl with the curiosity of a cat having free access to my domain.

Dawn closed the door behind her and turned to me with a look that was scary, as scary as she can look wearing nothing but an ex-boyfriend's football jersey and fuzzy orange slippers. The scary part came from the devilish smile. "I know something...I can't believe you did it!" she said, then said again, and again. She then stopped and picked up a white legal size envelope that wasn't there when I went to bed. It was huge. It must have barely fit through the mail slot.

"What the hell are you talking about in that tone of voice?" I yelled. "What did I do? I didn't do anything. What are you holding? What time is it?" Dawn, being Dawn totally ignored my pleas for information. "Please feel free to answer my questions in any order you wish."

"I can't believe you signed your contract!" Dawn screamed in that same high pitch tone that sounded like she poured Red Bull on her Cheerios.

"That's not an answer to a question, that's a statement that just brings up other questions. For instance what fucking contract?" She still wasn't listening. She's like I was when my parents talk to me with my headphones on while listening to Katy Perry.

"I got my bonus," Dawn continued. "Fifteen thousand...Fifteen big ones...Fifteen K...fifteen large...Fifteen...

"Okay Dawn."

"I never thought you would do it."

"It? What it? What it is it that I did?"

Dawn finally paused to take a breath. "The big it. Well, not the big it but the next biggest it."

"Dawn, so help me, if you don't stop talking Dawnie and start talking English, I can promise you that the jury of my peers will take into consideration my sleep-deprived state and your crazy-ass rambling."

"You signed Julian's contract."

"I didn't sign it," I said with defiance. "I didn't sign anything."

"Yes you did, you must have. Or...or...or, or, or." Dawn stopped jumping and you could see the light bulb go off. First her eyes widened, then her smile. "Oh my God! You slept with him. You had sex. How was it?"

"What...what...makes you think I slept with Julian?" I said turning away from Dawn hoping she didn't see the blush on my cheeks.

"Uh-oh. You didn't read your contract did you?" Dawn said with an impressive impersonation of my mother. "What, were you waiting for the Cliff Notes version?"

"Hey, you're not allowed to pass judgment without offering half-caff mocha with sprinkles. And besides Miss Procrastinator, your tenth grade teacher is still waiting for your book report on Moby Dick."

"That book had a misleading title, and we are so not talking about me," said Dawn as she walked into the kitchen and took out the instant coffee and two cups. "Do you have a copy of the contract here?"

"Top drawer in the dresser, under the bras and panties," I told her, "Why do I need to look at the contract, I didn't sign it."

Dawn came into my room and handed me a cup of coffee and then went to the dresser, opened the top drawer and giggled "Holy shit! You have panties in here that say 'Slippery When Wet.' They're cute."

"They're a gift," I said in irritation.

"From who? Perverted Santa Claus?"

"From none of your business...Now stop running your fingers through my undies and just find the contract, you know, that useless piece of unsigned paper," I said impatiently.

Dawn took out my leopard print bra, and after one final grrr sound, she pulled out the contract. She thumbed to the third page and handed it to me pointing at the fourth paragraph "Read!"

I absolutely hate reading legal documents, but I took a long drink of caffeine and read on. "In the event that a physical encounter develops between the party of the first part and party of the

second part, and said encounter leads to the act of coitus and/or fellatio, regardless of duration, the contract shall become bound and validated, regardless of the absence of a signature from either party." I looked up at Dawn who was trying to not laugh in my face, "What are coitus and or fellatio?"

"You're so naive about sexual terminology," Dawn said. "It's what boring people like professors and lawyers call sex. You know oral sex or ... conventional straight up sex."

"Why don't they just say intercourse and oral?" I asked.

"It's the same thing and sounds better," Dawn said as she sat on the corner of my bed.

"So...what did you do?"

"Coitus," my voice came muffled from under the covers of my bed.

"Spill," Dawn said eagerly, bouncing up and down on my bed in an effort to drive me out of the sanctuary of my covers. "And don't skimp on the salacious details."

"Let's just say I did it," I said, skipping the salacious details.

"Oh, come on. Was it terrible? Was it wonderful? Would you recommend the ride to anyone else in the future?" she asked excitedly.

I could go into every detail, every nuance of the experience, and she would think it was cool. Hell, she would probably carry me around on her shoulders chanting 'You go Cat... You go Cat', but I kept it brief. "It was...amazing...fantastic...mind-blowing."

"I knew it," Dawn said, "Your mind was blown! Was anything else blown?" I just stared at her. "Okay, no comment. Well I'm just assuming it was and move on. Here's a package from Sam, better see what secrets it holds."

Dawn leaned forward licking her chops like I opened the pirates' chest of gold or a sweepstakes envelope full of money. I ripped opened the envelope and out falls...money, huge amounts of money. Lots and Lots of hundred dollar bills and among the Benjamins was a note.

While I was waiting for my breath to return, I remembered what my mom always said. Read the card before playing with the gift.

*Caprice*
*Bring a list of your changes to the contract signing.*
*Dinner with Julian is at six o'clock in the garden suite.*
*Come and get a list of Julian's preferences.*
*Sam*

"Preferences?" I looked at Dawn. "What does this mean?"

"Seriously...You just unloaded a pile of bills on your bed and you're worried about the semantics of a love note?"

"It's hardly a love note," I told her. "It's more of a summons. And hey, I just found out that a wonderful one night stand has committed me to an ironclad relationship, so excuse me if I'm more gun-shy about the semantics. Now what the hell does Julian's preference mean? It sounds creepy."

"Come on Cat, you were just in Julian's bed you know him. He's not creepy," Dawn reminded me.

"It wasn't his bed," I said as my voice trailed off. "It was his...car."

"You did it in his car? Bitch, you are my hero. I want to be you when I grow up," she said in girlish admiration.

"Dawn, focus please...Preferences?" I reminded her.

"Chillax, it just means what the guy wants from you," Dawn said.

"See, creepy," I said, "It makes me feel like a whore."

"Hey," Dawn said as if she was insulted. "Some of your best friends are whores. And besides, you have a heart. You're a whore with a heart. They make movies out of people like you."

"How do I get out of this?" I asked after once again retreating to my sanctuary under my covers, "How do I go from property back to person?"

"Well, I can think of one way," Dawn said, "If Julian breaks the contract...But I really don't see that happening, he's totally into you."

"Wait, I just need Julian to break the contract?" I said hopefully.

"Yes. Why? What are you thinking?"

I didn't answer right away. My mind was racing with ideas. Dawn was watched my face for hints of what I was thinking, but my features kept changing from happy to confused to sad and back to happy. "I'm thinking we go get this list of preferences. Then we sit down and think of those things that guys hate about women, things that drive them nuts and wish they could build hot looking robots that can cook and are programmed to be open to any experience. After that we give Julian a demanding list."

"That might work, but the demands will have to be outrageous," Dawn said in surprise.

"Don't underestimate my ability to be a complete bitch," I answered, "Julian said he wanted a real girlfriend, so let's give him one with boobs and attitude."

"I don't understand. You don't like Julian?"

I started thinking about it, but I didn't answer, only said "Can you head back to your room? I'm getting dressed so we can go and get what we need from Jade's Inn."

"Head back to my room? Cat, we just stripped to almost nothing at the club. We were all over each other. Unless you're afraid I'll make a pass, I'll just wait here," she replied.

"Dawn, sweetie, you're not wearing pants."
Dawn looked down, looked up, smirked and left the room.

# Chapter 16:

# Meeting Julian's Father

The drive over to the Inn was filled with typical girl chatter about boys—how to find them, how to lose them, and how to scare them shitless. The plan to force Julian to reevaluate his desire to implement this ridiculous contract would call for a great amount of manipulation and cunning.

Fortunately, all women are born with these attributes. Dawn and I bantered back and forth with ideas, both funny and daunting, to add to my list of unreasonable demands. We drew upon our own experiences through the dating years, and also from pop culture, television, and movies. Particularly I Love Lucy and the latest teen girl power popcorn flick.

It was not as easy as I thought it would be. Usually if you want to lose a guy in ten days or less just tell them you want a commitment. Now, there I was running from a commitment by contract with what I would say is the hottest guy in existence. Either Julian needs therapy or I do.

I mean he has a list of preferences for a relationship? That cannot be sane.

Maybe I can start simple, like having his cell number so I don't have to go through Sam every time I want to talk or text him. At this point I think it would be naïve to think he doesn't have my number, so I should have his. I don't know if I will ever return a call but it's a matter of balancing the power of a relationship.

"How about more money?" Dawn suggested "Or jewelry! Nothing says I want you, I need you, I love you, like sparkles."

"I'm pretty sure that Julian's pockets are really, really deep, so he wouldn't miss the money. Besides, he has given me more than an enough. Call me hopeless, but I don't want Julian to give me jewelry unless he wants to, not because I made it a condition," I said.

"I know, I dropped Psych 101 as a major a few semesters ago, but I'm getting a mixed signal here," Dawn said smiling at me, "Contract bad...contract good. Are you looking for a way out of the contract or a way into his pants?"

Ignoring the question, I kept trying to figure out a way to mess with the male psyche as originally intended. "I really don't think I should ask for more money. He'll see my attempt as being a greedy, spoiled brat with a princess complex as cute, and then just give me more money."

"Don't you hate that, when people just hand over more money simply because you asked for it?"

"The money thing is out," I insisted. "We need something that will strike at the heart of a man's fear. Maybe something that I want him to do, but he will absolutely hate doing."

"In-laws," Dawn said.

"In-laws?" I questioned.

"Okay, not in-laws...yet. But there are few things that will scare the holy living shit out of a guy, and send him running to enlist in the Foreign Legion, than having to meet his girlfriend's parents, especially this early in the relationship," Dawn concluded.

"That would scare him off," I admitted. "How about I have to meet his parents?"

"That's just mean," Dawn said, "Here's an idea. What about, he has to meet your friends, and not just any friends, but friends who have been specially trained to be obnoxious, bitchy and judgmental. Tell him he has to participate in the girl's night out ritual where we will put him under the proverbial microscope and look for any chinks in the armor."

"Bullshit!" I said, "You just want him under the microscope so you can stare at him with lust in your eyes."

"I am offended! You are my best friend. I am here for you and ready to embarrass your potential boyfriend. The lust thing is merely a perk," Dawn said without an ounce of seriousness.

"Well, if you don't like that idea, how about he has to come over to your place, watch reality shows about fashion designers. And...and... he has to bring dinner or cook it himself."

"I like it," I said. "How about any role playing games have to be approved by me first?"

"Well, that's a given," Dawn said.

"Okay, I get to ask him one hundred questions that he has to answer honestly," I added.

"Oooo, I love that one. I think I'll add that on my next contract," Dawn said. "Just make

sure that the questions you ask are really the ones you want an honest answer to." I had to think about that one. She made a good point. "Here's another one," Dawn continued. "How about a week off from Julian during mid-terms and finals. As great as non-stop sex and dating is, you need time to cram for exams. Remember, it is also important to make your professors happy too...grade wise."

"I like that one also, practical and demanding...it's going on the list," I said. "So this next one is mean, but how about he has to go shopping with me."

"Oh God, that's perfect," Dawn said with excitement. "Take him to a lingerie store. Most guys turn red in those places. After about ten seconds they usually head to the nearest sports store or a place that sells pretzels...well, most guys. Although, I had this one boyfriend, who followed me into a Victoria's Secret, and when I put a lacy little number up to my waist and asked how it looked, we ended up doing it in the dressing room. So maybe not a lingerie store...Try a craft store, guys hate that," she concluded.

We pulled in to Jade's Inn and got out of Dawn's car. I suddenly thought out loud "If I have to wear a ring he has to wear a ring too." I said it under my breath, but of course Dawn heard me.

"What ring?" Dawn asked.

"Julian wants me to wear a ring, and as if the ring didn't say it enough, he told me no dating anyone but him in or out," I said. "It's like he's leaving his expensive mark on me, a warning to all others to stay away."

"Well, I'm sure it's a pretty mark," Dawn whispered as we walked in, "Wow, didn't know he wanted you that much."

Once we got inside, we followed the sound of ivories being tickled. After we came out of the hall we entered the main room and found Sam at the piano with his eyes closed like he was in a different world, a world where the piano man plays anything but Billy Joel's, Piano Man.

Dawn went to pull him out of his musical trance to let him know we were there, but I stopped her and shook my head. I was enjoying the show too much. So we parked ourselves on a corner couch and listened to the music. It was so beautiful. Sam should be headlining at Carnegie Hall, not at an Inn in Pocatello, Idaho.

When Sam hit the last note, it echoed throughout the room. He grinned, opened his eyes, turned around and saw us still swaying to the music. "Enjoy the show?" Sam asked.

Dawn and I stood up clapping "Very much so," I said. "You got some major talent there. How is it that you haven't landed a lady? A girl's imagination could run wild after seeing your magic fingers on those keys."

"I have to agree," Dawn said, "I'm feeling all tingly inside."

"Keep your wild imagination from running kids," Sam warned. "I'm glad you enjoyed it Cat." Sam turned from me but not before I noticed a sad look in his eyes. He turned those eyes to Dawn and asked, "Dawn, would you stay here while I take Cat to the office?"

"Oh sure, fine, I don't feel left out at all," Dawn said. "Whatever you guys talk about, Cat will tell me later after I peruse her with whiskey."

Sam put his arm around me as we walked down the hall. I felt nervous, like we were having a father/daughter talk about boys. I put my arm around his waist, I guess as a sign of trust more than anything. I trusted him and he could trust me. "Julian doesn't have to pay me...I would date him without the money," I finally said after a long trek down the hallway in silence. "You know, I really like him, that's why taking the money is hard."

"I know, that's why I like you, you're good for him," Sam said pulling me in for a one-arm hug. "You probably don't know this, but I have known Julian since we were kids, and I know his family really well. You will be good for him, Cat."

"I appreciate your confidence in me Sam, and your support. So you won't be surprised when I try to get Julian to break the contract tonight?" I asked hesitantly.

"I'm waiting for it," Sam replied with a knowing smirk on his face. "It will be...entertaining. Just remember Julian has some changes he wants to add to the contract too."

Sam opened the door to his office, and as we walked in Sam's words just kept repeating *over and over in my head Julian has changes... Entertaining...it will be entertaining.*

Sam took an envelope out of the top drawer of his desk and handed it to me. "Julian is expecting you to wear something ugly or ordinary like jeans and a T-shirt, just to turn him off. Trust me, it won't. I would like to give you some words of advice...go the other way. He wants you and he wants this contract, nothing will change that, Cat. Instead of dressing down, dress up, shock him. If you make him drool, he will want you more. The more he wants you, the more you can bargain for what you want," he concluded.

"I'll take that under advisement," I said thoughtfully. I kept turning the envelope over and over in my hands. I couldn't bring myself to open it, not yet. I wanted the contract broken, gone, history. I wanted tall, dark and wow with no legal strings attached so we could just be Julian and Caprice, boyfriend and girlfriend...not Mr. Julian and his hooker. I have been trying to come up with creative stipulations to this damn contract that would scare an ordinary man away, but of course Julian is anything but ordinary. And according to Sam, steadfast and determined to put this binding document into place.

"What you don't use is yours to keep," Sam said. I would be lying if I said I understood that, but I didn't say anything. I knew Sam understood how I was feeling, and I knew he sympathized.

I kind of think he wanted to comfort me and tell me everything will be okay. Maybe he wanted to tell me turn around and run far and fast in the other direction. But the practical, business side of Sam, Julian's friend and confidant, took over "Dawn can help you find what you need for tonight."

I left Sam in his office and walked back down the hall, feeling alone. The hallway seemed much longer than before. I finally made it back to find Dawn, and felt less alone in the world. I still had the envelope in my hand and it was still tightly sealed. I hadn't opened it, but I had a sneaky feeling what was inside. It felt familiar.

"Hey girlfriend," Dawn said after picking up the envelope and handing it back to me. "Are you okay?"

"The Jury's out on that one," I said, sitting next to Dawn.

Dawn couldn't take her eyes off the envelope. "Well it looks like you got a special prize. Is that what I think it is?"

"Probably," I said grudgingly, wondering how I got into this mess in the first place.

"And? Are you taking it out and playing with it?" Dawn asked buoyantly.

With reluctance, I opened the envelope. I knew if I didn't Dawn would have done it for me.

As I had figured, more money came tumbling out. Julian's list was in there too. I was curious about what was still inside the envelope, and by the time I got it out, Dawn had half of the money counted. "There's a couple thousand dollars here," Dawn said.

"Well, I guess I have a dinner date with Julian tonight. This is probably his way of saying to go out and buy something nice," I said with disappoint in my voice.

"Where, Rodeo Drive?" Dawn asked. "Where are you supposed to drop two grand in Pocatello for a dinner dress?"

"And shoes," I pointed out.

"Yea, that's true," she said pondering this.

I perused the list and tried as hard as possible not to pass judgment when an older man with a cane slowly made his way into the room. I jumped up and held the door for him. I would put this guy in his fifties, but a good fifty because he wore it well. His dark brown hair had a touch of gray that made him look like one of those guys who grew more sophisticated with age, while women just grew old. I was staring at him longer than I should have, not because he looked like a classy 1940s movie star, but because he looked familiar. I'm sure if he didn't have the gray in his hair he would look fifteen years younger, but he wouldn't look any better. There's something about him, something in his eyes that tells you he has seen and knows more then he lets on.

"Could you find Sam for me?" the man asked politely. God, his voice was sexy. Dawn and I just stared at him and each other, wondering if we were thinking the same thing. Is he a client that frequents this establishment? I can't imagine he would have a difficult time finding a lady if he didn't have one.

"I'll...get him," Dawn stuttered and headed down the hall, walking backwards, not wanting to take her eyes off the stranger.

"Would you like to sit down?" I asked. I couldn't help but wonder where I may have seen *this man before. Have I met him before? I would think I would remember a guy like this. I also* couldn't help but notice his cane. It had a silver tip and handle, and I could swear it looked like a bat with its wings folded in.

*"Thank you, Caprice," he said. He said Caprice! He said my name! Wait, what the hell? Who was this guy? Was he one of those guys from Bingo? I was about to ask him how he knew me,* when I heard Sam thundering down the hall. This guy must be somebody if he can make Sam come running.

"Dominic, it's been so long," Sam said breathing hard while shaking his hand. I have never seen Sam show so much respect for someone other than Julian.

"It's nice to see you too Sam, it has been a long time as well," Dominic said, "So where is my son, Sammy?"

"Upstairs in his office I think...want me to go get him for you?" Sam asked.

"If you could please...thank you Sam. I'll just wait here and talk to Caprice," Dominic said.

He then turned to me with this look of familiarity on his face. He knew me and I should know him, but from where? I liked the guy. Besides being great looking, he seemed pleasant. And Sam seemed happy I was getting along with this man, and that would have been cute if I knew why, but I didn't so it wasn't.

Before Sam could head up stairs Julian came through the front door of the Inn. At least, I *think it was Julian. Does Julian have a younger brother? That's not a younger brother, that's a younger*

*Julian! Holy shit, he cut his hair! I had been all over this guy when he looked ten years older than me, a mid-thirties, distinguished looking gentlemen, but now he looked mid-twenties and, well... still distinguished, but a younger distinguished. I wanted to be all over him again, try* out the newer model as it were. He was dressed in a perfectly tailored black suit, as usual, which is why he always looked distinguished. I wonder if he would look so distinguished in Bermuda *shorts and a tank-top. I would pay to see that. Maybe I'll add it to my list. God I'm so mixed up. The contract makes me want to run for my life and his body makes me want to play with him like an anatomically correct Ken doll.*

"Father," Julian said.

Father? As in dad? The lustful wrong feelings that I have been experiencing for the last few minutes was for the father of the guy that I had sex with last night? I wonder if one of the Chinese Circles of Hell is reserved for people like me.

Julian gave his father one of those manly three pats on the back hugs. "What are you doing here?" Julian asked, not noticing me until he turned to Sam. "Did you offer my father a drink?" Julian did one of those cute double-takes when he saw me. A small grin shown on his face, a brief smile he was trying to hide from his father. He was probably afraid to show any vulnerability. And while the smile was small, it was enough to give me goosebumps, and just large enough for his father to notice. Dominic just beamed back, probably knowing his son, while still manly, was also adorable.

"Did I hear what I thought I heard?" Dawn asked when she finally made it back . She whispered, "Is the hot guy the father of...that hot guy?"

"Yes," I whispered back.

"And Julian has an office here, like a head honcho office?" Dawn said in a shocked, but quiet voice.

"Apparently," I said being just as quiet.

Julian looked at his father, back to me, and then back to his father again. If he could keep one eye on me and one on dear old dad, I'm sure he would. He looked like he wanted to say something, but just couldn't find the right words. Thankfully, his father clued right in.

"Since my son is tongue-tied right now, let me introduce myself," Dominic said while he watched his son watch me. Was it possible that Dominic knew what I was thinking while I stared into the eyes of his son? If Julian was thinking what I was thinking then his dad wouldn't need to read our minds, it would be embarrassingly obvious. If Julian looks that good at that age, his *wife will be a happy Mrs. Julian. I wonder if I will be that Mrs. Julian. Oh my God! What is wrong with me?*

"Please Father...allow me the honor," Julian said before taking a big breath, and for some reason looking worried. "Father, this is Caprice Angela Talbot and Amber Dawn Ellis. Ladies, this is my father Dominic Hainsworth."

"It is a pleasure to meet you Mr. Hainsworth," I said politely.

"Yea, ditto," Dawn said. "I now see where Julian gets..."

"Down, Dawn," I whispered. "Don't make me get the tranquilizer gun."

"Julian you will have to bring Caprice to our house for dinner soon so the rest of the family can meet the new woman in your life," Mr. Hainsworth said. How did he know we were a *couple? We're not a couple. We're a potential couple. Then how did he know we were a potential couple? What does he mean I should meet the family? One night in a car and I'm meeting Mom and Dad and the rest of the Hainsworth horde? Jesus! Bring us out of warp speed*

Mr. Scott. Mr. Hainsworth interrupted the panic-driven rambling in my head.

"Caprice, I believe you know my granddaughter...Elizabeth. You helped her through a bad day she was having." Dawning comprehension hit me over the head.

"Oh yes, Elizabeth. She was the girl I met who was going from the Cheerleading competition to the Science competition. She got turned around at ISU so I helped her. She's seemed nice and smart. I watched the competition and she made me feel really stupid."

"You're being modest," Dominic finally said. "You were a tremendous help to her Caprice. Can I just call you Cat?"

"Yea sure, all my friends call me Cat," I said. I like Dominic calling me Cat. It means he likes me and he seems comfortable around me...that could be handy in the future. Julian moved next to me and put his arm around me and pulled me close. The little fire that ignited inside my inner depths was now getting hot enough that everyone around me should be wearing radioactive protection. I wonder if it's noticeable. At this point I have no idea who was talking, my mind was still in the backseat of Julian's car. I needed to relax...breath...listen to Julian's dad while thinking about ice cold drinks on the snowy banks of northern Greenland. However, the fact that Julian's arm held me tighter was not helping.

"Cat, my daughter and her husband would like to thank you personally, and Elizabeth would like to see you again," Dominic said. "Sam I hope you will come too." Really...a dinner *invitation? His granddaughter was lost...I pointed her in the right direction...It's not like I gave her mouth-to-mouth or saved her from a falling anvil.*

"Caprice and I will check our schedules and I'll call Emma to set a date for dinner," Julian said. "I will also make sure that Sam comes with us." Here I was thinking if I demanded a chance to meet his parents it would scare him away from this ridiculous contract. But now I was feeling trepidation about...everything. Oh well. The best laid plans of mice and overpaid escorts.

So here I am, jumping from backseats to backyards picnics. I need to get out of this room before Mr. Hainsworth insists I wear white and pick out patterns. "I...I have to get ready for tonight...our date... tonight," I said, and then without thinking, I kissed Julian on the cheek. I quickly turned to

Dominic. "It was nice to meet you. Please tell Elizabeth hi for me."

"I will. I hope my son is treating you well. If not, you let me know." Dominic said winking at me.

"I will," I said trying not to laugh, nasty thoughts in the back of my mind contemplating how I would really like Julian to treat me.

*Wow. Is he treating me well? Would Julian's fine upstanding father find it shameful to learn his fine upstanding son is paying me to have sex? A ready-made girlfriend bought and paid for?*

"See you tonight Caprice," Julian said kissing me softly on the lips. God damn it, I wish he would stop being so charmingly hot. I'm trying to muster up some righteous indignation here, assert my womanhood for the good of all womankind. I took Dawn by the hand and pulled her along with me out of Jade's Inn, leaving the three men behind.

# Chapter 17:

# Shopping

Dawn and I quickened our pace once we hit the parking lot. I should say that I quickened, Dawn was just trying not to trip while I dragged her like a child going to the dentist. Our departure from Jade's Inn felt more like an escape, an attempt to salvage my sanity. When we finally got to the car, I waited while Dawn searched through her cavernous hand bag trying to find the keys. "Wow, wow, wow!" Dawn said over and over again. "Julian works at Jade's Inn? Does he own it? I mean, his name isn't Jade, at least I don't think it is. Wow! I think he really likes you. Do you think there is anything he won't do to get you? Wow! How many women has he had over the years?"

"Shut up Dawn, excellent questions, the same ones I have bouncing around in my brain, and if I can find the courage I will be asking those questions tonight, among many others." I looked at the envelope again, turning it over and over. "How many women has he had?" I asked myself.

I don't remember if I said it out loud or not. I knew my previous night with Julian was great, it was amazing...but was it special? The romantic in me wanted to believe it was a singular moment in time shared by two people. The pessimistic realist that won't shut up believes it was a *rumble in a rumble seat, one of many. Was it special to Julian? Do I want to know the answer to that?*

There was a silence in the car, the awkward kind that Dawn doesn't like. "Let's look over his preference list, maybe it will give us an insight into his psyche and a hint at what we should buy for this evening's festivities," she pleaded. Looking at the list of likes and dislikes, which is just a list of dos and implied don'ts, I'm beginning to see the wisdom of Sam's idea that shock and awe would be better.

"Okay," I began, "His favorite color is blood red. Eww. He likes simple clothes? I wonder if that means simple on me or simple on him. I don't think silk black and blood red counts as simple. He seems to favor the smell of roses. I wonder if that's 'Blood Red Rose' or if any color will do. Well, here's something, he likes garter belts, that's simple."

"It's only simple if they are for you," Dawn pointed out, "Garters on a guy are really complicated."

"How do you know that?" I said in my silly voice.

"I...just...do and we are leaving it at that," She said with a note of finality in her voice. I decided to wait until she was drunk off her ass before I pressed for more details about this particular subject "What do you think of a nice simple cocktail dress, with a red garter belt, and red high heels to match, oh, and Rose Water perfume?"

"That sounds very...complex," Dawn said with just a hint of sarcasm.

"What am I supposed to do with the rest of the money?"

"I know this great charity you can donate it to, it's called 'New Dawn.' They do great work with struggling, but cute, college students who are in desperate need of designer clothing," Dawn said.

I just glared at her.

"You could just keep it," she suggested.

"I guess I can," I said as I lowered the seat back and attempted to reach under my seatbelt and into my pocket.

"What the hell are you doing?" Dawn asked as she started to veer off the road. "Can't you wait until tonight?"

"I'm trying to get my phone you perv," I told her, "Just keep your eyes on the road. I have questions I need to ask Sam."

I kept my eyes on the floor of the car, admiring my shoes while the phone rang. I have learned over the years if I keep my eyes down while Dawn is driving I won't see any impending catastrophe and try with futility to continually hit my imaginary brake. The phone rang a few times before Sam picked up. "Hi Sam," I said.

"Well hi Caprice, you sound nervous."

"Dawn's driving," I continued.

"Got it. I'm glad you called. I meant to tell you something, but you ran out before I could.

We have been looking at the room that you are designing and I believe it is ready for the next phase. I was wondering when you wanted to come and take a look at it?"

"Can you give me an hour and I'll be back there?" I asked

"Doesn't need to be today Caprice," Sam answered.

"I'm excited to see it and I just have to shop for tonight and that won't take long," I replied,

"So I'll see you in an hour."

"See you then," Sam said and the line went dead.

"So what's the what?" Dawn asked.

"We need to get this shopping thing done quickly," I told her, "The room that I designed is ready to go into the next phase. I want to get over there and take a look, see if I can get new ideas to finish the place."

"Well, I have to say that rushing through the whole shopping experience goes against everything that I believe and hold as true," Dawn pointed out, "But if we must we must, and you will owe me."

"I owe you? After Teddies'?" I said in exasperation.

"Well if you're getting picky...fine. We'll run through the stores, grab a bunch of stuff and hope it matches. By the way, I didn't hear you ask whatever question you would ask," Dawn said knowingly.

"Yea, I know, I forgot. I'll bring it up when I get there," I finished.

I really didn't have the time to hit every individual store across town to find each and every thing I was looking for. Also, Pocatello is not known as a shopping Mecca for designer clothes, so we decided to go to the mall and hope we could find it all at once. After an exhausting search through six different stores, most catering to teen and pre-teen—just to find a dress that I liked and Dawn didn't laugh at. Then, we moved to shoes. It took only three stores, a slightly twisted ankle and a slightly wounded pride to find the right footwear for that evening. I know I had an outer outfit that looked simple. Not sister wife simple, but something that Julian should appreciate. On the way home, we stopped at Daisy Mays Boutique for the under garments that were anything but simple.

When we left the lingerie shop my purse, weighed down by three thousand dollars was now about six hundred dollars lighter. I turned to Dawn, whose eyes were roaming back and forth between the road and the new nightie she bought that was draped over the stirring wheel.

"I still don't know what I'm going to do with the rest of the cash."

"Wow," Dawn exclaimed with exasperation. "If only everyone in the world had that problem. If you're not going to donate to a worthy cause or put it in one of those fucking swear jars every time you stub your toe, think of Daniel, or watch an episode of Meet the Kardashians, you can always..." She stopped talking and stopped driving.

After slamming on the brakes and crossing over two lanes of traffic that others drivers foolishly thought they had a right to be in, she pulled off to the side of the road and pointed her finger to the right. When I finally opened my drenched eyes, I saw what grabbed her attention away from the finer points of driving school.

It was as if a light came down from the heavens just to illuminate Tiffany's. Once again unto the breach dear friends, and into the chair of the master of fingernails and hair. I scrambled to find my phone while making a less than graceful exit from the car. "Sam, can we make that two hours," I said and hung up before he could say huh.

I felt an overwhelming sense of excitement, and only a tiny sense of shame, knowing that I was about to tell Tiffany. "Spare no expense on us."

"Ready?" Dawn asked.

"Yes, I call it friend appreciation day for not killing me."

"Well the day's not over yet?"

When we left Tiffany's my purse was once again lighter, but my fingernails were longer than I have ever seen them and were painted the same color as my toenails a deep scarlet red polish that made them feel like armored-up weapons of mass destruction.

After Dawn drove me to my car and I grabbed an arm full of new clothes that I threw into the backseat, I headed over to Jade's Inn. I was eager to see my new room so I may have exceeded the speed limit just a tad. When I got there I headed straight for Sam's office, but he wasn't in. I figured he was waiting for me in the new room I was going to be working on, so I headed down the hall practically skipping as I went. I was looking forward to talking about the room design, talking about real work, talking about getting paid for real work that didn't involve taking my clothing off.

When I walked past the Garden Suite, I noticed the door was open bit and the light was on.

As far as I knew, most of the rooms were vacant. Could Sam be inside? I opened the door just enough to stick my head inside. "Sam, are you in here?" There was no answer so I stepped inside.

The room looked like a seventeenth Century French Garden—the kind of garden that has a bubbling fountain under a tree. This one happened to be half-in and half-out of the wall. I have to wonder if the sound of the fountain keeps customers up at night feeling like they have to pee.

Near the other wall was a full-size white gazebo, and then if you turn the corner you see one of my favorite items—which any self-respecting seventeenth Century garden should not be without—an oversized jetted hot tub. And off to the left, you find a shower and a sauna. This room allows you to relax and go back in time a few centuries, or it's a real nice place to make a porno.

I didn't find Sam traipsing through the garden so I wanted to leave, but I had to stop and check out the castle painted on the wall. This was a detailed, beautiful picture that had—like all the other designs on the wall—Dawn's autograph below it. She does good work. It was while I was imagining the knight in armor and the princess in the castle that I felt his breath, his silent presence behind me. It was like medieval magic, a wizard quietly coming out of the mist on the Moors, alluring and creepy. I didn't turn around. I stared at the mural and I'm sure he was too. I wonder if he was imagining the same thing I was, in our own little world.

Just having Julian next to me gave me goose bumps. I shook my head as a foolhardy attempt to get him out of my thoughts. I could feel his eyes on my neck, studying each goose bump, and each little goose bump grew and multiplied just as he reached out to softly stroke my throat.

That's when I turned to him, and the look in his eyes startled me. No man had ever looked at me that way...there was hunger in his eyes. With his hand still gently on the side of my neck Julian pulled me towards him. Our lips suddenly met and all I wanted was him.

I felt his lips on mine and felt my knees go weak at his touch. I brought my hands up to his arms, suddenly feeling the need to hold on to something so as not to fall over. I grasped his upper arms and felt how strong he was. My hands moved up to the back of his head, making the kiss tighter, more passionate. He felt me pull him closer to me and it instantly drove him over the edge. I felt him harden against me, as he held me closely and kissed me so hard it felt like he couldn't get enough of me. His tongue flicked out of his mouth and ran across my lips.

I parted my lips as he darted his tongue in, exploring every inch of me. I made a low moan in back of my throat as I felt things that were new to me. I had never been kissed like this before. I kissed him back with all I had. My fingers were locked in his hair, my tongue finding my way into his mouth. He kissed my face, chin, neck. I found his lips on my throat, his tongue caressing my skin. I felt so weak with yearning and I longed to do things with this man that I had never *imagined. I wanted him to take me, to have me. I have to stop this, before I'm out of control. Someone stop me!*

"Julian we need to stop," I finally managed to say, breathlessly.

"Why, no one's here?" he asked softly as he kissed my neck down to my shoulder, moving my shirt aside and working his way down.

"I'm here...to see Sam," I stuttered. God I was enjoying these lips going down my shoulder, or I was until he pulled away. My heart was racing when I saw him move to the door of the suite and close it.

"I believe you're here to see me...I'm the one who approves room designs," he said smiling.

"Really," I said while creative and kinky thoughts of how to put this garden to good use danced through my head, "Why are we in this room? This room is perfect."

"Would you believe that it was just last night I had a dream of you and I in the French Garden suite," Julian beamed and pulled me close to his body. "I just wanted you to know," he whispered. And before I could whisper back, he started kissing my lips again. I so wanted to be a part of this decadent dream sequence, but the reality of the contract kept fucking things up.

"I want you too, Julian, and I...really mean that," I said breathlessly. Julian picked me up in his arms still kissing my neck and pulling me closer to him "Oh, okay, but...one condition...It's just us, just you and me. No contract. No money on the nightstand."

"As you wish Caprice, if that is what you want," he said simply. For a moment I was standing there in his embrace, staring into his eyes—and without seeing him move  –I realized I was being carried in his arms. We were headed to a huge mahogany four-post bed with heavy velvet curtains the color of burgundy wine.

"Caprice," Julian breathed my name as he ran his fingers through my hair and his tongue slowly parted my lips. I moaned softly. I could feel him harden again with my body rubbing against his. I placed my fingers in his hair while his passionate kiss covered my mouth. Julian rolled me onto my back and leaned over me, trailing his lips and his tongue down my cheek, to my collarbone, and then my shoulder. I felt his warm hands on my waist, under my shirt, pulling it slowly up my body past my bra and over my head, thus revealing my skin that ached for his touch. He was so amazing, every inch of his face a perfect statue, like a classical Greek god. I found the buttons on his shirt and undid them. Then pushed his shirt back and ran my fingers over his smooth, hard chest.

Julian slowly glided his hands down my sides, sliding his fingers inside the waistband of my pants, circling to the front and undoing the buttons. Ever so slightly, he slowly pulled my pants down, tenderly enough to tickle every inch of my skin from my hips to my toes. I gasped with pleasure at the feeling. My bra was next, his nimble fingers undoing the hook with one hand, while the other was caressing my back. I was amazed at his gentleness. He ran his massaging fingers all over my satin panties before sliding them down my legs, leaving me naked. Our lips danced together softly, until I realized my hands were pulling the zipper of his pants down. Julian groaned and deepened the kiss immediately. Our passion was soft, our embrace gentle, until everything became desperate, as the storm reached the garden.

I could feel how much he wanted my body. I followed his lead and trailed my tongue down his throat to his chest. I bit his nipple playfully and his muscles all jerked. I ran my mouth all over his skin while his fingers desperately found the soft spot between my legs. Julian shoved his fingers into me, making me cry out in pleasure. I was more than ready for him. Julian positioned himself on top of me and I, unable to stand it any longer, opened myself to him. As our eyes locked, he slowly thrust himself into me.

My nails dug into his back as he moved in and out and back in again. I lifted my hips to meet each of his thrusts, allowing him deeper and deeper access inside of me. I cried out in desire as he grew more urgent, harder, and faster. It was in that moment that I no longer knew where I was or how long Julian had been moving inside me. I was lost in that moment and didn't want to be found. Our bodies just kept moving, thrusting, devouring until the moment I knew he could not hold back any longer. I was groaning with pleasure, enjoying every inch of him. I felt the climax begin to grow deep inside, the warmth that built in my belly started to spread throughout my entire body. "Oh God, please," I screamed with intensity as my nails dug deeper into his back as if I was trying to hold on to the world Julian had brought me back into. He pulled me closer to him, on the verge of coming as well. We rocked back and forth as we continued to go at a frantic pace, as we came together, totally lost in pure ecstasy.

We didn't move. We just lay there trying to get our breath back. I never knew what it was like to want the world to stop in one moment, but I did then. Julian pulled away from me rolling me on my side and brushing the hair out of my face. "Caprice," he whispered.

"Hi there," I quietly said. I watched the beads of sweat roll down his face, which means I did a good job. I reached up to wipe the sweat away from his eyes so that he could continue to look at me lovingly. When I brought my hand to his face I froze. The red on the tips of my fingers was not the polish, and it was dripping down my arm. "Oh my God," I yelled. "Are you okay? Did I do that to you?" I quickly turned Julian around and discovered the bloody red tracks that I left on his back. "I am so sorry. I guess I got caught up in the moment. I didn't realize..."

"Relax, Cat," Julian said softly. "I am alright. I look at these as a warrior's wound. The scars of passion that I am proud to wear." He could see the concern and guilt was still plastered all over my face. "I was led to believe that chicks dig scars."

"Not when we are the cause of them," I said bluntly.

"Well as you can see I am fine. I want to know how do you feel, Caprice,". I just beamed at him. "Do you have any regrets?"

"Other than causing you grievous bodily harm, no, no regrets," I said cuddling up to the side of his body, "Do you?"

"Never," he said simply.

"Do you think we should get back to work?"

"Never." Julian exhaled. "Or maybe in a while. For now, let's just stay here and revel in each other."

This is one of those times where you want to hit the stopwatch and make time itself stand still. You can go for years, or a lifetime trying to find that one place you can call home, and here it was. Here I was, home in his embrace. It felt wonderful, but...I had to ask. "Do you own Jade's Inn?"

Julian hesitated and tensed up, but only for a moment. "More like the CEO of a company...It's a family business or businesses," he said and relaxed more. I don't think I have *ever seen him this content, this happy. Should I take advantage of his current state of mind, or should I just lay here and be content myself? Hold him, cuddle? That would be the romantic thing to do. Nah, I needed to push the advantage.*

"Julian, you do know that I'll be your girlfriend...without the contract, ring and all."

Again, a hesitation, but longer this time. Julian tightened his embrace before saying "No, I want the contract."

"Why, you don't believe I'll stay?" I asked, hurt.

"I believe you will stay for a while, Caprice. Then you will leave," Julian said looking away.

*Wow, he is self-conscious. His confidence is not as hard as nails, but soft and mushy like mine. I* decided not to push the point so I changed the subject.

"Have any of your girls that you dated met your parents?" I asked with a sheepish grin.

"Yes, one other," Julian said quietly, "And it was my father she met. My mother died some years ago."

"Oh, I'm sorry," I said, choking on my proverbial foot.

"It's okay," he said smiling. "Like I said, it's been...a while. And just to give you a heads up and make you nervous as hell, it will be my whole family you will meet. All my brothers and sisters, and their families too."

I tightened around him in fright, "You're kidding, right?"

"Nope," his smile became less charming and more smart-alecky, "See why the contract is a good thing for us?"

"It doesn't cover family." I said in indignation.

"It does now," he said simply.

After great sex I'm usually relaxed. Not so much now. However, I could still feel myself drifting off to sleep with images of judgmental family members dancing in my head. Maybe I can come up with some fun new exotic disease before this happened.

# Chapter 18:

# The Room Design

The sheets were soft and cool, like a summer breeze that cradles you, and no matter which way I turned or stretched, I could move freely and enjoy this wonderful sensation. This told me two things. One is that I'm not in my own bed, and two, I'm alone in this bed. My arms and legs were flailing about like I was trying to make a snow angel, confirming what my eyes remained afraid to open and discover for themselves. Julian was gone. I called his name, but there was no answer. I crawled out of bed wearing nothing but a puzzled look.

Where was Julian?

Where was my underwear?

Relying completely on luck rather than memory, I was able to find my bra draped over a small statue of a naked wood nymph, and my panties hanging over the peep hole on the door. I'm not going to try and remember how that happened.

I finished getting dressed and consoled myself with the fact there was no money waiting for me on the nightstand. Wow, how romantic. I was plotting which route out of the building would allow me to leave without being seen. I was not in the mood to be seen. When I opened the door I saw Julian, standing there with a smile and a tray of cheese, fruit, a bottle of wine with two glasses. He was also carrying three big files.

"I'd like you to stay, we have things to discuss," Julian requested as he came into the room and closed the door behind him.

I couldn't tell by the tone of his voice if that was an urgent request or an order. "Is that an expensive bottle of wine?" I asked, not trying to sound too bitchy.

"It is," he said as he sat it on the table near the bed, and then looked at me hopefully.

"I'll stay," I finally agreed, my inner bitch at bay. However, I felt nervous.

When someone says we need to talk, they usually want to talk seriously about their relationship. When they say we have something to discuss, they want to talk business. Since the heart of our relationship is a business contract, I wasn't sure what to expect. "What are we discussing precisely?" I asked.

Julian set the tray on the bed and patted the bed and winked at me to join him. It appeared to be an open invitation fraught with meaning and innuendo, or maybe he just wanted me to sit. I slowly sat next to him, keeping an eye on his hands which unfortunately grabbed a wine glass instead of my leg. Julian poured some wine and handed me the glass.

"We can talk about our contract tonight," Julian suggested in a voice that sounded happier than I was used to. Before I could respond, he took a piece of cheese and put it in my mouth. I managed to eat the cheese by chugging half a glass of wine, and maintained my cool while asking an important question in a casual way. "Have you ever been in a contract with anyone else?"

"Yes, many times," came Julian's casual reply.

"God Julian, with so many clichés to choose from, which one do I start with? How about 'I'm not going to be another notch on your expensive hand-crafted bed post?'" I stated getting ready to leave. Julian stood up in front of me smiling a big smile, like he had no clue I was considering kicking his nuts up through his tonsils. "Look Julian, I will always remember this day and you, but I can't ..." Julian grabbed my arms again, pulled me in and kissed me.

"Hey, if you wanted to shut me up..." I started again, and then he kissed me, shutting me up entirely.

Julian pulled away "You are absolutely adorable when you're angry, which means you're also confused. At the moment, I can guess your confusion is making you angry, which means you're incredibly gorgeous." He put his hands on my face and pulled me in for another, all too brief kiss. "Now," he said in a calming voice, "I deal with contracts in my life and I work constantly. I have contracts with accountants, real-estate agents, insurance agents, and...room designers."

Well I was feeling foolish. I wanted to apologize and I was sure a certain amount of groveling would be involved, but before I could say anything, another kiss. "I have never entered into a contract with a woman before," Julian said, "At least not a romantic one...for lack of a better word."

Julian stood up and poured himself another glass of wine "To be honest, there have been women in my life. They come and go. They see me and they like what they see. I know, I sound conceited, but it's true. They see me but they don't know me, they don't want to. They're drawn in by the mystery- –maybe because their own lives aren't going the way they want...they're bored. They're bored with boyfriends, lovers, routine, and they see me, someone who looks handsome but not entirely...safe. It doesn't take much after that, a smile, a wink, a drink and they stay for a night, maybe two."

I don't know if I'm supposed to feel sorry for the guy, or buy him a beer and say you're the man. "So let me get this straight," I said, "Beautiful women meet this tall, dark, handsome, rich, mysterious stranger, have sex with him and then decide he's not good enough and they leave...or are you the one who decides they're not good enough and you slip out under the dark of night?"

"Believe it or not they are the ones who usually leave," Julian said as he turned away.

"Why?"

"I don't know," Julian replied. "Maybe the truth about the Inn is too much of a challenge to their moral standards."

"Really..." I asked, "They come to this moral epiphany after a one night stand with a total stranger?"

"Hypocrisy is alive and well—even in Pocatello," Julian said.

"And that's why they leave?" I asked again.

"I don't know. Maybe...they realize that after a night or two the mystery isn't so mysterious, the danger less dangerous. They had their fantasy and reality takes over," he said sadly.

"What reality?"

Julian looked back at me for a moment and then turned away again. "The reality is...you're the one I take home to Mom and Dad."

"I don't believe that."

"That's why you're different," he said, "That's why you're here. If I knew you'd stay after you got to know me, the real me, the contract wouldn't be necessary."

"I have to admit," I said, "You never struck me as being insecure. That must be the 'real you'. The one you hide behind the chiseled body and perfect hair the way others guys hide behind fancy cars they can't possibly afford."

"You know this contract doesn't just protect my fragile feelings, it also protects you," Julian reassured me. "You can ask for anything and I'll make it happen, but the contract... it has to happen, or...I can't..."

"I know better than to suggest therapy," I said. "So let's take a look at the contract...for the rooms." Julian grinned and pushed one of the envelopes toward me. I grabbed the file and opened it. A puzzled look came over my face as I read. "This isn't my room."

"No it's not. It is a room that was done nine months ago and it's just not doing as well as we had hoped. I thought that perhaps you could bring your considerable expertise to bare and offer some helpful suggestions." Julian sat next to me "This room is called the Bachelor Pad. It's supposed to be a single man's room from the 50s or 60s with all kinds of electronic gadgets that come out of the walls or floor. You know, like the 'Space Race' mentality, the kind of thing that is supposed to impress the ladies and make them want to sleep with you. It worked for the first two months but I guess it lost its charm—I'm not sure why."

"Really?" I said with a smirk, "I shouldn't pass judgment until I see the room, so this is me being totally nonjudgmental. Based on what you have told me, I'm guessing that it lost its charm because it never had any. What do you say we go take a look at it, before I pass final judgment?"

In a most gentlemanly fashion, Julian held out his arm for me to take "Come with me, and thanks for holding your opinion until all the facts are in."

We made our way down the hall, arm in arm, and it felt nice, so nice that for a moment I couldn't remember where we were headed or why. The look of blissful obliviousness was noticed by Sam, who winked as we strolled passed him. Julian and Sam nodded in that manly way all men do. The purpose of our walk returned to me when we reached the door to the room known as the "Bachelor's Pad," the door that had a rhinestone-studded heart shape around the peephole. "Oh God," I said under my breath so quietly no human could hear.

*"No hasty judgments, remember?" How did he hear me? What does he have, bat ears?* Julian opened the door and turned on the light. Finally, I get to pass judgment. I have to give credit where

credit is due. The authenticity was amazing. It was like a time slip to a 50s, male, midlife crisis. If you think a 50s bachelor pad wouldn't be complete without a black leather couch, you would be right. The coffee table and two end tables look like they were designed by two guys sharing a doobie. There's wood paneling on the walls that could not have been easy to find.

Julian led me to the black leather couch. "Come sit with me," he said. I sat next to him, making myself comfortable, and watching him open a hidden panel in the arm of the couch. With one push of a button, the couch moved forward with us on it and the back dropped and we were suddenly sitting on a bed. The lights dimmed and the wall on the far side of the room turned to reveal a full bar.

I got up and went to the bar and was pleased to discover that it was fully stocked. I opened a bottle of wine while watching Julian press yet another button. The music started, and not just any music but Barry White, and the lights changed color in perfect rhythm. I poured myself a glass of wine, took a drink and put it on the bar. "Okay...I'm sensing a theme. The more cool toys, the better chance to score. I believe, I have figured out the problem. This room is a one-sided fantasy. If you'll pardon the terminology, it's a beaver trap waiting for an unsuspecting, gullible girl to walk in wide-eyed and waiting to be manipulated," I said bluntly. Maybe I've had more than my fair share of wine today.

Julian didn't say a word—I had left him speechless. I tried again, more tactfully. "Look, I'm sorry, but you wanted me to see the room and give an opinion. I can work with the place, but I'll need to know if you want to keep some of this stuff or can we erase the drawing board and start again."

"Maybe you can give me your ideas on how to fix it either way. A nip/tuck here and there or a complete do over," Julian suggested.

"I can if you don't want it right away," I told him, "It will take some thought, and I believe we have a date tonight."

"Agreed. You can think about it and let me know, but for the moment would you like to see your room?"

"Yes," I said. Julian took me by the hand and led me back to the hall to the room I was designing. On the way, we passed a number of the cleaning staff who were more interested in us than any work there. This made me ask "Why are people stopping and looking at us?"

"Because you're cute," Julian said.

"That's not it, what's going on?" I asked again.

"I suppose it's possible that they are staring at me. I'm walking in the hall, practically skipping, hand-in-hand with a beautiful woman. I'm happy. Or maybe it's just that I'm not wearing a tie...either way they are not used to seeing me like this. I guess it's not being professional. They see a change and want to know who did it?" Julian concluded.

"So you're telling me that you're professional all the time? Wow, that's no fun. So this is a shock to your crew here, to see a smile on your face. Do you think they like it or are they possibly scared?"

"I like to think that they are happy to see me happy, if that doesn't sound too corny," he said as he put his arm around my waist, which made everyone in the hall stop and stare. Their eyes followed us until we got to the room, and I felt better when we got inside. Once inside, I found what I was expecting, an unfinished room. The walls had a fresh coat of paint, but no murals yet, *and I was happy to see I got the bed I asked for. I need to figure out a clever way to camouflage the hot tub and big screen TV that you wouldn't find in the forest of Sleeping Beauty.*

"I have a file here," Julian said, "It has sample murals that you can go through to see if you find something you like. There are crowns and other accessories in there too if you think that we need them. As far as the murals go, we prefer to use the artists that work here first before we contract out to the public."

"That's not a problem," I said knowing Dawn could paint anything I wanted. I sat in the center of the floor and spread out each of the samples in front of me, the entire time under the watchful gaze of my employer. I could not tell if, in his mind, I was impressive or amusing. It was driving me crazy and I was grateful when Sam came in and told Julian there was an important call he had to take.

It was much easier to get work done with Julian out of the room—all that staring and ogling he was doing, and, admittedly, I was also doing out of the corner of my eye. I was matching mural samples to wall color and bedding and towels and carpet and fixtures for the bathroom. I would come up with great ideas and an hour later throw them out because they were pure crap.

My mind was drifting through the world of Sleeping Beauty—or the world as I perceived it at that moment—when a voice came from the other world. "Cat, I think it's time to stop," Sam suddenly said, making me jump. "You need to get ready for your date," I looked at my cell. I've been in this room for three hours?

"Okay Sam," I said, sounding like I was twelve, "Time to return from the fairy princess land to the two hundred and fifty dollars a night room. So, where's Julian?"

"Getting ready for the showdown tonight," Sam said with a smile that quickly disappeared when I glared at him. Apparently he forgot how I felt about our arrangement.

"Oh yeah. I guess I need to remember to bring my reading glasses and a pen with plenty of ink. Out of courtesy, I'll leave my lawyer at home." I could tell Sam was not appreciating my dry sense of humor. "So would you like to see my ideas on the room? That way you can tell me what

Julian might think since you know him way better than I do." Sam came and sat beside me and just listened to what I had planned, and when I was done reading all the sticky notes I had to translate because the handwriting sucked, I handed him the file.

"So what have you decided to do tonight?" Sam asked. I wondered how long he has been waiting to ask that.

"I'm taking your advice and dressing up."

"This should be fun to watch. "

"It should break up the monotony of being a mediator slash secretary," I told him. Bleeck! I *think I need a shower after the day I've had. I gather up my stuff. "See you tonight," I gave him* a quick peck on the cheek. "You know, I'm not sure why, but I feel safe around you like a dad or something."

"I feel the same way about you," Sam said, giving me a hug too. "Tell you what, tonight I'll throw you a wink if there's a good chance you'll get what you're asking for."

"Well aren't you just the sweetest little teddy bear. And here I thought you worked for Julian, not me." I gave Sam another kiss and was leaving when I turned back around "You know...an idea just hit me for another room...tell me what you think—Vampire."

"Excuse me," Sam choked.

"Vampire," I said again, "You know...like Dracula, or we could use Dark Shadows as a design idea."

"Are you serious?" Sam asked.

"Sure, why not?" I said, "Vampires are really in right now and who wouldn't want to be seduced by a dashing mysterious vampire with hypnotic eyes? I remember seeing that version of Dracula with Frank Langela. Wow! He can bite me anytime."

After a long pause Sam finally spoke up "So...write it up, and when you're done, give it to me. I want to watch Julian's face when he reads that one." Sam chuckled and I started wondering if he was just humoring me. Maybe this was a bad idea.

"Why," I asked, "Julian does go for the vampire vibe, doesn't he?" I was just guessing, but with the way he dresses, he looks like he could be auditioning for the mascot of the next vampire craze.

"I wouldn't say that." Sam said, "How do you feel about them?"

"Vampires? I fantasize, dream, and read about them like most women. Having a man in tune with your thoughts and feelings, and being more than just together—really together, blood and all—would be amazing." Sam was just sitting there smiling, watching me go off on a tangent about fictional monsters "Yeah, I get it, they're not real, but I can dream. Anyway, I better get going before I'm late for my date."

On my way home, I started thinking of that question about vampires. I dreamed of Julian as a vampire, but to be fair, I also dreamed of him as a pool boy. I had to laugh at myself. I read too many of Laurell K. Hamilton's books. Next, I'll be dreaming of Julian as a Fey and giving him magic.

My thoughts turned from vampires biting my neck to a date biting my neck. I knew I was going to need help if I wanted to be ready in time, so I grabbed the cell phone and called my wing man.

"Hi Cat," Dawn said in her perky voice.

"Hi. I need some help getting ready tonight?" I begged. "Please."

"I was waiting for you to ask." Dawn said. "My date starts at ten so I have time."

"Is it Kurt?"

"Yep."

"I'm almost there," I said, stopping outside the Stevenson Building. I ran to the building and up the stairs and met Dawn at my room. I took a fast shower and blow-dried my hair while Dawn laid out my dress and all the clothes for tonight, including the under garments.

"I have always wanted to do your eyes." Dawn said when I walked out in my bathrobe.

"Tell me you mean that and you're not just coming on to me," I said quickly.

"Hey, put it in park party girl. I just love you as a friend and a blank canvas. So what do you say?" Dawn said.

"Yeah, well, after all we been though the last couple of weeks the least I can do is let you express yourself artistically using my eyeballs. So go ahead and do the voodoo that you do."

"I wish I had more time," she said smiling at me. "Maybe next time, since I'm sure that there are going to be many more dates. So...subtle or slutty?"

"I'm thinking more on the subtle side. Don't want to frighten the man."

Once she started it was fun to watch, when I had my eyes open. Surprisingly it didn't take long, although it did look like it. "I have this lip stick that will look great on you," Dawn said when she was halfway out the door "Be back in a minute."

I went into the bathroom and put on a blood-red dress that tied around my body. When I bought this dress at Purple Moon in the mall, I admit I wasn't just thinking about how comfortable it was, or how easy it is to move around in. I was thinking about how easy it would be to put on a show, and how easy it would be to get out of.

# Chapter 19:

# Unwanted Company

I heard the knock on the door.

*She's knocking? She just barely left a few minutes ago. It is out of character for Dawn to* think she has to be polite and knock. "Come in Dawn, it's not like I locked the door behind you." Then I heard the door open, but I didn't hear Dawn rushing in here with the lipstick at the ready and telling me to pucker up.

"Dawn..." I asked uncertainly.

I heard the door close.

I heard the door lock.

"Dawn?" I questioned again.

"Hello Caprice," Daniel said.

I came from the bathroom to find Daniel standing in my room and locking the bolt lock of my door. The cold sound of the lock sent an equally cold shiver down my back. This is not good.

"Get out of my room Daniel," I said to sound brave and determined and ever threatening. It didn't work.

"Cat, we have to talk," he said with a nervous smile. "You...you look great by the way. Are you going on a date with your new boyfriend? Is he the one you're dressing up for?" Daniel sounded like he was trying to control his anger before it burst out of him.

"Yes, Julian will be here any minute. You need to leave Daniel," I said firmly.

"No, I don't think so," Daniel said with a frigid air in his voice. He was walking closer to me, stepping slow and deliberate. Soon he was right in front of me, staring, smiling, and frowning and the same time. I heard the doorknob rattling.

"Cat let me in," Dawn yelled, "What's going on?" Daniel turned and unlocked the door and Dawn pushed it open, but Daniel stopped it. Dawn took a quick glance at me and I mouthed help *me*.

"Dawn, Cat and I have some things to discuss," Daniel said in a matter-of-fact voice, as if we were still dating. Daniel slammed the door, but Dawn put her foot in the way. Only for a moment though, until Daniel kicked it out and pushed the door closed.

"I'm calling the cops." Dawn yelled through the door.

I didn't make a sound. I didn't move, but I wanted to. I wanted to run as fast as I could past Daniel and out the door. I could tell by the look on his face he had no intention of letting me run away from him, or run to Julian.

"I miss you," Daniel said, which turned my blood cold, "Cat, you will always be mine and nothing will keep us apart. You know I have been in contact with your parents. They like me. Your mom said that I had to show you that I still love you...that I want you back."

Before I knew it, Daniel was back in front of me and his lips brushed against mine. The taste was brief but bitter and left me wondering what he would try next. A single tear slid down my face. I don't know if he saw it, and if he did, I don't know if he cared. It probably made him feel proud, or worst...aroused. Either way he grabbed me by the hair and pulled my face close to his.

Then he said "I am sure that after a time I will be able to forgive you, Cat, for walking out and leaving me. But you must be made to understand that you are wrong and why you are wrong and why you must never leave me again."

"Are you fucking serious?" I practically screamed, "You broke up with me. You left me! Why can't you let me be?" I was shaking like a leaf and he knew it, but I needed to keep yelling.

I needed him to keep arguing to give Dawn time to come back with the police—just keep him talking.

"No!" Daniel shouted, his face turning red, "You can't...I never want to see you in...that club again. God! Dancing like a slut, like a whore in front of my friends, in front of strangers, dancing for that...man. That shit needs to stop and stop now," Daniel clenched both of his fists and turned from me, his breathing heavy but calm. "Do you have anything to say to me Cat, after everything you have done?" he said, ignoring every word I said. He had been childish and stupid like this before, never this angry. I had always caved and give him his way just to shut him up. Not this time. I was not the same person I was a week ago.

"Daniel, this is my home, not your home, not our home. There is not our home anymore. There is no us anymore. I did not give you permission to come into my room—I gave Dawn permission but not you, now get out of my room!" I was shaking more now, from head to toe, and the tears where flowing more when I noticed Daniel's eyes turn cold...ice cold. I was making him madder, and I knew what was coming next. He grabbed me, pushed me hard against

the door.

"You don't get it do you?" Daniel screamed angrily, "I can get to you any place any time. Nothing can keep me away from you." Daniel squeezed my arms tighter as if to emphasize the point. His eyes grew more lifeless as he looked at me. "How many times did you let that man fuck you?" He drew his hand back ready to hit me, and then slammed it into the door behind me.

"You let him put his hands all over you, but you belong to me. No one else can touch you. Do...you...understand?" he raised his hand again, only this time he didn't slap the door. The sound of his hand across my face echoed throughout the small apartment. He has hit me a couple of times in the past but as soon as I crumbled to the floor he would stop. I always thought it was my fault and he was always drunk, but this time I knew I did nothing wrong. I backed up and grabbed the only thing in reach, my backpack. I swung it at him. I think the shock that I even tried knocked him off balance more than anything. All it did was make him more enraged. This time he doubled up his fist and slugged me so hard I flew against the wall and crumpled to the ground.

The grin on his face was terrifying as he bent down to get a closer look at the pain he caused. He was like a wolf that could not only smell the fear but bathed in it. He reached out and wiped away the tears before grabbing my throat. Without even thinking I swung at him. My hand slashed across his face in an attempt to wipe the grin off his smug face. Daniel cried out in pain and fell back to the floor. I raised my trembling hand and saw the blood dripping from my fingers. The fingernails that drew blood from Julian's back in a moment of pure ecstasy drew blood from Daniel's face in a moment of pure anger.

Grabbing me by the hair, he pulled me up again until he could see the fear in my eyes and the blood trickling from my quivering lips. I tried to get the dizziness to go away after he pulled me up so I could fight him off. Then I saw his face there was no sympathy on Daniel's face when he looked at me, just a smirk before hitting me again with his fist. It sent me flying over my bed to the side of the wall. When I hit the floor I landed hard on my side...and on my phone in the pocket of my dress. I quickly pulled it out, hit the first number and left it on the floor just before Daniel grabbed me by the hair and pulled me up.

I choked on the blood in my throat and screamed "Help please! I'm at my apartment..." I don't know whose number I dialed. I don't know if they heard me, but Daniel grabbed for me again and I push off the bed to grab my pillow so I could block the next hit I knew was coming. He hit me before I could yell again.

I barely heard a pounding at the door above the ringing in my ears "The cops are coming,"

Dawn shouted through the door. "Let her go or I'll kill you before they get here!"

I staggered to the far wall trying to keep as much distance between us as possible, giving me a chance to breathe and him a chance to realize what he was doing and hopefully come to his senses. Then I saw Daniel's eyes and knew he would go to prison, be found insane, which he is, and be out in two years, free to find new women to obsess over. I would be dead. I'd never see Julian again. He would be alone.

"Caprice, I love you. Just hold on, help is on its way." That was Julian's voice. He sounded so worried...he sounded like he loved me...he sounded so far away.

"Caprice, get away from the door..." said more voices. The voices should know the door is the least of my worries. And then with a deafening crash the door burst off its hinges. The voices came rushing into the room, and they looked like Dawn and Julian's father. Dawn ran to me and Dominic ran to Daniel, pulling him away from me with enough strength that Daniel flew over the bed and came crashing to the floor.

First came the sound of breaking bones, followed closely by Daniel's cries of intense pain. Daniel managed to pull himself to his knees, then his feet, and fueled by stupidity and the adrenaline of anger, he took off after Dominic, screaming like a Banshee. Sam came rushing through the door next, ducking just in time as Daniel flew over his head and slammed into the opposite wall where he fell limp like a ragdoll.

"Oh Jesus, Cat, are you okay?" Dawn cried, "Please, honey, tell me you're okay." She grabbed a tissue and carefully pressed it to my mouth, dabbing off the blood.

"I'm...I...don't know," I stammered, still shaking. "I guess...I'm alright," I stammered. I looked over at Daniel. "That asshole wouldn't happen to be dead would he?"

"Unfortunately, honey, no," Dawn said "However, if all of you people can clear out of here for a few minutes, he will be. I promise it will hurt like a motherfucker."

I was considering Dawn's gracious offer, but with all noise we made, Campus Security showed up. Dawn went to talk to them, attempting to explain the noise, the blood, the dents in the wall, leaving me alone with Sam and Dominic. I couldn't stop shaking, even in the embrace of Dominic, who grabbed my blanket off my bed and wrapped it around me. When one of the campus cops approached me I backed up, a new found instinct. He stopped for a moment and then took another step forward and I took another step backward, pressing myself against the wall.

"I won't hurt you," this blond kid assured me. He seemed kind enough, he sounded sincere, and yet I found myself trying to back up through the wall.

The blond security guy, whose name tag read Brandon, was standing nearby not talking to me, while his partner, a dark haired kid named Phelps, was checking Daniel's pulse and scratching his head wondering who was responsible for his current condition. Dawn was talking sufficiently fast to confuse the security men while leaving out the details, which was working well until the real police showed up.

The first police officer through the door noticed me immediately, and when he started walking toward me, I moved behind Sam and he took a step back. "Ma'am, I just need to see if you're okay, if you need medical attention," he said calmly. I couldn't say anything. I just stayed behind Sam as I watched more people come in, more than there was supposed to be. People I didn't know started talking to me, but I couldn't understand them. In all the confusion, another officer came up from behind me and barely touched my arm. I screamed.

Everyone went silent. The police officer lifted his hands up to show he wasn't touching me.

"Leave her alone!" Dawn yelled protectively.

"This is my job, to get her help and to find out what happened?" the male police officer said.

"Your job!" Dawn shouted. "My friend Caprice here filed a report on the asshole out cold on the floor and the police didn't take the report because you said he didn't touch her. He has been following her all over town and the police said there was nothing they could do until he hurt her. Well guess what? Daniel did this and you could have prevented it. So right now you're not helping her, you're freaking her out. You need to back off and give her time!" Dawn said, daring the next person to speak and defy her.

Dawn was so enraged she had tears in her eyes. She sat next to me shaking as much as I was. She held out her hand, not taking mine but waiting for me to take hers. When I did, I held it tight knowing that Dawn would never hurt me. "Honey," Dawn said in a soft voice, "Can you tell the nice police officer what happened?"

With Dawn there looking over me, and Dominic, and Sam, I felt safer. I don't remember when I started talking, or why, it all came out like a robot without emotion. When I was done the cops had their story, they had Daniel, and Sam had a tear in his eye at my recount.

"We need to get her to the hospital," came yet another unfamiliar voice from the door. This short medic pulling a gurney headed in my direction. I must look pretty bad if he was coming for me instead of the unconscious guy on the floor lying there looking like a pile of dirty laundry.

Before the eager medic reached me, he was intercepted by Sam. "Do not try and touch her unless she's okay with it," he said in a low but intimidating voice. "Whatever you need to do, you need to ask her first and you need to explain everything you're doing and why.

Understand?"

While the tone of Sam's voice was subdued, it still captured everyone's attention and brought a halt to whatever they were doing. The momentary silence was broken by one of the braver police officers "Are we going to have to ask you to leave?"

There was no expression on Sam's face when he looked back at the police officer. I had no idea a blank stare could be so scary, and by the look on the cop's face, he didn't either. "Let me be clear. My friend has been traumatized, and you will not add to that trauma. You will take this slow or I will be contacting my lawyer."

"We are trying to help her," police officers said, "Now you want to bring an ambulance chaser into this?"

"My lawyers do not chase ambulances...they catch them," he said in a tone that made everyone around him scared shitless.

I was starting to feel sorry for the young medic. "Tell me sir," he said finally, "are you related to this woman?"

It was Sam's turn to hesitate this time. He turned to look at me and that's when I heard a voice in my head. *Let them believe Sam is your uncle, that way he can stay with you.* The voice I usually hear in my head is more paranoid and critical. This voice was not mine.

"He's my Uncle," I said meekly.

The medic gave a conciliatory nod to Sam, and Sam gave me a friendly smile. "Honey, I'm going to pick you up and move you to the bed so the medics can look at you, alright?" His arms wrapped around me and I grabbed for him and he picked me up and carried me to the bed, but when he laid me on the bed I couldn't—I wouldn't let him go. I hugged him and I didn't want to stop, because I felt safe.

"Okay honey, we're here," he whispered. I finally let go, too tired to hang on. He turned to the medics and police who were all just staring at him. "Remember, let her know what you intend to do before you do it," Sam reminded him with a glare.

I held my hand out to Sam and he took it, and squeezed it. They are not here to hurt you, *Caprice, let them help. Sam will not leave you.* Sam will not leave me. I knew that, but it wasn't Sam who said it. The unfamiliar voice was back. The voice was calming and reassuring, and the fog that plagued my brain cleared because the voice became familiar. I knew who it was. It was Dominic.

The next voice I heard was one of the medics talking. I'm not sure what he said, I really wasn't listening.

"I need to take your vitals," he said again.

Sam gave my hand another reassuring squeeze. "Let them examine you and I promise they won't hurt you." I knew they wouldn't hurt me, with an uncle the size of Sam standing over me like a guardian angel. I knew they would treat me like their grandmother's finest china.

While I lay there having my pulse taken and wounds bandaged, a thought came to my mind.

*Where was Julian? Why wasn't he here?*

Through a great deal of effort I managed to sit up. I wasn't supposed to, but I did anyway. I looked down at the blanket Sam had put around me, and regretted not staying on my back. After seeing all the blood, I wished I was unconscious. It only took a moment and I was.

◊

I had no idea where I was before I opened my eyes. I still had no idea where I was after I opened my eyes either. All I knew was I felt the same familiar sickness I felt when I was a kid, lying in the back seat of my parents' car on the long road trip to my aunt's mountain cabin.

Clearly I was in a moving car, but why were the other people in the car staring at me? "Cat, you're in an ambulance," Sam said, unable to hide the concern in his voice. "Dawn is calling your mom, and she and Geri will meet us at the emergency room."

I was strapped with my head stuck to something that was keeping me from moving or breathing comfortably, so it was difficult to get my next question out. "Where's Julian?" I finally managed to ask, "Is he here?"

"Julian and his father are on their way to the emergency room, sweetie," Sam said gently. I reached for his hand and he softly took it.

"Please don't let go," I asked before things started going black.

"You have my word..." was the last thing I heard Sam say.

Sam was as good as his word. When I woke up in the emergency room groggy as hell, I could still feel Sam grasping my hand as tightly as he had in the ambulance. Through a foggy haze I could make out that Sam was not alone. There were two figures standing near him, and one of them sounded like she was trying not to cry. The last time I heard that whimpering was when Geri broke up with a guy that had a flaming skull tattoo on the head of his penis.

"Hey, sweetie, how do you feel?" I heard Dawn suddenly ask.

"Like someone beat the shit out of me," I said throwing a smile out hoping it cheered them up, "How do I look?"

"Well, I've seen you look better," Dawn said with failed sarcasm.

"If you think I look bad you should see the other guy," I said teasingly. I was expecting a laugh, but instead Geri cried harder. "Come on, I can't look that bad? Where's a mirror? I need a mirror." If my appearance can bring one of my best friends to tears I needed to see before Julian did. I didn't need him running away screaming.

"I'm not sure that this is a good time, maybe in a couple of days," Dawn suggested. If they were trying to be reassuring, it wasn't working.

"Sam, will you give me a mirror?" I asked again, looking at him with what I assumed were black and blue puppy dog eyes.

"I agree with Dawn on this one," Sam said firmly, "But, if you really do want one I will find a mirror." With that, Sam stood there waiting for me to tell him to get one, but obviously hoping I wouldn't.

"Sam, I want to see what I look like, before he gets here, before Julian sees me like this," I said resolutely, but not feeling that way.

Sam could see the fear in my eyes, hear it in my voice "I assure you, Cat, Julian will not care what you look like, but if you really need to see yourself then I'll go get a mirror." He turned and walked out of the room as the one person I did not want to see right now walked in. I looked away when Julian stood beside my bed. I wanted to hide under the covers, retreat into another world like I did in my own bed in my apartment. The room went quiet.

Julian touched my arm. "Honey, are you going to look at me?" he finally asked.

"No, I can't," I said. I didn't want him to see me. I knew he knew what happened...and that it wasn't my fault. But if he sees me and turns away...I just couldn't take it.

Cat, can you hear me? I don't know where Sam was, but his thoughts were suddenly in my *head Believe me, nothing will change if he sees you. He is in love with you...no matter how you look...no matter what mask you wear...he will see only the true Caprice. He is here because he loves you and needs to know that you're going to be okay. As you know Caprice, I am aware of how you feel about Julian...you can't hide it from me...or from yourself anymore...* Sam's thoughts finished in my head.

*You know Sam...you can be a real rat bastard when it comes to the Jedi mind tricks. Yeah, I* know how I feel, I said with my own thoughts. Then I turned my head to look into Julian's eyes. He beamed and he bent to kiss me, but stopped.

"Can I kiss you?" he asked in a sweet, low voice.

"You better," I warned, and he followed my warning. The kiss was on my cheek which was good because my lips remained swollen. But, when he rubbed his face against mine I just wanted to grab him and ask everyone else to leave. It felt so good to have him touch me. When Julian heard Sam come back in the room, he pulled away. Sam's timing could have been better.

Sam had a mirror in his hand, but he hesitated before handing it to me. I reached out, and Sam placed it in my palms. I held the mirror and it reminded me of the small makeup mirror I use on the weekend. It felt so light resting in my palms. I just needed to turn it around and see what everyone else was seeing...just turn it around... Finally, as I found my courage, Geri reached out and grabbed one of my hands. "I think you can wait a couple of days. I mean Julian is clearly head over heels, and whatever is there will heal. You can wait," she said trying to persuade me against my actions.

"The police officers took pictures of me, but I didn't see them," I said stubbornly. "They're evidence, like me. But I did see how they looked at me when taking the pictures. I want...I need to know what they saw, what you see now but are too polite to admit." The room was silent, awkwardly silent, like everybody was waiting for someone else to say something. I took advantage of the momentary hesitation and turned the mirror around. The tears started and didn't stop. My eyes were black, both of them. I had a fat lip but I had guessed as much. The large black and blue bruises were probably the first thing people noticed, or perhaps my swollen nose that was as red as Rudolph's. My ears are the same brown color as my cheek, and just as painful. I reached up to touch my battered flesh, but suddenly moved my hand away as if it had been burned.

I now noticed my tears were getting my ugly hospital clothes all wet. Julian reached out and brushed them away, but they continued to fall like raindrops. The totality of what had just happened sank in, and I cried harder. Julian reached forward, encircling me with his arms, and gently pulled me to his chest just letting me cry in his arms.

I had no idea when all the others left the room, but I noticed they were gone when the nurse came in. I heard her clamoring around with a tray full of scary hospital crap. She turned around holding a syringe like it was a weapon poised for attack. She saw the less than confident look on my face and turned to Julian who shook his head before the nurse injected whatever was in the syringe into my IV. First I felt heat rolling over my body, which I hope like hell was normal, then I felt like I was floating around the room, like a cute little fairy with wings.

I may have been stoned.

"I feel weird," I said to Julian. "Is this what three days at Woodstock felt like?"

"No," Julian said. "That was...never mind. I really think that you need to get some sleep honey. You'll feel better and I promise I will be here when you wake up..." he said reassuringly. *I had no idea what Julian just said, but that's okay, I needed to get some sleep anyway. It will probably do me good...I hope Julian will be here when I wake up...*

*I'm hearing a voice soft, concerned, and yet still sexy. Am I still buzzed? "Caprice...Caprice* honey, can you open your eyes please?" came Julian's voice calling to me from the darkness. I seem to remember opening my eyes used to be so much easier. But with my eyes closed, I could see him, remember him, his wise and mysterious eyes, his wry smile that hid a world of secrets. I knew Julian was there and I really would like to see him for real, but my head was killing me and for some reason my face felt numb. Oh yeah, Daniel... "Caprice...love...please wake up..."

"Well, since you asked so nicely," I whispered. I slowly opened my eyes and felt a cold shiver race through my body...another strange room, not the place I started flying around like a fairy—this must be the place I landed. White ceiling, white walls, an antiseptic smell of death and nurses...I'm still in the hospital. My ugly hospital gown was replaced by a cleaner uglier hospital gown, but my IV accessory was still attached.

I moved my head around. It hurts when I move it too much, but I managed to see Sam looking as worried as ever, and next to him was Dominic looking more relaxed after throwing Daniel around like a bratty girl who got the wrong doll for her birthday. I gave them the best smile I could pull off before turning to see the one who had been holding my hand all this time.

When I managed a smile, Julian gently pulled me in and wrapped his arms around me, trying not to squeeze too tightly.

"Hello Caprice," Julian said.

"Hi," I responded meekly.

How do you feel? Dominic asked politely...but in my head, not aloud.

"Like shit. Why, how do I look?" I asked jokingly to the room.

"Excuse me," Julian said puzzled, then asked, "What?"

"I said I feel..." I began, and then stopped as I realized Julian's confusion at my statement.

Wait, was he talking to me? I heard...oh crap...Another meeting of the minds.

*I apologize for the intrusion, Dominic said again in my head.*

*Warning, I thought back in response. Maybe a telepathic knock on the door would be nice.*

*There could be sexual situations and adult language going on in my brain. Not a good time to waltz in unannounced.* Noted, Dominic replied respectfully.

How are you doing this? I thought finally, only because my curiosity overpowered my fear.

*An old family...secret, he replied. I am curious, has Julian attempted to communicate with you this way?*

*I think so...I can usually tell what he's thinking anyway. It's in his...body language. Does that count? Do you want me to try again? I asked Dominic.*

*Yes, just open your mind to let him hear your thoughts, Dominic said.*

*Okay, here goes...Holy Shit, I can't think of anything to say...I mean anything can pop into my head...I can't control it...What if I start thinking of stupid stuff like shopping at K-Mart or tampons? Oh God...what if he can hear me...How do I turn this mind shit off?*

"Relax my dear," Dominic said, "It takes practice."

I looked up at Julian...oh hell...who was looking at me with a smile on his face... A smile that says this young beautiful girl I have fallen for is off her rocker! I bet he picked up every embarrassing thought. Something he can remind me of for the next several years.

*Alright...Julian, I really would like a kiss but I'll settle for staring into those dreamy eyes of* yours. Julian bent over my bed with his hands on either side of my swollen face, and his eyes locked on mine looking deep like he was trying to see my soul. He then leaned forward and kissed me on the cheek...was it because he read my thoughts? I mean me wanting a kiss is kind of a given, and I always want to stare into his dreamy eyes any way. It doesn't take a mind reader to see that!

"So you think my eyes are dreamy, huh?" Julian whispered. I didn't know what to say. I was amazed and admittedly scared. A single tear fell from my cheek. I don't know why, I really don't. Julian reached out and wiped the tear away "Please don't cry...this is a happy moment."

"Well that answers that question," Dominic said. "She is of our blood."

*What the hell did he say? Did he say our blood like...are we related? Oh shit! Oh shit! Oh shit! We're like cousins or something. I've died and gone to the Jerry Springer show!*

*No, Julian and you are not related in...the way you think, Dominic reassured me.*

*Is this really happening? This isn't some party trick you can only catch on a late night talk show is it? Can all of you hear my thoughts, cause that makes me want to consider a lobotomy?*

Maybe this was just a dream, the kind of weird dream that freaks you out but you still want to stay asleep, just to see how it ends.

*It's not a dream, my dear. It's a gift, one that you have always had just never used...you needed to wait until you're ready.*

Now I know this is bullshit! I shouted. Well, I shouted in my mind anyway, does that count?

I then said aloud "You mean to tell me that I have always had the ability to read the thoughts of the geeks in my class who finish their tests in fifteen minutes and spend the rest of the hour trying to nonchalantly look down my shirt? I could have aced my way into thousands in scholarships instead of working for assholes. Don't tell me—that would be using my superhuman powers for personal gain instead of for the greater good, right?" Dominic's chuckle turned into a full heartfelt laugh, while Julian and Sam smirked trying to keep their laughter to themselves...it didn't work.

Julian ran his fingers through my hair and I closed my eyes wishing he would do it again and again. "I know you just woke up, but you need to get some rest," he said. "I will be here while you sleep and when you're awake." I decided to close my eyes, clouding my mind with thoughts of counting sheep instead of naked Julian's running their fingers through my hair. Eventually, sleep found me.

Later, I opened my eyes to find Sam asleep in what looked to be an uncomfortable chair. Julian was in my hospital bed lying next to me, his arm wrapped lightly around me like he was trying to protect me from the world outside. I didn't want to wake them...I enjoyed watching both men sleep— like protective guard dogs you don't want to wake because they look so cute.

I pondered my present situation as the darkness of night moved into dawn through the window. It was a glorious escape from all that had happened. I found myself truly inspired... something inside me had woken up. I let my fingers dance and glide across the skin of Julian's arm, and what poured out from the depths of my soul was pure magic. Julian is magic to me. It is in this heightened state of euphoria I realized I had only been keeping Julian at arm's length...

I love stepping into a place where time and space blur and are faded into the distance of where my dreams take me. It is that lovely place where all things are possible, and my imagination is filled with inspiration of what our life could be together. My thoughts drip into my fingertips and slide into

Julian's flesh, where he can read them. This new found realization tastes so sweet...Sleep my love, Julian said in my head as I escaped once again to dream land.

# Chapter 20:

# Meeting Family

Wow! That was a weird ass dream. Jesus, did the nurses slip a mickey in my IV again, or sprinkle magic mushrooms in my tapioca? Against my better judgment I began to wake up, with the help of someone pushing and poking me towards consciousness. I thought I could pretend to still be asleep in hopes that they would go away, until they started talking. I recognized the voice. I used to pretend to still be asleep every morning before school, but I could never fool her.

"Hi, honey," I heard my Mom say in her oh-so-sweet-voice. I'm not saying it was the sound of her voice that made my head feel like it was going to explode—it could just easily have been the way I jerked my head around to see her standing there. "I want this man out of this room right now," she said as my eyes rested on her. Yeah, that's my mother. Isn't she a ray of sunshine? She has the superhuman ability to embarrass the shit out of me, both with her attitude and her appearance. I'm laid up in a hospital bed and she is here in her blue jeans that are one size too small, ten years out of fashion for her age, with a way too tight shirt. I don't mind the heavily dyed hair style pulled back off her face with curls in the back. Lots of women have the long finger nails, and probably colored toes too, but her attempt to look younger is a failed experiment in my opinion.

When I turned to see Sam, I smirked just to let him know that he shouldn't take her too seriously—I never do. "Hey," Sam said smiling back, "How are you feeling?"

"Like someone beat me up." I said, "Thank you for helping me."

"Cat, are you listening to me?" my mom said.

Here is a brief history on she who calls herself "Disappointed Mom." Besides her unhealthy obsession with the illusion of youth, she is a strong-willed woman who firmly believes that it's her way or...well...no way or...just her way, and if that creates problems in the long run...oh well, just get over it. She has expectations about how people, all people—family, friends, strangers—should live their lives in predictable patterns. She sets the example of predictability in her own relationships. Boyfriend, husband, ex-husband, new boyfriend-repeat—not a good atmosphere to raise a child in. I have three other half-sisters and half-brothers, all from different fathers, but just one overbearing mother. We can and have considered starting our own support group.

"Is this the new boyfriend Daniel was talking about?" Mother squawked. Frankly, I really was not in the mood for her and didn't give a damn if she liked Daniel. "If you had gone to the school your stepfather is teaching at this would have never happened," she scolded, as if I had planned on getting the hell beaten out of me. It's always a stepfather. Does my Mom even know anything about my biological father? All she ever told me was a name. You really can't make a father out of a name, can you?

"If God would have seen fit to castrate Daniel with a lightning bolt, this never would have happened," I finally replied in frustration.

"Daniel was your boyfriend...he cares about you," Mom said with a straight face as if I deserved this.

"Are you fucking kidding!" I screamed.

"Caprice, watch your language," she said ignoring me completely.

"Watch my language? Are you fucking serious?" I looked her straight in the eye, which I used to be afraid to do. "Daniel is the reason I'm in here. Look at my face Mom, look close...the fat lip, the bruises, he did that to me! He did that to your daughter!" I said in fury.

Anyone with a shred of decency could have picked up the frustration and sadness in the room. Naturally Mom didn't, but Sam did. "I know we've never met, but Caprice has been through a lot and she doesn't need this right now," Sam said politely but sternly. "I'm sure her doctors would agree," he said with a note of finality in his voice, and it was kind of scary.

Wow, look at Sam standing up to her, standing up for me. Good luck. I remember asking my Grandma if she was always this difficult, and she said only during high school, after she hung out with the "wrong" crowd. I guess there were drugs and alcohol involved since Grandma said she just wasn't the girl she raised. Of course my mother had a different version of her youth, but I never could believe her. In her mind the fault was always someone else's, never hers. Unless she gets a visit from the ghosts of childhood past, I don't see her changing any time soon. I really just want her to keep her life to herself and let me keep mine.

"I am Mrs. Jessica Smith, Cat is my daughter and you have no relation to her so you need to leave this room right now," she said coldly.

"Well Mother, let me introduce you to the person who is as good as my family here," I said angrily. "This is Sam, the man who saved me from Daniel beating me to death. I feel safe around him, more so than all those 'stepfathers' I have had to put up with—got it!"

My mother looked at me with a complete lack of sympathy. "Oh Caprice, you're exaggerating about stepfathers and I'm sure about Daniel too," she said this as if being in a hospital bed was a normal part of relationships, and as though I hadn't spoken.

Thankfully, Mom didn't hear the fuck you that I screamed in my head, but I know Sam did. The short cough I heard from him wasn't a cough as much as it was a suppressed chuckle. If my mom could hear thoughts like me, we would be fighting for the next twenty years about the last twenty years, and my head hurt too much for a knock down drag out fight right now. I kept my mouth shut, looked away, and hit the nurse's button under the blanket. I noticed Sam staring at my mom, but not with anger, with rather a mild curiosity.

"This may be presumptuous of me Caprice, but may I ask who your real father is, or do you know?" Sam asked with hesitation in his voice. I looked at my Mom and knew she had to put her two cents in before I could answer that question.

While Sam may have hesitated in asking me the question, my mother had absolutely no problem in responding quickly. "It's none of your damn business." I didn't have to rely on mindreading tricks to know that was exactly what my Mom was going to say, but I was curious why Sam was asking.

"His name is Wyatt McGill," I told him verbally, not mentally. "Talbot is the last name of my first stepfather. He adopted me when I was three."

"Wyatt Edward McGill?" Sam asked with a serious tone that got my attention and my mother's too.

"Yes...Do you know him?" I asked him in a soft voice. My mom suddenly got really quiet while waiting for him to answer the question.

"Do you know where he is from?" Sam asked, looking from me to my mom.

Sam just gave my mom an excuse to vent, not that she ever needed one. "He is from Lava Hot Springs, the bastard. I haven't heard from him since he found out that I was pregnant and then told me he had a business trip." My mom's arms were flailing around like a fly was buzzing around her head. "He said he would be back in a week, but never came back."

When I was younger the only information my mom offered up on my birth father was his name—that's it. So it turns out that Julian's family are from Lava Hot Springs and Sam too. And now the father I never knew comes from the same place.

The question of my parentage came to a stop when a blue-eyed, blonde-haired nurse walked into the room wearing Winnie the Pooh scrubs. She must have come from maternity—I liked her. "Hi I'm Meg." The room was silent, all eyes on the nurse. "Umm, there are flowers at the front desk for you, but no one knew if you're allergic or not." I waited for half a second to let my mom field that one. Nothing.

"I'm not allergic," I said, "Can I get something for the pain?"

She took out the blood pressure cuff and put it around my arm and gave me the required nurse smile. "I'll check with the doctor and see what you can have." When the cuff was through squeezing my arm in half, she put a thermometer in my mouth. "Are you hungry?" she asked me while checking the reading.

"Not so much," I mumbled, trying not to spit out the thermometer.

"Well, everything looks good here, but if you want to get out of the hospital you need to keep food down," Nurse Meg said.

"I'll eat," I said realizing it will be so much easier to run from my mother when I'm not wearing the ugly hospital clothes.

"Good girl," she said, sounding like she was still in maternity. She opened the door in an attempt to leave, but was blocked by a large vase of flowers and an oversized Winnie the Pooh bear. The flowers and bear stepped aside to allow the nurse to leave and then found their way to the table beside me. I had to smile—Julian knew me so well. My mom was smiling. She doesn't know Julian at all, but by the way she is looking at him, she wanted to, intimately. This scenario is so familiar to me and so is the look in her eyes. It's the same look she gave my last stepfather and the one before that...and the waiter at the pizza place where I had my ninth birthday party. I guess it's too much to hope that she will remember she is married before bending over to pick up the handkerchief she pretends to drop.

During my momentary lapse into the fantasy world where Carol Brady was my mother, Sam took my hand, but he was tense, I could feel it. I don't think the tension was because of my mother. I think it was at Julian's sudden presence. Sam had not taken his eyes off Julian since he entered.

"Hi honey," Julian said as he bent to give me a light kiss on the cheek. I guessed the smile on his face was more for my benefit—his way of hiding the pain of seeing me here like this.

Even with my mom here I wished Julian would give me the kind of kiss you feel all the way to your toes...the kind of kiss that declares to all other women in the room "Yes, he is mine, we're together, and stay the fuck away."

"Mom, in case you haven't guessed, this is my boyfriend Julian," I said, "Julian...Mom."

"You can call me Evelyn," she said, smiling for the first time.

We needed to get back on topic before Mom tries to slip her phone number into Julian's back pocket. Sam was still holding my hand, but he wasn't looking at me. He was looking in the corner, staring at nothing. I asked "So my dad...Sam, please tell me, do you know him?"

"Sam, what's going on?" Julian asked, looking from me to Sam and back to me.

Sam hesitated like he was searching for the right words. "I know who Caprice's birth father is...it's Wyatt." There was a look on Julian's face I have never seen before. Shock, clearly, but there was something else.

"Really," Julian said, "Are you sure?"

"I felt a connection to her but I thought it was...." Sam suddenly ended.

There is more drama going on here than anyone is letting on. "Can someone tell me what's going on?" I asked in frustration, "Someone tell me." Sam looked into my eyes, and then finally said plainly "Caprice, your father is...my brother."

"He was my...he was...your...who?" I was...well, stunned doesn't seem adequate. Wyatt and Sam are brothers? "Wait, Sam is actually my uncle?"

My mother, not wanting everyone to forget she was there in the wake of our conversation, had to remind everyone why she had earned her bitch title. "That can't be. Wyatt is white and you're not." There are many abilities beyond my mother's grasp—tact is one of them.

Sam had to force back the bitter taste of my mother's naive prejudice. "My mother is white. My father is black. Wyatt is my half-brother," he said slowly and deliberately. His acidic tone was not lost on most of those in the room, but dear old Mom still had a blank stare. Sam decided to press forward "I have some questions to ask you Mrs. Smith. Maybe it would be better somewhere else." He tightened his grip on my hand before letting it go and walked to the door and held it for my mom. I was expecting my mother to put up some resistance, to keep up the façade that she was in control and doesn't do anything unless it's her idea, but she left without saying a word. Sam is a true miracle worker.

Mom left the room, and Sam was about to follow when he stopped. He knew I wanted to ask something, like I was wearing a question on my face.

"Sam..." I began.

"Yes sweetie," he said expectantly.

"Where is my birth father?" I asked, not sure I wanted to know the answer.

Julian took my hand, saying nothing. Finally Sam said, "Wyatt was...killed in California,"

However, the question I was wearing was still there. How? Sam answered "It was just a case of being in the wrong place at the wrong time. He was on a business trip, and was supposed to return later that week, but...he didn't. Wyatt did tell me that he had gotten a girl in town pregnant and was planning on marrying her, but never told us her name. None of us knew he was in a relationship. After Wyatt died we tried to find your mother but...couldn't."

He stopped. Sam didn't want to continue the story when he saw a tear running along my cheek. It was perfect timing when Nurse Meg came in caring two pills and a glass of water, a feast fit for a future manic depressive. Sam winked at me encouragingly as he closed the door after Nurse Meg left the room.

Julian and I were alone. I took my pills and drank my water. I frowned for a second or two and then cried, cried for the father I never knew. He didn't leave my mom, he died. My mom had said all these bad things about him for years, making me feel like I was abandoned...it was all a lie. Julian just held me tight, his shirt soaking up all the tears shed for someone I will never know, but who wanted to know me. "Wyatt would never abandon you," assured Julian's voice in my thoughts.

"I have so many questions." I told Julian while he graciously wiped my tears away. "Sam has all the answers. Did you know Wyatt?"

"Yes, Sam's mom and my mom are really good friends, more like sisters. We all grew up together. I knew your father very well," Julian said kindly.

It goes without saying that this was not the time or place for math. So of course I started thinking, if I'm twenty-three and let's say Wyatt was about nineteen, which would make Julian in his forties. Wow, how old is he...?

"Your grandmother is still alive," Julian said quickly, strategically interrupting my train of thought concerning our age difference.

"Really, does she know about me?" I asked.

"Yes, she does. When Wyatt died, his mother searched tirelessly for your Mom. She looked everywhere and hired a private detective." I feel like I have been caught in a twisted family reunion. My mom shows up for the sole purpose of pissing me off, and I find out that I have an uncle with a patriotic name who I secretly thought of as kind of hot. I need a drink.

Me too, Julian thought.

"Oh God, did you hear..." I asked.

"Yes," he said.

"Even the part about..."

"Yes," he said again.

"Our secret?"

"Our secret."

There was a welcomed knock on the door and Julian's father Dominic walked in with flowers "Hi Caprice, how are you feeling?"

That was an outstanding question. Let's review. I hurt in more places than I know. I just found out that my boyfriend was old enough to be my father, but Sam's my uncle, that's a  positive. My birth father was killed before I was born. Let's see...oh yeah, my mom wants me to go back with the guy who beat the shit out of me.

"I'm fine," I said dropping my head back on the pillow. I'm anything but fine right now and I'm sure they were aware of it. Then I heard a chuckling in my head.

You can't lie to me, Dominic's voice echoed in my head, Now let's see if you can talk back to me, and just think what you want to say to me...

Can Julian always hear my thoughts? I asked, looking at Julian and smiling like I was innocently asking about the weather.

No, only when you really want him to. However, in time he will always be able to hear you.

I'm still not sure how I felt about that.

You're a kind girl Caprice...your grandmother can't wait to meet you.

"I appreciate the sentiment," I said. "But we are getting off topic."

Your father had many gifts and it looks like you have some of them too. Dominic said.

Before he could explain further I could feel the meds Nurse Meg gave me kick in and I became very tired Just rest, we can talk more later, and I'll answer all your questions.

There exists a realm somewhere between the world of the awake and the world of those who are asleep. When you're in this realm, you feel like you are drifting between the other two. When you think you might be asleep you hear things like "Father, I want her, I can take her pain away," and "My love, I love you," and you wish you were awake.

There are times when you are sure you are awake and you hear, "I love you too," and once you realize you are the one who said it and you don't know why, you hope you are asleep and dreaming. It had to be these kick-ass pills.

Rays of beautiful early morning sunshine made their way between the blinds of my hospital room and straight to my barely opened eyes to remind me of a new day and also that I had one hell of a headache. I took a few swings at the sunlight to make it go away, but that didn't work. This was probably because Julian was still holding me securely in his arms. I can't tell if he is laughing or irritated.

"Hi Love, you're awake," he said softly.

"Unfortunately. Where's what's her name?" I asked.

"The one that gave you birth?" Julian questioned.

"That's the one," I said dazedly.

"She was here," Julian said." She kept checking on you, she kept arguing with the doctors and nurses, as well as complaining that your being here was your own fault and not Daniel's."

"And where is she now?" I was hoping he was going to say gone.

"She's gone. Every time she came in she saw Sam. As much as she wanted him out of the room, she realized he wasn't going to leave you...so she did," Julian said with a note of humor in his voice.

"Sam deserves a raise...can you see to that?" I insisted.

"Of course," Julian agreed. "Is there anything else I can do?

"I want to get up," I whispered, not wanting to wake Dominic who was still asleep on a corner cot. I was too eager to wait for Julian to help so I swung my legs off the bed and braced myself on the nearest table, which I just remembered is on wheels. Julian moved fast enough to catch me, and I mean fast, but I wasn't fast enough to catch the specimen cup that hit the floor with a resounding crash. The good news is that the cup was empty. The bad news is that Dominic was no longer sound asleep.

"Maybe we should ask the nurse if it is okay for you to take a stroll," Julian suggested, pushing the call button.

Nobody gets it—I have been lying in this bed for hours and hours, getting poked and prodded by nurses and doctors instead of my hot boyfriend. I need a road trip, even if it's to the local vending machine, or my bathroom where I can get some alone time. As much as I appreciate the concern behind all those eyes watching my every move, I really think some "me time" could be therapeutic. I hope no one will be offended if I ask them not to follow me. That way I can sit semi-comfortably, grab some toilet paper and make a list of questions and concerns.

One, ask the doctor what works and what doesn't? Two, is Daniel sharing a cell with a leather-bound Satan worshiper who is not afraid to show his feminine side? Three, can I get the complete biography on my father and grandmother from Sam? Four, can I continue with school without begging for a tutor from the nearest grade school to help me with my studies? Five, the contract —the elephant in every room that Julian and I are in. If I sign it, which I am tempted to do, can I add a clause that requires Daniel to stay at least three planets away from me? Yeah, I probably can't put that into a legally binding document, but a girl can dream can't she?

My imaginary list was interrupted by a knock on the door. "Good morning, my name is Monica, your nurse on call for today until Meg arrives later. I am here to make you comfortable. If you need anything just give me a buzz. Would you like to take a shower or a sponge bath?"

"I'd love to give you a sponge bath or we can take a shower together." Thankfully this offer came from the mind of Julian and not the nurse. He looked at me with a smile and a blush when he picked up my thoughts of how much I would like him to join me in the shower with a really big loofah. Sam remained quiet, giving no hint at all if he was eavesdropping on our shower scene. Maybe he's just sorting out his feelings about his brand new, fully grown niece. And while we were all deep in various thoughts, Nurse Monica was still talking. "...and your doctor will be in at nine to check on you. So how are you feeling today?" The perky brown-haired, brown-eyed girl finally took a breath, waiting for me to answer. Before I could say anything, I had a thermometer in my mouth and a blood pressure cuff in a death grip on my arm.

"Knock, knock..." Geri said before coming in the room with an arm full of balloons and another Winnie the Pooh. You can never have too many Winnie the Pooh.

"Where's Dawn?" I asked.

"She really wanted to be here," Geri said "She had a test today in her Economics class. You remember how much of an asshole Professor Adehlson has become since it was pointed out to him that his toupee wasn't fooling anybody—there's no way he was going to let her make it up."

"Well," Monica asked again, "What about the shower?"

"A shower sounds soooo good. Better if I can take it on my own," I stated. I can see the dilemma on Nurse Monica's face. Her Nightingale oath probably tells her that she has to watch her patients splash around in the tub to prevent injury, but she can probably tell by the look on my face that if I have to have someone in there with me, I'd rather have Julian as my lifeguard.

However, at this point I'd rather not have Julian, or anyone else see me in the buff until I know how bad the damage is.

I have high hopes that the sound of water jetting out of the shower and hitting my head will drown out the sound of the voice in my head, a girl's voice. He is so hot—I so want to jump his bones...what am I thinking he's not interested in me... I can't blame Geri for what she is thinking, but I need to learn to control the way I use my brain like a toothpick—picking crap out of other people's minds. Every time we walk past a bevy of babes I'm going to hear a chorus of he's hot, I want him, and can he lose the bitch he's walking with?

You can imagine how surprised I was once I realized that her thoughts of lust were not directed towards my beau, but towards Sam. She likes Sam...she really likes Sam!

I did not see that coming, but it's kind of cool. I decided to shoot her a thought of encouragement. Why don't you ask him out? My timing could have been better. Geri was taking a sip of the Coke and ended up spitting it out all over the floor. Yeah,

Sam will find that attractive, I mused to myself this time.

Geri was staring at me, not realizing she just spit on Nurse Monica's shoes. Oh my God, she thought. You heard me, and then talked to me in my head. You're one of us... One of us? That's unsettling, from a friend. I'm waiting for everybody in the room to start chanting "one of us...one of us..." If the nurse joins in, I'm leaving. I have been told that I am 'of the blood' Geri, but I don't understand it. Do you know Julian and Sam?

Julian is my cousin and Sam is a friend of the family.

Well shit. Geri noticed the look on my face, and feared it as well as she should. Before I called our friendship into question, Nurse Monica spoke up. "I'm going to get some towels for your shower and my shoes. I do have to be close by while you're in there in case something happens." She left the room. Time to verbally ask some questions.

"Julian is your cousin and you didn't tell me. You didn't think that was something Dawn and I would want to know?" The question was more forceful than I had intended, but this was big news for me and Dawn.

"That's why I didn't tell you, you'd freak, and guess what...you did." Geri said. I can understand that and I think I would have not dated Julian if I knew it would be like dating your friend's brother...so not going to happen.

"Again, that's why I never told you," Geri said, continuing to read my thoughts. There has got to be a way to block my thoughts from them all.

Supernatural drugs, keeping some annoying song sung by an annoying puppet from an annoying kids show stuck in my head. I so needed a break from my life. There was a knock on the door that raised my hopes, but it was just another doctor, at least, as far as I know. I have never met him but everyone in the room was cordial like they have met, probably while I was out cold.

"Hello, how is my patient doing today?" he asked. He seemed nice and casual in his blue jeans, plaid shirt, a belt with an enormous buckle that has a picture of a guy on a bucking horse, and to complete the western ensemble, cowboy boots. I bet there is a cowboy hat on the hat rack in his office. If it wasn't for the lab coat I'd have thought he took a wrong turn at the rodeo. The long gray hair in a pony-tail made him look like a wise old medicine man from the movies.

"The last time we met you remained unconscious, so let me introduce myself. I'm Doctor Frederick Jensen. I have been the family doctor for Dominic and your grandmother for a long time. Dominic brought me in after you came to the ER. Then your grandmother called me after talking to Sam. If you have a problem with this please let me know now."

I looked over at Julian who gave me a nod. I turned back to the doctor. "If Julian trusts you, that's good enough for me," I told him plainly.

"Good," he started thumbing through the chart he had in his hand, "How is your head?"

"I have a headache," I said, not knowing if it was from Daniel's rampage or from the flood of family history I have been bombarded with in the last twenty-four hours. I needed to talk to the doctor without everyone in the room.

"I'd like to have some privacy so I can examine Caprice," Dr. Jensen said. Wow, just like that. Let's try that again. I need Johnny Depp's phone number...Nothing...Well, give it time.

Geri was the first out the door. "I'll be right out here if you need me," she said. Yeah, I'll bet. She knows I'm pissed about her withholding vital gossip, and since she has always believed there is no problem that can't be solved by sprinkles on a donut...I'm guessing that she will be in the cafeteria looking for the bakery section.

Julian did the quick reassuring grip of my hand before letting go and reaching for the door. I could hear his quiet thoughts. If you need me just think of me and talk...Don't worry, Dr. Jensen can be trusted. I'll be right outside the door on my phone trying to find Johnny Depp's number.

My smile hurt a bit, but it was worth it.

Sam was not so easy to get out of the room. He just sat in the chair not wanting to leave, like he didn't trust the doctor. However, Dr. Jensen said, "Sam your mother asked me to come and see her, that's why I'm here. I will be gentle. She will be fine with me and if she needs you she can pop right in your head and call to you." Holy shit, how many people know about this mind chat thing? That must be why they asked for the country doctor to be here.

Sam got up and gently kissed my forehead. "Don't be afraid to contact me if you need me, I'm just a thought away." He is so sweet, like the dad I never had.

"Can you keep the door open so you can hear everything?" I asked Sam. I knew I wanted to talk to the doctor alone, but the thought of being alone in the room with a man I just met was scaring me. He was not Daniel. He was a doctor who helps people—who helps my family. And no matter how many times I said that, I still wanted the door open.

"Just keep the link open. I can hear your thoughts and will be in the loop," Sam said. It helped.

"So doc," I said, "Tell me what's wrong with me."

"You got beat up by an asshole," he said bluntly. "However, I'd like to try something—just bear with me..." And just like that he was in my head too. This is too weird. I'm sure there has to be a capacity limit on the number of people running around in my private thoughts. If you can hear me, lift your left arm up, Wasn't there a scene like this from an old Frankenstein movie? I exhaled and lifted my left arm like a good little monster. Interesting, can you talk to me?

Okay, here's a curve ball. Why doesn't Sam like you? I asked. I could hear Sam grumbling outside.

Dr. Jensen hesitated before answering I'm married to your grandmother, which I guess means I'm your grandfather. Sam is still trying to get over the fact we are married, but after ten years you think he would realize I'm staying around for the long haul.

Oh my fucking God. Are you kidding me? They write shit like this for soap operas. I can't wait for Nurse Monica to come back in and say "Hi cousin how's your headache?"

Dr. Jensen could see my exasperated frustration and decided to employ some bedside manner. Well...granddaughter, "I know this is overwhelming, and we probably should have waited until you're stronger before laying all this on you."

"Yes, you should have," I said aloud. "You could have waited until I was discharged and given me the medical bill just to soften the blow." Dr. Jensen backed up when I took a deep breath. "Moving on...So what's the prognosis?" I queried.

"Well, you have a concussion and bruised ribs, but most of the cuts are superficial and the bruises will go away in time." He said then stopped and looked at me, "Listen, if I had known you're my granddaughter I would have never treated you in the first place, or...I don't know, maybe I'd have gotten here sooner. This is just as new to me as it is to you." He looked at me up and down. "This," he said waving his hands, "All this will heal in time, but to be honest, I worry more about your mental state of mind. Sam and Julian are as well. I really think you should talk to Emma."

"Who the hell is Emma?" I ask, five minutes from utter exasperation at learning more family secrets.

"She is Julian's sister, and she's a physiologist," he said simply.

"Of course she is," I said, "If she's Julian's sister she probably knows I'm fucked up in the head. Why doesn't she just use some kind of Vulcan mind-meld to fix me?"

"I don't think..." Dr. Jensen began.

"Wait," I said curiously, "Why are you worried about Sam and Julian?"

"When you were assaulted by Daniel, Sam and Julian both had a psychic connection to you—they felt what you felt," Dr. Jensen said, "That kind of emotional trauma will stay with them for a long time. Please give them time. I have no doubt that it will be a long while before they will let you out of their sight again."

# Chapter 21:

# The Test

"I did the blood work and you are Sam's niece and my granddaughter. Julian on the other hand is a friend of my family so if you don't mind my asking, how do you feel about him?"

*Oh shit, he wants me to know what I think of Julian. Everything I think of Julian? All of the...Julian with his big...me without any...Oh crap! And just like that I locked my grandfather* out of my X-rated head. He smirked at me. He knew. I blushed.

"I don't know if I love him or not," I said in a low voice like I was trying to save face. "But I do feel something for him...something strong considering the short time I have known him."

"Well, Dorothy will love you," the doctor said.

*This next thought went out to everybody. Now who is Dorothy? Somebody please tell me that Dorothy is not the Dorothy, the one from Oz who I pretended to be on a stage in front of a bunch of horny horn dogs?*

Sam was quick to chime in. "She is your Grandmother."

"Oh...okay. Could everyone who didn't know, forget the Dorothy on stage thing?"

"Also," Sam continued, "Dominic has talked to your teachers and you have two weeks off to recuperate. They will send you your homework."

"Thank you," I said, "and all my teachers agreed to this?"

"I'm sure they did, Dominic can be persuasive." Dr. Jensen said, "By the way, your grandmother wants you to come home with us to stay so she can get to know you and we can help you recover. I believe both Sam and Julian have different plans for your recuperation, so the question is, do you want to stay in the hospital for one more day to get more rest or do you want to be released? Keep in mind that if you are discharged, you will need to stay with someone for a couple of days due to the concussion, and you will be in pain for the first three days. It should get better after that."

"So how long will it be before I feel better?" I asked. "You know, walking without a limp, looking in the mirror without screaming?"

"Two, maybe three weeks if..." then he stopped, as if he was listening to something in the distance he was straining to hear. "So would you like to stay with your grandmother during your recovery?"

"I don't think Sam or Julian will like that...and I don't really know my grandmother or you well." That was my polite way of saying I wanted to go back to my dorm room. It's small but I can be my own miserable self and not pretend to be fine when every square inch of my ass hurts.

"I don't want to meet my grandmother looking like this. I want her to like me."

*Your Grandmother is usually nice and at times cantankerous, Sam explained. She is particular about the ingredients she puts in her homemade dishes, but not about family. She will like you. But all things considered I do want you to stay with me. We have rooms at the Inn and this way we can keep an eye on you. We can have Geri stay if you want.*

Sam, it wasn't your fault, he heard my thoughts...I know he did, but I just don't know if he *believed them. If you and Dominic hadn't gotten there when you did, things could have been...*

Sam kept quiet so I turned back to the doctor.

"What do I call you?" I asked. I have never had a grandfather...my mom's dad died before I was born. My grandma, Hazel, has been gone for a long time too. I miss her so much.

"You can call me grandfather or Fred or Doc...it's up to you but I like grandfather the best, maybe grandpa." Grandfather said. "Grandpa sounds like I'm old...Grandfather sounds like I'm old but wise."

"Well Grandpa-father-doc, as much as I enjoy hot and cold running IVs, and nurses watching me pee, I believe I'd like to take my leave of this establishment. I think I feel better staying with my uncle Sam at the Inn for now if that will be okay." I tried not to think of the hot and cold running Julian that will also be at the Inn. Instead, I focused on how safe I always feel around Sam, before I knew him as Uncle.

"I'll get your discharge papers, but I wanted to mention that there is something I can give you to help you recover faster if you would you like to try it?" I know I could feel the tension from Sam in my own mind as if it filled the whole room. I wonder if anyone else felt it. "If you want to try it ask Sam or Julian and they can get ahold of me. And don't worry, I will talk to your grandmother and explain why you didn't want to stay, I'm sure she will understand."

I haven't met Grandma Dorothy yet, but I could tell that she had the ability to reach out across great distances to make me feel guilty. Is this some special power that all grandmothers have? Since I wanted to feel safe and not feel guilty about wanting to feel safe, I needed Sam and Julian. Sam, Julian, you can come in, I thought at them, and there they were.

"As I am sure you know, Caprice has decided to stay with you two." He cleared his throat before continuing, trying to cover his disappointment with an authoritarian voice in search of sympathy. "This means you have to keep a close eye on her, take her temperature, watch what she eats, and just be nearby." Then the doctor turned to Sam. "I on the other hand have to deal with your mother. As a consolation, you have three days to get her to Lava to meet Dot or there will be hell to pay, and you know I am not exaggerating. Three days." Once again I was wearing my confused face. "Dot?"

"My mother's nick name, everyone calls her that." Sam said. Then, yet another knock sounded on the door and Geri came back in with a sprinkle covered donut in hand. It was funny the way she snuck it to me without the doctor noticing.

Accepting the donut was like accepting her apology for leaving me out of the events of my own life. I accepted the donut with grace and then asked her a question. "Geri, can I stay with you?" I thought staying with her, away from the distraction of guys would give me the chance to get my head straight and ask important questions I will disguise as typical girl talk.

"Well, I have classes and you need twenty-four hour care," Geri said. "I think the Inn is a good place because there is always somebody there. I can come see you after classes."

Since everyone could hear my thoughts, I might as well tell them how I felt. "I don't want anyone to see me like this, and I am not allowed to be alone. I get that...sort of. I don't like it, but I don't have to. So I need to stay some place where people can keep an eye on me, but can't see me. I know I want to leave this place, but where do I go?"

"I have an idea to that," Sam said "more like a compromise..."

"What is it?" I asked eagerly. I know there is no way in hell I will go back home to dear old mom. I'd rather stay here with Nurse Monica than go back to that.

"We put you up in one of the rooms at the Inn." Sam said "The Romeo and Juliet room or the Garden suite room or even the Bachelor pad. All these rooms have intercoms, we leave them on all the time and you can be alone. You just call if you need anything."

"The Romeo and Juliet room has marble stairs and I don't know if that will be good for her." Julian said. While they were debating the pros and cons of marble steps my head went to the Garden Suite room and the fun Julian and I had there. It seemed like so long ago now. I couldn't stop the blushing. No one noticed since they were now in conference about the dangers on the Bachelor Pad, and then went on to arguing about what room I should stay in without asking my opinion.

I looked at Geri and smirked while I took small bites of donut. She smirked back and then I felt what I can only describe as a knock on the door of my head. I opened up to Geri who wanted a one on one.

*When you come to visit someone's brain, isn't it customary to bring a bottle of wine? I* asked her.

*The next Chardonnay is on me"* Geri said. *Listen, I hope you're not thinking about going back to your dorm room, at least not until after everything calms down. If you're at the Inn it will give me a chance to come see you without Dawn finding out that I know about what she is doing at the Inn.*

*You have known about the club the whole time and didn't say anything to either one of us?*

*Yes, I knew and honestly I wanted to tell you, but I was afraid Dawn would think I was doing the same thing she was doing and that I do not want.*

I pictured Geri with Dawn and me on the stage, or in a bordello room watching or...participating in any and all activities. I drove out the images as quickly as they came in.

When I looked up, Geri was trying to give me a reassuring smile. Geri, I don't know what to do?

I couldn't stop the tear before it fell and was noticed by everyone in the room. The arguing stopped and was replaced with silence and pity.

"Sweetie, relax," Sam said sympathetically. It didn't help. I just shut down, closed my mind to the reality that is my life...no thoughts, no talk, I only wanted me in here. Maybe shutting everybody out was rude, but I didn't care.

"What would you like to do, love?" Julian asked. Sam just waited for an answer.

No more silence. "I'll stay at the Inn," I said quietly. "I need my laptop, my books, and clothes...Geri can you get them for me?"

"Of course, anything else you need?" Geri asked.

"Whatever you think I need," I said. "Can you stay the night at the Inn too?"

"Geri, it'll be good for her to be around family," Julian said. "If you are worried about what people like Dawn might think, just tell her you are there for Cat."

"I'll stay, but in my own room." Geri said.

"Thank you," Julian said

I guess we had everything settled. Everybody knows what everybody else was doing. I'll have a room and around the clock attention. They probably have a "Cat Watching Schedule" all made up.

There was a knock on the door and Nurse Monica came in "I have your discharge papers." And just like that, I was released.

I can go to my room.

I can try to get some sleep.

I can try and not have nightmares.

The third floor hallway was long though it only had six other doors besides the one Sam, Julian and I stood in front of—my home away from home. Geri was on her way to my dorm to find me some clean clothes. I really hoped I did my laundry before any of this started. Dominic told me he had some things to do, but he would be back. He wanted to talk to me about my new family. I hope I'll be ready to listen.

Sam unlocked the door, pushed it aside, and stood back to let me go in first. Under normal circumstances it would be romantic for Julian to carry me across the threshold—there are times I miss normal. Once I made my way in, Julian set me down and turned on the lights. This was not a theme room, but more like a small apartment that was bigger than my dorm. It had the typical couch and loveseat in the living room, but unlike most living rooms, this one had a hot tub. The huge television on the wall and a fire place made it look like a perfect mountain getaway. Sam gave a brief tour showing me the two bed rooms, one with a king-size bed and the other with two queen size beds. The bathroom was big, and I loved the way the bathtub and shower were separate, but the coolest piece of furniture outside of the bathroom was the massage table. We walked through another door into the small kitchen with all the normal amenities. The tour was over and I made my way back to the front room and crashed on my new couch in exhaustion.

"Is there anything I can get you?" Sam asked.

"Thank you guys," I said sincerely. "But all I want is a shower. Can you give me some privacy?" I was cleaned up, wiped down, and sponge bathed in the hospital, but his scent, the feeling of Daniel's foul touch was still on me. This feeling may not go away with a shower, no matter how hard I scrub, but I still had to try.

Sam took me by the hand and I could tell he wanted to give me a hug. He wanted to make it all go away. If only he could. He stepped past me and moved to a door I thought was a closet. It wasn't a closet. "This is my room," Sam said, "I will be working from here and you can come and get me if you need me, or just knock and I will be here."

Julian moved to the other side of the room to yet another door. I had an idea of what's behind it and I was beginning to wonder if there are any closets in this place. With a wink and a smile he opened the door to what I can only imagine is his room, conveniently located next to mine. "This is my room. If you have any problems you can also come see me. However, I do not want you to think that this is the only reason to knock at my door."

"Julian," Sam said.

"She's an adult," Julian said.

"I know she is," Sam said. He wanted to say more...I know he did. The look on Sam's face, in his eyes meant he was not happy about...something.

"Have I missed something?" I asked looking at both of them.

"No sweetie," Sam said. But once again the look in his eyes betrayed what he was saying, and that's when it dawned on me. Sam saw me as a struggling college student that became what was essentially a paid escort to his boss. While he was okay with it at the time, my uncle Sam now sees me as his niece, not one of the girls working at Jade's Inn.

"There's a robe and other supplies in the bathroom and if you need anything just call me,"

Sam said as he walked into his own room and quietly shut the door. Julian stood by the door to his room, waiting, waiting to find the right words to say, or waiting for me to say the right words.

I sort of beamed at him and he turned and walked into his room, accepting that a look is worth a thousand words—a thousand words that all say there was nothing you could have done.

I locked the door to my room, and I locked the doors to both Sam and Julian's rooms, and then I unlocked them...I don't know how many times. I made my way to the bathroom, undressed and took a long hard look at the person staring at me in disbelief from the other side of the mirror. I couldn't breathe...not until I turned away. I didn't take the time to count the number of bruises...it was too hard to tell if they were a bunch of little ones or a few big ones. Look at *the bright side girl...at least you have a nice living space to hide your bruises in.*

The water from the shower was warm. It felt good at first to clean away the dirt and grime, but once I started scrubbing harder and harder, I realized that bruises and past mistakes do not wash off. The parts of my skin that weren't bruised began turning red, becoming raw and painful, and my tears mixed with the water from the shower. My crying became uncontrollable and I slowly slid down the wall of the shower to the floor, the water still beating down on me like rain.

Then I heard footsteps.

I didn't move. I didn't want to make a sound. I knew there was no way that Daniel could have gotten in here. There's no way he could have. The footsteps stopped. The door to the bathroom open and I wanted to scream.

A thought came to my mind but it wasn't my own. "*Relax Cat, it's me,*" Julian said. "Are *you okay? I could feel your pain and...can I come in?*"

I was curled up on the floor of the shower, helpless. I didn't want him to see me like this. I wanted to get up. I tried, but I couldn't, and I cried again. The water stopped, and when I looked up, there was Julian with a towel. He bent almost touching me on the shoulder, but hesitated

"Can I help you up?" he asked. I shook my head and he reached and picked me up, grabbed my robe, and took me to the front room held tightly to his chest.

"Caprice breathe, take a deep breath," Julian said in a calming voice. I relaxed into him, pressing against him, trying to get as close as I could. I breathed deep, taking in that familiar smell of rain. I wanted the smell I loved all over me instead of the smell of Daniel, the smell of pain, anger, and regret. The bastard left his mark on me, the bruises, cuts and his smell...I wanted if off.

Julian looked nice in his slacks and blue dress shirt, and I didn't want to get him all wet as he carried me. "I'm okay," I said trying to get out of his arms, but he just held me tighter.

"You're not okay," Julian said. "Don't you understand? I can feel what you feel...you can't hide it from me." He brought his lips to mine and kissed me. At that moment, that's all I needed—to know I was loved and to know I was safe.

"Julian," I said. "Please take the pain away." To be honest, I don't know why I asked him that. Well I didn't ask, I told him, as if I thought he could do something. I guess I thought if anyone could make this go away with just a touch, just a word, it would be Julian.

"I would, love, but you don't understand what that will mean," Julian said kissing my cheek.

"What is there to understand?" I asked. "I can feel him, Julian, and I want that feeling to go away..." I was wondering if he understood I meant I wanted him. I needed his hands all over me, touching me gently, softly. I wanted him to show me I could still be loved.

"You have to allow yourself to heal first, my dear," and there was a hint of disappointment in his voice which told me while my health was his priority, he still misses knocking boots.

I get that the sex would be better if it didn't hurt every time I took a breath, and that orgasms are only a temporary pain reliever, but it could be therapeutic for my mind, soul, and self-assurance. I started thinking about what Grandfather said in the hospital about a way to heal faster. I looked to Julian. "Is there a way I can heal faster?"

Julian took my hand. He looked into my eyes and then looked away. He did everything but answer my question. Finally, he coaxed out, "Let's wait for my father to come back and we will discuss it."

"I would argue with you about this, but to be honest, I'm just too tired right now. So you win this time, but don't get used to it."

"How about this..." Julian said, "I'll get you one of my T-shirts and sweats. That way you won't have to be in the robe. Or I can find you some of our theme clothes?"

*Theme clothes? So I can dress as a hooker, a Catholic School Girl or Marie Antoinette as* part of my road to recovery? "Your T-shirt and sweats will work for me," I said, thinking this could be a roundabout way of getting his clothes off.

"Are you hungry?" Julian asked. Under normal circumstances his feeble attempt to change the subject would have failed miserably, but as it turned out I was hungry as the grumbling in my stomach could attest. "I'll take that as a yes. What would you like?" he prompted.

"A peanut butter and grape jelly sandwich sounds great," I said.

"PB and J, really? I think we can do better than that," Julian said. "Ask for anything and I can get it for you, anything at all."

When I was a kid and I was feeling low, bad grades or stupid boys doing stupid things at school, or just a rainy day on Monday, peanut butter and jelly or toasted cheese sandwiches dipped in tomato soup made me feel better. I usually had to make them myself, but they worked.

*"I want comfort food. Either peanut butter and grape jelly sandwich, or grilled cheese and tomato soup would do."*

"So grilled cheese and tomato soup it is," Julian said. He bent and kissed my forehead, which was probably the only sugar I will get for a while. "I'll put an order in with the kitchen, then I'll be back with some clothes, but the Marie Antoinette outfit sounds like fun. All those slips." he winked. He can hear me even when I don't want him to.

Just as Julian left, a knock came from Sam's door and he walked in with something behind his back. I hope he wasn't going to ask me to guess what he had or to pick a hand. "Close your eyes," he said. I tried to see what he was hiding, but I gave up and closed my eyes. He handed *me what felt like a DVD case. Oh God. I hope this isn't an embarrassing slid show of me when I was too young to tell the adults to get that camera out of my face. "I thought you might want to* watch this." I opened my eyes to see a Winnie the Pooh DVD called Pooh's Heffalump Movie. I as feeling better. The last time I saw this was with my sister a couple of years ago.

"Thank you, this is perfect. How did you know?" I asked.

"Geri said it was one of the movies you watch when you're having a bad day," Sam said.

"I thought it might help you to relax. Is Julian getting you lunch?" There was a tone in Sam's voice lately every time he mentions Julian.

"Sam...I thought Julian was one of your really good friends," I said "So I don't understand why you're having such a problem with him now that you know that I'm your niece. Did you lie to me before about him being at good guy?"

"Julian and I are more than friends, more like brothers and best friends in one," Sam said.

He fidgeted, looked around out the window with the drapes closed, at the TV that wasn't on, at his wrist that didn't have a watch. Sam looked like a father searching for the words to explain the birds and bees to a wide-eyed innocent kid, knowing that once he does, the kid will be just less innocent. "There's a way things happen in our family when it comes to...dating and... I will admit that I was protective of you when you just..."

"When I was just another one of the girls?" I inquired.

"You were never just one of them," Sam beamed. "But, I watched over you before I learned that you were my niece and now I watch you closer." I wonder if there was a point that Sam was trying not to get to, "Julian is a good man. He really is."

"Then what is the problem?" I asked. Before anything further was said Julian returned with an oversized dark gray T-shirt and black sweats. I took them, said thank you and made my way toward the bathroom.

"Cat, I can have someone go buy you some clothes or anything you need," Sam said.

"No, that's okay," I said. "This will be fine until Geri comes back," I closed the bathroom door and became more and more excited about wearing Julian's clothes.

Kinky...maybe...Weird...no, after making sure that the sweat pants would fit. I slowly, very slowly pulled the T-shirt over my head, smelling his scent as it glided past my nose. I felt better.

It was easier to imagine his arms around me and I felt...happy for the first time in the last forty-eight hours. I picked up a brush and forced myself to look in the mirror. When I walked back out of this room I wanted to look close to the way I looked before, the same way I looked when Julian saw me for the first time. It wasn't easy.

Somewhere between the waves of self-pity came the smell of toasted cheese. I walked out of the bathroom to find four peanut butter and grape jelly sandwiches sliced in quarters, eight grill cheese sandwiches cut in half, and tomato soup with a glass of milk and what I thought was tomato juice. "My nieces really love this stuff too," Julian said after handing me and Sam a heavy white plate with gold trim, fancy for soup and sandwiches. I take two halves of grilled cheese and a couple of the PB and J. With the guys watching my every move I smile and grab another PB and J. Hey, I'm the patient here...I don't have to be polite. Julian handed me a glass of milk before giving Sam one of the glasses of tomato juice and taking the other for himself.

After I got the bowl of soup I took off my slippers and curled up on the couch.

"May I sit next to you?" Julian asked with a slight bow. He didn't have to ask me twice. I moved over closer to Sam who put his arm around me allowing me to rest my head on his shoulder.

"Ready to watch the movie?" Julian asked hitting the play button on the remote. There was Winnie the Pooh filling every corner of the seventy-two inch screen. For the first time, I felt safe and loved with my three favorite guys—Sam with his arm around me, Julian with his hand in mine and a silly old bear. Could life get any better?

# Chapter 22:

# Family History

I woke up to find my head in Julian's lap which explains the great dream I wish I could get back to. I looked up at Julian and he beamed at me. "Have a nice nap?" he asked, with one hand on my shoulder and the other on the keys of his silver laptop computer.

"Yes, I had a good nap," I admitted. His one hand continued to move across the keys of his computer quickly—it's kind of impressive to watch. "What you doing...if you don't mind my asking? I realize it's none of my business," I said.

"I needed to go through my email, business stuff you know," Julian said closing the top of the computer, "How are you feeling?"

"My body is stiff," I said. "My head's not hurting right now, which is surprising and cool, so don't say anything. I don't want to jinx it."

"Good, because I want to teach you something before the others come in," Julian said in a low voice like he was passing on state secrets or the answers to the mid-term, "I know you're having trouble keeping people out of your head."

"No kidding!" I said pointing to my head, "I thought it was crowded in here when it was just me and my own neurosis. If there is a way to keep people out without knocking I'd love to learn how to do it."

"Your brain is an easy thing to work with if you don't think what you do and just do it," Julian said, "Understand?"

"Yeah, you just called me simple minded," I said.

"No, that's not what...I didn't mean...in general people...Okay sorry?" he attempted to explain.

Well that was fun to watch.

"Let's try again," Julian said after collecting himself. "When you concentrate on a particular thought or action it's harder to block someone from hearing those thoughts." Julian stood up and paced. Something was making him nervous. "You will be learning family history and while you are learning this, there may be memories of you and I and the things we...have done, and you will want to block these thoughts and images. I will try and help you. Just try and keep just me in your head during the learning," he stated.

"Excuse me teacher," I said with confusion, "Isn't that the problem? If I keep you in my head, I started thinking of the Garden Suite and the back seat of a shiny Mustang? Keeping you in my thoughts is easy...keeping your clothes on while in my thoughts will be a bitch."

Julian stopped pacing and knelt in front of me, "When I say keep me in your thoughts I mean keep my thoughts in your head. It's a connection between you and me, and it needs to stay open. If you think of that connection, I can help you block the other thoughts."

"Does Sam know we slept together?" That question just popped out there before I could reel it back in.

"He knows that the contract is in effect but not signed so he knows something happened. I just don't want everyone knowing everything," Julian leaned forward and kissed me. "Your clothes are in your room. As much as I like seeing you in my clothes, you can change whenever *you want.*" *My bra and underwear would be good. That whole blocking thoughts thing would come in handy right about now so he doesn't know I'm going commando in his sweats.*

"I'm getting dressed, but I think I'll keep the shirt," I said and headed to the room to change.

"If you need any help, Commando, I'm more than willing," Julian sneered. I giggled and closed the door behind me, calculating the amount of time I needed to spend in a tanning bed to camouflage my embarrassment. With my arms held wide, I dropped back on the bed and grabbed a pillow and crushed it into my face and let loose with a scream that was as quiet as I could manage. Since the pillow wasn't suffocating me fast enough I threw it to the floor and with great deal of pain, pulled the sweats off. I reached for the skimpy, see-through, pink panties that Geri picked out —thanks for that—and with effort pulled them on. Trying to put on the bra hurt more, so I gave up and grabbed a tank top. Since my chest has an obvious reaction when I'm around Julian, I needed layers, so I threw on Julian's shirt over the tank top. Last but not least were my jeans, my tight, ass-hugging jeans. There was no way, so I found my oversized purple Pooh bottoms and put them on.

I was attempting to brush my less than cooperative hair when I heard a knock on the door to the apartment, followed by the voices of Dominic and Geri saying hello to Julian. After I heard Sam come through his door, the next thing I heard was Geri's thoughts of Sam. They were sweet and X-rated at the same time. Who knew she would be so cute when she's turned on. I never thought of it before, but she would be my aunt Geri. While I was deciding how I felt about that, there was a knock at the door and Aunt Geri walked in before I could say come in.

"Hi Cat, how's your head?" she asked.

"You really need to tell him how you feel about him," I said aloud.

"Are you ready for all this?" Geri asked, ignoring my advice. I sat on the bed and she looked at me with concern in her eyes, "Dawn will be by after she's done with her last tryst with Kurt."

"To be honest Geri, I'm not sure what I'm ready for," I said. "It's like everyone was in on one big secret except me and I kept saying I wanted to know too, at least until they said 'Okay we'll tell you', and now I'm not sure. It's scary." Geri just looked at me without saying a word, but I could tell she knew what I was talking about.

The thoughts of secrets in my head were interrupted by the thoughts from Julian. *Love, what you will learn is something you can't talk about outside this family. Some of what you hear...most of what you hear will be hard to believe at first, but it's all real. We are sharing information with you the same way we do with all the girls that turn seventeen, but since you are new to all this it will be difficult to understand. If you have questions, ask. Then like that, Julian* was out of my head again. How am I supposed to get used to this popping in and popping out crap?

"Ready?" Geri asked as if I was walking the Green Mile. Julian didn't exactly put me at ease with his cryptic words of encouragement.

"Ready or not, here I go," I said boldly, which was contrary to how I felt. When we walked into the living room all the men who were seated stood up like perfect gentlemen, or like they would start an intervention. Sam and Julian each took a step to the side so

I sat between them. Sam and I sat while Julian made his way to the door, and just before he reached for the door knob, there was a knock. Julian opened the door for a lady that I have never seen before, but when Sam saw her he got up and met her at the door with a kiss on both cheeks.

"Caprice, this is your grandmother Dorothy," Sam said.

Unless this woman takes showers in the fountain of youth, there was no way she was my grandmother. Yes, she had brown hair like mine and yes she had brown eyes like mine, and she was my height, but she looked like she was in her forties. So unless she gave birth to Sam when she was five, this was not his mom.

I looked at her and she looked at me. I was wondering what moisturizing routine she uses and I was sure she was wondering why I was looking at her the way I was. Eventually, we both grinned, but my smile quickly disappeared and I took two steps back when I remembered the *bruises. Child...it's okay, the bruises will go away in time, said a new voice in my head. There* was care and concern in the thoughts coming from this woman who has never seen me before, and I think some of the concern was coming from her worrying what I was thinking of her. I *loved your dad so much and I tried to find you after he died, she thought.*

"I know," I reassured her, "Sam told me, and if you're worried about Sam taking care of me, don't be. He has been like an uncle to me before I knew he was my uncle."

"It's not that. I have known I had a grandchild out there and I looked for you. And now by fate or chance, Julian has found you, Sam has met you, and Geri has known you for years. I just had to meet you too. I know that photo albums can scare young people away, but I brought one that has pictures of your father. I thought we could sit and go through it and talk," Dorothy concluded.

"Ever since I learned of your existence I wanted to meet you too," I said, "But not like this, not looking the way I do." She took a step toward me and I didn't move. She slowly reached out and touched the bruises ever so slightly, and I felt the same thing I feel when I touch Sam...home, a safe place. I never really felt this way at home, but I did with Sam.

"You can, Caprice..." She handed the photo album to Sam and opened her arms. When I walked into them I felt the same way I felt as a little girl being hugged by my other grandmother.

*I have heard some say that a grandmother's love is unconditional...I think it might be true.* "It is, in this case...it's unconditional," she said.

Sam came up and joined in on the family hug. We stayed this way for a while until grandmother decided it was time for a history lesson. "Time to learn who you are child." And with that we all sat, Sam and I on the couch and Grandmother on a cozy chair Julian had put in front of the couch. Once Julian sat on the other side of me, Grandmother looked at us both, "You love him."

For the first time I admitted what I felt, so I locked everyone out of my head allowing only *Grandmother to hear. Yes, I love him. It's crazy...I shouldn't love anyone right now...My head is not exactly on straight. I feel like I'm going nuts and he says he still loves me. My life has been turned upside down, I have more baggage than an airport and he says he still loves me. It's hard to believe him, but I can feel it...he loves me. I hope I'm not overwhelming her. I haven't talked with anyone in my family like this since my grandma Hazel.*

*You obviously loved your grandmother very much, and I'm flattered that you see some of her in me, that means a great deal to me. As for Julian, he is good man and I can tell he loves you and trust me, he will not run away from you for any reason. And Sam will be protective because he loves you too. You have a family now...It's up to you how much you take from this.* I knew she meant every word, but my face didn't light up. My reservations were still there and she knew it. She had a sad look on her face, but didn't ask any more questions.

"Well are we ready to start?" Dominic asked, with the positive demeanor of a politician who was giving his constituents the good news and the bad news. Julian took hold of my hand and I squeezed harder than I should. If Geri was nervous, sitting kicked back on the loveseat, she was hiding it better than everyone else. Once he noticed that everyone was seated and relatively comfortable, Dominic pulled out a large, old looking book. From the writing I saw on the weather-beaten pages, it looked like a diary. Dominic began to read it.

*This is the Diary of Elizabeth Hainsworth, Dated seventeen seventy-one*

*I'm writing this diary to help you understand what happened at this time in my life. I sometimes feel that it didn't really happen, but it did. I'm starting the diary on the day I thought it all began. I want you to know I have no regrets about what happened to me and my family. I loved my husband much and would not have changed what happened in my life. All I can say is you have a choice to make. I hope you pick what's right for you.*

*French Naturalist Georges Louis Lecterc De Buffon traveled to the new world with his assistant Dominic Hainsworth Jr. (my husband) to study bats. Mr. De Buffon learned of a bat that could drink the blood of a sleeping animal or a person without awakening them. He classified them as a Vampire bat. However, he was unaware that Dominic had been bitten by one of these bats, and changed. Dominic felt his strength increase. He became more aware of his surroundings. His knowledge of everything around him grew. When Georges became sick and was close to dying, Dominic, having studied the Vampire bat, had learned that if a Vampire bat licked an opened wound on the animal or person that was sick, certain properties in the saliva of the bat would make them well again. Dominic tried it and George's life was saved.*

"Dominic, was this person your grandfather?" I asked.

"No, he's not my grandfather," he said.

I heard Grandmother whispering in my mind like we were in a library. *Let him finish this page dear. If you have questions ask this way for a while.* Then Dominic continued to read.

*Dominic never got sick again. However at first, he craved raw meat and blood, but shortly after, he was able to satisfy his craving with one cup of blood a day. He saw changes in himself that he didn't understand.*

*Okay, eww! I was stunned into silence. Blood? Raw meat? I don't know what I was having for dinner tonight, but I definitely know what I am not having.*

Just listen, Caprice, said Julian's thoughts, followed by a quick squeeze of my hand.

*Dominic returned to England with Mr. De Buffon. My husband told me that he would be going back to the new world, but this time I would be coming with him. The*

*New World was a beautiful place, full of wonder. It was not long after our arrival that I became pregnant and had our first child, a son, Dominic Hainsworth III, born March thirteenth, seventeen sixty-seven. We were so happy on that day, but our joy did not last. Our son became sick almost immediately. No one could tell us why he was so sick.*

*Several weeks had passed and our little Dominic was not getting better. Dominic wouldn't eat anything. Then one day, while I was getting dinner ready, Dominic brought him a bottle, but the milk was a different color. He said he put something in it to see of little Dominic would drink it. I gave our baby the bottle and the baby drank, and wouldn't stop. It's the first time he showed any kind of appetite. I looked at Dominic, knowing he knew something. He had to explain to me what happened when the Vampire bat bit him, and how it changed him. When little Dominic's fever had finally broke, we could tell that it was the blood he needed. I would think that I would be frightened by what my husband had become, by what my baby was, but I was not. I don't fear them.*

*We started giving a little bit of blood to the baby in his bottle and he got stronger as the days passed. As time went on we realized that we had a strong healthy son.*

*On April thirteenth, seventeen sixty-nine we had a second child, Emma Ann Hainsworth. We feared that she would require the blood as well, but she didn't. She was a healthy baby girl without it. But a year later when we had a third child, John Hainsworth, on May tenth, seventeen seventy, he did need the blood to live. We had three more children Amy, Henry and Julian. All the boys needed blood, but the girls did not.*

*Having had six children, I of course began to show the marks of age. It was at this time that I realized my husband did not. I was four years younger than Dominic, but he didn't look a day older than the day he returned to me in England, after his adventures in the New World. I felt so much older, taking care of my children and helping Dominic work our farm. My body did not handle it well, and I grew weaker day by day. The doctor said that I had Scarlet Fever, and that I didn't have a great deal of time left. I wanted to be there for my children, watch them grow. I knew what I had to do. I asked my husband to bite me too. I wanted to see if it would change me. Dominic set it up as a second wedding. My friends thought it showed he really loved me, knowing I did not have time left. He had the kids go to my friend Dorothy's house. Dominic and I were alone. He gently bit my arm and I felt no pain. He drank my blood and I fell asleep. When I awoke the next day, I felt so different. I was stronger, healthier and I was finally free to walk without my chest hurting.*

*It is important that whoever is reading this remembers, I asked him to bite me. This was my decision, and I stand by it. Now I have the same Vampire bite as my husband and the boys. My girls picked up some of the traits that the boys did. They never got ill. They too would remain strong.*

I sat in stunned silence, but only for a moment...then I giggled. "So there was a vampire bat...and blood. You know what this sounds like?

This sounds like one of those old black and white horror movies with that guy, Lugosi or something. He's this old vampire." I stopped laughing when I looked around and noticed no one else was. "Oh come on, it's like you get bit by a vampire bat and then you're a vampire. I mean, it's just a movie...holy fucking shit! Are you telling me this is real? Fangs, coffins and the sucking of..."

"Yes Caprice, they are real," Dominic said.

"I need to sit," I said in shock.

"You are sitting, sweetie," Geri informed me.

"Oh...well, good," I was the center of attention. Everyone was waiting for me to say something coherent. I looked at Julian, and Geri and then the old book. "I will give a dollar to the first person who laughs and tells me that this is just the way our kooky family initiates the new kids."

"Honey, I understand this is great deal to process," Sam said, "If you can allow Dominic to continue, you may understand more and if you have any further questions you can ask them when he is finished," Sam said.

*In seventeen seventy-five, Dominic joined the continental Army and became an officer to fight against the British. He served under Colonel William Prescott. Dominic was there when the Colonel said his famous line "Don't fire until you see the whites of their eyes!" The Red Coats won that day.*

*It was when Dominic was away that I first felt I had to tell someone our unusual lives together. My best friend Dorothy's house was set on fire because she burned the fields so the British could not get the food. The British soldiers were angry and beat Dorothy. I remained so furious because I knew Dorothy was alone with her six children. Her husband Lt. Robert Carter was killed just two weeks earlier at the battle of Bunker Hill. I brought Dorothy and her children to my home. Dorothy was near death from wounds. I decided to send the children outside. Dorothy remained asleep, tossing and turning, no doubt reliving the nightmare of the attack on her. I bent and gently licked Dorothy's wounds. She immediately began a more restful sleep. It was not long before she got well again, but she didn't regain her strength. I sat with Dorothy one night after the kids went to bed, and I told her how different I felt after what Dominic had done for me.*

Grandfather looked up from the diary "From what Elizabeth tells me, the talk went well." He said it like a fond memory.

While Dominic briefly strolled through memory lane, I realized that the people in the book, who were from a different time, were also in my living room. The mother of the guy I slept with hung out in the age of George Washington. Dorothy, my grandmother, could have literally gotten an invitation to the Boston Tea Party, but she was too busy at home discovering her best friend was a freakin vampire. Were you shocked when you found out? I asked my grandmother in her head.

*Not shocked. It made sense after all I saw. My children had lost their father...I didn't want them losing me too.*

So Lt. Carter is my grandfather who died in the Civil War. That's good to know. I was getting eager to hear more of this story.

*It was a shock when Dorothy learned of my family secret, but I could not see fear in her eyes. We always had a close friendship, and I could tell she was happy for me. I could also see that she was growing weaker. She beamed at me and put her hand in my hand as if to reassure me that she would be fine. I guess I wanted to be sure too. I raised her hand up to my mouth. I kissed her inner arm, and then I bit her.*

*Dorothy got well and we moved her family into my house. It became our home.*

*Dorothy and I even built three more rooms onto the house by ourselves. We were both less lonely.*

"Elizabeth bit you?" I asked my grandmother. She just shook her head.

*I knew I was not going to tell anyone else, but Dominic was not there and had no clue what was going on. The more things that happened to people, the more the secret came out.*

*Dorothy and I turned fifteen women to help keep the family together.*

*A portion of these women were left behind with kids and didn't have the ability to work a farm and help keep the family going. Out of the fifteen women, only four husbands came home. We as women worked together to get things done. We took turns on the farms, and one of the women, eighteen year old Emma McGee, was a teacher and taught the kids during the day. She was not married and became very sick. The kids were so upset and this was our only way to fix the problem.*

*We had our way of doing things after working together for eight years. When the men came home they had trouble accepting it at first. A share of the men got jobs in town because we needed money to pay the taxes on the land. It was the women that worked to make sure everyone had everything they needed.*

Dominic put the diary aside and said, "After slavery was outlawed in Massachusetts, we had two African American families with a total of thirteen kids that needed food and shelter. They were willing to work for money or food. Elizabeth, with her big heart gave the men work on the farm, and the women work helping in the house. She insisted that the children be in school. Most of the townspeople believed the kids should be working, but Elizabeth would not hear of it. She wanted them to learn to read and write. Most of the African Americans at that time did not know how to read or write and Elizabeth didn't think it was fair. Our community was getting bigger and bigger."

"I met and married Sam's father ten years after this. When we all moved to a new place away from all the prejudice," Grandmother said, "So I know you have questions."

"Questions? You think I might have questions?" I asked with as much sarcasm as I could fit in my huge attitude. "If you want I can write them so you can take a few days to answer them. Maybe we can start with am I a vampire? Are vampires born or just made in a really gross way? Do vamps die or live forever?"

"The males are born this way, the females are not," Dominic said while I had my fingers in my mouth feeling my teeth. "While you do carry the gene that passes on to ninety-nine percent of the male children, you yourself are not a vampire, but can be turned into one. There's one other thing you should know...For some reason, we are not sure yet why, there are more males than female born into the family. This is why we do arranged marriages." If I was drinking booze, and I really, really wish I was, I would have spit it out. I locked down my thoughts as fast as I could. "As far as vampires living forever, and we prefer vampire not vamp, we age very slowly and it is harder to kill us, but it can happen."

"Yeah, yeah, yeah...about this arranged marriage?" I asked with fear and righteous indignation, "I'm sure I must have misunderstood, or were you just channeling the you of two hundred years ago?"

Dominic paused for a moment until he realized there was no way to explain an archaic notion like arranged marriage in the politically correct twenty-first century. "You're one of us so you fall under this rule. It's one female for every three males."

"I get three husbands? Like a reverse Mormon thing," I uttered, shocked as I said it.

"No, no, no," Dominic said quickly, "I'm talking about statistics. One girl to every three guys, sorry to get your hopes up."

"Scared stiff is more like it...One guy is enough for me!" I said, "With all due respect to the family history in matters of the heart, who is it that you think I'm going to marry?" I think with the pointed question, there is an understanding that I wanted nothing to do with this arranged marriage crap. Then it dawned on me—Geri isn't married. I opened my mind to her. You're *not married, right? Holy shit girl are you married? Were you set up in all this arranged marriage bullshit? With all these dirty thoughts you've been having about Sam and you have a* Mr. Geri at home. Shame on you, I scolded. I was about to find out that Geri was not who I thought she was.

# Chapter 23:

# Geri's Thoughts

First of all, Cat...Shut up. I am not married, and the dirty thoughts about Sam were not meant for your mind. Now, the arranged marriage thing is a tradition, but you don't have to agree to marry the one who has been arranged for you, you can say no, you have that right. No one here is going to make you do anything you don't want to do. As corny as it sounds, just follow your heart and you will know who you love. I wish I had an arranged marriage set up for me at a young age, she said with finality.

My eyes narrowed, but never left her eyes. I was waiting for a laugh or at least a chuckle. It didn't come. A young age? You're a few years older than me. Then I paused and so did she

"Please tell me we're about the same age. Tell me you haven't been twenty-three for two hundred and twenty-three years."

Hey, I'm only twenty-three. Why, how old do I look? she asked sarcastically.

"You look young," I reassured her, "You look young and too Twenty-first century to buy

into an antiquated ritual like arranged marriages. Is that really what you wanted?"

When I was turning eighteen I really was upset that I didn't have a boyfriend, or at least someone who was hopelessly infatuated with me, besides the creepy kids with the majority of their body parts pierced who craved to introduce me to their dead cats. I have seen only girls in our extended family that were involved in arranged marriages and they were happy—still are. My younger sister, who just turned eighteen, is part of an arranged marriage and is so happy that it makes me want to throw-up. And like any good friend would do, I laughed.

"So I guess that makes you pro arranged marriage?" I asked.

Very much so...I tried guys at school, then college, now internet sites and all I want is that man over there. Geri said looking at Sam with longing. Cat, he's hot Then I froze when I heard my grandmother's voice.

"We have had someone that is interested in marrying you," my grandmother said with a straight face, "However there are other gentlemen that have learned about the latest addition to our family and want to meet you." My eyes widened as she said, "Right now I don't think you should worry."

"Oh really, well we need to come to an understanding right now," I demanded. "I'm marrying who I want. Maybe I've met him, and maybe I haven't. It might be sometime in the next week, it might be sometime in the next decade. I mean no offense and don't get me wrong I do want to get married someday. I have to admit that when I was a little girl dreaming about wearing the gown and strutting down the aisle, it would be with the man of my dreams, not my family's dreams!" The room was at a loss for words, but my curiosity got the best of me.

"Just for the sake of argument, who is this guy that may be the man of your dreams?" asked Dominic.

Before anyone dared to answer that question, Geri popped back in my head and she was not happy. So you have a suitor, someone who wants you. You will be married before me. What's wrong with me? She said in utter frustration.

There is nothing wrong with you, I said trying to console her since this seems to be really hard on her.

"This is not the way it's supposed to be done," Sam said, "Cat, you were not raised the way the rest of us were raised so things will be different, but please let us tell you more."

"Your life is yours, my dear," Grandmother said, "I know your life has been turned upside down, but it is yours. We want to be a part of it, and if possible to make it better. You have money from your father's trust. You can go to school, work towards any degree that you want and not have to worry about working in lousy jobs with rotten bosses. There is a great deal the family can offer you."

On my pros and cons list of being in this family, the no more lousy jobs and bosses definitely goes on the pro side, but I don't mind working some jobs. The money may be pathetic, but it was mine and I earned it. The all-expense paid scholarship was nice, but I needed more backstory on vampires since they only existed in books and movies until about an hour ago.

"Can you explain the vampire thing more?" I asked, "For instance, shouldn't there be more vampires?"

"Remember in Biology class when we went off topic about Porphyria disease?" Geri asked me, sufficiently distracted from her plight of being boyfriend-less.

"Yes, it's one of the talks you don't forget, putting some fact into fiction," I said.

"Well, remember the gross part of the conversation about how the disease causes the skin to be sensitive to sunlight and mild sun light can disfigure the skin, causing the nose and fingers to fall off and make the lips and gums shrink so the teeth look like they are bigger?" I shook my head wanting to thank Geri for putting that image back in my head after it took weeks of internet shopping to get rid of it. "Well this is close to what happens to us if we don't take blood. Don't get me wrong we still have to eat, you can't live on blood alone. Have you ever been sick?" Geri asked.

"Not really, my sisters and brothers would always get sick but I didn't," I said.

"This is one of the things the bite gives us, better health,. It did something to our parents' DNA and it transferred to our DNA from mother and father to baby," she said.

"Every member of a family has a unique talent. With all families, once you're married to your spouse and drink of his blood, you can read his thoughts. Of course your family has always been able to read the thoughts of not just your family, but other families too," Geri concluded, completely winded.

This sounded like a crummy commercial. Did Geri know she was making a pitch? Caprice, you have won an all-expense paid lifetime with a family of bloodsuckers. Here is your prize package, intrusive, non-verbal communication, a great health care plan, and a special talent to be named later. The trouble with commercials is that they never give you the flip-side. They never tell you why the glass is half empty. "So are there people that have died from being bitten?" I asked.

Dominic decided to chime in, giving Geri a chance to catch her breath, "Yes, so we don't turn people unless we check out their DNA, particularly with females since there are so few that are born into the families...some are brought in through biting. We want to make sure that they are safe."

"That's good to know," I said, then I turned my attention back to Geri, one of my best friends that I hardly knew. "While you have been describing everything, Geri, you've been saying 'we' a great deal. I don't mean to be judgmental and I don't want to label, but are you a vampire? Is it okay to say vampire or is that too pop culture? Maybe I should say Undead American."

"Undead is an invention of novelists and Hollywood writers. Vampire is fine and no, I am not one yet. If I can't find my love by the time I'm twenty-five then my grandfather Dominic will turn me if I ask him to." The only real sympathetic look

I was getting from everyone was coming from Grandmother

"You have been through so much my dear," she said. "All this family history is probably not helping, but we can make it better. Do you want to be healed?" She gave me a reassuring look like I was eight years old and she was putting a Band-Aid on a booboo. "We can have you looking and feeling like your old self in four hours if you want. You can be ready to meet a few boys who will be coming in to patrol tonight. They are anxious to meet you," she concluded.

"What is the patrol?" I asked. I had one of those headaches that only pretend to be small before sneaking up and kicking your ass, aggressively announcing it is really a migraine.

"In our lives, with the sweet comes the sour. There are some within our ranks who have bitten people just to control them and their 'unique talents,'" Geri said using air quotes. "The men in our clans who are not married serve two years or longer in a patrol, as a way of identifying these people and taking care of them."

Well, that's a scary thought that my fucked up brain was turning into a nightmare tonight "I don't want to be the pooper of the vampire party, but I really do not want to be the bachelorette meeting all the potential bachelors. Believe it or not guys are not on my list of things to do right now. Sorry for the poor choice of words."

"You don't have to date them, just meet them," Sam said "So we are sure..." I hate it when he stops, like he catches himself before he'll reveal some top secret plans. I know it would be impossible to keep my mind on the guys who just want to meet me when there is one out there who has said he wants to marry me.

So in the last two days I went from having really no family to having a very big one with customs that make Big Fat American Greek Wedding look like child's play. Thinking about this shit hurts. I need to get back to normal first so I can have a decent nervous breakdown when I realize all this scary ass shit wasn't a bad dream. All this had to wait until I felt better, but I can't escape it or wish it away, so I thought I would ask another question.

"So how do I get back to normal?" I asked to no one in particular.

"Yes, my dear, there is a way to speed your recovery," Julian said, "But Sam doesn't want you to go through with it. Once you're bitten, you have to be bitten by the same person until you're turned."

"So the way I can heal quickly is to be bitten...by a vampire? Maybe we should wait for FDA approval of this procedure." No one was laughing. "Okay, let me understand this, rule number one when it comes to biting is that once I have been bitten, that same lucky vampire has to be the one who bites me again to turn me. Why?"

"Because that person will be protective of you and if you have someone else bite you, you will get sick," Julian said.

"I'll bite her, I don't want her suffering, it will easily fix the problem," Grandmother said,

"This will also protect her."

"No, you can't," Julian said abruptly. He didn't say anything after that, not for a while. He paced back and forth and around in circles. There was a secret in there dying to get out and Julian didn't want to let it, but he gave in. "Dorothy, Caprice has been..." Before he had a chance to finish, there was a loud crash and Julian, who was standing in front of me, was now being pressed tightly against the wall by Sam.

"You have taken from her...When?" Sam demanded with such anger. I had no idea what the hell was going on. Took what? I don't remember Julian taking anything from me except maybe my breath the first time I saw him without a shirt...or pants.

"It was before I knew who she was...before the contract...before you met her." Julian mumbled under that hand of an angry Sam. They both looked at each other with an intensity that was scaring the shit out of me. I was sure there was a fight about to break out if I didn't do something.

I struggled to stand up, and that got them looking at me instead of each other. "What has Julian taken from me?" I asked thinking if they believe it was my virginity, they should know I misplaced that several years ago.

"Your blood," Sam said before turning back to Julian. "Julian when did you take her blood? It is against our laws to take a female's blood without a contract." Sam's voice was thundering like one of those scary judges from a long time ago that wore the creepy wigs. Hopefully the rest of the Inn thought we left the TV on.

"I have a contract, not signed, but I have one," I said quickly, hoping it would defuse the situation. It didn't. If anything it may have made it worse because now my grandmother froze, and then she looked pissed too.

"Julian, you understand what this means?" Sam said waiting for the right answer to come from Julian's lips.

"I had planned on it all along...I just wanted her to love me back first. It would make it so much easier on her and me if..." Julian sat down on the loveseat away from me looking down at the floor. Sam sat down next to me and took my hand. I could tell by the look on both of their faces they were mind melding with each other and I could not hear them. It was my turn to get pissed. They were talking about me in that weird non-moving lips way, but I was right here. I felt like a little girl whose parents are fighting to decide who the child will live with.

"If you people do not tell me what the hell is going on in the next five-fucking-seconds, I'm deciding my own future and no one will like it!" I yelled, and not just in their minds, but loud enough for the neighbors to complain.

Julian looked at me with steely eyes and then got up, went to his room, and a moment later returned with a small box. He stood in front of me for a moment, turning the box over and over in his hand before finally handing it to me, "Open it."

The box was ornate, but not so much so that you would think it came in place of a prize in a ring toss game at the carnival. While the design looked old, the box looked new. It was a nice box, but not one that I was expecting to find a ring in. First came shock, that Julian would have the nerve to give me a ring, and then came awe because it was a cute little ring. The best part of the ring was that it didn't have a diamond because I didn't feel like kicking Julian's ass before running to my room and lying on my bed, catatonic for a week. It was a gold band, and a silver ribbon that weaved around it. There were two hearts on the band and between them were words that read "Forever Love."

It was sweet...and familiar.

Dominic and my grandmother looked at each other, while I was looking for a knife to cut the tension in the room so I could breathe easier. "Julian, why didn't you say something?" Dominic asked.

"I sensed that a block had been put up in her mind," Grandmother said, "I thought someone was helping her get over what happened."

"Do any of you have any idea how annoying it is to have a room full of people talking about you like you're five years old or not there at all?" I yelled. "Now somebody needs to tell me what all this means. Why is this ring familiar? Why are people talking about blocks in my head, which by the way is insulting?"

I'm in a room full of vampires and I think I had them scared. "Show her," Sam said finally. "Now!"

"It's not so bad once your eyes adjust..." Came a smooth voice behind me—or was it in front of me...?

I jumped and my heart nearly stopped. It was as if the night itself was speaking directly to me. I whipped around to see who had scared the shit out of me, but no one was there. I turned again, twisting myself in a knot. No one was there, just me and the night. I started running to the big McDonald's sign across the street from the university when someone stepped out in front of me with the biggest, deep milk chocolate brown eyes—Eyes that were staring straight into me, as if they were staring into my soul. I strained to speak, but couldn't. I craved to run, but my legs

wouldn't budge. He stepped closer, and I could see him better.

Thick black hair fell past his neck, running wild around his head, and his skin was like fine white porcelain. His eyes were dark as the night around us, and his long dark coat only hid him more against the dark backdrop of night. My mind quickly flashed back to my self-defense class.

Being alone in the dark with a stranger was one of those unsafe situations they talked about avoiding. Lesson one was don't walk around alone at night. Well too late for that, dumbass. Lesson two was run for your life!

Finally, with painful effort, I managed to swallow. I still couldn't move or take my eyes off of him. I watched him moved closer and closer. His lips parted as if he was directed to speak, but he said nothing. His mouth continued to open and I saw his teeth, two in particular. They were white and growing longer. Okay, that was not normal. Now his lips were on my neck. I couldn't move. I felt terrified. I felt anxious. I felt teeth biting into me.

I finally managed my first words. "Ow! What the hell?" Who did this guy think he was, trying to make a meal out of me? I pushed myself back in an attempt to get away from him, but it wasn't working. He was not small...at least a foot taller than me, and his embrace was tight, rock hard tight.

Suddenly I stopped struggling. I stopped moving. It was as if I stopped existing in the real world. I was somewhere else, some place I had never been before. It looked like a farm, horses and buggies and amber waves of some kind of grain. It was like I was watching a movie from inside the film.

I could see the strange man, but he was much younger, no more than seventeen or eighteen. He was sitting with a girl on a porch and they were holding hands. It was like a period film. I mean this house looked like it was straight out of Little House on the Prairie, complete with a porch swing the couple was sitting on. I had to admit, it was kind of sweet, and I could feel the excitement they were feeling from just holding hands together.

It's such an incredible feeling to be young and in love.

Then things suddenly became fuzzy and I felt something else, pain, emotional heart-wrenching pain. I saw a younger Dominic with a younger Julian "I should have bitten her. Why didn't I do it?" The young man cried.

"She didn't want this," his father said in an attempt to console his son. Who were they talking about? Were they talking about the girl he was holding hands with?

"I loved her so much, and we had this beautiful little girl together, and now she's not here to be a part of us, to see our child grow up, laugh, cry, sleep, and live. She is so beautiful when she sleeps. Amy died giving birth to this amazing little girl. It's not fair. How am I to live without her, Dad?"

"Amy wanted you to take care of your child and make sure she will be safe. Amy left some part of herself behind to love. Don't hate your little girl because she took your love away. Amy would expect more from you than that, son," the man said.

"Dad, I've loved her since we were kids. I don't know how to live without her..." he trailed off.

"You and your daughter are still part of our family. We will help you," Dominic said, laying a hand on his shoulder, "Let's go in and see that little girl. Did Amy and you come up with a name?"

"Yes, I am letting Amy have her way this last time," he stated.

"Think of it this way, you will have a great deal of stories to share with your daughter, and she will need them to know the kind of person her mother was..." And then it was like the lights slowly dimmed before coming back on. I saw that same Julian, older now, and all he was doing was working, working here and working there. There didn't seem to be anyone new in his life except the girls he would bite from time to time. There doesn't seem to be any sign of a relationship, not even sex, just sadness and loss. I didn't know why, maybe I was a sucker for a hard-luck case, when that case was gnawing on the base of my neck, but I wanted to make his pain go away if it was just for one day...one hour...one moment.

Then the lights went out again, but they didn't slowly come back on, except for the big glowing yellow M for the McDonald's sign down the road. "Who is this Daniel?" Julian asked.

"Huh? Oh, Daniel is my ex-boyfriend as of today. He broke up with me," I said distantly, as if I wasn't the one answering the question, as if the answer was drawn from me. Then he growled, really growled. "You bit me. Who the hell are you?" I said through my dazed thoughts.

"Like that's not the most obvious question to ask," he presented me with an incredibly seductive smirk, showing his fangs glistening in the moonlight. I felt my chest tighten with a strange feeling. Was that fear or my own curiosity that had gotten the best of me? "That Daniel guy should be shot for what he did to you."

"Well thanks, but I don't know if he should be shot. I was thinking of something with spiders and snakes and....wait. How do you know Daniel?" I asked.

"I saw him and you," the stranger said.

"When? Where?" I asked, each word clearing my thoughts.

"Just now while I was..." He must have thought better about continuing that statement.

Wait, so when I went on my little field trip through his past, he was watching my sad and pathetic life? It's like I got to watch a sad historical romantic epic while he was stuck in a crappy theater with sticky floors watching a stupid teen flick staring a bimbo.

While I was waiting for the Twilight Zone music to start I wondered why he was asking about Daniel. What the hell was happening?

I finally found my voice, "If my question is that obvious...why don't you answer it?" I spat defensively, trying to move in my angry frustration. I could slowly feel my courage come back to me and it replenished my senses.

He only chuckled again "I planned on eating and then leaving you, but now I need to know more about you."

"What is your name?" I asked wanting to know who he was and what the hell was happening to me. And why, why, why did I want him all over me again? Did I feel sorry for him?

Did I feel sorry for me? Would a hook up with a stranger make me feel needed again? Maybe I was just horny.

I stepped back slightly, attempting to keep my balance as waves of dizziness washed over me. "My name is Julian...Hainsworth." He dropped his gaze, bowed to me and then stepped forward and started looking over my body with a hungry expression that ended with his dark eyes staring into mine "And you are...?"

"Caprice," I replied simply, feeling weak and light-headed. Then I remembered that no matter how hot this guy was, I was pissed. "That hurt and I'm still bleeding," I said with more fervor in my voice, which was contrary to how I felt "You know, they have Big Macs right across the street."

"Caprice, that's a beautiful name..." he purred, still creeping closer to me. I wanted to back away, every instinct told me to, but I didn't. He moved to my neck and licked it, lapping up the blood as if it were nectar from a succulent fruit. Then he gave me a kiss on my cheek as the feeling slowly flooded back into my legs and I felt myself move back as he moved forward. He lashed out, grabbing me and pulling me in close to him, then pressing me against the nearest tree.

I gave a slight gasp as I lost my breath for a moment. He released my arm and leaned in closer, pressing his body against mine, pinning me to the gigantic trunk, the bark pushing deeply into my back. His expression was brutally intent as a terrifying hunger danced somewhere behind his eyes.

"Does fear excite you?" his voice cooed, resembling velvet but with a note of warning like the sting of a bee.

I should have been afraid. I should have been shaking with terror. I should have been checking my purse for mace. But instead I was fascinated by this strange dark creature standing before me. Maybe it was the heart-shattering let down of my romantic life and the recent betrayal in the movie theater Daniel had just dealt me. Or, was it the "movie" I just received in my head that led me to believe he would never hurt me? I swallowed again "What kind of a question is that?"

He laughed a silent laugh again. "It's a simple question..." Looking down at my body he lifted his hand, placing the tips of his fingers against the warm flesh of my bleeding neck, then trailed them down over my shoulders, grazing my breast, then under my shirt, across the open flesh my belly, over the fabric of my skirt, finally stopping on the hem of the material. He left his hand there instead, looking up at me with a knowing smirk sliding across his face. "...and I think it does...I think fear does turn you on, Caprice." I felt my heart thump fiercely, and my breath grow ragged in excited fear in anticipation of his next move.

"Did you ever think it might be you making me feel this way?" I pointed out, hoping he would get what I meant. I wanted him to keep going.

He pressed himself against me more, leaning in close to barely brush his lips across my neck, sending a shudder down my spine and a cascade of goosebumps across my skin as he spoke.

"I want you...but I need you to want me too," he said simply then pressed his mouth to my neck, kissing me forcefully, causing my blood to rush from my neck more. I couldn't stop a moan of unexpected pleasure from escaping my lips, and soon completely gave in to his seduction. Not thinking, I tilted my head up slightly and offered him the rest of my neck to bite.

As I felt Julian's fangs gently nibble at the soft flesh beneath my ear, I also felt his hand slide up my right thigh. The tips of his fingers teased the sensitive skin on my inner leg, and a strangled whimper slipped from my throat. He pulled himself back to give a small laugh of satisfaction.

"You're awfully warm...you want me just as much as I want you...Just say yes and I will," he purred, his hands slowly sliding my panties down over my thighs, letting them drop to the ground below. I quickly shoved them out of the way as his hands kept my thighs apart. One hand slipped upwards, sliding higher up my leg to my center, stroking the heat that was pooling between my legs.

"And awfully wet..." he purred again, "Your body is betraying your inner thoughts and desires."

Another dizzying moan escaped my lips. I was unable to say anything, not wanting to stop him. And quite honestly, I needed to take the pain we were both feeling away for this one night.

"I am completely positive...I want you," I finally managed to say. His lips returned to my neck and shoulders, caressing my skin with passionate kisses and gentle bites. I could feel the scratch of his fangs brush my delicate skin, finding my pulse point, but not breaking the surface of my flesh.

Suddenly, I felt his fingers slip into me and I gasped as they worked themselves slowly within me, and as his thumb stroked my center, heat rose inside of me. I closed my eyes again, letting my head fall back and rest against the tree in ecstasy. My heart pounded harder as his fingers worked faster and faster.

"Oh God..." I moaned. Was I really having a one night stand with a stranger, a stranger with fucking fangs? Fangs? The little devil on one shoulder was of course saying "Yes, go for it." While the angel on my other shoulder was saying "Are you fucking kidding? Have you seen him? Go for it!" I gave my common sense the night off as I was becoming more excited by Julian's movements.

He slowed his fingers and carefully withdrew them, still massaging my sensitive center.

Overwhelmed with lust and an insatiable carnal hunger, Julian finally removed his hand completely and instead used it to unbuckle his pants just enough to unsheathe his own massive length. I instinctually reached forward to grasp him. His sheer size and breadth surprised me and I looked at him longingly.

Moving both his hands back under my skirt, he pushed my thighs apart and positioned himself directly above my slick opening, which was more than ready for him to enter. My chest grew tight in anticipation, and my center ached for him to enter, fearing that his more than ample member might cause me intense pain. I whimpered in wanting and fear, and he pulled back to face me slightly. Julian's own expression looked overwhelmed with his desire like my own, yet slightly surprised. Nothing could stop him, but he must have found it curious that I wasn't afraid, but instead completely lost in the moment. The desire in his eyes expressed a longing that had not been satisfied for centuries.

Leaning in, he gently pressed his lips to mine and sucked on my lower lip. Julian covered my mouth with his and swallowed my cry of surprise as he thrust into me. My entire body tensed up, feeling his shaft fill every inch of me. I wanted cry out again—half in pain, half in longing— but I couldn't. He groaned into my mouth, lavishing in the intense pleasure of my body surrounding him. My back arched against the tree and his hands slid around my waist, pulling my body as close as possible, and entering me as deeply as I could allow.

His thrusts grew stronger and faster, bringing both of us closer and closer to release. His lips finally left mine and returned to my neck, his tongue darting out to taste my skin and the fresh blood now rushing down my neck. This caused moans to escape from my lips, my body experiencing something I had never gotten from Daniel, something I always longed for but never received.

Unable to take it anymore, Julian was coming to his breaking point, as though his bloodlust was growing stronger than any other lust his body could control. As he held me close to him, he moved within me, his length sliding against my tight throbbing walls. In an explosion of the most intense pleasure I have ever felt, I contracted around his length and Julian groaned again before finally plunging his fangs deep into my throat.

I cried out in a deadly mix of pleasure and pain, succumbing to him completely as he drew life from my body. His fangs pierced my soft flesh, and he drank deeply from my neck. I felt so intimate with him, like for the first time I was whole with someone, though he was drinking my blood. I wondered what it might feel like to drink from him too.

The movie started again. I could see and feel everything he felt a long time ago. I never knew how much a man could feel. Then I saw us in the back of a car, this time it was me ravishing him and him saying next time it would be slower.

Everything appeared to be moving quicker now. I saw a ring, a beautiful ring with a band of both gold and silver saying "Forever Love," Julian putting it on my hand while we were in bed together, and then it all came to an end.

He finally withdrew his fangs, slowly and carefully, and with that the movie was gone, leaving me wanting more, like the film broke before the ending. Was it something yet to come?

Was that my—our, future together? My body slumped against the tree, unable to stand. I might have fallen to the ground if Julian hadn't been holding me tightly while he was still inside me. Julian pulled back slowly, sliding his manhood from the depths of my sweetness. My cyes were closed and my mouth slightly open, panting for breath.

Julian began redressing himself, but didn't let go of me. I opened my eyes again and looked at him. My body was still clutched in his arms, held tightly to his chest. Those milk chocolate brown eyes danced with something strange that looked deep into my soul as a weak gasp escaped my parted lips. He looked into my eyes and smirked, then winked at me. There was something else behind his eyes, a type of knowledge that implied there was a new world that I may soon be intimately acquainted with. Everything in his visage said that this was far from over...

He gave me a strange look, a look both of longing and...familiarity before he said, "In all my years wandering this earth, there has only been one other person to accept all of me, including my dark side. Until tonight I didn't think I would have found another..." I was completely bewildered, at an utter and complete loss for words. Then Julian fiercely clasped my cheeks in his hand and said in a low, whispered voice, "Caprice, after I finish talking and leave, you will remember none of what happened between us tonight. All I want you to remember is what your last thoughts were before we met, as you left the theater. Remember that you headed back to Daniel's apartment... Thinking this is not our apartment. Not our home..."

I don't know if he will be coming back tonight, but I can't let him see me like this. Okay, this is fucking ridiculous! The hell with Daniel, breaking up with me just like that, no explanation, just "You need to leave." I have to look for a new job and look for a new place to live. This day has not turned out the way I thought it would...

Julian smirked as he placed these thoughts into my memory, and he smiled with a look as if to say reading my thoughts was like reading a familiar book. I didn't want to forget. I had to remember. I wanted to read the next chapter of this story. I wanted go on reading it for all eternity...

I suddenly asked in a heartbreaking voice, "But...why? I don't want to forget you...I saw the ring."

Julian caressed my cheeks softly and said, "What ring, love?"

"You gave me a ring Julian. Was it all in my head?" I said shaking, thinking I just lost something amazing.

"No, but I want you to forget Caprice," he said and he kissed me long and soft, "Because I want you to find me on your own." Then he looked deep into my eyes and whispered in a rush,

"The next time you hear my name, you will be intrigued and want to meet me, do you understand?" I was nodding my head in silent affirmation with tears threating to spill down my cheeks as I did. I felt like I knew this man, like I had been waiting to know him my entire life.

"Caprice, what is your full name?"

"Caprice Angela Talbot...Why?" I said.

"Because sometimes fate needs a little help," Julian winked at me knowingly.

"Caprice, I will meet you soon. I will never take your memories like this again. I promise you this, and this is a promise I intend to keep. This is only the beginning, my Forever Love..." and with that, he walked away. But not before turning and looking at me one last time before he melted into the darkness of the night.

# Chapter 24:

# Lost and Found

Then like that the memory was gone. What was that? Where am I? Where was I? "Did that really happen?" I thought I kept that last question to myself but apparently it was heard loud and clear, because everyone was staring at me, except for the two guys who should answer the question. They were looking at each other—hoping the other would answer first. I looked to Sam, but only briefly before turning my lethal gaze on Julian. He and I knew he was the one that needed to answer me.

"Yes, it's real...it really happened," Julian said quietly. I knew it was real, I didn't want it to be, but I could feel how real it truly was. I wasn't looking at Julian any longer...I was staring at my ring. It was beautiful. It was perfect. I put it back in the box, closed the lid, and handed it back to him.

"Who saw what I just saw?" I asked. There was only one good answer to this question. The last thing I needed was my grandmother looking at me with a smile and saying "Good gracious my dear, you're kind of a slut. Props for keeping your balance..."

"No one but you and me," Julian said looking nervously at me.

"Thank God," I gasped. Everyone was still looking at me, but now more out of curiosity and embarrassment.

Julian had the box in his right hand, then his left, and back to the right. He sat down and after a moment handed the box back to me "This belongs to you." Great, he did not just give it to me that way. I saw how he did it in that flashback. I don't know all the details but it was more romantic than this. I guess he figures since he was smooth and suave the first time, he got it out of his system and now he can just be practical. I didn't say a word but the look on my face was worth a thousand tantrums. I set the box on the table, never taking my eyes off Julian.

"Do you have a daughter?" I asked bluntly.

"Yes, I have a daughter, her name is Lily. She's completely grown, and has children of her own. She is a teacher at a nearby high school," Julian said. He said it calmly, but the fear I saw in Julian's eyes was unexpected. He was afraid that once I knew what he was...how old he was...that he had a daughter and grandchildren...I would leave him. But it was the look on Sam's face I couldn't understand.

"That's what you got out of all this!" Sam said.

I felt so raw at this point I just want to crawl under my bed and hide. "I understand the vampire stuff now...well, some of it," I admitted. "I really don't want to believe it, but that doesn't make it any less true." Again there was silence. Everyone was expecting me to say more, to give some kind of conciliatory speech like "I give up, you win. Yes Virginia, there are vampires and for some fucked up reason—I'm in love with one!" My Abnormal Psych professor would love this shit. I didn't have a speech, just a request. "I need to talk to Julian alone."

"Caprice, you need to be bitten," my grandmother said, "You're not looking well." Really, I don't look well? Could it be the mother lode of crap that just got dumped on me, or maybe it's just the sniffles?

"Look I know, I get it, one bite and my complexion will clear up and I'll feel the irresistible urge to do hand stands. Right now, I just want to talk to Julian," I said before turning to Dominic.

"But before you go, does it have to be him? I mean, how sick would I get if someone else bites me? We're not taking a Linda Blair head spin followed by a course of pea soup, right?"

"It will be worse on you if someone else bites you," Dominic said, "If you do not wish for Julian to bite you, it would be better for you to wait."

Wait. Wait for how long before deciding it is time to have sharp teeth sink into my skin in order for me to feel better? I should wait a while to give my brain a chance to wrap itself around that concept. "Okay, but I need to talk to Julian alone," I said again. I felt like yelling my request for privacy, but I was afraid my head would explode all over the white carpet and I really didn't need the maids pissed at me.

Sam was the first to move to the door, the door that led to his room. He opened it and waited. One-by-one Dominic, Grandmother and Geri slowly shuffled towards the open door, not saying a word, and the door closed behind them without making a sound. The box was sitting on the coffee table. I was staring at it and it was staring at me. It wasn't an imposing box, just decorative and...cute—inside was everything I ever wanted. Inside this little box was a world I never knew existed, and yet I wanted it. I was scared to death of it. However, all I had to do was open it. All Julian had to do was present it to me, the way I saw him do it...instead of just handing it to me like a newspaper after he read the sports. All he had to do was let me keep my memory instead of locking it in a decorative little box.

Julian cautiously moved to the couch at the opposite side of the room from where I was sitting. "How could you do that to me?" I asked. Julian was about to answer, but not before I asked him—at the top of my lungs—all the questions that were on my mind. "You erased my memory. Why would you do that? And what's with the ring? No bell-ringing, angels-singing event when you give it to me? You basically just tossed it to me like a Cracker-Jack prize!" I was livid. I wanted to kiss him and kick his ass at the same time. He tried to answer, but I cut in again.

"Look," I said in a more civilized tone, "I can live with the less than imaginative way you gave me the ring, I'm a big girl, but taking my memory? I don't know what I'm supposed to believe! The only thing I can think of is we met...there was magic and heavy breathing, but when the magic was over you decided that I wasn't worth a second thought. You wiped my memory so that I wouldn't show up on your doorstep like a pathetic little girl wanting more than just a one night fuck!"

Once again, before Julian could come to his own defense with a tirade of man-made excuses—or drop to his knees and beg for forgiveness—I made a beeline to the bathroom. I couldn't remember the last thing I had to eat until now. Julian was right behind me trying to keep me steady until I pulled away from him. I really didn't want him to touch me, but when the bathroom starts spinning like that... He grabbed me before I could object, and helped me find the couch.

Julian sat down, closer to me this time. He still looked miserable, heartbroken after I unloaded on him. I put my hand on my forehead pretending to scratch and I left it there to hide the tears. No matter how hard you try, sometimes you can't stop them. I turned anyway, but he still reached around to catch one of the falling tears. When I turned back I could see his pain.

"Why...?" I asked in a whisper.

"I wanted you to want me, need me, and love me without the magic that the bite holds," Julian said, "When I bit you, I knew we were meant to be, but I wanted you to get to know me before you found out."

"What you thought was that I would be fine with you erasing my memory like a teacher at a chalkboard. I have no doubt you were hoping I would never remember. Well guess what!" I yelled through my tears, "I remember and I am not fine with it. Get out and leave me alone and tell the rest of the family to stay out. I need to think."

I walked over to the open window, never seeing or hearing Julian leave, but knowing he was gone. I watched the dark clouds swallow the sunshine, turning the day prematurely to night. I could smell the rain coming.

The air was fresh, like the memory of Julian. This just made my head start spinning like a top. I closed my eyes and opened them slowly and made my way to the bedroom where I found the bed. The window to the room was open and a gentle breeze made its way in carrying with it the scent of Julian, or was it just my imagination since I couldn't get him off my mind? The sound of the rain had always been comforting to me, before today anyway.

There was a pain in my chest that began to grow, and I don't think it was the metaphoric pain of heartbreak. The window was open and the air was coming in, but I couldn't seem to breathe. I needed to get out of this room, out of my own small box that was getting smaller and smaller, and get into the open air.

I opened the door of my room and checked the hallways. I don't know what I was thinking, it's not like you can sneak around in a building full of mind-reading vampires. The best you can hope for is that you scared the shit out of them with all the screaming and they know enough to leave you alone. I made it to the stairs without being noticed, but these weren't the stairs leading out to the real world where everyone believes that vampires are only found in books and movies.

These were the stairs to the roof.

I have always fantasized about being up on a roof with a guy...I've seen it so many times in the cheesy romantic comedies. One table with dinner and a burning candle in the middle, and of course moonlight. After dinner, dancing, followed by two courses of sex, and considering the king-sized bed frame and the roses adorning the open walls around it, I'm sure this roof is just another choice for the guests of Jade's Inn.

The rain was coming down now, falling right in line with my tears, hiding them, which really didn't matter since I was alone—no one to see me cry. I wrapped my arms around myself, listening to the rain and the soft sighs escaping my lips as the breeze grew stronger and caressed my skin. The rain was colder than I thought, and not as cleansing as I had hoped. But, what did I expect? Did I think the rain was going to wash way the memory of Daniel, the feeling of betrayal from the one who was supposed to love me, the reality of vampires? There is no intent in rain, it just falls, and no matter how hard it falls it cannot wash away the truth.

Shivering slightly, my flesh tingled as goose bumps chased over my body, rain pelting against my skin, I closed my eyes and tilted my head back, sighing deeply as the rain caressed my face and trickled down my neck. I was still wearing Julian's shirt, but it was becoming more and more see-through as the rain continued to be more and more relentless. I tilted my head back again and shivered slightly as the wind brushed up my clothes, pulling them tightly against me.

"You need to come inside," a voice echoed through my head.

"Julian," I said sighing. Hearing his voice should have been annoying, but it wasn't. I still should be angry with him, and I was, but the sound of his familiar voice brought back a memory, a memory of the smell of rain whenever I was near him, a smell that now surrounds me in the darkest storm. I was wrong. There is intent in the rain, at least this rain. I think Mother Nature was trying to tell me something like "Pull your head out of your ass kid. You may not get a second chance at happiness."

There is a question I've been waiting to ask, but never could. There were always people around. I asked in my head Julian, you're the one that Grandma was talking about aren't you, the one who asked to marry me?

Yes, of course I am my love, Julian said sedately. God I am stupid, of course it was him, who else would it be? He just wanted me to fall in love with him, no tricks, no magic—just him.

First you have to fall in love with the man—it made it easier to fall in love with the vampire.

All this thinking about my feelings crap, while helpful, was exhausting. I needed to get back inside. I felt his eyes on me. Maybe I don't need to go back inside. .

I turned around and immediately knew it wasn't Julian. I caught my breath, bit my lip until it bled and watched the man slowly move closer to me. His movements were deliberate, but not hurried. I turned and tried to run back inside, but I couldn't get my feet to move. My eyes widened as the man stopped in front of me. I looked up at the face of Daniel.

"I...thought you were in jail," I said in a low voice. The grin on his face was familiar at first, but it kept growing.

"I was in jail. I was in jail with drug dealers and thieves. They didn't have separate cells for innocent guys who just wanted to get back with the girl they love. I would still be in there if it weren't for a mysterious benefactor."

"Who would have helped you get out?" I asked, half in fear, half in curiosity.

"Who indeed, that's the mystery in 'mysterious benefactor.' Who could it be? How about my parents? How about your parents? Your mom has always liked me, Cat. Think about your friends, I know a lot of them, could one of them ratted you out? Here's a thought...how about your lover, Julian? Maybe he thought he didn't want you anymore. I mean look where you are, up on a roof, by yourself, in the rain."

I backed away, but there was nowhere to go. "What do you want?" I said, while my mind thought frantically of escape.

"What's mine," he said with a knowing grin.

He moved faster than I remembered he could, and before I knew it, he was on top of me,

"Okay, here's the plan. You will tell the cops that this whole thing was a mistake, your mistake, and that you should never have left me." This cannot be happening.

"How did you know where to find me?" I asked, hoping that by giving him time to brag, it will also give Julian time to get up here.

"Again, the mysterious benefactor, this person—or persons—knows a lot about you Caprice," Daniel said, water dripping from his hair and face like slime. He glared intimidatingly at me, saying "I'm all wet Cat, thanks to you. I have been outside this Inn for hours, walking around it three or four times looking for a way in—looking for you. I gave up until you helped me by coming up here to the roof all by yourself. When I saw you, I just climbed the fire escape and here you were, crying tears for a lost love. But who is the lost love, Cat? Is it Julian or could it be me?"

I could feel every part of Daniel on top of me—every disgusting, revolting part. His face was only inches away, his breath polluting the air between us. My breath quickened then stopped when Daniel leaned closer and whispered in my ear, "I have a surprise for you." I know my mind was open, Julian must have heard everything, but I was screaming at the top of my mind's thoughts anyway.

His lips were the first to touch my neck. When I felt the tip of his tongue I closed my eyes and tried to push him off. He licked across my pulse point, and that was when—in horror—I felt his teeth. "Is this what you want, Cat?" he whispered creepily. "Is this what you're into now? Is this what he gives you?"

"How?" I asked, my voice shaking with the very syllable.

"How what, Cat?" Daniel was much louder now. "How did I know what he is?" Daniel sat up, all his weight on my waist. "Do you think I'm stupid, Cat? Is that what you think?" His face turned red with anger and his hand was shaking as he raised it up. He brought it down with fury and hatred, but it was stopped an inch from my face.

Daniel turned and saw anger greater than his own. Julian pulled Daniel off and threw him into the storm. I couldn't see him hit the far wall, but the sound was certainly deafening. After a moment, I saw Daniel stagger forward. "I know what you are," he said, but those were his last words. Julian crouched down like a wolf ready to attack. His mouth opened wide, his fangs came out and I swear I heard him growl like a wolf. In a blink of an eye, Julian was holding Daniel in the air by his throat. For that brief moment, the air was filled only with the sound of rain, not the sound of Daniel's scream as he was thrown high in the air, and over the edge of the roof. But of all the sounds, the one I will remember forever was the sound of Daniel hitting the pavement with a sickening thud and crackle of bones.

I will never take standing up for granted again. I stopped trying, and just lay there with Julian over me—not the worst position to be in. All my anger, and my hurt and bitterness were being washed away by the rain drops. How could I ever stay mad at him? I loved him. I reached up and caressed his cheek and ran my fingers softly over his bottom lip. I still wanted and needed to know so much. So many questions to ask, but where do I begin?

Before I could get one question out, Julian had his fingers over my lips and said, "No, honey not now." The sensations from just the simple touch of his fingers against my lips took my breath away. My knees trembled as the dampness of the rain trickled down my body. I knew he saw the reaction of my body shining in his dark brown eyes. He was as gentle as possible when he picked me up, like a really cute baby bird, but the pain shot through me, like being hit in the stomach by the cute little bird's angry mother. "We need the doctor now," Julian insisted.

I wasn't really unconscious. I just kept my eyes closed while I was in my lover's arms, but when I opened my eyes I was in my room again watching my grandmother and Geri running around grabbing blankets and sheets like I gave birth in the back of a Buick. As much as I loved my grandfather he really needed to stop poking my stomach or I'd have to send him to his room.

Every touch made the pain grow worse, not better. "Caprice needs to be bitten now," Grandfather said urgently.

Before things started getting weird, I needed to know something "Where's Daniel?" I asked. I knew he hit the ground pretty hard, but I have seen too many scary movies to not be paranoid enough to believe he could be coming around the corner at any time.

"He's dead," Sam said simply.

"Are you sure?" I asked, still worried.

"Yes," Sam said, ending any doubt. I was able to breathe for a second. I was surprised how easy it was, to feel relieved that the man I was living with a short time ago is dead.

"I don't want to be turned yet," I said in a whisper. I looked to Julian but he was trying to close his mind to me...it wasn't working. I knew what he was trying to hide, but you can't hide that kind of pain. He looked the same as he did before...when he lost the love of his life.

"We will try to heal you first, but biting you might be the only way to save you," Grandfather said.

"Try first," I said out loud, but my thoughts were with Julian and his thoughts were with me.

He wasn't trying to hide them anymore. Julian watched Amy die and he blames himself, he believes he could have prevented it, and now he was watching me. "Julian, if the healing doesn't work...bite me...save me..." He just stiffened and shook his head. "Julian, you will bite me if I need it," I commanded him.

Julian took me by the hand, but he turned away. He was trying to hide his tears this time, but I saw them, we all did. "I will not let this happen again," he said under his breath. His one hand was holding mine while his other was caressing my arm. He brought his head down and softly kissed my wrist and left his lips there feeling my pulse. His lips then moved up my shivering arm, leaving goosebumps as he went. It was then that the look in his tear-filled eyes changed.

They were intense, frightening, and inviting. His mouth opened, his long teeth dripping with anticipation. "I love you, I won't let you die." In an instant his teeth sunk into my arm, blood dripping down, the muffled scream that escaped my lips was not from pain, but pleasure.

I have the weirdest fucking dreams, and it's not like I go out and hunt for wild mushrooms.

While these dreams do get bizarre, I wake up angry simply because I wake up. Sometimes, when you find the right dream, or it finds you, you never want to leave. As much as I didn't want to depart from this particular vision, I opened my eyes and sat up in bed.... It wasn't my bed though. Then my memories came flooding back, memories of teeth, blood, and pain. I immediately ran my hand up and down my arm, but there was nothing there—no marks, no pain.

As a matter of fact, there was no ain...anywhere.

I lay back down and rolled over, still surprised that my body didn't hurt, and more surprised to find there was something under the covers. I knew exactly who it was. I slowly peeled back the blankets like I was opening a birthday present. Just what I always wanted, a mostly naked man. The pearly light of the full moon shined through the open window and illuminated Julian with an unearthly glow. I thought my "present" was asleep until he turned to me and said "Sorry Caprice, I didn't mean to wake you, I'll leave."

I reached for him. "No, don't go...stay with me..." I begged, and Julian lay back on the bed next to me saying nothing. With the distraction of my new and improved body, and the hunk lying next to me, it took me a while to realize I was no longer in Julian's shirt, or my tank top with the Winnie the

Pooh pajama pants. I was in a long silky white night gown that brought up an interesting question. "Who..." before I could get the words out Julian answered my inquiry

"Geri and your grandmother." I relaxed again.

"What's the matter?" I whispered sleepily.

"Your mind has been shut down since you told me what you wanted. I just laid here and watched you," he told me as he gazed into my eyes. "I was wondering what you were thinking...what you were dreaming...it was nice not knowing. It makes you more mysterious." I closed my eyes and snuggled closer against him as he took a deep breath and relaxed. I didn't realize how tense he was until that moment. I followed his movements as his hand traveled over where the bruises used to be...it felt amazing. Julian rolled over on his side, away from me and I pressed myself against his hips. I traced my hand up his muscular leg and over the waist band of his silky boxer shorts. Honey... Sweetie... Man-o-mine...Don't ever erase my memory again, got it?" I declared in a cute yet stern voice. Julian chuckled.

"Trust me...I'm not pissing you off like that again." Wow, he is trainable! We continued to lay there together in silence, hands caressing each other, and then I asked that one question every woman asks and every man loathes. "What are you thinking?"

"I was just thinking about you, thinking how lucky I am because I get to keep you forever..." he muttered to himself. I stiffened against him.

Then he said quickly "Caprice, I'm sorry, I'm being silly." He pulled himself closer to the curve of my hip and he laid a hand on my arm again—just held his fingers in place. I lay silently pressing myself against him "Tell me...please," I pleaded.

"No," Julian responded.

"No, you're not going to tell me, or no I'm not a vampire," I stated with some irritation.

"You're not a vampire...yet, but you will be someday," he told me with confidence. If it hasn't happened yet, I still have a choice, no matter how cocky and self-assured he sounds.

"And how can you be so damn positive it will happen?" I asked. It was one of those questions where you want to know and you don't want to know simultaneously. But, since it's a question of whether I belong to the same species I belonged to yesterday, I thought I would be sure.

"I saw it when I bit you," he told me.

Well that stopped me cold. "Julian, you should know that I don't want to get married, after all, I am a Twenty-first century woman..." I began. Of course the real reason I found married life less than blissful, was because of my mother. After seeing what she did with her multiple marriages, I was turned off to the concept all together.

"Well, love," Julian said, "There is one thing that you should know about being a vampire. I have all the time in the world, and...." And after that, he left the room.

Before I could feel too abandoned, he returned with one hand behind his back. "...And I'd like nothing better than to give you all the time in the world to decide." He brought his hand out from behind his back, holding the pretty little box I recognized. I sat up and watched Julian open the box and pull out the ring.

This is what I remembered.

My breathing stopped when Julian got on one knee. "Please wear this ring as a symbol of my love until I can replace it with your wedding band." He took my right hand and slipped on the golden ring with the sliver ribbon running around it, and the words that made my heart stop— "Forever love."

"If I'm wearing a ring, then so are you," I commanded.

"I thought you'd say that," Julian said. He stood up and went to the top drawer of the dresser, then took out another small box and handed it to me. I opened it and found a ring that matched my own. It was larger but had those familiar words "Forever Love" engraved upon the precious metal circle.

"Look inside the band," Julian said. I looked closer and found written on the inside "Julian loves Caprice."

"Is this inside my ring too?" I asked curiously.

"Yes it is," Julian answered then handed me his right hand and I slipped the ring on his finger. "Forever Love," he whispered and bent down and kissed me. "Are you ready to sleep?"

"Wait, why the right hand and not the left?" I asked

"Because we are not married yet."

The tiniest hint of a smile played against my lips. I gently placed my hands on either side of his face and pulled him closer to me. He kissed me, softly and I kissed him softly in return. We pulled back from each other, staring deeply into one another's eyes. An intense heat instantly filled the room, but our eyes never left each other. Then our lips slammed together fully, deeply, and passionately. As we kissed, I quickly became aware of how hard he was. I lifted my hips, waiting, wanting, drawing him to me, and aware of the fact I had no underwear on. I didn't stop until he was deep inside of me. He pulled back, sliding all the way out, leaving the tip kissing between my lips.

With an unbridled passion he thrust deep inside of me again and again. We cried out in unison as my hips rose up to meet his. It really felt as though we were made for each other—for the first time I truly realized this fact. We increase our pace, our bodies finding each other's rhythm and responding to it with passion. I looked up into his eyes and grinned before wrapping my legs around him and flipping him onto his back. I knelt above him, placing my thighs on either side of his hip. Looking up at me, he said "You're my one and only love. Be gentle, you can really hurt me like no one else can..."

I leaned forward supporting myself with my hands I pressed against his hard chest while I raised myself up and dropped down onto him. I whispered, "make me forget." I leaned up and kissed him deeply. He rolled to his back and pulled me on top of him, pressing our bodies close, yet skillfully never leaving my lips. One arm hugged my waist tightly as the other caressed my face gently. For that moment in time, all else stopped. Even though, it seemed as if time only progressed for us

I trailed kisses to the tender part of his neck, just above his collarbone. Julian hissed a soft breath and I could feel the goose bumps rising on his skin. I continued random kisses along his chest and neck. His hands roamed the skin just beneath mine, I pressed myself once more to him, and kissing him with everything I had. His heart beat a steady tempo against my chest, and we caused it to quicken when Julian slid my thigh up to meet his groin. He let out another soft hiss. Smiling to myself as my own heart rate increased, I sat up a bit and took in the look on his face. It was kind and gentle, but the glazed-over look in his eyes made an ever-so-great contrast.

I raised myself off him wanting something more from him. I kissed his neck and continued kissing down to my favorite part of him.

His eyes closed as his breathing quickened. I slid his member through my hand and immediately kissed the length of the shaft. I felt various muscles in his body tense and relax, and I got a twisted sense of pleasure in knowing that I was the cause of it.

I had planned on maintaining this sensuous torture, but Julian quickly and unexpectedly rolled me over, pressing my back to the bed.

I shivered as the blanket had long been forgotten. "Let me help," he cooed in my ear. And, placing himself at my entrance, he eased himself in, taking care to my reaction. Once I adjusted, I nodded my head and kissed him once more. He pulled himself out a bit before reentering each time with a slightly firmer force He increased his pace, as he felt himself getting close. He knew I was too. Suddenly, my walls tightened around him, and my back arched. I was spiraling into the unknown and I let out a loud moan to match. That was all it took to send him spinning out as well, he released into me, groaning loudly as he thrust his tense body once more before collapsing in a heap on top of me.

He kissed my forehead gently once more before rolling over again, pulling me as close to him as possible. The stars shone brightly from the window giving a glow on our bodies. He grabbed at the forgotten blanket and covered us both, and Julian took a deep breath and whispered, "I love you," then fell asleep.

Drifting away to sleep, I was happy I had finally found the right dream.

# Tammy Godfrey

Residing in Pocatello, Idaho, Tammy L. Godfrey is currently a college student at Idaho State University. After spending sixteen years in the military, Tammy decided to follow her heart's desire and pursue a professional career in writing. Tammy resides with her wonderful husband, who spends endless hours dealing with her habit of being on her laptop all night writing. She also lives with three dogs and two cats who would prefer Tammy gave them all the attention rather than her computer. Tammy is currently working on her next novel and working on a degree at Idaho State University

### Books by Tammy Godfrey
A Soldier's Wish
A Soldier's Love
A Soldier's Eyes Are Smiling

Combat Boots & Mistletoe
Combat boots & Reunions

Promises Kept
Promises Broken

Welcome to Jade's Inn

www.ingramcontent.com/pod-product-compliance
Lightning Source LLC
Chambersburg PA
CBHW031305280626

47169CB00017B/108

9 7 8 1 6 3 5 8 1 0 3 2 5